Keepers of the Ancient Wisdom

(Kalie's Journey Book 3)

Sandra Saidak

Uffington Horse Press San Jose, CA

CreateSpace Edition

Published by Uffington Horse Press, San Jose, California, USA

ISBN: 978-0-9863385-0-2

Learn more at: **www.sandrasaidak.com**

Praise for the Kalie's Journey Trilogy:

Book 1 *Daughter of the Goddess Lands*:
A masterful epic journey about trauma, healing, love, hate, and the loss of a prehistoric world we can never find again. Debut author Sandra Saidak mesmerizes with clear vivid prose and heartfelt emotion.—Valerie Frankel, author of *From Girl to Goddess: The Heroine's Journey in Myth and Legend.*

Not every author can find a way to tell a new and challenging story, or should I say stories, since our heroine Kalie is a storyteller herself. So many novels follow the same tired formulas, with the same happy (and boring) endings…But Kalie is neither a warrior princess waving a sword or a beautiful seductress dressed in shimmering gowns. Instead she's someone who must overcome her own terrors, even as she finds herself assuming the role of a reluctant heroine.—Sam Barone, author of *The Eskkar series.*

Book 2 *Shadow of the Horsemen*
The story of Kalie continues in Shadow of the Horsemen, and what a story! This book is full of feeling. I returned to it every chance I got, and when I wasn't reading, I found myself wondering what was happening. The first book was good, but Saidak really comes into her writing in this second book. The world is vibrant and the characters are fully three dimensional - even the most minor character was someone I felt like I could actually talk to. Please tell me there will be a third book!—Marlene Dotterer, author of *Moon Over Donamorgh*

Books in the Kalie's Journey Series:

Daughter of the Goddess Lands
Shadow of the Horsemen
Keepers of the Ancient Wisdom
Oathbreaker's Daughter (short stand-alone, set in the same universe)
In the Balance (Short story collection; title story in set in Kalie's universe)

Other books by Sandra Saidak:
The Seal Queen

Praise for the Kalie's Journey Trilogy:

Book 1 *Daughter of the Goddess Lands*:
A masterful epic journey about trauma, healing, love, hate, and the loss of a prehistoric world we can never find again. Debut author Sandra Saidak mesmerizes with clear vivid prose and heartfelt emotion.—Valerie Frankel, author of *From Girl to Goddess: The Heroine's Journey in Myth and Legend.*

Not every author can find a way to tell a new and challenging story, or should I say stories, since our heroine Kalie is a storyteller herself. So many novels follow the same tired formulas, with the same happy (and boring) endings...But Kalie is neither a warrior princess waving a sword or a beautiful seductress dressed in shimmering gowns. Instead she's someone who must overcome her own terrors, even as she finds herself assuming the role of a reluctant heroine.—Sam Barone, author of *The Eskkar series.*

Book 2 *Shadow of the Horsemen*
The story of Kalie continues in Shadow of the Horsemen, and what a story! This book is full of feeling. I returned to it every chance I got, and when I wasn't reading, I found myself wondering what was happening. The first book was good, but Saidak really comes into her writing in this second book. The world is vibrant and the characters are fully three dimensional - even the most minor character was someone I felt like I could actually talk to. Please tell me there will be a third book!—Marlene Dotterer, author of *Moon Over Donamorgh*

Books in the Kalie's Journey Series:

Daughter of the Goddess Lands
Shadow of the Horsemen
Keepers of the Ancient Wisdom
Oathbreaker's Daughter (short stand-alone, set in the same universe)
In the Balance (Short story collection; title story in set in Kalie's universe)

Other books by Sandra Saidak:
The Seal Queen

Acknowledgements:

For this final novel of the Kalie's Journey trilogy, I can only repeat my thanks to everyone who has made it possible for me to get this far: all the members of the Whensday People writing group (especially Adrienne, who created the map), my wonderful family, all my teachers back at Aragon High School—most notably Dr. Philip Fisher, who was able to turn an Amazon review into a reprise of an English lesson I remember from 1976—George MacDonald and Donji Collumbine for technical wizardry and artistic genius, and finally, all of you who have read the these books.

Dramatis Personae:

People of Aahk who followed Kalie and Riyik west:

Warriors:	**Women**	**Children**
Borik	Brenia	Yarik
Garm	Tarella	Sirak
Durak	Darva	Myla
Zanal	Danika	Liara
Malor	Sarika	
Yanal	Agafa	
Garak	Varena	
	Saela	
	Katya	

Healers of Green Bower:
Shula
Andor
Laissa
Galla
Josan
Jaleen (a merchant)

Survivors of Kalie's mission from Book 1:
Larren
Alessa
Kestra

People of Stonebridge:
Nara – Senior priestess
Ilara -- Priestess
Orin—Senior priest
Bodon--Priest

Janak--Smith
Sarella--Midwife
Ranal--Hunter
Taran—Varena's suitor
Noris—Varena's suitor
Martel—Brenia's suitor
Nyssa—Martel's sister
Jula—Basketweaver
Minda—Jula's daughter
Casim—Wandering storyteller
Ruleen—Leader of those opposed to fighting
Analie— Warrior-in-training
Ladoka—Warrior-in-training

Kariik's people:

Warriors:	**Women**
Lornak	Elka
Kelvin	Kara
Hysaak	Gallia
Artev	Miona
Alrik	
Charnak	

Otera's followers:

Malana
Lanara
Valeska
Derona
Erobia
Danarie
Griva
Trisa

Map

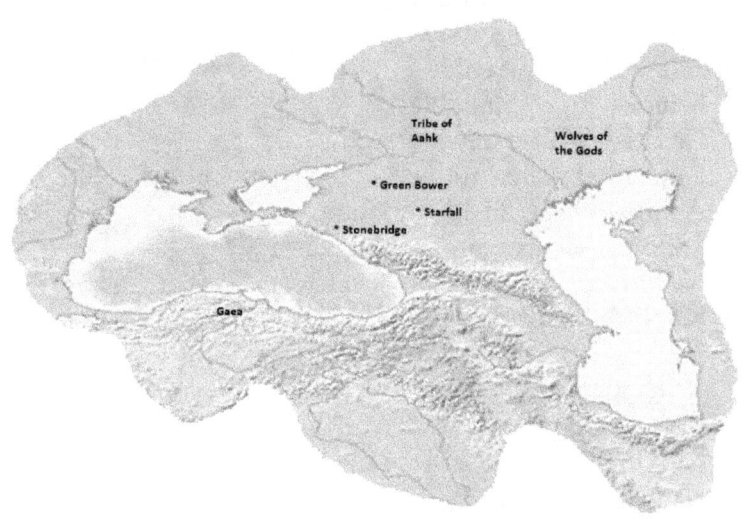

Prologue

Varlas, king of the Wolf tribe, stood on a low hill and surveyed the burning tents and broken bodies of the tribe he had just defeated. He heard the screams of their women as his warriors took their pleasure, and watched while his own women took his flocks to the greatest prize he had won this day: a tiny stream flowing with fresh water. That stream—the only water within a two day ride—meant life for his tribe. For a few more days, at least.

A scattering of snow mocked him. He needed water for his people, not more drought. Brown and brittle grass chafed their legs and arms in the strangely dry winter. The land was dying. And from ancient tales of similar disasters, Varlas knew that if they didn't move west, and take the water and grass that still remained, their flocks, and their horses, and then finally the people would die as well.

But the western steppes were drying, too. Not as badly as here; there would be water and grazing for their animals in the spring—once they had taken the land from the tribes who called it home. Varlas looked upon the prize he had just won, and cursed the demons who swallowed the water from the land. Demons who dared to prevent a king from enjoying the fairest of the women and many skins of kumis and all the other treasures that were now rightfully his.

Because this victory was not as his others had been. As Varlas proudly watched his oldest son, fresh from his first battle, thrusting into a comely girl no older than thirteen, and probably a virgin, judging from her strangled sobs, he knew she would have to be left behind with all the others. There was no food to spare for new slaves. Their weakened animals could not carry any treasure beyond food and water. To be brought so low, after all his father and grandfather had paid in blood and courage to earn this tribe the name of Wolves of the Gods stung deeply, and was an insult to the gods themselves.

So Varlas, mightiest king of the grasslands, would do what none before had done: he would take his people and leave the steppes.

Everyone had heard the tales of the land to the west, where the water never ran dry, and where food and gold were said to be as plentiful as grass was on the steppes. The western tribes raided there, but none had stayed, and for good reason. It was also a land to fear, filled with mists that swallowed horses, and forests where a man could go days without ever seeing the sun. Automatically, Varlas looked up at the bright winter sun, the clean lines where endless brown grass met endless blue sky. To leave the land of their ancestors was unthinkable. But to stay meant death.

And there would be rewards for warriors who rose to such a challenge. They would be masters of a land no one else possessed, and few would dare try to take. Varlas knew about the dirt-eaters: strange men, if they could be called men at all. They lived by grubbing in the earth like worms, too weak and cowardly to fight as warriors and take what they wanted. Some even said that women ruled them. Varlas snorted. If that were true, this strange land was his for the taking. But he also knew that only a fool believed every wild tale that he heard.

Varlas watched his two wives watering their flocks. One had been his boyhood love, and had given him five children, including his firstborn son. The other was young and enticing, and made him long for his bed in the middle of the day, though she had given him only a daughter so far. The slaves, bent low beneath the weight of the full water bags they carried, had dwindled to only three. The others were dead, along with Varlas's favorite concubine.

In the west, he would give both his wives the life they deserved. Slaves, to see that his queen spent her last years in comfort, while he covered his younger wife in jewels and furs. Over time, there would be more wives, and sons to make him the envy of all men. And many barbarian slave girls, eager to please him. Or they would meet the fate of all who displeased the King of Wolves.

His fears calmed at last, Varlas went to his tent where the daughters of the former master of this land awaited him. He was a king, and to ignore the prizes allotted to him would anger the gods. And he would need their favor if the daring course he had set his tribe upon was to succeed.

Chapter 1

The people stood in a tight, fearful group beside the river and gazed at the trees on the other side. Behind them was nothing but an expanse of withered brown grass, stretching unbroken to the eastern horizon. Kalie turned back to the river, and then glanced at the sun sinking behind the distant hills beyond.

"We will make camp here," she said, turning to address the group of nearly seventy men, women and children. "Tomorrow, we will find a fording spot and cross into the Land of the Goddess. There, we will be safe."

Not everyone seemed convinced, but they began to go about the work of setting up camp, for that was something everyone—whether they had been a warrior, a slave or a wife in the tribe of Aahk—knew how to do. Camp consisted of a small fire, a good supply of driftwood and dried dung to keep it going, and enough flat ground for everyone to roll into their blankets and sleep in relative comfort.

The smell of roasting meat—from one of their last goats, Kalie knew—made her mouth water, while at the same time made her smile. Riyik, once a nomad warrior, now Kalie's lover and life-mate, was turning the meat on a spit. He was cooking! Something no warrior of Aahk would even consider doing when there were women around, and now it was, well, perhaps not natural, but he did it. And it smelled delicious.

"So this is…what is the word?" Garm asked, pointing to the dense stand of trees across the river.

"A forest," Kalie answered, supplying the word that did not exist in the nomad's tongue.

"And big water? Is called river?"

"Yes!" Kalie was pleased that so many were learning her language. Of course, with some words, they had no choice. No one from the grasslands had seen a body of water so long and wide that it appeared endless, and would never dry in summer.

Two young women stood beside Kalie, staring into the bright water, which now reflected the setting sun like a flame. "It is like blood," said one of them, spreading the fingers of her right hand in the sign against evil. The other woman only shook, too frightened to speak.

"Not blood," said Kalie. "It is the birth-waters of the Goddess. When we cross this river tomorrow, we will be born again into a new world. A world of hope and joy. A land where we will all cast off our fetters."

The women, both junior wives in their old lives, seemed offended by Kalie's terms but neither spoke. They had, after all, chosen to come with her.

Kalie turned back to the camp where most of the women were busy unpacking the horses, filling their nearly empty water skins from the river, and adding what little they could to the goat meat for their supper. The few provisions they had been able take with them when they fled the land of Aahk—hard cheese, curds and grain—were long gone. They had foraged what they could, but this far from home, the horsewomen recognized little that was edible. Only their diminishing flocks of sheep and goats would feed them until they reached a village where the animals could be traded for the vegetables, fruit and grain of Kalie's childhood.

"You there," Danica called to one of the women. "Come help with sick ones." While most of the women set to work easily, some of the former slaves tended to stand still, looking around with interest, but doing nothing when they stopped for the night. It's not that they're lazy, Kalie thought. It's that they have no initiative. They're not used to working without someone yelling orders—usually delivered with slaps and kicks. Fortunately, Danica, who had been the daughter, then wife, and finally mother of chiefs, was very good at delegating.

Kalie went to help Sarika, who was making a meaty broth for those who were ill. Her greatest worry was for Agafa who had once been a proud and beautiful dancer; the prized possession of a chief. When Agafa had grown too old to please her master, his spiteful new wife had convinced the chief to cast Agafa into the shadows rather than selling her. Essentially a death sentence, it meant she had no home; no place in the tribe. As she reached old age— a time that would have guaranteed her a respected place in the Goddess Lands to the west—Agafa was forced to depend on the compassion of people who had none, and hunger and exposure had taken their toll.

Now as Agafa collapsed shaking into the blanket spread for her, she was aided by two of the most compassionate people Kalie had met—in this or any other land—who were also the best healers in the party. Sarika, once Danica's slave, had appointed herself Agafa's chief caregiver, helping her walk during the day and plying her with potions at night.

Brenia, Kalie's sister-by-marriage, assisted Sarika, and worked to keep Agafa's spirits up, as she walked beside her with a quiet grace that never failed to impress Kalie.

Others requiring healing included one of the men who had a cut that had begun to fester, and two of the children who had picked up fevers. The others, to everyone's amazement, suffered from nothing more than weariness and fear. And that, Kalie thought as she returned to the riverbank and gazed longingly at the maze of beautiful, familiar trees, just across the river, would soon be remedied.

Larren waddled over to where Kalie stood, toes nearly touching the water. Kalie smiled at the only other person here who could look at a forest and see home instead of an alien landscape.

"I told you your baby would be born free, in our homeland," Kalie said.

"We're not there yet," said Larren, placing a hand on her huge belly. For a moment, she glared down at the bulk before her. Then her gaze softened and she smiled.

"How much longer?" Kalie asked, trying not to show her nervousness.

"At least a moonspan. Don't worry; I won't have it on the trail. You were good enough to keep me from killing this baby and myself when I lost hope. I can at least return the favor by not making our escape any more exciting than it already is." Larren sighed and rubbed her back as they walked. "I just wish Alessa was here."

"So do I," said Kalie, thinking of the gifted healer who had set out with them on their mission to defeat the horsemen, more than a year ago. Alessa had

refused to leave their enemies, still convinced she
could somehow turn them into friends. Kalie gagged
as if she had tasted something sour, and then turned
her thoughts back to the pregnant woman beside her.
"Sarika and Brenia are both skilled healers."

Larren nodded. "They have been very helpful.
And very kind. Strange that all that time I was Itaak's
slave, his hateful wife…two of the cruelest beasts ever
to foul the body of the Goddess…all that time, there
were people like Brenia and Sarika, living in the same
camp; the same stinking tents. And I never knew it."

Kalie had no answer to that, so she squeezed
Larren's hand.

"Is it the same forest we crossed on our way to
the steppes?" Larren asked. "I remember crossing
several streams, and at least one river. I just don't
know if it was this one."

Kalie nodded. She was equally uncertain.
Normally, this would not be a concern. But winter
was fast approaching, and more important to Kalie,
she had promised herself that Agafa would live to see
the lands of the Goddess. Turning her back on the
river, Kalie went to sit with the sick woman. Sarika
was adding the last of the honey to willow bark tea for
the children with fevers, while Brenia, kept Agafa
propped up as she coughed, wiping blood and phlegm
from her mouth. Kalie picked up one of Brenia's jars
of salves and began rubbing Agafa's feet with the
sweet-smelling mixture.

When the coughing subsided, Agafa winked at
Kalie. "That feels good, but I'll die in your land, not a
stone's throw away on the wrong side of the river. So
don't start anointing my body yet!" She tried to look
fierce, but was nearly purring with pleasure at Kalie's

ministrations.

"We prefer to use such arts for the living, rather than the dead," said Kalie.

"Such sensible people," said Agafa. "Another thing I think I'm going to like about your home."

Brenia massaged Agafa's hands while Kalie finished with her feet. They worked in companionable silence until Agafa fell asleep. Then Brenia and Kalie went to find their collection of children. Yarik, Riyik's three-year-old son by his late wife, was now Kalie's step-son, but he still felt closer to his aunt Brenia, who had raised him since his mother's death. Kalie had come to love Yarik, whose club foot she had been treating, nearly as much as Varena, the child she had adopted while still living as a slave in Maalke's tent.

Kalie looked at the young woman who walked about the camp, seeing to final chores, and reassuring those who still feared the noisy flowing water—and nearly everything else they saw. Varena had been an unwanted, half-starved slave girl when Kalie had met her barely over a year ago. Now she walked tall and proud among those who had once been her masters, her unbound hair blowing golden and free behind her.

And then, Kalie thought as she settled Yarik in his blankets beside his cousin Barak, there was Brenia. Married to a cruel and selfish warrior since she was fifteen, Brenia had been pregnant many times in the eighteen years of her marriage. But as her husband never tired of reminding her, only one had survived, and that one had not even arrived until Brenia was nearly thirty— an age when most women of the steppes were old and dried out. Yet Kalie considered Brenia to be one of the most beautiful women she knew, her skin still clear and white, and her long red hair no longer hidden by a veil. But Brenia carried her beauty more in her quiet dignity, graceful stride and kind heart.

And now that she had finally taken her son and left her brutal husband, Brenia had gained the one thing she thought she would never have: a daughter. It had been nearly two hands of days since they had fled the tribe of Aahk when Kalie had discovered that a girl of about nine years was not the daughter of one of the many women who had followed Kalie into the unknown. Liara had simply walked away from the tent in which she had been a slave since the day of her birth, and joined those risking their lives for a chance at freedom.

Hard-working and silent, Liara had been terrified she would be left behind when her secret was discovered. Instead, Brenia had adopted her, as Kalie had adopted Varena. Such a thing would have been unthinkable to even one as unusual as Brenia had she stayed with her tribe. But now, it seemed, anything was possible.

When the two little boys and the older girl had fallen asleep, and even Varena had been convinced to come lie down beside them in her own blankets, Kalie looked over the mass of humanity who had left everything behind and followed her on this desperate journey because Kalie had promised them a better life in the west.

She prayed that she would be proven correct.

Kalie had just decided that she would check on the watch, and then find her own bed, when Riyik appeared beside her, like a shadow thrown against the darkness by their one fire.

"We crossed farther north last time," he said, answering the question that had been bothering her since they came to this place. "But it's the same river. Your home—our home—is not far."

And Kalie realized that there was in fact one other besides herself and Larren who had traveled this way before. Riyik had been here. Years ago, when he came with Haraak to raid her home. She did not want to think about that now.

Riyik saw her expression and misunderstood. "You fear being so close, that something will happen to take it all away. You would swim that river tonight, if you could. You would run through the forest until you found your people, wouldn't you?"

So perhaps he had not misunderstood. "We've come so very far," she said. "But until I see a village or town, full of safe, happy people running to welcome us, and not a burned out ruin, I will not truly rest."

Riyik wrapped his arms around her. Kalie hesitated only a moment, and then melted into his embrace. If Riyik noticed her hesitation, he said nothing. "Come to our furs and I will watch over you until you sleep."

"But you must sleep as well," Kalie whispered. "Tomorrow, I shall count on you to watch over us all."

Riyik kissed her and she did not flinch; in fact, she felt warmth spreading through her body. "Then let us find a way to help each other to sleep."

As he led the way to their bedrolls, Kalie felt a moment's uncertainty. Then she forced it down. The monsters who had made the joining of men and women into a thing of pain and dominance would not destroy what she and Riyik had. She would join with him tonight in joy, even if she had to fight a war to do it. But she hoped for the day when there would be no war. When loving a man was as natural to her as it had been before she had met the horsemen.

Chapter 2

The next morning, everyone rose alive and well, and the river, fording spot and trees on the other side had not vanished in the night like a cruel trick. "I've got to get home before the strain of this journey drives me mad," thought Kalie, rising from her empty furs. Riyik was already seeing to the horses, and explaining the crossing to those who were awake to listen.

When they finally lined up to cross, women and children first, men walking their horses behind, things went surprisingly smoothly. Some wanted to argue when Kalie insisted everyone remove their clothing and carry it in bundles on their heads, or allow the horses to carry it. "The air is too cold to travel in wet clothes," she said firmly. "And the water is cold as well. You'll want something warm and dry when you reach the other side."

Kalie and Larren found it amusing that both men and women were uncomfortable crossing naked, although for different reasons. The women had been conditioned from birth to keep their bodies covered— especially when men were present. The men were afraid of unknown water-beasts which might attack their manhood—and of the cold they feared would shrink it.

Eventually, everyone made it across. Laughing and shivering, they dried themselves, climbed back into their clothes—many adding extra layers in the biting air—and hurried to resume their trek. The brisk pace set by the leaders helped everyone warm up. Even Agafa had energy, insisting the cold water and vigorous rub-down Kalie had given her had restored her health.

The going was easy at first. Level ground and sparsely dotted trees—many of which were losing their brown leaves—gave the travelers little trouble. Kalie inhaled deeply of the rich earth scents and felt a sensation that took a moment to identify.

She was home. Perhaps not out of danger; perhaps even bringing danger with her in the form of nearly seventy nomads, many of whom she barely knew. But the sights and smells were familiar. The birdsong was one she recognized. The touch of rough bark and the whisper of falling leaves gave her a sense of peace that she had thought was lost forever. Kalie stopped to wrap her arms around a sturdy oak, and the feeling increased.

Not everyone was so happy. The refugees from the steppes clustered together, walking in silence and staring about the trees as if they expected monsters to jump out of every shadow. Children whimpered and clung to their mothers. Kalie was certain that many were wondering why they had come here, and she hoped to have something wonderful to show them soon.

Still, she was pleased to see that some in the group were gazing about with eyes wide with wonder. Some were even smiling. Varena gaped at every new sight and sound as if they had been designed just for her. Danica peered intently at everything, nodding from time to time, as if confirming a particular story her grandmother had once told her. A few of the bolder children made a game out of jumping from shadow to shadow.

The animals, however, had only squeals and

whinnies to contribute.

"The horses are afraid," commented one of the warriors.

"They don't like this strange place," said another, looking nervously at the trees, and making the sign against evil.

"Look, nuts!" said Larren.

Kalie looked up. Larren had found a walnut tree. It was late in the season, but a large quantity of edible nuts still clung to the branches. Although wary, the people of the steppes were also hungry, and eager to supplement their nearly all meat diet with something familiar. The variety might be new, but nuts themselves were something they ate back home.

Some of the more resourceful members of the party began looking for fallen branches to knock down the few on the lower branches. Kalie and Larren grinned at each other. "That's not how you do it," said Larren, grabbing a low-hanging branch, and trying to hoist herself up.

"Don't even think of it, Larren," Kalie said, putting a restraining hand on her friend's arm—and another on her protruding belly. "Next year, all right?"

Larren pouted, but Kalie knew it was half in jest, and delighted in the change she saw in the woman. The resignation and despair that had filled Larren's soul just a moonspan ago were gone, and the woman she had been before was peeking out like a sun long hidden by clouds.

Kalie grabbed at a branch and leapt up to crouch on the one beside it. Years out of practice, and not nearly as gracefully as she intended, it felt good none the less. *This is freedom*, Kalie thought almost giddily as she continued to climb. "Get out some baskets," she called down, but Larren and Varena were already getting them. With their food nearly gone, empty baskets were plentiful.

Kalie began picking nuts and tossing them down to the women below. Soon, Varena tried to follow Kalie up. After two failed attempts, Riyik lifted her up, and held on until she was nervously perched on a low branch. "Just be careful," he told her. "I promised your mother I'd get you to her home in one piece."

Next, one of the older boys tried, and showed impressive skill for one who had never climbed a tree before. Two more boys followed, and then a girl hitched up her skirt and joined them, moving as nimbly as a squirrel. Her mother's scandalized shouts to get down fell on deaf ears, perhaps because there wasn't a man to back her up.

"That's enough for one tree!" Larren called, as more began to climb. "We don't want to break it." She pointed to a second nut tree. While not as rich with food, it gave the remaining bold adventurers something to do. The children soon had a competition going, each trying to gather the most nuts. Most of the adults who braved the climb were more interested in getting a good view of this truly new world.

Nearby, they found a nice spot to rest and eat their prizes. A spreading beech tree crowned a low hill, its branches still covered with golden leaves, and a small spring flowing nearby. As the travelers settled beneath it, the air was soon filled with the sounds of shells cracking open, food being shared and people exclaiming over the abundance and sweetness of water in this land.

One of the men gingerly plucked a leaf from the tree, examined it closely, and then threw it away in disgust when he saw it was just a leaf.

Riyik and some others laughed. "Were you expecting real gold, Durak?"

The young man, only just initiated into the ranks of warriors the year before, looked angry at being laughed at. "Haraak told me that gold grew on trees in this land," Durak said defensively.

Riyik's laughter vanished. "Haraak was a liar and a traitor," he said coldly. "And those were not even the worst of his faults."

"But there is gold here, isn't there?" asked another warrior, older than Durak, but clearly oblivious to the tension that had just manifested. "That is why some of us came. Well, one of the reasons, at least."

Riyik and Kalie exchanged a glance, and Kalie found her good humor slipping away.

"We came here for many reasons, Zanal," Riyik said, meeting the eyes of each of his men. "But all of us came looking for a life we could not have amid the violence and deceit of the tribe of Aahk. Kalie and I explained the rules before we left. Perhaps now would be a good time to review them." He gestured for Kalie to speak.

Wonderful, she thought. *It's cold and everyone wants to move. We need food and shelter, and we'll need the help of other people before winter sets in.* She looked at the sky and saw the rainclouds moving in from the north. The weather would turn tonight; tomorrow at the latest.

But Riyik was right. They would meet people soon, and they could not risk any kind of misunderstanding. Kalie rose to her feet.

"The land you have entered is filled with many treasures." She gazed at Durak, then Zanal, boldly meeting their stare until both men looked away. "Gold is one of them, but not the greatest. If you wish for gold you may have it, but only if follow our rules. Touch nothing without asking. Then ask what you must do to acquire what you want. If the person you ask does not know the answer, he will tell you who does. Just remember: that person will as likely be a woman as a man. That is our most important difference from your world. "

Everyone had heard this before, but there was still some shocked laughter and nervous whispering. Then Danica asked, "What other treasures will we find?"

Kalie smiled. The woman was shrewd. Danica knew what Kalie was going to say, and had no need to hear more. But for many in their party, the land in the west was only vague myth and children's tales. Now that the running was over, they needed to understand what their decision to come here would bring them.

Kalie took the half-full water-skin she had been drinking from and went to the little spring to fill it. "Never going thirsty again, for one," she said. "And food in plenty, although I can't promise you will never go hungry. But you will live with people who will share their food through good times and bad. People resourceful enough to solve any problem that comes their way. You will have freedom—not just from slavery, for there is no slavery in this land and never will be—but the freedom to choose how you will live, what dreams to pursue, what you will contribute to the community. That, I think, is the greatest treasure of all."

After that, there was a murmur, as people spoke, sometimes to Kalie, sometimes to each other. "I was never a good warrior," one man was saying. "I wanted to learn to heal, not kill." "I want to learn how to make food come from the ground." "I want my baby to live."

And so it went, until they all stood up to resume the journey.

The discussion was well-timed, for that afternoon they began to find signs of human habitation. A footprint in the carpet of fallen leaves, a scrap of cloth torn from a garment by a thorny bush. Then they came to a well-used track through the woods, and from just beyond, in a grove of apple trees, the sounds of laughter and challenges, and the dull thud of fruit striking baskets. Nearly full baskets, if Kalie's ear was not too far out of practice.

She was about to suggest that only a few of them move forward, when there was a sudden silence, followed by a flurry of movement. Then a group of children emerged from the trees, and froze in amazement at the sight of a large number of strangers, accompanied by huge animals none had ever seen before.

Then they all disappeared down the track at a run.

Chapter 3

At Kalie's insistence, the women and children walked in the front of the group, the men walking the horses behind. It was the opposite of how things would have gone in the land from which they had escaped. There, it would have been mounted warriors approaching the camp or settlement, women and children far behind, or hidden.

"They were afraid," said the woman beside Kalie, almost accusingly. "You told us strangers were welcomed, and that your people feared nothing."

"The children have only gone back to their village, Tarella, to tell the adults that guests have arrived," said Kalie. "So they can prepare a welcome."

"Or a defense," said Durak.

Kalie and Larren exchanged a worried look. Neither of them knew what had happened here over the last year. Children would normally show more curiosity than these had.

When they reached the village, however, Kalie and Larren both sighed with relief. Standing before a neat collection of rectangular wooden dwellings, a group of two men and three women stood unarmed and smiling, ready to greet their guests. Behind them were gathered the rest of the population—including the children who had been picking apples.

The oldest man and women stepped forward, both wearing the brown and green robes of the priesthood. "Greetings in the name of the Goddess," said the woman.

"Welcome to the village of Green Bower," said

the man.

Their smiles were genuine, but strained. Taking another look, Kalie could see why. Behind her were nearly seventy people, and over half that number of horses. The village of Green Bower contained barely more; perhaps one hundred people. Even if their harvest had been good—and Kalie seriously hoped it had—she could not possibly ask them to strain their resources by feeding and sheltering this many.

Beside both the priest and the priestess, an acolyte stood, each holding a large jug of what Kalie guessed would be fruit juice, or perhaps whatever fermented specialty this place had to offer. Both the man and woman seemed at a loss to know who to offer it to first, or what to do when it ran out.

Smiling, Kalie stepped forward. "My name is Kalie, and I have just returned from a long…stay…in the east. I have returned with many good people who seek a new life. For now though, we seek only a night's shelter and a place in your temple for a few who are sick. We have sheep and goats to contribute to a meal we might share tonight, and many stories to tell."

"Of that, Kalie, I have no doubt," said the third woman, who stood a little to the side of the four clerics. Unlike priest's robes, this woman wore a short-sleeved dress of white linen, a heavy blue shawl thrown over her shoulder for warmth. "You left Riverford, with thirty women, yet here you are with many more. And most, I'd dare say, are not of this land."

Kalie stared, but could not recognize the woman who spoke.

"I am Shula," the woman in white said helpfully. "A healer. I was in Riverford to help with the crisis, which I am sure you well remember."

"I do indeed," said Kalie. "Forgive me, I do not remember you."

"You had much on your mind," said Shula. "And I was not one who supported your mission. I called it madness and left the city soon after you and you followers did. Where are they now?" she asked, eyes searching the crowd.

Larren, who had been standing with two other pregnant women, stepped forward.

Shula started to speak, but the priestess cut her off. "These people need a place to stay and a proper meal," she scolded gently. "And shelter from the storm." At that, everyone looked up at the looming clouds. We made it just in time, Kalie thought. But how much can a place like this spare? The two acolytes began working their way through the crowd, offering each person a sip from the pottery jugs they carried.

"And you said there are sick among you?" Shula's pale skin was red with embarrassment. "Please bring them to the temple. Follow me." Whatever else the healer said was drowned by the orders of the other leaders, as the warriors were led to an area outside the village, but sheltered by trees, to set up the tents. Women and children were sent in groups to various dwellings. Kalie and Larren assisted the sick to the temple.

Kalie glanced back once, and saw an eager group of children following the horses, and pelting the warriors with questions. Most of the men were patiently answering, while at the same time managing to keep the children away from sharp hooves. There was none of the yelling or hitting that would have been viewed as normal in the tribe. It suddenly struck Kalie that she was home, and it had not changed. Even if she had, this world was welcoming her—and the people she had brought. She wanted to weep and laugh at the same time.

This feeling intensified when the party reached the temple. Inside, everything was as Kalie remembered: a warm and comforting collection of rooms, with the walls painted in soothing shades of green and blue. Heat and light were provided by the fire that burned before the simple altar, adorned only by a statue of the Goddess in her form as crone. There was the sharp, clean smell of moss and herbs, neatly stacked in bundles and jars on shelves along the walls, and, most important to Kalie, the sight of at least six beds made up with linen sheets—all of them empty.

"I was afraid the temple would be too small to accommodate everyone," she told Shula. "For a village this size—"

"We serve several isolated farms, and a nearby fishing village," Shula explained, as she got everyone settled, and directed her staff, which consisted of two other healers and a young apprentice. One of the sick children seemed to be on the mend, but the other had gotten much worse. He and Agafa were examined first, while the little girl, sitting on her mother's lap, insisted she felt fine and wanted to play with the children who lived here. Malor, the injured warrior, insisted the others be treated first, although Kalie could see he was burning with fever.

"The midwife will be here soon," Andar, a young male healer, told Larren. "You should lie down until she gets here." Larren agreed a little too quickly for Kalie's comfort, who wondered just how difficult the journey had been on her friend. Unlike the nomad women, Larren was not used to grueling travel while pregnant.

While Kalie acted as translator, an older woman with long gray hair tied back in a neat bun bustled into the room. No one needed to tell her this was the midwife, as the woman took in the entire room with bright dark eyes that missed nothing. She went to Larren without a word and began to speak with her quietly. Kalie faltered in her translation of Shula's questions to Agafa and one hand strayed to her belly, as she briefly considered requesting a word with the midwife when she was done with Larren.

Self-consciously, Kalie forced her hand to her side, and focused on the work at hand. There was much of it. In addition to four patients in serious need of attention, two other nomads entered the temple: a warrior who had been stoically ignoring bad stomach pain for the past three days and a fragile slave girl of about thirteen, who did not wish to trouble anyone, but thought she was having a miscarriage.

The midwife helped Larren to move to a stool, as both the bed and her assistance with translation were needed. While Larren helped with the man, Kalie knelt beside Saela. "Why did you tell no one you were pregnant?" she asked, as the midwife gently examined her.

"I was afraid you would not take me with you if you knew the truth," Saela whimpered.

"But at least three other women in our band are pregnant!" said Kalie. "They would have helped you; all of us would have."

"But you might have asked who the father was." Saela cried out then, and after that, all her focus was on the pain, and the tiny, unformed creature her body fought to expel. Kalie assisted the midwife until it was over. Once Saela had been given a soothing draught, and fallen into a peaceful sleep, Kalie and the midwife had a chance to introduce themselves.

"I am Laisa," said the midwife.

"I am Kalie. Will she be all right?" Kalie nodded toward Saela.

"I believe so. Although she was far too young—not to mention undernourished—for a baby. Whoever these people to the east are, I can see why so many chose to move west. Did she give you any explanation for why she hid her pregnancy? What frightened her just now?"

"Something about the baby's father."

"What does that mean?" Laisa was clearly baffled.

Kalie sighed. She wanted to enjoy being home, not explain the hell she had just left to someone who had no way of comprehending it. "My guess is that the baby's father was Saela's own father. Either that or a man who told her he'd kill her if she told anyone he'd raped her."

Laisa stared at Kalie for at least thirty heartbeats. Then she looked at Larren, as if expecting a reasonable explanation for Kalie's outrageous statements. "I think it was probably her father," Larren said quietly. "They always blame the daughter in those cases. Usually, the girl is killed."

Kalie wanted to hug Larren for the simple act of supporting her statement. Eight years ago, when Kalie had returned from her first time as a captive of the beastmen, few had believed her tales of what she had seen, and no one wanted to hear such horrible stories; surely, they thought, it was nothing more than the ranting of a deranged woman. This time, Kalie was not alone.

"Perhaps we should see what is happening outside," Laisa said at last. "Everything seems under control in here."

Kalie looked around, and saw that Sarika had joined the healers, competently assisting in their work, asking questions with her limited command of the language she had studied during the journey, and looking like she never wanted to leave. Checking the row of beds, Kalie could see that everyone was now sleeping or resting comfortably. The healers were busy cleaning up or grinding herbs for more medicines. Kalie smiled wearily. "May the Goddess bless you all," she said.

Outside, the sun was setting in a brilliant display of color among the storm clouds. In the cleared space in the center of the village, a feast was taking shape. A large bonfire was laid in the center of the clearing, waiting to be lit. In front of each house, a smaller fire burned. Each one contained some kind of food roasting above the flames, frying on rocks beside them, or baking underneath. Kalie stopped in the middle and looked around, taking it all in.

The smells were intoxicating, as was the pleasure the local people were taking in showing their guests around. Children were running everywhere, and in the blur, Kalie could not easily distinguish native from foreigner. She took a moment to marvel at that fact. Then Varena and Katya detached themselves from a group of local girls and ran up to her.

"Oh, mother, you were right!" Varena began ecstatically. "Everything you told me—"

"Did you know about this?" Katya cried, waving her hand to encompass the village. Like Saela, Katya had been a terrified wraith of a slave girl when she left the tribe of Aahk. Now for the first time Kalie had known her, Katya spoke louder than a whisper—and had even interrupted someone.

"Did you know?" the girl repeated. "About how the people here live? How women just speak when they feel like it, and go where they want? I haven't seen a man hit a woman since we got here! I haven't seen anyone hit anyone, not even a child, but it can't be like that all the time, can it? And look how men and women both are cooking! And they think it's all normal. I asked if the men who cooked were slaves, since no men are slaves back in the tribes, and no one knew what I meant!"

Varena put a restraining hand on Katya's shoulder, as if afraid the girl would leap across one of the fires. "Kalie has been telling us about it since she came to our clan more than a year ago," the young woman said in slow, measured syllables. But even Varena could not repress a grin as she looked around.

"I know she told us," said Katya, reclaiming some of her dignity. "But Kalie's a storyteller. It's what she does. This…" Katya trailed off; trying to grasp the words she wanted.

"What did you expect?" Kalie was genuinely curious. "You risked your life to run away with me. Why take such a risk if you didn't believe my stories were true?"

"Well," the small, dark-haired girl rubbed her chin with one hand and seemed to be thinking very hard. "Someplace better, of course. Food, and short winters, and people who were kinder than back home. But I still thought they'd be people. I mean, people are the same everywhere, right? Some are good and some are bad. But there's always a few who run everything, and who take whatever they want and push everyone else around. I didn't think that would be different anywhere."

"Why did you think I would bring you here if that's how it was?" asked Kalie.

"I just thought the people who owned everything here were your kin, and you'd make sure they sold me to someone kind. Or that you would keep me as your handmaid, like Varena.

At that, Varena bristled and was about to speak, when several village elders approached them, with Riyik and some of his men following at a respectful distance. "We would like to begin," the priestess told Kalie. "We are blessed with dry weather for a little longer. It is good that we can all share a meal together outside, where everyone can hear your news and your stories."

"And we have many questions for you as well," Kalie said. "But for now, your generosity and hospitality are more than enough."

"We thank you as well for the gift of so many fine sheep and goats," said the priest, gesturing to where several animals were turning on spits.

Riyik and Kalie grinned at each other, while the elders, with the help of musicians playing flutes and drums, called the people together.

"Some things truly are the same everywhere," said Riyik. "Those sheep and goats were as tough and mangy as any animals I've ever seen. Yet that priest thanked us exactly as a clan chief would have when presented with the same gift."

Kalie smiled. "Of all the things for our two peoples to have in common, I'm happy with good manners. And you may be surprised. Our cooks take tough meat as a special challenge. I can't wait to see what they've come up with."

"I can't wait to taste it," grumbled Borik.

At that moment, the priest and priestess together lit the bonfire.

"May the Goddess bless this feast, as we welcome our visitors from the east," said the priestess. "May she spread her bounty over all who come to the fire."

"May we join together in harmony, this night and all others," spoke the priest. "Let us begin."

Chapter 4

People began moving among the hearths, taking what appealed to them. Most —both local and foreign—had their own plates, cups and eating knives. Those who did not were given them by their hosts. Kalie had been relieved to learn that the harvest had indeed been good, and the meal reflected it. There were many varieties of bread, and even more kinds of meat. Vegetables such as beets, leeks, mushrooms and cabbage made up dishes that were strange to the visitors, but brought tears to Kalie's eyes as the taste brought back memories. Apples, pears and nuts lay piled in softly glowing mounds. There had even been time to turn some of them into the luscious pastries Kalie had often longed for during her captivity.

Kalie and Riyik were seated on woven mats beside the village elders. At first they spoke only of the harvest, and of the region around Green Bower. Kalie learned that they had returned to her homeland far to the north of where she had left it. Her home village of Tall Oaks was many days south, and a bit to the west. If they were to walk due west for about six days, they would reach the Black Sea at the northern tip of its eastern shore.

"I had hoped to reach Gaea before the winter," said Kalie. "It's the only city I know of large enough to take in this many people." She glanced around at the nearly seventy men, women and children she had brought out of the steppes. They were scattered among their hosts, all talking eagerly, different languages hardly a barrier—except among the children, where it was no barrier at all.

A white haired woman, probably the oldest person in the village, shook her head. "Gaea is on the southern shore of the Great Water," she said, using the local name for the same body of water. "You will not make it there before winter."

"But there are many large settlements along the eastern shores, just south and east of here," said a portly, middle-aged man. "You can easily reach them in a few days."

"That would allow us to break our people into smaller groups," said Riyik, managing the local tongue well. "Less of a drain on resources."

The elders nodded, some with evident relief that the visitors did not plan to stay in Green Bower for the winter. Kalie had to smile. Had she not been prepared to lead this group away in a few days, these people would have felt obligated to keep them until spring, whatever the cost. If Kalie needed any further proof she was home, this was it.

Shula arrived from the temple, somewhat out of breath, and carrying a plate of food. The elders made room for her to sit beside Kalie. "I must return to the temple soon," she said. "But I did not want to miss your news."

That was a cue if Kalie ever heard one, but the priestess spoke first. "The others will not leave the temple?"

"Andar will likely stay all evening. Food has been brought to him. Galla and Josan have already come to the feast, and Josan has returned to the temple. Sarika is getting food now, but I think she will return as well." Shula turned back to Kalie. "She is a most remarkable healer. Ignorant of much knowledge which I take for granted, yet knowing things no one here has even thought of! I look forward to learning all I can from her, and sharing what I know. From what you told us in Riverford last year, I did not expect to find skilled and dedicated healers among these people."

Kalie was taken aback. After a moment's thought she said, "I have learned much about the people I once named beastmen. Many of them still deserve the name. But many others do not." I only hope I brought the right ones to my home.

"There is always much that different tribes can learn from each other," said the priestess.

"How are the sick?" Kalie asked.

"The children will both be fine," said Shula. "I believe the man with the cut will recover in a few days. The poison was in his blood by the time he reached us, but he is strong, and already responding to the medicine. The young woman, Saela, too, will recover, with proper food and rest."

"And Garak?" Riyik asked.

Shula nodded around a mouthful of food. "Yes, the one with stomach pains. We had hoped it was only bad meat, but now fear it may be more serious. That is why Andar will not be leaving the temple tonight. He believes that Garak suffers from a swelling of an organ within his belly. I, too, have seen such things before. If it continues to swell, it must be removed before it bursts and kills him."

Riyik set his place down on the ground before him, and had to swallow his last bite several times. "Can such a thing be done?" he whispered, his face white.

Shula set down the goat's rib she had been stripping with her teeth. She put her left hand, the hand she had not been eating with, gently on Riyik's arm, and met his gaze. "Andar has done so before, and the patient lived. Your friend could not be in better hands."

Kalie remembered, a long time ago, or maybe just the summer before last, when she had counseled a man with a similar condition at a temple of healing far across the world. She hoped Garak would not require such extreme measures. But if he did, she prayed he would live, and that all the people who had come from the tribe of Aahk would take it as a sign of what was possible in the Land of the Goddess.

Only one person had not been mentioned. "Agafa?" Kalie whispered, fearing the answer.

Shula's face became carefully neutral. "You must have known when you brought her here that there would be little we could do." Her words, although not what Kalie wanted to hear, were laced with compassion.

"She did not want to die a slave," Kalie said, blinking back tears. "She wanted to see this world, and know it was real."

"And that much she has done. She will do more, Kalie, especially if she is not forced to travel any further. If Agafa stays with us, we can help her manage her pain without dulling her senses, and she can enjoy all the village of Green Bower has to offer."

"I had hoped to show her more of our world. Temples and cities and the Great Water. But…if she stays here, could she live through the winter?"

Shula thought her words over carefully. "It is possible. I cannot promise."

Kalie felt a rush of joy that Agafa might live to see the dancing that would happen at the Spring

Festival; hold the first new flowers in her hands before she closed her eyes for the last time.

Sensing her emotions, the elders waited a few more moments, but the feast was winding down, and there was much to be done before the rain began.

"If you and your friends might tell us something of this land from which you came?" the priest began carefully. "And what brought you here?"

"Of course." Kalie rose to her feet. A moment later, Riyik did as well.

Silence spread in ripples throughout the gathering. When she had everyone's attention, Kalie spoke. "Thank you, people of Green Bower, for your kindness and generosity. I was born in a place not far from here, and I understand that such things are normal; to be expected. But I have brought with me people from a distant land, where the ways are very different."

Her words provoked a storm of questions. Things people wanted to know, but had been prevented by good manners from asking, were now shouted from the crowd. They wanted words like "war" and "slave" explained, and reasons for the frightening scars they had seen on many people, and how tattoos were made.

Maybe I should start with tattoos, thought Kalie. It's the only thing I'm not already sick to death of explaining.

"Perhaps I should speak this time?" Riyik asked quietly. "If you could translate?"

Kalie nodded, relieved. While Riyik had a good command of her language, he was much more articulate in his own, and this was not the time for mistakes.

Riyik began by holding up his plate and cup. "This feast which you provided for strangers is the best example I can think of to show how different our two peoples are." His voice travelled well, compelling in its exotic sound. Kalie's voice matched his for strength, bringing Riyik's words to the farthest edge of the gathering.

"In the tribe from which I come, people also gathered beneath the sky to enjoy great feasts. But in those feasts, no strangers would have been welcomed—only the members of our own tribe."

Riyik continued. "Cooking was done by slaves, who were watched carefully, to make certain they ate nothing while they worked. When all was ready, the chief and his warriors would arrive, and then the feast would begin. The chief would have first choice, taking as much food as he wished, followed by all of his men, based on their status. After the lowest ranked warrior had eaten his fill, their wives could help themselves, usually taking food for their children. Slaves and their children got what was left."

Kalie scanned the faces of the crowd. She saw what she expected: anger, confusion and disbelief. At least this time, the questions all came down to a single word: why? "Why do you live like that?" came from the crowd in several variations.

To her surprise, Danica stood and walked the short distance to where Kalie and Riyik stood, leaning heavily on her cane. Several villagers moved to help her but Danica shook them off, muttering. This brought smiles to help ease a tense situation: Danica was acting like any revered old woman of the land.

Signaling for Kalie to translate, Danica addressed the assembly. "You ask why life is so different where I come from. Why there is cruelty and want; why people are divided. But you cannot truly understand without seeing this land for yourselves. It is a harsh place, and only the strongest people can live there. That is what we are taught since birth. But it is true, in some ways. For there will never be enough for all, and there will always be many who are not strong enough to survive. We learn to accept death at an early age.

"There is never enough of anything in that land: water, food, grass for the animals, protection from the elements. Perhaps we were once more like you, but over time, the people became as the land: brutal, treacherous, and proud of the power to inflict pain."

"So why not simply leave?" shouted a girl of about twelve years. In the utter silence, Kalie heard the gasps of nomad women and children at the girl's boldness.

But Danica grinned, and swept her hand toward the visitor's tents and horses. "We did, and here we are! Some of us, at least. And we thank you for offering us a new way to live."

The crowd laughed, but there was a nervous edge to some of it. Kalie wondered if one of their hosts would ask the logical question of how many more refugees they might expect, but for now the people here still had questions about how such a place as the land of Aahk could exist.

"If there is little to go around, then sharing is even more important," said the priestess. "That is a lesson we learned long ago. All is not prosperous here, either. We have known the hunger that comes when crops fail or illness strikes our animals. Yet our

Goddess, and those She chooses to speak through, have taught us that cooperation and sharing are necessary at all times. And even more so when times are hard."

"How could anyone let a child go hungry if there is any food at all?" cried a woman.

"What kind of man abuses the very image of the Goddess Herself?" asked an old man. "Do you treat your own mothers as Riyik and Kalie have described?"

Kalie and Riyik looked at each other helplessly. Riyik tried to signal Larren to speak, while Kalie looked toward some of the women from the steppes. But they were not used to addressing large groups; many feared to speak at all. That Danica could do such a thing was surprising enough, and she had the highest status of anyone present.

Then, from across the gathering came a single guttural word. "Horses."

Everyone turned to see a brawny, dark-haired nomad who stood at least a head taller than everyone else.

"Horses," Borik repeated. "When you ride a horse, the world looks different." He fumbled for words. "You feel stronger, faster, like a god. A man feels like he can do anything from the back of a horse. And some men do bad things, even thinking they are good."

Kalie gaped, and Riyik had to tap her shoulder to remind her to translate. She did so, all the while wondering what was happening. She liked Borik, and knew his loyalty to Riyik was beyond question. But he rarely spoke, and she'd always thought he'd had more strength than intelligence.

Now people were casting fearful glances at the large animals grazing peacefully near the tents of the nomads. Borik followed their gaze and let out a frightened yelp. "It's not the horses' fault!" he cried, looking as though he wished he'd said nothing. "But Lady Danica said we might have once been like you, and I think she's right, and you asked what changed and so I—" Borik began to stammer, looking around seeming much like a frightened horse himself. Kalie was overwhelmed with the desire to run over and hug him, but she had to seize the opportunity he had given her.

"Borik is right!" she called out, pitching her voice so all could hear. "Both about how the taming of the horse changed the men, and that the horses themselves are innocent. They are powerful creatures, but like any power, they can be used for either good or ill. The outcome depends on those who control them."

She stopped then, as a buzz of conversation made addressing the crowd impossible. But that was fine; Kalie knew the people here needed to discuss what they had heard. Someone handed her a finely carved wooden cup, just as she realized how drained and thirsty she was. She took a large sip, expecting water. Instead, sweet, mellow apple juice slid down her throat, tasting like comfort; like the whole season of harvest she had missed. She finished it slowly, taking time to savor the taste—and the possibilities.

When the talking wound down, the leaders of the village stood to call an end to the feast—and the discussion. Before they could a young woman asked one last question. "Why do only men ride? I got to pet one of your horses, and anyone can see their backs are designed for women! In fact, isn't it dangerous to let your men ride?" She sent a puzzled look at the nomad women. "Won't all that bouncing hurt their balls and make it hard to give a woman—"

"Yes, we have much more to talk about," called the priest. "But for now, let us show our guests to their beds, and applaud them for leaving behind such a place, and seeking a new life with us."

Some seemed inclined to argue, but the first drops of rain were falling, and they still needed to clean up the remnants of the feast. But the look of so many blushing warriors and grinning women was one Kalie would remember with satisfaction for the rest of her life.

Then she found the leaders of the village staring at her with an intensity that halted all levity. "Will there be more?" asked the oldest woman. "Will others follow the path you have blazed, seeking sanctuary? Or perhaps, other things?"

It was not possible to lie to that gaze. "I would not have led them here if I thought so," Kalie said. "We left the tribes fighting among themselves, and I pray, too weak to threaten this land."

"And if any more were to come," said Riyik, his arm coming protectively around her waist. "We would make sure they were those who are seeking shelter and offering their strength—and no one else."

Kalie prayed their small band was enough to make it so.

"Come," said the priestess, as the rain began to fall harder. "Let us sleep. We will have many days to discuss these new tidings."

Chapter 5

The storm lasted three days. While many people stayed inside, especially the sick and elderly, the folk here were used to rain, and had no intention of being confined to their homes until the blizzards came, and snow sealed their doors shut. As for the nomads, this storm was little more than a shower compared to what they were used to.

Kalie spent most of her time in the temple, dividing it between the section devoted to healing, and the large room where the council met. The morning after their arrival, Kalie and Riyik were invited to attend a meeting.

While their best clothing was stained and travel-worn, a good night's sleep indoors, and a hearty breakfast of hot porridge and leftovers from last night's feast had them looking better than when they arrived the night before. They had even bathed, in a small tub of hot water, provided by their hosts, a charming elderly and childless couple, who were happy to have Brenia and the two boys as well. Kalie's brown hair was neatly braided down her back, and Riyik had trimmed his beard and bangs, while his black hair was held back in a tooled leather headband of his own making.

The temple chamber, though large, was filled to capacity. All five council members were present, along with the priest and priestess, and about seven or eight villagers who Kalie guessed were concerned citizens. Larren—and to the couple's surprise—Borik were also there. Larren sat amid a pile of cushions, close enough to Laisa that Kalie wasn't sure if the midwife was there as part of the meeting or to keep an eye on Larren. Probably both, she decided.

After invoking the blessing of the Goddess, the priestess began the meeting. "Is there anything else you wish to tell us of this strange land and people from whom you have fled?"

Again Kalie and Riyik looked at each other, and again, Riyik spoke. "My former people are violent and do not share well. For now, we believe they are busy fighting each other. Should the day ever come when they come west with thoughts of conquest, we would like you to be prepared."

"Prepared?" scoffed an old woman. "To do what? Flee into the forest with what we can carry? Leave our animals and homes to these monsters, and hope they will be satisfied with that?"

"That is one option," said Kalie. "Another would be to learn ways to protect yourselves; to convince the beastmen that they would be happier if they went somewhere else."

"If they are as skilled in this thing you call war as you say," said a man with the grace and bearing of a hunter, "we cannot possibly stand against them! We are few, and when it comes to defending ourselves," he growled angrily. "There is a boar that has been ravaging the countryside. We have not even been able to kill him! Two good men who tried are dead."

"That is something we can help you with," Borik said excitedly. "When the rain slows, the warriors of Aahk would be honored to kill this beast for you."

The man gazed at Borik as though trying to determine if he was serious—or perhaps if he was right in the head. Well, thought Kalie, Borik's used to that.

"We would appreciate your help," the priest said smoothly. "With the boar—and perhaps with these other threats you mentioned. You said that you are looking for a new home. All of you?" He looked toward Kalie and Larren. "You two are of this land. Do you not have families somewhere?"

"My village was destroyed last year by the raiders who took us as slaves," said Larren. "All in my family were killed." Riyik winced, but quickly mastered his expression.

"I have relatives in the village of Tall Oaks," said Kalie. "I do not plan to return there, but I would know how they fare, if there is any news."

Several people turned to look at a young woman of perhaps eighteen summers. Beside her sat an elderly man, with a weather-beaten face and thin wisps of gray hair tied behind his head. "This is Jaleen," said the priest indicating the young woman. "A trader, who recently returned from a long season of travels to the south and west, with a band of other traders."

"This past summer," began Jaleen, "we stopped in Tall Oaks. All was well there, although we did hear the story of traders who went east one year and never returned, and the young woman who came back injured in body and mind. That would be you, Kalie?"

Not trusting herself to speak, Kalie nodded. She felt Riyik's comforting hand closing around hers.

"Were there any more recent such tales?" Larren asked. "Or stories of attacks by beastmen?"

"Nothing like you have described here," said Jaleen. "But we met a traveler from the south, and he told a strange tale of something that happened in a village at the foot of the great mountains at the end of the world.

"He told us that last winter a small group of half-frozen travelers were found in the snow outside the village. Only eight could be saved, the rest had already perished. Their clothing was unfamiliar, and they spoke no language anyone knew. And the storyteller told of large strange beasts on whose backs they rode." Jaleen stopped, her eyes widening in sudden understanding.

"I now see he meant horses. Although, at the time, I imagined something very different." Kalie clutched Riyik's hand, and felt her stomach do the same to her.

"They cared for these strangers until they regained their strength," Jaleen continued. "But then, we were told, they behaved most rudely, especially the men. Apparently, the people put up with it for some time before the village Mother decided they would have to leave. None of us could understand that part. What could anyone do that would possibly make a village willing to send them into the snow in winter?"

In the silence which followed, Borik gulped loudly. Kalie might have done the same, but her mouth was too dry to swallow.

"Did they leave?" asked Larren.

"That's where the story became muddled. It seems that some did, and some stayed. But there was some kind of fight between the village Mother and the leader of the horsemen—and that a child was killed. Accidently, we presume."

Or not, thought Kalie.

"Please remember that the man who told us

this story was not present for these events," said
Jaleen. "It was something he was told—by someone
else who may or may not have been there, either."

"Have there been any other stories of strangers
from the east?" asked Riyik.

The people in the room looked at each other,
but all shook their heads.

Laisa spoke up. "Well now all of us are here,
to witness with our own eyes and ears the real men and
women of the east. It is clear they are not monsters,
and equally clear that they need a place to live.
Perhaps we should now work on that."

There were many nods. "We cannot take all of
you into this village," said the priestess. "But perhaps
some of you will stay? Shula tells me that your two
men and the crone may not be moved for some time.
Also that the healer from the east wishes to stay with
us."

"Larren should not continue her travels until
after her child is born," Laisa added.

"Many of the children have expressed a desire
for Borik to stay," said the priest.

Kalie found she could still feel surprise—and
even the desire to smile. "Oh?" she asked, one
eyebrow raised.

"They like to climb on me," Borik muttered,
red faced, yet still looking pleased.

"We will need directions to the settlements
which you recommend, for those who do not stay,"
Kalie addressed the council. "Which will be most of
us."

There was further discussion, during which a
mid-day meal was brought in by several older children
and two women to supervise them. The meal and the

meeting finished together, and the people walked out of the temple to see that a heavy mist had replaced the rain for the moment.

Borik went to find men to help him hunt down the boar. Kalie and Riyik wandered through the village and talked.

"Was it Yuraak, do you think?" Kalie asked.

"The timing is right," said Riyik. "He disappeared last winter, with his entire clan, to seek treasure in the west." Riyik sighed. "It sounds like most of his people died before they even reached that village."

They watched people of both tribes taking advantage of the brief respite from the storm, to move about the common area, or from house to house. Children from the village hurried to see the horses, or ask if they could spend that night in the tents. The door of one house was flung open to let in fresh air, and Kalie saw Danica seated on a cushion, drinking tea and apparently telling her life story to a large number of village women. The women sipped their tea and passed around baskets of dried fruit and nuts, listening with interest. Varena sat beside Danica, translating.

The door to another house opened, and Brenia walked out. She stopped to greet her brother and his wife. Kalie was about to ask Brenia what she thought of this new world, but Riyik beat her to it. "Is it everything you expected?" he asked.

"It's too wet to know!" Then Brenia laughed at the expressions on the couple's faces. Kalie had forgotten how lovely the older woman was when she smiled. She had smiled far too rarely in their last season in the east. "It's beautiful," Brenia continued, almost reverently. "The land, the people, the things they make—even the things they say! Yarik and Barak are inside, playing with a large pack of children. I wanted to go to the temple, to check on the sick, and the woman whose tent, no, *house* we were in said I should go. But I could stay with the children if it's proper."

"The boys will be fine with whichever family they're with," said Kalie. "Here, children are raised by the entire village. And you should feel free to go wherever you like, Brenia. In fact, I'd like to go see how our people are doing, as well."

"Go ahead, both of you," said Riyik. "I want to check on this boar hunt that's shaping up, and practice my speech on some of the locals. Let's just hope I don't say anything that gets us thrown out." Gray eyes twinkling, Riyik took his leave.

In the temple, Kalie and Brenia found a buzz of activity. Since the place was dry and warm, and held a group of visitors who couldn't go anywhere, several villagers had found reasons to come and visit. A group of local children were on the floor with the two recovering nomad children, teaching them how to play a game which involved moving black and white chips of stone around squares drawn on a large, flat piece of leather. Malor and Saela both sat up in bed, learning the local language, and trying, though both were a bit baffled, to understand some of the local customs.

"Where is Agafa?" Brenia asked Shula.

"In the First Shrine, taking instruction in the Mysteries," the healer replied, somewhat distracted, as she took an inventory of supplies.

At Brenia's inquiring glance, Kalie explained. "The First Shrine is the first room built in any temple complex. Often underground, or in a cave, if the temple is built close to one. In larger settlements, there is often one for men and one for women. It's where children are taught our faith, and where boys and girls go for their initiation into adulthood."

"And a woman Agafa's age has gone there for instruction?" Brenia asked in surprise.

Kalie grinned. "It seems our friend has decided to do more than die here. I think she means to start truly living!"

Brenia shook her head, but was clearly happy with what she was hearing.

Then Andar appeared looking serious. Upon seeing his expression, Shula abandoned her supply shelf and hurried over. Kalie and Brenia followed.

"I will have to operate on Garak now, while there is at least some light," Andar said. "Joran and Galla have gone to prepare the room. Please get the Speakers, and come assist me."

"Of course." Shula hurried away.

"The Speakers are the priest and priestess you met yesterday," Kalie explained as both she and Brenia followed Andar.

"Should we be doing this?" Brenia asked anxiously.

"We both have some skill at healing," Kalie said over her shoulder. "And I have assisted in such operations before." More like observed, Kalie reflected, but she still hoped to be able to help.

The room that had been set up was large, with a western facing wall which could be removed to gain all the light an afternoon could offer—even a foggy one like this. Word had spread, and now it seemed like half the newly increased population of the village crowded outside, hoping for a glimpse of what was to happen—and the miracle everyone hoped for.

Garak lay on a table, pale from the sleeping draught he'd been given.

"He should be quite insensible to pain," Andar explained to the watching crowd as the priestess poured water from a sacred spring three times over his hands. Then Andar went to the altar where a block of shiny black obsidian waited next to a stone hammer. With a few quick, efficient blows, Andar created a razor sharp knife.

"Why does he do that?" Brenia whispered.

"To cut into a human body, a special knife must be made. It may be used only once; Andor will bury it after the procedure."

"But why?" Brenia persisted.

Kalie shrugged. "I don't know. It just seems that more patients survive when it's done this way."

The priest and several acolytes stationed outside began beating a simple rhythm on hide-covered wooden drums.

"Everyone may help," the priestess explained to Garak's friends, who stood watching mutely. "Simply join with us in our prayers." With that, she began a simple chant, which was picked up by the crowd. Some of the easterners backed away and remained silent, fearing their presence and that of their foreign gods might endanger Garak. Others joined in the chanting.

Sarika was allowed in the room with Kalie and Brenia, but in the end, they only watched. With steady hands, Andar and Shula cut into Garak's body with the new obsidian knife, and then found and quickly removed a strange-looking bloody mass, which an attendant caught, while Shula held the wound closed and Andar—his hands never shaking—sewed the two sides together with sinew.

The priestess brought the chanting to a close, amid a collective gasp of the watching crowd.

"Now we will wait and see," said Andar.

Garak was constantly attended by healers, but all others were kept away. "The more people near him," explained Shula, "the more likely evil spirits are to enter his body. In his weakened state, they could easily kill him."

Garak survived the night, and awoke the next morning, although he was groggy and in pain much of the day. He was beginning to feel better when several jubilant and mud-covered hunters emerged from the heavy rain, bearing the body of a huge boar, and eager to start it cooking. Finding enough dry space to cook it was a problem for the villagers, but one which they eagerly embraced.

Kalie looked from a miraculously recovering Garak, to the happy villagers who had been rescued from a dangerous menace, then calculated that the meat the warriors had brought in was nearly enough to make up for what the visitors had consumed.

Overall, things were going quite a lot better than she had hoped for.

Chapter 6

Two days later, sixty-two of the people who had arrived four days earlier offered heartfelt thanks to their hosts, and prepared to depart for the west.

Malor and Garak would be staying. Unbelievable as it seemed to the newcomers, Garak continued to recover. Still, it would be many days before he could walk, let alone ride. Malor was recovering well, and might have travelled on, against the healers' advice, but decided he didn't want to.

"Perhaps a true warrior of Aahk would ignore the pain and lingering weakness and mount his horse," Malor told them. "But I have seen stronger men than I die from cuts like I had, once they turn bad." He turned to Garak, propped up on cushions and sipping broth from a bowl with shaky hands. Then a young woman took the bowl from Garak and fed him. "And I have never seen anything like what they did to Garak. He should be dead. If these people allow it, I will study healing, and perhaps, one day, work such miracles myself."

Much to the disappointment of several children, Borik decided that his duty was to follow Riyik, but he promised to visit again if he could. A warrior named Yanal took his place, promising to teach any children interested how to ride, and whatever warrior's skills the people would allow. Everyone feared they would one day be needed.

Larren decided to stay and have her baby in Green Bower, and Agafa, would be remaining for the rest of her life.

Saela would also be staying, despite a lifetime

of teaching that told her a woman who was not strong enough to walk to the next camp after a miscarriage was unworthy to live. She sat up in bed sewing woolen cloth. "Even after all your stories, Kalie;" said Saela, "I never believed such people could be real. I still marvel at their kindness—to me! A slave-girl! But the healers cared for me like I was the wife of a chief. They say I will still be able to have children. But only when *I* decide I am ready. And if I decide I am never ready, they tell me that is fine, too." She shook her head, as if some things were beyond even fever dreams.

"What are you making" Kalie asked.

"A dress. For me." Saela's voice dropped, as if speaking aloud of such generosity would make it disappear. "I was not used to not working. Laisa brought me mending to keep me busy, and said I was very good." She blinked back a tear; Saela was not used to compliments, either. "Now she says I can learn to make cloth their way, and teach them how to make felt. I have always loved to sew."

"I have decided to stay as well," Sarika told them, already wearing the linen shift of a healer.

"Were you going to ask my leave?" Danica asked, looking dangerous.

"No," replied Sarika, looking Danica in the eye, and for once looking equally dangerous. "You were a kind mistress, and I wish you well, but I am no longer a slave. In this land, I make my own choices, and I choose to stay here."

Everyone, even the villagers who barely understood the stand-off, held their breath as they watched.

Then Danica grinned, showing the black

stumps of her teeth. "Good! Now I know we are truly in the land of my grandmother!" Then she gave Sarika one of her best amber bracelets and bid her farewell.

The party traveled west into the forest. There was frost on the ground and frost in the air anytime anyone spoke. But the going was not difficult and full winter not yet here. After five more days of travel, they reached the heavily populated land along the streams that fed the Black Sea.

Everywhere they stopped, they were made welcome, and at nearly every stop, more of the people from the east found homes. In a few places, they were turned away after one meal and a night's rest by people who feared bad luck, or the taint of violence, or the horses. But they still had time before winter closed in, and Kalie thought it was important that no one stay where they—and their new people—weren't entirely comfortable. "More important than making a good marriage, eh?" Riyik teased her.

"As long as they don't have to go through what we did to find the perfect match," she replied with a grin.

In one village they heard a story of raiders from the east, riding strange animals, and attacking a town to the north. It seemed much worse than anything Yuraak's tiny band could have done, but as always, no actual witnesses were present.

"We're heading north and west," said Riyik. "We'll find out soon enough."

Kalie kept them moving until at last, only fifteen of them remained to reach a land of hills clothed in trees, many of which stayed green in the winter. Here, just a half day's walk from the sea, they found a clear stream dancing over rocks, and spanned with a bridge made of blocks of stone. No one—not even Kalie—had ever seen such a thing before. And since they only had five horses left, they took the chance of crossing the bridge. Everyone made it safely to the other side.

There, crowning a low hill was the place Kalie knew she and these last seekers would find a new home. Easily seven times the population of Green Bower, the town of Stonebridge was a place of fine homes and temples, with a large open market in the center. Sheep and goats grazed on the grassy western slope of the hill, and in the meadows that sloped gently down toward the sea.

Once they were seen, the party was soon surrounded by excited people, welcoming them and exclaiming over the horses. Townspeople draped shell necklaces over everyone's heads. Kalie guessed they'd have been made of flowers if it had been summer. Everyone was escorted to the traveler's temple, where a council of elders, and a headman and headwoman greeted them. Since it was winter, no other travelers were staying there, and everyone was able to find room to sleep in the spacious accommodations afforded all travelers.

They left their few possessions in the temple, and then broke into smaller groups for a tour of the settlement. A young priestess named Ilara acted as a guide for Kalie, Riyik, Borik, Tarella and Garm.

"Since it will likely rain by sunset, we can't have a town-wide feast in the open air, as we would like, with so many visitors," Ilara explained. "A small feast will be served in the council chambers, for you and our leaders. But everyone will be using the arrival of visitors as an excuse for a celebration." Ilara smiled, and a pair of dimples appeared on either side of her pink mouth. "If you don't mind the rain, all of you should go from house to house, introducing yourselves, sampling local delicacies and sharing the songs and stories of your homes."

Riyik, for all that he thought himself worldly by now, had the look of a pole-axed ox. "Our flocks are gone, we have nothing to offer these people—not even token gifts—and they still treat us like royalty," he whispered. "I keep thinking this will turn out to be some misunderstanding—and the important people they're actually waiting for will show up and kick us out."

"This isn't like Green Bower where seventy of us descended on a village of one hundred," said Kalie, as they were escorted to a place where they could bathe. "The opposite, in fact. Fifteen of us, and seven hundred of them. And they're all stuck here for the winter. They already know we're from a place none of them have even heard of, which means new stories, exotic music, and a new language for those who study such things. Not to mention new skills and interesting discussions."

"But sharing food at the start of winter? Aren't they worried about shortages before spring? After all, I've seen what your people consider a 'small' feast."

Kalie turned to speak with their guide.

"She says this town is prosperous—" Kalie began.

"I haven't seen one of yours that isn't!" Riyik sighed.

"They raise sheep and goats, and grow fruit and nuts."

"Where?" Riyik looked around for orderly

groups of trees.

"All around us," said the priestess. "In the forest. Some are wild; some we have planted. Over time, it's become a fact that nearly every tree surrounding the town gives us something useful."

"What about grain?" asked Garm. "I haven't seen any fields."

"We grow a small amount of grain here," explained Ilara. "But for most foods we trade, except for fish, which we find in plenty just a half day from here."

"What do you trade?" asked Tarella.

"The things we make. Jewelry, cloth, pottery, stonework, leather," she eyed the visitors' clothing. "I'd say you can teach us a few things about making leather. And that other thing you wear?"

"Felt," said Kalie. "Yes, we would be happy to teach you our skills, just as many of us are eager to learn yours. " Already she could see who might have a talent for certain of the skills the priestess mentioned. Since most of the people Kalie had brought here had little interest in farming, a town based on trade was the perfect place for them.

"What is that terrible smell?" Tarella exclaimed, stepping back from a plume of steam which appeared to be coming from the rocks on the hillside below them.

The priestess grinned. "That is where we bathe."

She was clearly about to launch into an explanation, and Kalie had no wish to deprive the woman of her fun, but she couldn't help herself. "Hot springs! You have hot springs here!"

"You know of them?" Ilara asked, surprised.

"I know of few others, and none close by."

Kalie closed her eyes, inhaling the rotten-egg smell of sulfur, remembering her years spent in the mountain village which took its name from the healing waters of the nearby hot springs. "It was long ago," she said as memories washed over her. "And very far to the west. But I think that every day since I left, I've missed the feeling of soaking in hot water that comes from the ground. Especially in winter."

"Then you should be very comfortable here," Ilara said, smiling. "There are towels waiting, along with soaproot and lavender, and room enough for your entire group." At Tarella and Garm's startled—and clearly uncomfortable—looks, Ilara grew flustered.

"I do apologize," she said quickly. "Is it against your customs for men and women to bath together?" she asked Kalie.

"It's the stink," Tarella explained with less tact than Kalie might have wished for. "How could something that smells like that make anyone clean?"

Garm just stared at the steam as if a dangerous beast lurked beneath it.

"I assure you, Tarella, the smell does not stay with you," said Kalie. "There's actually a kind of magic in it. The water feels wonderful, and when you leave, you'll swear you've never been cleaner. It can even heal illness!"

Tarella and Garm looked skeptical.

"Most of these people have never immersed themselves in water before," Kalie explained. At Ilara's confused expression, she added, "Water is scarce where they are from. The women use a kind of cleansing paste on their bodies."

"I'd like to learn more about that," said Ilara,

with unfeigned interest. To the others she said, "There is no need to try it until you are ready. If you two would follow me, we can return to the temple, and you can bathe there."

"Borik, you'll probably want to go with Tarella and Garm," Kalie said, shooting a meaningful look at the big man.

"Oh no, I'd like to try…" Borik stopped as Kalie's expression finally registered.

"I'll come back later," Borik said quickly, following the others.

Riyik glanced at Kalie, amused. "Something I should know about?" he asked.

"Oh, just some things I heard about at Hot Springs," she said with a mischievous smile. "You see, couples quite enjoyed bathing together. Something about the water adding tremendous pleasure to the act of joining. Of course, I never had a chance to find out for myself, as I was unattached the whole time I lived there, and I didn't care to watch others, although many people did in that part of the world. It could all just be rumors."

"Somehow I doubt that," said Riyik, picking his way down the path carefully until they were in a large stone chamber. The air was hot and steamy, despite the frigid cold just above them. Conveniently placed stones led to the large, nearly circular pool in the center. Riyik had his clothes off faster than Kalie would have thought possible.

"While we figure out the truth of those things you heard," he said, slowly untying the laces that held Kalie's dress together, "why don't you tell me about this interesting custom of watching other people bathe?"

Chapter 7

For the next several days, Kalie felt as if she
were living her life backwards. Everything she had
taken for granted growing up—from the excitement of
meeting new people, to the freedom to walk where she
chose, to the necessities of life just being there for the
taking—were all back. All she had to do was slip back
into that manner of living.

It wasn't as easy as she thought it would be.
Then again, it hadn't been the first time, either.

Riyik teased Kalie that if she hadn't been busy
showing fourteen other people how to do it, she'd have
forgotten how to live in her own home.

There was some truth to his words, Kalie
thought as she led people around the town, explaining
the importance of keeping clean, of looking people in
the eye (difficult for the women) and how to find
useful work. Introductions were easier here than in the
horse tribe, since the touching of palms and a single
word of greeting would suffice for everyone except the
revered elderly. But convincing the women to touch a
man or initiate a conversation proved challenging.

Finding permanent living space proved
blessedly easier.

Garm and Durak both expressed an interest in
learning metalworking. Since the town only had one
smith, and he was currently without an apprentice, the
smith was happy to take both men into his home, and
begin teaching them. Much to Kalie's surprise,
Tarella quickly found a family of jewelry-makers who
invited her to live with them while she learned the new
craft.

"I didn't think you were interested in such things," Kalie said, as she helped Tarella move her few possessions into her new home. "Or that you would feel comfortable living with so many men not related to you." The family consisted of three grown brothers with a much younger sister of about eight years old, and their grandmother, who might have been considered a suitable chaperone by the tribe, had she not been nearly blind and bedridden.

"You told us we had to learn new ways," the younger woman said as she tossed her pale blond hair behind her, apparently quite comfortable without a veil. Tarella's hips swayed suggestively as she walked, and she clearly liked the attention it drew. "Besides, I'm the only woman here without a mate or children. A large family is a good opportunity for one like me. They will need help with the old woman, and the little girl should not grow up with only men."

Kalie had her doubts about Tarella's motives, but wanted too much to believe her words to question them.

The rest found homes soon after they arrived. Three houses stood empty. One, abandoned for some time, was going to be knocked down for usable materials. Instead, Borik and Zanal moved in, and set about repairing it, with help from local carpenters. Kalie, Riyik, Varena and Yarik moved into a home in far better shape, as the woman who owned it had recently died, and the relatives living with her had all moved into other dwellings.

The remaining women—Brenia and Darva— moved with their children into a house built for a newly joined couple, who had tragically drowned in the Black Sea in the early days of their marriage.

"This place is cursed!" whined Darva. "Their ghosts don't want us living in their home when they can't! I can feel it."

"I would think the feel of all these luxurious furs on your new feather bed would drive out all other feelings," said Brenia.

"It does help," admitted Darva, as she ran her hands along the finely stitched fox pelts, and a whole blanket made of lush winter rabbit. The bed, large enough for Darva and both of her children nearly filled one of the two bedrooms in the stone and wood house. Kalie and some locals were setting up smaller beds in the second, smaller chamber for Brenia, Barak and Liara. "I just wish I could stop fearing we're being readied for sacrifice."

Tarella pursed her lips in disapproval, as Darva explored the rest of the house with even more excitement than her children. She squealed in delight at the dishes of food brought by neighbors and left by the indoor hearth. She opened boxes exclaiming at the treasures within. One held a mirror of polished copper, and Darva nearly dropped it upon seeing her reflection for the first time.

"That woman is a slave!" Tarella exclaimed. "Brenia should have the larger room with the finer bed!"

"There are no slaves here." As Kalie reminded Tarella of that simple fact, she wondered how many more times she would have to repeat it.

"And Darva has had a harder life than I," said Brenia, joining them in the main room, and gazing at the woman of twenty-five years who looked like a skeletal crone. Most of her teeth were worn or missing, and her black hair lay in tatters around a face pinched with hunger and deprivation. "Let her enjoy a few luxuries for now. You certainly are, Tarella."

"I was born a chief's daughter!" the blond woman cried, outraged.

"Until you were captured and made a slave," Kalie reminded her.

"Not a slave for long! Old Gorik made me his concubine." Tarella picked up the mirror that Darva had discarded and gazed at her reflection. "If he hadn't been so old and sick when he rode to battle, I might have stayed with him, and won him away from his old goat of a wife. But I knew he'd never survive, and then I'd just be some new man's prize. Better to come here, I decided."

The mirror revealed a calculating smile on the beautiful woman's face. "Arbela did me a favor when she slipped me that potion that caused me to lose Gorik's baby. Here I am, still firm and unlined, ready to find a new man. One young and virile this time. And I will give him many fine sons." She chuckled, setting down the mirror, and twirled around, her arms flung wide, as if to embrace her good fortune. "Oh, if Arbela could see me now!"

Kalie and Brenia exchanged a look that combined amusement, outrage and disbelief. Kalie was about to speak, but Brenia simply put an arm around her and led her outside. "Come now," said Brenia. "Let's you and I enjoy some luxuries ourselves. We should have at least a few days before one of these fools starts trouble for all of us."

"Do you really think we have that long?" Kalie sighed.

"Absolutely! How about a soak in the hot springs before we stuff ourselves with more of that amazing food and wine tonight?"

"Sounds wonderful," said Kalie.

As it happened, the next few days passed without incident, and everyone enjoyed them. Kalie watched the newcomers carefully as they settled into town life. After showing everyone the community storage sheds filled with grain, fruit, nuts and dried meat, and explaining that everyone could come and take what they needed, Kalie was rarely anywhere else, making sure none of these people—so used to hunger—took more than their fair share.

"It hasn't been a problem," Martel assured her. He was a pleasant featured man with thinning blond hair, just entering into middle age. "Do you really think it could be?" They sat on a stone bench outside the main food shed, where the roof sloped out above them, providing shade. Normally, someone kept watch when supplies were brought *in*, not out, to keep track, and inform the people of surpluses or shortages. Kalie had requested someone be on hand at all times to "answer any questions the new residents had."

"There are people here who have never had enough to eat," she said. "Others who see the world only as predator and prey. I want them to learn there are other ways, but that won't happen if they cause people here to go hungry at the end of winter. Have you spoken with any of them yet?"

Martel nodded. "Zanal has shown several of us some ingenious ways to make tools from bone and horn. We are thinking of forming a group to make a large quantity of them over the winter, for trading in the spring."

Kalie smiled. This was exactly what she had

hoped would happen.

"Borik, too, is a most interesting man," Martel said, stifling a laugh. "Probably the biggest man anyone here has ever seen. The children adore him. He plays with them and teaches them to ride those strange new animals. And he has much to teach us about hunting in the winter. I think you have little to fear in terms of shortages, Kalie, with the meat he and those he hunts with are bringing in."

"The firewood, too, seems much appreciated." A few days earlier, after the first snowstorm of the season, Borik had found a fallen tree near the edge of town. Using nothing more than a sledge of hides, he had dragged the entire thing to the center of town, where Kalie and Martel could now see it.

"That was quite a feat," said Martel. "He's not a man of words, though." Martel's fair skin went pink. "I meant no offense," he said quickly. "Not everyone has the gift to learn a new language right away."

"He would not be offended," Kalie assured Martel. "Borik was not a man of words in his own language, either. His greatest gift is his strength, and I can see now that he delights in using it for the good of others. That was not something he could easily do where he came from."

"I am surprised," said Martel. "From what I have heard about that far-off place, strength seems to have been greatly prized."

"It's the using it for the good of others that was…complicated," said Kalie. "They are very competitive in the grasslands."

"They seem to hold very odd views about men and women, as well. Most of the women have been hard to get to know. I'm told their customs are quite...strict...about keeping separate from men not family. I spoke with Brenia a few days ago. I showed her where to find wool and flax for spinning. My life-mate, while she lived, quite enjoyed making cloth, and I insisted Brenia take her old spindle and loom, since they're doing no good in my house. The next day, she came to my door with a wonderful meal she had cooked, and gave it to me—but would not enter my home to share it!" Martel looked at Kalie as though for an explanation, then looked away. "But you have nothing to fear. Their ways may be strange, but these people have much to offer, and most of them offer it freely. They will do well here."

Kalie leaned back against the stone wall, feeling at peace. Perhaps she really could stop worrying.

Not likely.

She saw Riyik coming toward her, and waved. He was in a group of three men and one woman. They stopped by the storage shed. "I'm going to meet master-carver Lowek," he told her. Kalie realized that the others in the group were probably all carvers. "My friends here tell me that our work session will probably end with an invitation to stay for supper, and that I should speak with you." Riyik paused, looking uncertain. Kalie suppressed a smile. He apparently didn't know if he was expected to ask her permission, or invite her to join them. *Oh, if his spear-brothers could see him now*, she thought.

"Go, enjoy," she said. "I have plans tonight, anyway."

Riyik was clearly relieved, though he looked askance at the thought of his wife having plans he didn't know about. Kalie looked up at the snowflakes that were beginning to fall. Everyone outside hurried to finish what they were doing and get inside. She and Martel stood, and with hurried farewells, went their separate ways.

A few hardy souls were still hacking pieces from the tree Borik had retrieved. Kalie saw that one of them was Varena, and that she had already accumulated a sizable pile.

"Varena, let's go inside!" Kalie called over the wind. "You have more wood than you can carry already."

"No, I can do it." Varena bundled it all together with a leather cord, exactly as if she had still been living on the steppes.

"There's more here than we need," said Kalie.

"Most is for other families." Varena adjusted the huge pile on her back, trump- line across her forehead. "Go home, Mother. I'll be there after I've delivered all of this."

Kalie picked up the pieces that had fallen from the bundle. "Varena, I think you work harder now than when you were a slave!" she said, coming up beside the young woman.

"That's because here, no one forces me to work, or is mean to me! When I do anything helpful—even when it's learning things that are helpful to me—people are nice! They even give me things in return!" The beautiful parka Varena was wearing, made of sable fur and trimmed with ermine tails and ivory beads, attested to that.

When all the wood had been delivered, mother and daughter returned home. Varena went to collect Yarik from the neighbors while Kalie built up the fire. While the little boy played with the new toys his father had carved for him, Varena began preparing dinner. Kalie quickly noticed she had more food than the family could eat—even if Riyik were to be home.

"Are we having company?" Kalie asked innocently.

"You told me I could invite people whenever I wanted," Varena said nervously. "And I provided most of the food."

"Of course, dear," said Kalie. "But it's also customary to check with the others who live with you."

"Is it all right?" Varena asked anxiously, all pretense of being a confident, independent woman gone. "There's only three or four coming, and Jolie and Cobin are going to teach me to play the flute. I milked both mares today, and I'm going to show them how to make curds, and Borik brought over two ducks, so we'll have plenty—"

"It's fine," said Kalie. "Just tell me sooner next time. And…you're not planning to show them how to make kumis, are you?"

Varena made a face. "Gods, no! Besides, Jolie is bringing wine, which is so much better. Have you ever tasted it? Her father trades for it all the way to the Great Salt Waters in the south!"

Kalie decided not to spend the evening meditating in one of the temples as she had planned. Chaperoning Varena and her friends would be more fun, not to mention important. And, very likely, more healing.

Chapter 8

Trouble, when it finally arrived, came from a source no one had expected.

It was on a cold, clear morning, while everyone was preparing for the Winter Festival, that a young boy came running into the gathering space outside the main temple, shouting that someone was hurt, or hurting someone, and would someone please come?

Many people were about, preparing the temple for the upcoming festivities, so in only moments, the child, who had slipped in the snow, and was trying to right himself, was surrounded by concerned people. "What is it, Vasar?" asked one of the temple acolytes, as he helped the child to his feet.

"It's Sirak!" cried the boy, shaking. "He's hitting Lalia with a stick! And the other boys are just watching!"

"Show us!" commanded one of the senior priestesses. It only took the mention of the boy from the steppes—Darva's eleven year old son—to send Kalie racing after the crowd which was following Vasar. The boy led them to the forest outside the town. There, between two large trees, partially hidden by some leafless bushes, stood a circle of boys—all of them from the town.

In the center was the only outsider—Sirak. At his feet was a screaming girl, trying to protect herself from the stick Sirak was viciously wielding. "This is what happens to a girl who meddles in the affairs of men!" Sirak shouted, swiping the stick across her back. He handed the stick to the boy closest to him. "Now, you, Josan! Teach this girl some respect.

Soon, all of them will learn—"

Sirak broke off when the priestess grabbed the stick from Josan, and Janak the smith grabbed Sirak from behind, pinning both his arms. The steppes boy fought, but as he lacked the muscles and training of a grown man of his tribe, could do nothing to break Janak's hold. He resorted to shouting profanity and threats which Kalie prayed no one here could understand. From the expressions on the faces of the other boys, however, it was clear Sirak had been teaching them the language, as well as the customs of his people.

Several people were helping Lalia to her feet when a scream pierced the air. Zola, Lalia's mother, was running toward them. Beside her lumbered Borik. From the disarray of their clothing and way they moved together, it was clear what they had been doing. Under any other circumstances, Kalie would have been delighted. Although...Borik? And Zola? Kalie shook her head. *Later.*

"You will each have a turn to speak," said Nara the Priestess. "But I remind you that you are all in the presence of the Mother of All. She hears; and She knows what is in your hearts.

They were in the main chamber of one of the smaller temples, this one dedicated to settling disputes. Sirak and the five boys involved were seated on the floor to the right of the altar. Parents of the boys sat against the wall a short distance away. To the left of the altar, Lalia, whose cuts and bruises had been treated, sat on her mother's lap. Borik had wanted to stay, but Zola had coldly asked him to leave. Only Kalie and Riyik were allowed to attend as representatives of the newcomers—a job neither relished at the moment. Because this problem involved customs and people who were unknown to the people of Stonebridge, two priests joined Nara to resolve what otherwise would have been handled by the families themselves.

Kalie scanned the expressions on the faces of the parents. Most ranged from outrage to shock to concern. Only Darva looked afraid, and even that warred with anger. She looked hopefully toward the two men seated before the altar, but scowled when the woman continued to speak.

"Josan?" prompted Nara.

The boy stared at the floor. "Sirak started teaching some of us about the ways of his people a few days after the new people came here." He risked a glance at the priestess, then at his mother. "Everyone said we had to teach them our language and our ways, and that we should learn theirs, too!"

"When did the secret meetings begin?" asked the priest named Bodon. "Nylan?"

"Just a few days ago," replied the boy, more puzzled than worried. "He told us that we were the best of the boys here, and he was going to teach us the way of the warrior. Those who did well would rule as chiefs, when all the priestesses were gone."

"And what is a chief?" asked Bodon.

"I don't know," said Nylan. "That's why I went to the meeting! I wanted to learn more. Sirak says that in his land, men make all the rules."

Nara looked at each boy in turn. "And when you heard such things, why did you not tell an adult? Did you not realize the wrongness of such ideas?"

The boys shrugged and looked at each other.

"Sirak said that only men could ride horses and win glory and rule over other men," said another boy, probably the youngest. "I don't know about that other stuff, but I want to ride a horse!"

"How did the attack on Lalia come about?" asked Orin, the second priest.

The boys shifted uncomfortably but said nothing. "Sirak?" asked the priest.

"I don't have to tell you anything!" the boy retorted.

"You are correct," said Orin. "I simply wanted to give you a chance to help yourself, since your lack of respect will work against you. There's only one person whose words we need to hear now. Lalia?"

Before the girl could speak, Sirak shouted in disbelief, "You're going to let *her* speak? A stupid girl? One who's never even learned to obey a man?"

"Sirak, do you truly not understand how much trouble you are in?" Riyik demanded. "Or how much trouble you've brought to your mother?" Although technically a breach of protocol, no one objected. In fact, Kalie suspected this is what the others in the room had hoped for.

At the mention of his mother, Sirak looked afraid for the first time. "I…was only trying to teach them a better way to live."

"My son speaks the truth," Darva began.

"You will have your turn," Nara told the former slave. "Now then. Lalia?"

"I just wanted to know what they were doing. Everyone wanted to meet the new children, but there's only two girls, and they don't say much. Sirak was fun at first. He knew lots of things, showed us new games. But then he said no girls could play!" Lalia looked around, as if daring the adults to believe such a thing. "When I saw him taking a group of boys into the woods, I followed them. Then I heard what Sirak was telling them, and I knew it was bad, so I tried to leave. To tell an adult." Here Lalia glared at the boys who should have done the same. "Sirak grabbed me and—" Lalia's voice caught. "He hurt me! He wanted the others to hurt me!" Her voice was swallowed by a sob. Zola hugged her daughter.

"Josan?" asked Bodon. "If others had not stopped you, would you have struck Lalia with the stick?"

Josan looked like he was about to cry. The word "no" formed on his lips, and then he looked at the statue of the Mother Goddess on the altar, and quailed. "I don't know," he whispered.

Kalie felt everything she had worked for dissolving in the wake of those three simple words.

But the townspeople surprised her. The parents of the boys looked upset, but not ready to drive out the foreign demons. Some seemed embarrassed for their children, but most looked like they were remembering their own youthful mistakes. Was this kind of thing possibly more common than Kalie remembered?

"You were right to include Sirak in your play, and to learn of his ways as well," said Nara. "But as you heard his words, there came a point when you needed to show him that some of those things would never be acceptable here. Who can tell me when that was?"

The boys looked at each other. "When he said there would be no more priestesses?" ventured one timidly.

"When he told us only men should decide things?" asked another.

Sirak looked at them with contempt, and then turned away.

"Correct," said Nara. "And if he continued with such talk, what should you have done?"

"Told a mother or father?" said Nylan.

"Yes! These things are small, and part of how everyone learns—even adults. But when Sirak struck Lalia, then it became serious. Why did no one stop him?"

The boys looked at each other, and it became apparent they themselves did not know.

"Were you afraid of Sirak?" asked Bodon.

More uncomfortable shrugging and furtive looks.

"When something like this happens, you might not feel you can handle it yourselves," said Nara. "And that is all right. But you should have run to get an adult, as Vasar did." Nara and the priests looked proudly at Vasar, who only looked uncomfortable.

Nara gazed at each of the other boys in turn. Some squirmed, but none looked away. "To atone for your mistake, you must each seek an opportunity to do a good thing for someone in this town. And, you must each apologize to Lalia for not protecting her." Nara turned to Darva. "Do you have anything to say on this matter?"

Darva looked like a cornered beast. Kalie saw her consider and discard many plans before she spoke. Then, before the startled people nearby could stop her, Darva leapt at her son, slapping him hard across the face and bursting into tears. "Oh, I am cursed!" she wailed. "Your wickedness will cost us our lives.

These people welcomed us, and now they will cast us into the wilds to die!" Then she sat down, rocking back and forth and crying.

"Parents, take your children home, and discuss these matters further," said Nara, loud enough to be heard over Darva's wailing. As the room cleared, she went to Darva, offering her a scrap of cloth to dry her eyes. "We will not send anyone in the wilds to die," she said firmly. Darva's tears cut off instantly.

"Although I suspect you already knew that," Orin said drily. "Despite your impressive performance."

Kalie shot the priest a look of admiration and began to relax. "We still have a problem," said Nara, moving to sit beside Darva and Sirak. "Both of you still live by the violent ways which you have sworn to leave behind. Therefore, we will help you reach your goal by sending each of you to live with a different family. It is likely this will help you learn our ways more quickly, as living with only others of your people has not."

Darva finally revealed a genuine emotion: outrage. She hid it quickly behind fear, which Kalie guessed was no less real. "You would take a child from his mother?" she whispered.

"Temporarily," said Orin. "And you will still see each other. But this way you can get the help you need, while learning useful skills, so you can contribute to the community." *Smooth*, thought Kalie. He doesn't mention that Darva was nearly the only one of the nomads who had done little to no work since their arrival. Her opinion of this man grew even higher.

Realizing she had just been outmaneuvered,

Darva cried, "What of my daughter, Myla? She is only six, and—"

"I'm sure she can remain where she is," said Kalie. "She gets along well with Brenia's two children. We would have to ask, but I believe Brenia would be happy to care for Myla until the family is reunited." Privately, Kalie hoped Brenia would be allowed to keep Myla permanently, as little as Darva seemed to care for her. Sirak was her sun and moon.

"That would be agreeable," said Nara. Darva shot Kalie a look of pure hatred, but Kalie only smiled. Had they not been in a temple, she might have stuck out her tongue instead.

"Might I speak with my son in private before we are separated?" Darva asked, holding back a sob.

The three clerics agreed before Kalie could voice her objections. While they began to discuss possible placements for Darva and Sirak—a clear message that the meeting was over—Darva led her son out of the temple, in the direction of the woods.

"I've heard there are some good places to pick mushrooms that way," Kalie told Riyik, hurrying in the direction Darva was headed.

"Do mushrooms grow in winter here?" Riyik asked doubtfully.

"I'll go find out!" Kalie called over her shoulder.

Darva checked behind the trees carefully to make sure they were alone. She chose her place well, Kalie thought from her perch high in the biggest tree, and praying Darva did not look up. But in the steppes, danger rarely came from above.

Sirak looked deeply troubled, and for a long

while, his mother just held him. Only when he pushed her away, assuming the look of a man who would not allow himself to be babied, did Darva speak.

"You must be more careful, son. Convince these people we truly believe their nonsense, and then you may begin again. But when that time comes you must do a better job of choosing your followers."

"I will never find boys I can make into warriors here!" Sirak growled. "These people are sheep! You heard them: that old woman told them to run when there is danger! And that traitor, Vasar, actually did! Although, it might have been more fun if they had all run off like rabbits. Then I could have done more than just hit that little bitch." To Kalie's horror, Sirak smiled, as if imagining what he would have liked to do to Lalia.

"That may be," Darva said firmly, drawing his attention back to her. "But you have no one else. The steppes are closed to us. And there is far more to be had here for a strong warrior and his clever mother than in that retched place we left behind."

"Maybe," Sirak said doubtfully. "But this place is strange. And breeds weakness. How long am I to bow to women? And useless men who bleat?"

"For as long as necessary." There was an edge of command in Darva's voice. "Listen to me, my boy," she said, softening. "One day, you will be king of this land. The first king these fools have ever known. And when you rule, they will rush to learn our ways. But until the time is right, you must be patient. Let no one know what we are planning."

Sirak's back stiffened, and he puffed out his chest. "A warrior never lets his enemy see his true thoughts. They will know nothing, Mother." Then he glared at her. "And you will never strike me again. Is that clear?"

"Of course, my king," Darva said smiling, as they made their way back to the settlement.

Kalie waited until they were long out of sight before climbing down her tree. None of what she had witnessed should have surprised her, but...

A figure stepped out of the shadows at her feet. She nearly screamed before seeing it was Riyik—less than two paces away. He still moved like a warrior, she thought with admiration.

"Interesting," was all he said. Then, after a pause, "I had no idea she was so ambitious!"

"Nor I. I do not think it will come to anything, especially once we warn people of what to watch for. But that boy is dangerous. He could cause a lot of damage before anyone sees him for what he is."

"But it's his mother who rules him for now. If she were to find...other uses for her energy...he might be left adrift. And more easily influenced in other directions."

"How would we manage that?" asked Kalie. "Darva is a true woman of Aahk. She places all her hopes in her son."

Riyik smiled at something only he could see. "I have an idea."

Chapter 9

Riyik did not share his plan with Kalie over the next few days, but she was far too busy to press him. The preparations for the Winter Festival were enough to keep everyone busy, and for Kalie, an errand that could no longer be put off.

One cold, snowy morning, just three days before the longest night of the year, Kalie took Yarik to the temple of healing to be checked by one of the healers, and fitted for new shoes. While his limp was still pronounced, he could walk without a crutch, and rarely stumbled. While a kindly old man massaged Yarik's club foot, assisted by a young woman who could always make the boy laugh, Kalie went in search of the midwife.

She could no longer delay confirming what she already knew.

"Yes," Sarella the midwife said with a smile, after completing her examination. "You are most definitely pregnant! Is this really your first?"

Kalie nodded, distracted. "I did not think I would ever…be able to…"

"At your age, I'm not surprised. What are you, twenty six summers? Twenty-seven?" When Kalie continued to stare out the door at the snow-covered ground, the woman's expression changed. "You're worried. What is it? Is this not good news?"

"It is good news," said Kalie. "It's a miracle! After the damage the beastmen did when they raped me all those years ago, I thought I would never bear a child. But…I can't be sure this is Riyik's baby—" Kalie broke off at the sight of Sarella's expression.

She was a healthy, attractive matron, who had
probably borne several children of her own, and had
dedicated her life to helping other women bring forth
their own. But here it was again: the disbelief; the
discomfort. Kalie was speaking of things that made no
sense in this world; worrying about things that had no
basis in any reality this midwife knew.

After thanking the woman, Kalie took Yarik's
hand and led him out of the temple. She could see the
difference in his gait at once. Yarik now walked
perfectly normally, laughing and turning, delighting in
what he could now do. Kalie watched him play in the
snow with some other children, and thought about
having a child of her own. This baby would be her
third child, yet the first of her body. What would it be
like? What would Yarik, who would be nearly four
years when his new sibling arrived, think? Or Varena,
who, at thirteen, was already an adult?

Yarik fell in the snow, and Kalie scooped him
up. She was setting him back on his feet when Brenia
walked by. At Kalie's expression, she stopped.

"I'm pregnant," Kalie said by way of greeting.

"That's wonderful!" said Brenia. Then her
face fell. "But you're afraid it's not Riyik's." It was
not a question. Brenia knew of Haraak's rape, just
days before Kalie had consummated her marriage to
Riyik.

"It would be a shame if I had to think of
Haraak every time I looked at the child I've waited so
long for. And more so if Riyik did."

"Riyik will love the child no matter who the
father is," said Brenia. "And so will you."

"Yes, I think I will," said Kalie. "But Riyik?
That is not the way he was raised."

"But he left those ways behind. We're in your world, now, Kalie. My brother will not let you down." Kalie wondered just how many meanings Brenia had attached to her words. "Although it might help if you had some privacy when you told him."

Brenia waded into a swirling ball of children and picked up Yarik. "Would you like to spend the night with Barak?" she asked, dusting him off.

"Yes!" cried the boy.

"Thank you!" Kalie called to Brenia's retreating back.

"A baby!" A grin spread slowly across Riyik's face. They were in the main room of their house. Kalie had not yet begun preparing dinner, and she hoped Varena would be away a while longer. "When?" asked Riyik, picking Kalie up and spinning her around.

"Whoa, put me down! I haven't thrown up yet, but—"

"Sorry, I'm just excited." Riyik set her carefully on a large cushion by the hearth.

"I am, too," said Kalie. "Sometime in the summer. And I wish I didn't have to say this, but we don't know if you're the father."

Just as she had feared, Riyik's face hardened. "I had forgotten about Haraak."

"I'm glad. I wish I could as well. As far as I'm concerned, and by the customs of my people, you are the father, Riyik. But I know it's different where you come from."

Riyik paced, thinking deeply. Kalie sat in silence, watching the play of emotions across his face. "I love you, Kalie, and we live in your world now," he said at last. "Perhaps it's best if we never know. The child will be my son,"

"Or daughter," Kalie said, smiling. Then, troubled again, "And we might find out when it's born. Haraak had red hair—"

"As does my sister."

Startled, Kalie could only nod.

Riyik took her in his arms. "Our first child, born in the first year of our life together. That should be the only thing we think of."

And that, Kalie decided, was a very worthy goal.

The day of the Winter Festival dawned soft and misty. Kalie felt that the weather reflected the magic and mystery of the occasion perfectly. But there would be snow later, and likely freezing wind. Due to the large population, the people of Stonebridge had developed the custom of holding a short ceremony in which everyone gathered outside in the center of town for the blessing which marked the turning of the season, then retreating to the temples and individual homes for a long string of parties and events.

Kalie strolled through the town about an hour before sunset, watching the final preparations, and making herself available to help if the need arose. She had just come from a soak in the hot springs, and was wearing a new woolen dress, dyed a deep red. While officially in exchange for healing teas she had brought the weaver's sick daughter, Kalie knew she had gotten the better deal. It was time she found useful work for herself, rather than helping others to find it. But that could wait until tomorrow.

She paused by the grove of trees which grew

around the main temple. All but one was bare of leaves. Towering above the others was a tree with needle-like leaves which stayed green all year round. Soon it would be covered with rush lights and tiny oil lamps, just as the similar green trees outside of town were already covered with brightly colored decorations and offerings.

Varena came by dressed in a stunning outfit made entirely of the winter fur of reindeer. The long tunic, pants, and boots covered Varena from the neck down. But not, Kalie saw, like the shapeless felt robes of the women of the steppes; rather this showed off the girl's fine figure. And later, when others would be wrapping themselves in fur mantles, Varena would still be warm enough to stay just as she was. Especially if she did a lot of dancing, which Kalie suspected she would.

"You'll probably want a hat of some kind," she said. Varena wore only a string of shells in her lustrous gold hair.

"Eventually," said Varena, with a toss of that hair. Compliments had made Varena rather vain about her hair. But if she caught a cold it would be an annoyance, not a death sentence, as it might be for a slave in the steppes, and Kalie wanted her to enjoy tonight.

Varena looked up at the evergreen tree. "Mother, I wanted to tell you before the festivities started. There is a boy here in town…" She trailed off, uncertain.

Kalie smiled. "There always is. In your case, many boys who have noticed you. So who is this boy who convinced you to notice him?"

"Taran. His family fishes the river in the warm

seasons. We've been gathering a lot of firewood together."

Kalie stifled a laugh at the sudden image of an entire forest stripped bare. "And has he asked you to meet him alone tonight after the dancing?"

"He asked, but…I said no. I said I would dance the first dance with him, and that seemed to make him happy. It's just that…I'm not ready yet."

Kalie put her hands on Varena's shoulders and looked into the younger woman's eyes. "And that is a good thing. What troubles you? Did he try to pressure you? Did someone say something mean?"

"Oh, no, nothing like that. But I like him, and I think I want him to be my first…" Varena blushed. "Isn't it amazing to be speaking like this? Choosing who I will give my virginity to? And then calling him my first? Not husband, or master, or the only man I will ever lie with?"

"I thought about such words every day I lived with the tribe of Aahk," said Kalie.

Varena shivered. "I don't know how you survived it, knowing that life could be like this, and having it all taken from you. It was easier for the rest of us. We never knew such a life was possible!"

Kalie thought of the things Varena had witnessed—and experienced. "Are you afraid you'll never be ready?"

"What? No, of course not! It's just that I've decided I want my first time to be at the summer festival. Where we can be out in the forest, under the moonlight, when it's warm."

Kalie laughed. "That sounds wonderful! And very much like my first time." It would also be the anniversary of Varena's womanhood ceremony, when

Kalie had risked death to show the women of Aahk how to find and celebrate their own power. She hugged Varena, whispering a prayer she would enjoy that time of transition as much as Kalie had.

"And what about you, Mother? And Riyik? Jolie told me that at festivals, there is much…sharing of bodies. Even couples who are married may choose other partners."

"That is true all year," said Kalie. "But more so at festivals. Especially this one, at the time of darkness and death. It's a way for people to join together against the darkness; a defiance of death by summoning new life."

"So will you…? Or Father?" Kalie couldn't tell what answer Varena was hoping for, but it sounded like more than idle curiosity.

"Your father may of course do as he wishes," Kalie said, then stopped and considered her words. "I suppose in that way, it is much like life on the steppes."

"Except that here, the woman's consent is what matters."

"True! And as for me…well, pregnant women usually refrain. And besides, I will be busy listening for gossip or complaints that might tell me of any further trouble."

"Oh, Mother, you should relax and have some fun! We're safe now; there's no one chasing us. Darva and Sirak are no threat to anyone, and everyone else is making friends and becoming a part of things. You should too!"

Kalie smiled. "Your father said nearly the same thing to me just yesterday."

"You should listen to us."

"Let's go home and check on the food," said
Kalie. "Brenia and I are making extra for Borik and
Zanal, since neither can cook, and it would be bad luck
for any house to be without food to share, tonight."

But as they reached their lovely home, from
which heat and good smells were wafting, Kalie
thought that what she really needed to do was listen to
Riyik and Varena. She would think about it.
Tomorrow.

But tonight, she would simply be happy.

Chapter 10

"On this, the longest night of the year, let us offer our own light, to the Light which will return, little by little, each day, beginning with tomorrow's dawn." The priestess intoned the ancient words in a darkness that was nearly total. Not a single fire burned within any home in Stonebridge. Then she hung a tiny shell of burning oil on the highest branch of the evergreen tree in the temple grove. One by one, every priest, priestess and acolyte did the same, until the tree glowed like stars on a summer night.

Next, the youngest acolyte came forward with a burning brand, and lit the bonfire in the center of the marketplace. The people murmured as the fire took hold and climbed above their heads, declaring to the heavens their intention to fight darkness with light. When it was burning well, and the falling snow popped and crackled in and around it, one member of each household lit a torch and held it carefully as they walked to the kindling that waited in each cold hearth of the town.

"May I take the torch?" Varena asked, noticing that many of the torchbearers were those newly initiated into adulthood.

Kalie wanted to say yes, but customs ingrained in her since birth would not allow it.

"Your mother carries life within her," explained Jula, their neighbor, whose family made baskets and brooms. "It's best if she is the one to bring the fire to your hearth." Jula's own daughter, Minda, was also pregnant and carried the fire that would light their hearth.

Varena nodded, content to walk behind Kalie and Riyik, and keeping a firm hold on Yarik's hand. Now that the children around him made him welcome in their play, rather than hitting him and calling him names as they had on the steppes, Yarik did his best to be everywhere at once and explore everything.

When the four of them entered their dark home, Kalie knelt beside the hearth and dropped her small torch into the center of the waiting wood shavings. As the light grew, a table laden with food came into view. It had been Riyik's idea to make as their contribution to the feast meat cooked in the manner of the steppes. Now, as Kalie took in the rich smells, and the table that seemed to groan under the weight of it all, she was glad he'd thought of it. The people here needed to know that not everything about the horse tribes was bad. Kalie needed to remember it as well.

"You don't need to wait for our first visitors," Riyik told Varena. "If your friends are waiting for you—" A knock sounded at their door.

"I think they're here," Varena said with a grin, running to fling open the door and greet whoever stood on the threshold. Soon, the town was transformed into a vibrant, glowing place of laughter and energy. People worked their way through home after home, eating, drinking and talking. Once everyone had the chance to sample everyone else's cooking, it was time for the many entertainments to begin. The dancing Varena had spoken of earlier would occur outside, later in the night, when people were warm enough from wine and food not to care about the cold. For now, people gathered in every temple large enough to hold a crowd and watched the truly skilled perform. Each temple boasted something wonderful: storytelling, dancing, music, guessing games and riddle contests.

Kalie was spellbound by one storyteller in particular. He was a visitor who had arrived the day before with a small entourage. While his fellow performers provided background music and pantomime to enhance his stories, the stranger held the audience in thrall. He was tall and muscular, with flashing dark eyes, and his neatly trimmed beard and mustache seemed to call attention to his mouth as he spoke. Most impressive to Kalie was the way the teller's voice changed as he became by turns, a goat, a wolf, a duck, a grouchy old man and, at one point, the Goddess Herself.

When the performance was over, Kalie rose to her feet and cheered, along with most of the audience. "Would you like to speak with him?" Riyik asked her. "One storyteller to another?"

"Later, perhaps," said Kalie, noting the large crowd of admirers surrounding the man. "When he is not so busy. What would you like to do next?"

"I thought I might try my luck at the riddle contest. I should at least be able to gage my ability with your language, and maybe confound the locals with a few riddles they haven't heard."

"I think I'll do some more visiting," said Kalie. "But I'll join you later if I can. Oh, and remember: any riddle that mentions a bird which dies in your hand—the answer is a snowflake."

"I think that will be the answer to a lot of them tonight, but thank you." Riyik brushed her lips with his and hurried to his next destination.

Kalie wrapped herself tight in her sheepskin cloak—one of the few things she still had from the steppes—and wandered around outside. Swarms of people, dressed in a rainbow of bright clothing made from everything from fur and wool to linen and leather, played in the snow and ran in and out of buildings. Borik, red faced with exertion from the snowball fight he was having with several children, was dressed in nothing but the leather shirt and pants he wore when he rode in from the grasslands. Zanal, dressed more sensibly in several layers of locally woven cloth and a wolf skin parka, worked with a group of both children and adults at constructing houses and animals from snow.

Kalie stood where she was, turning slowly to take it all in. All over the world, she thought, people are, at this moment, celebrating the turning of the season. Even in the grasslands. The only difference is, here I am free. She flung out her arms, and spun around, much as Darva had done in her new home, just to take in all the blessings surrounding her.

And as if the thought had conjured her, when Kalie came to a stop, the first person she saw was Darva. The woman looked far less happy now, as she trudged toward one of the temples, carrying a large jug. Apple cider, Kalie guessed, to refill the cauldron of the delicious hot brew that was probably empty again.

For the past eight days, Darva had lived in considerably less lavish circumstances, with a family of five women, who had zealously undertaken their job of teaching her the joy to be had in working for the good of the community. Kalie knew that Darva was well fed and not mistreated, although it was hard to tell any of that from her sullen expression. Kalie looked around for Sirak, her other concern, but did not see him.

She had just decided to go look for him when she spotted Brenia, and began to move through the snow in her direction. Halfway there, she realized Brenia was not alone. She was speaking with Martel, and even in the dark night, with shadows dancing from the light of the bonfire, and those that shone from open doors, Kalie could see the adoration in the man's eyes as he gazed at the dignified red haired woman.

Brenia caught sight of Kalie and quickly handed Martel a ceramic cup. "There's the friend I promised to meet. Thank you for the drink." She moved through the snow toward Kalie at an impressive speed, but still with that unconscious grace Kalie had noticed the first time she met her.

"Were we supposed to meet?" Kalie asked innocently.

"I just wasn't sure how else to get away," Brenia said. They began to walk, and Kalie did not suggest going inside, sensing Brenia might want to speak in private, and perhaps wished for some frigid air to cool the blush on her face.

"Was he bothering you?"

Brenia shook her head. "He's very nice. I enjoy talking to him."

"And he obviously enjoys talking to you. He's a widower, as I'm sure you know. I don't think he has any children."

"No, none. Which is sad. I've seen him with the village children…and…with mine, lately. He's been coming to visit, bringing gifts, and oh, Kalie, I don't know how to tell him to stop!"

Kalie stopped and looked her friend in the eye. "Are you sure you want him to?"

"Kalie, I'm still married to Hysaak!"

Kalie barely controlled a yelp of disbelief. But that wouldn't help. So, she calmly asked, "How do you reason that? He threw you away before we left."

"I know," sighed Brenia. "And I know that I threw away the laws and injustice of my homeland when I came here. But marriage is for life. We don't have this...what do you call it here? Separation?"

"Of course you do! Hysaak already did it. In your land, any man may put aside his wife whenever he chooses."

"But a wife can't put aside her husband!"

"Here she can. And surely, even by your laws you became free to remarry once Hysaak threw you away!"

Brenia sighed. "I was free to end my life in to avoid further shame. Or live with my brother, if he was willing to take me in."

"Which he did! Can't Riyik just give you permission—"

"It doesn't work like that! Or maybe now it does. Maybe I'm just not ready."

Kalie relaxed. "That, I support. I'm sorry if I pushed you just now."

"How are you feeling?" Brenia tactfully changed the subject.

Kalie's hand slipped inside her mantle and settled on her belly. "Quite good, actually. No morning sickness yet."

"You're lucky. I was sick all the time with my first two. Barak's the only one I wasn't sick with."

"I'm too busy being sick with worry about troublemakers here. I don't know what's going to happen with Darva and Sirak, and I'm afraid Tarella is turning out to be nothing but a parasite."

"Tarella won't be a problem," said Brenia firmly. Even as she spoke, Tarella spilled from one of the temples, leaning heavily on Varian, the oldest of the three brothers she was living with. Both were laughing and appeared quite drunk. "As long as she keeps him happy in bed, and he keeps her in jewelry, everything works."

"And the rest of the family? I've heard complaints that she eats—and wears—more than she works. "

"They will work it out as a family," Brenia said firmly. "Isn't that what people do here? Let's get out of the cold!" They went into one of the temples where a musical performance had just ended. People were heading outside to the bonfire where the dancing was about to begin. There was still food and wine on the table—the only furniture in the room, so Kalie and Brenia went to help themselves.

"And then there's Darva."

"I'd be more worried about Sirak," said Brenia.

"My thoughts exactly." They left the temple to watch the dancing.

To Kalie's surprise, Darva was outside watching as well—and looking like a completely different person than the sullen woman helping with the cider. The visiting storyteller was beside her, wrapping her in a cape of rich fur, and saying something that made Darva laugh.

"You must teach me to dance in the manner of your people!" the handsome man said as he led Darva to join the other dancers." Darva blushed, and protested she could not dance. "Then I will teach you ours," the storyteller insisted.

Kalie and Brenia exchanged a baffled look. Then Kalie saw Riyik across the open space. Standing with him were Zanal and the priest named Orin. It was the identical grins all three shared that told her something was going on.

She marched up to them, Brenia walking behind her with her usual dignified gait. "All right, what are you three plotting?"

"Remember when I said I had an idea about how to handle Darva?" asked Riyik. "There it is."

"Seduction by storyteller? Interesting. But I don't see how—"

"Kalie," said Zanal. "What is the one thing an ambitious slave girl from the steppes dreams of all her life?"

"You mean other than a son to win wealth and luxury for her? To find and marry a prince, I suppose."

Riyik pointed to the dancers, who were beginning to move to the music. The storyteller spun Darva with a skill that would have made the least competent dancer look good. "Behold!" called Riyik.

"But he's not a prince!"

"He's not particularly interested in women, either," said Orin. "But Casim cannot resist trying a new role, and he playacts better than anyone I know. For the rest of this winter, he's going to stay here and court Darva, telling her fine tales of his great ambition to become king, which of course, no one in this part of the world understands."

"How lonely he must be." Brenia sighed,

catching on to the plot. "An oddity among his own people. No one understands him at all—until the right woman comes along."

"And Darva will be only too happy to assure him that she understands him perfectly," said Zanal. "And then she will tell him all about how things work where she comes from, and why those ways are so much better."

"All right," said Kalie. "I understand that Darva will be too busy plotting with her future husband to plot with her son. But what happens when she learns that Casim is not going to become king? Or marry her?"

"Casim is more than a storyteller," said Orin. "He has been called to mediate disputes all around the region of the Great Water. He has a special way of listening to people which grants him a deeper understanding than most of us have."

"It is our hope," Nara said, joining them. "That Casim will find a way to open Darva up to new possibilities, even as she tries to do the same for him. At the very least, he thinks he can help her overcome her maddening fears that cause her to see everyone who walks on the earth as either predator or prey."

"But what does Casim get out of this arrangement?" asked Brenia.

"He will learn new stories," said Orin. "More than that, really: an entirely foreign way of viewing the world. Can you imagine what someone like Casim can do with that? The stories he will create? The roles he will inhabit? What he learns from this playacting will influence his craft for the rest of his life."

"Brilliant," said Kalie. "Insane, perhaps, but

brilliant. And Sirak?"

"The boy is a natural leader," said Orin. "We are seeking positive directions for that gift. After tonight, thoughts of the people will turn to spring. And the warning our new friends have brought." He looked at Riyik, Zanal, and Brenia with piercing eyes.

"We must discuss it further," said Nara, "but I believe that we will soon seek your services in preparing ourselves for less friendly visitors from the east. And since only the men and boys are trained in this art you call war, there are only five who can teach us. Or six if Sirak can understand that he is needed as well."

"Which may well be all he needs to change his path," said Orin.

After a moment, Riyik said, "I think I've had enough celebrating for one night." Kalie, too, was ready to go home. It had been a night of revelations. As they wound their way past the dancers who whirled in a broad circle around the bonfire, Kalie saw Varena dance by, hand in hand with a tall young man, probably just a few years older than she was. They stopped to watch for a moment, and then continued on to their home. The air between the dwellings smelled of clean cold air and wood smoke.

"You could go back if you want," Kalie said. "The celebrations will last until dawn."

"You could as well," said Riyik. "We may have married in my world, but I told you at the time I would accept the customs of yours. If there's someone else you want to spend the night with—"

Kalie stopped him with a kiss. "I've got all the man I need or want right here. But as our child grows, I may have less desire—or desirability—and you are a man, with a man's needs. If there is someone else you want, tonight, or anytime, it will be all right."

Riyik wrapped his arms around Kalie as they reached their door. "I have all the woman I need right here. And we don't need anyone's customs to tell us what to do about that. It's the longest night of the year, and there's still plenty of if left."

They went inside and closed the door behind them.

Chapter 11

For Kalie, the second half of winter was a quiet time of letting go: of the desperate flight from captivity that brought her to this new place, and of her fears that she had brought danger to her home. She finally took the time to get to know people—not just the leaders and those she could discuss the dangers of the east with—but people who became her friends.

Casim turned out to be as interesting as Orin had claimed, and Kalie spent many hours with him, exchanging stories, and watching in fascination as Casim convinced Darva that she would soon be queen of the land. Most intriguing was how Casim—and his entourage, whom Darva viewed as his servants—subtly conveyed the notions that empathy and responsibility towards one's people were requirements for ruling. That certainly wasn't the way it was where Darva was from. But it became clear over time that it left an impression on her.

Durak left the forge soon after the Winter Festival. Janak had kept him on even after it was clear that the young man had no aptitude for the craft, and was only there because he wanted gold. When the smith caught Durak stealing a pouch of small nuggets, Janak ordered him gone. Durak seemed inclined to argue, but Garm, who had developed both a love for the shaping of metals and a great respect for his teacher, hurriedly found Borik, who escorted Durak from the forge, and then went to inform Riyik of the situation.

Kalie heard about all this after the fact, for which everyone was grateful. By the time she did,

Durak, sporting a black eye and a slight limp, was already moved in with Borik and Zanal. Kalie was in no mood for Durak's apologies, but she calmed down considerably after speaking with Janak and Nara.

"I hope you know I don't blame you for Durak's actions, Kalie," Janak said.

"Nor for any actions but your own," said Nara. "Which are of course, above reproach," she added when she saw Kalie's expression. "Surely you have not been away so long you have forgotten our basic beliefs?"

They were sipping tea in a one of the smaller temples, where the Goddess in her form as mother presided.

"I brought them here. And I..." she struggled, having to rely on a word from the language of the horsemen. "I vouched for them."

"They are not the first strangers to join our community," said Janak. "We are familiar with the process of mixing in new ideas and new ways. It's why most of us choose to live here, and not a small village."

"But no one, I think, are as different as those I brought," said Kalie.

"Most of them are doing fine," said Nara. "They have found joy here, and they bring it to others. Although I must admit, the local women are benefiting far more than them men!" She laughed. "Those men, except for your partner, Kalie, act like they haven't seen a woman in a full turn of seasons! It's been the most exciting winter most can remember—on that score, at least. Borik, especially. That man has stamina to match his size, and every woman here wants to find out what he can do."

"I hope he hasn't…disappointed anyone," Kalie said, thinking of the damage a man of his size— even a gentle giant like Borik—could do if he wasn't careful. And self-control around women was not something he would have learned on the steppes.

"I haven't heard any complaints." The old priestess grinned. "But then, I haven't tried him myself. Yet."

"I was surprised that it was the men who were so eager," said Janak. "From what you've said about those bizarre rules of theirs that bind women so much, I would have thought they would be the ones wishing to try as many men as possible. Yet Tarella and Darva each stay with one man, and Brenia and Varena choose to sleep alone."

"Though I think many men hope to be the first one Varena chooses when she is ready," said Nara.

"I think the same might be said of Brenia," Janak said—a little wistfully, to Kalie's ears. "But most are stepping back, out of respect for Martel."

Kalie really wanted to ask about that, but instead asked, "Have there been any…misunderstandings? Men who do not give pleasure, or fail to understand what 'no' means?"

"You would have definitely heard if that was the case," said Nara. "Stop worrying, Kalie. You brought the right people, and taught them well about our ways."

Kalie relaxed into her cushion, and savored her next sip of tea. Stop worrying; it would be a fine thing, if only she knew how.

"The council has discussed the issue of preparing for possible unpleasantness with some of the less advanced horsemen," Nara continued. "There is some dissent. Many of the elders feel that preparing for violence will, in itself, cause it to happen. But they have agreed to let those who are interested learn to use weapons and ride the horses. We will have a meeting with the entire town soon."

Janak snorted. "It's not as if half the boys and girls aren't already learning those things—and many of the adults as well. We will have some holdouts—but most are in favor of being prepared. I wouldn't worry about some of these newcomers not learning a trade, Kalie. I think they will more than earn their keep by sharing these skills that they alone are masters of."

As winter slowly marched toward spring, Kalie spent less time worrying, and more time focused on the changes happening in her body. Riyik seemed to enjoy them as well, and was the most considerate of husbands, rubbing her feet, and bringing home delicacies that the other women insisted would help with the pregnancy. While he spent long hours instructing the people of the town in fighting and riding, Kalie's only real work was collecting food from the storage facilities—aided my Martel, who refused to let her carry anything heavy—and cooking meals for her family.

She spent most of her free time with other pregnant woman, and mothers of various ages and experience. Everyone was willing to offer advice, or lend a sympathetic ear when Kalie felt sick, or wondered where her energy had gone. Brenia was a frequent visitor, often bringing all three of her children, as Darva had yet to reclaim Myla, and of course, she always brought food.

Winter was also a time for two or three families to share an evening meal together, and Kalie always offered her stories for entertainment. Varena was in high demand for the fine singing voice she had only recently discovered she had. She sang the songs of her homeland, blended with the new ones she was learning, while she played the stringed instrument called a lyre, to a growing audience.

"Not so different from winter where you grew up, is it?" Kalie asked Riyik one night as they returned from an evening with a large family of musicians, who insisted on keeping Varena for the night.

"Except that those gatherings were usually just for men is your unspoken message, dearest?" he responded with a twinkle in his grey eyes.

"I guess I just never get tired of dwelling on the differences," Kalie sighed.

Kalie and her family shared many meals with their closest neighbors. Minda's baby was due in early spring, and she had no plans to start her own household, or involve anyone else in the child's life.

Kalie finally asked her about it one day while they were alone in Minda's house, weaving baskets. "Did something happen to your baby's father? Or between you and him?"

"I don't know who the father is," Minda said, finishing a basket and biting off the extra length of straw. "I didn't want to know, so I made sure to share the Goddess's Gift with many men."

"Why don't you want to know?"

Minda shrugged. "I like things simple. I've always wanted children; I just never wanted a life-mate. I knew I'd be happy living in my parents' house, raising one baby, then another, until they have children of their own. My grandfather is thrilled that he's going to live to see his first great-grandchild. Helping raise it might help him live longer."

Kalie couldn't argue with that, and had no wish to. She just got up to stretch her back, and basked in the warm glow of the love and freedom that surrounded her.

One night, as a blizzard raged outside—the last one of the season, Kalie hoped—she and Riyik snuggled close in their bed of rich furs: sheepskin, reindeer, and wolf. Yarik and Varena were asleep in the next room, and a fire of fragrant apple wood branches warmed the cozy little house. Kalie was reminded of a dream she had on her last night in the steppes; the night, she hoped, her child had been conceived.

"Do you miss your old life?" she asked Riyik.

"Never," he said, holding her tighter.

"Do you wonder how the others who came with us are doing in the villages and towns where we left them?"

"That I do. In the spring, I hope to ride a circuit and visit them. There may be news of the tribes, further east. I don't think it's a question of if they come; I think it's a question of when."

Kalie shivered and pulled Riyik closer. "So you plan to make sure that everyone we brought here is doing his job to prepare a defense?"

"Yes," said Riyik. "This town is built on a hill. When the river runs high, it can only be reached by that bridge. This might be the most defensible place we've yet seen."

"The bridge is strong enough to hold horses and riders," Kalie said sadly.

"But only one at a time. I walked around the entire town yesterday. I think we can make it so that the bridge is truly the only way in. With enough good archers, we can pick them off as they attempt to cross, until they grow tired and leave, or run out of men."

"Then they will move to an easier target," said Kalie.

"That is our next problem to solve," said Riyik. His confidence was contagious, and Kalie soon fell into a peaceful sleep. Now it was Riyik who stayed awake worrying.

That blizzard was indeed the last one of winter, and soon the signs of an earth reborn were everywhere. A new energy filled the people, including Kalie. As her pregnancy progressed, she was soon past the time of morning sickness and afternoon naps. The first time she felt the baby move was on a morning when they were both still in bed, so Riyik got to feel it, too. They both walked around with silly grins all day.

"I'm going to Green Bower to visit Larren and the others as soon as the paths are clear," she told Brenia and Varena one day.

"The village closest to the steppes?" Brenia asked doubtfully. "That doesn't seem safe, especially in your condition. If an attack comes, it will likely be there."

"All the more reason to make sure they're prepared." Kalie found herself unreasonably angry at her friend for reminding her that the world in which she had grown up, a world in which a pregnant woman had no fear of walking for ten days across the land, no longer existed.

"Please, Kalie, let the men do that," Brenia said, her thread tangling, then breaking, from the spindle she had become so adept at using.

"I want to go before I'm too far along to travel. I want to see Larren's baby, and maybe even see Agafa, if she still lives. And I want to see how the others are doing. The warriors won't leave the steppes until late spring at the soonest, and then they still have to get here."

"Which they can do more quickly on horseback, than you can on foot," said Varena.

Kalie stopped arguing, but no one was foolish enough to believe she had changed her mind. But first the rains needed to wash the snow away, and then the rains themselves had to stop. And of course, before anyone went anywhere, there would be the Spring Festival.

To prepare, people cleaned and aired out their houses, and outdoor hearths were rebuilt and laid with kindling. Children made a game of slipping in the mud, and seeing who could go home the dirtiest. As in every year, they only played that game once, remembering, as they did every year after the fact, the fun really wasn't worth the scolding they received afterwards. New clothes were made, and each home's garden was prepared for planting, along with the few community fields and gardens.

A few days before the festival, a group of travelers arrived. Kalie saw them crossing the bridge over the now flooded river as she left her garden, nearly as muddy as the children. The men were riding the horses on a circuit around the town, testing the best of the boys and girls who had been learning all winter how to leap on and off a moving horse. This added to the excitement, and at the same time made sure everyone had a turn to ride without tiring the horses.

"See!" she told Brenia. "There are women and children in that group, and it's not even fully spring yet. If they can travel now, surely I can!" As Kalie looked closer, she saw that the group was made up only of women; four of them.

Brenia frowned, and Kalie didn't think it was because of what she had said. Her gaze was fixed on the new arrivals. "There's something wrong," was all she said.

"What?" Kalie stared but couldn't see anything behind possible tiredness in the gait and expressions of the party as they left the bridge and walked the short distance to the town.

"I think I'll head for the hot springs and have a quick bath," Kalie said. "I don't want to greet visitors while I'm covered in mud." She thought of the dress she had just finished making: blue wool, which fell in pleats from the collar, to provide plenty of room for her expanding body. I'll wear that, she thought.

As she started on the path to the bathing place, one of the riders, a young boy, and probably the least experienced, also caught sight of the travelers, and distracted, missed the moment he was supposed to jump down, throwing the girl who was supposed to jump up off balance. She yelped as they collided, and the horse, shied, barely avoiding a collision with the horse behind him.

And then no one was thinking of the horses because the woman in the lead of the party let out the most terrifying scream Kalie had ever heard.

Chapter 12

Her bath forgotten, Kalie joined the others who had heard the scream and were running towards the travelers. One of them looked like she was ready to turn and run back across the bridge. Others were urging calm, and sending pleading looks toward the people of Stonebridge.

Nara was there, along with Orin and several healers. Of the four arrivals, two were visibly upset, one was trying to calm them and the forth—the one Kalie had thought was a child—stood frozen, her face blank in a way Kalie remembered all too well.

"Whatever the trouble," said Nara, "you are safe here. Please come with us to the temple, and tell us what is going on."

The woman in the lead of the column was a giant of a woman, adding to the impression that some of the others were children. She had pretty, pale blonde hair, which was cut oddly short. She ignored Nara and stared at the group of riders, who were now clustered, along with their horses, some distance away. "They're here," she said in a voice devoid of emotion.

"Horses," whispered Kalie. "Beastmen," she said in a louder voice. "She must have heard the stories! Raids, outcast bands…" Kalie was looking around, wondering who best could talk to this woman, when suddenly a tall presence was looming over her.

"I didn't hear stories!" the woman nearly spat into Kalie's face. "I met them personally." With one hand, she pulled open the front of her tunic, showing a disfigured breast. It took Kalie only a moment to realize the damage had been done by human teeth.

With the other hand, she brandished a long spear. "I am Otera, and I made a vow to meet them again—and greet them with this!"

"Some of them wish to greet you as well," said Kalie. "But not as they once did. Those living here now are here to help. To make sure what you have suffered will never—"

"Yes, I have heard!" Otera snapped. "A story has made the rounds of a group of brave women who went to take battle to the enemy. But instead, they brought the enemy to us—and blazed a trail from the barren east to the heart of our rich and fertile lands, inviting every last monster from that land to come and help himself!"

There was a moment of shocked silence. Then Orin spoke. "I remember you, Otera. Though you've been gone for nearly three years, do you not still see those you love gathered here? Is this how you wish to greet them? Have you nothing to offer your people but anger? Nothing for our new friends but insults?"

That silenced Otera—for a moment. One of the women with her quickly spoke up. "I am Lanara, a healer from the village of Waterfall. I can explain some of—"

"Lanara is here to act as guardian, and make sure the rest of us don't disgrace ourselves too much," snapped Otera.

"We clearly have much to discuss," said Nara. "Let us find you lodgings in the temple of travelers, and hear each other's news."

"We have no need for lodgings!" snapped Otera. "We will go to my home!"

"Gods, no," moaned Brenia.

"What?" asked Kalie. "It can't be your house

she means. It was built for a young couple who died."

"Were you once a merchant?" Brenia asked
Otera. The tall woman's head snapped back at the
sound of Brenia's accent.

"Oh, Goddess," moaned Kalie. "Borik, Zanal,
and Durak. They're living in her house. Just what we
need."

"We fixed it up," Zanal said, coming forward
with a conciliatory smile. "Come and see what we've
done with the place—"

Otera raised her spear and advanced on Zanal,
who wisely backed up. Nara, joined by most of the
priesthood and several of the oldest men and women
of the town moved to stand between Otera and Zanal.
"If you truly mean to harm someone with that spear, it
will be one of us," said Nara. "Is that what you
want?"

Otera lowered her spear, but showed little
shame. "My grandmother?" she asked.

"I am sorry, but she rejoined the Goddess
nearly a year ago," said Orin.

"My brother?" asked Otera. "My cousin
Elien?"

"Those should have been the first words out of
her mouth!" someone whispered. Kalie turned and
saw Martel beside her, looking at Otera in disgust.

"Your brother lives in a small fishing village,
two days south along the coast," said Orin. "Elien left
to look for you last summer. Perhaps we can locate
her, and let her know you have returned. But it the
mean time, you will need a place to stay. The house
belongs to you, and you may return there, but the three
men who lived there now have, as Zanal said, worked
hard to restore it. It stood empty for many seasons."

"I will not share my home with one of them!"
Otera shouted, not looking at the horsemen.

"I do not think that will surprise anyone here,"
said Janak, keeping a firm grip on his smithing
hammer, and an eye on Otera. "But you have
information we need, and we have all wasted enough
time on…unpleasentries."

"Let us go to the temple and discuss this
calmly," said Nara, hobbling over to Otera, and taking
her firmly by the arm. Not even Otera, it seemed,
would refuse to help an elderly priestess walk to her
temple.

A short time later, over thirty people were
gathered in the largest meeting room, with the rest of
the population of Stonebridge gathered outside,
awaiting news.

"It was early last summer," Otera began. She
was calmer now, sipping tea, and speaking to those she
remembered from when she lived in this town. Lanara
sat beside her. Given Kalie's vast experience with
healers, it was easy to see that Lanara was one. After
some argument, it had been decided that the settlers
from the east would be allowed to attend the meeting.
All but Tarella, Brenia, Darva, Durak and the children
were present, sitting along a side wall, so Otera and
her companions could ignore them if they chose.
Kalie noticed that they rarely did.

"I was trading amber I had gotten in the north,
in a town called Baratan, east of here." Otera frowned,
remembering. "A little to the south, too. It was about
this size, and I was trading amber for copper tools and
a very fine type of leather they made there."

"Was this town in the mountains?" Kalie

asked, trying to create a map in her head of where the nomads had struck. "Or could you see mountains from there?"

"There were mountains, but farther south," Otera said, annoyed at the interruption. "It was our last day; we were making some last minute trades, and packing. Sometimes I wonder…if we had just left a day earlier…" She shook her head. "They came in the morning. On those creatures you call horses. They were like a storm; like a giant wave."

"How many?" asked Riyik.

Otera glared at the horseman, and for awhile it seemed would not answer. Finally, not looking at Riyik, but at Nara, she replied. "I was too busy fighting something that never should have happened to count them. More than ten; perhaps as many as twenty. They killed people, as you may have heard. They knocked down buildings when they could; burned them when they could not. People tried to run, and the monsters ran them down with their horses. They laughed."

Otera's voice had grown flat; detached. Kalie recognized her own voice in the other woman. She closed her eyes as the words she herself had once spoken filled the room. "They forced themselves on women. Even children. Boys and girls. They laughed a lot when they did that as well." Her breath caught then, and when she tried to sip tea from her cup, Otera spilled it. Someone brought her a cup of plain water, and Otera drained it in one gulp.

"I survived because one of them hit me so hard he thought I was dead. When I woke up, I found a few others alive like me in the wreckage, and a few who had managed to hide." She nodded toward two of her silent companions. "Valesca and Derona were among those." The beastmen took our animals with them—and at least ten women. Some of the women we found dead along the route they rode over the next few days. Some, we never found."

"Where did they go?" asked Garm. "Was it east? Back toward the grasslands?"

Otera was silent, but Lanara answered. "Yes, they went east. I came with some others of my village to help, after the first survivors reached us." Lanara's face twisted into a grimace, which she relaxed with effort. "We followed their trail—it was easy enough with all the earth those animals churned up—and found another place they attacked. It was a small farming village. Two days beyond that, the grasslands begin. We stopped following and returned to Baratan, with the dead and injured we had collected."

For awhile, everyone sat in silence. Otera had retreated inside herself in a manner with which Kalie was painfully familiar. Finally, Orin said, "At least we have some solid answers now, and not just rumors."

"Do you recognize this group of attackers from Otera's description?" Janak asked the easterners, although his gaze was on his apprentice, Garm.

"Based on what Otera has said," Garm answered, "I believe this was an outcast band searching for wealth and territory."

"How can you know that?" demanded Ilara. "They could just as easily been from your own tribe!"

"Former tribe," Nara began.

"We already know that Yuraak—a chief from our former tribe—led a handful of survivors to Shining Mountain, where, thank the Goddess, the people were able to handle them on their own," said Riyik. "Since the attack Otera described happened nearly a year ago, and involved enough warriors to make up a clan, we know they were not of Aahk. The disappearance of another entire clan would have been noticed."

"They might have been from one of the other tribes Haraak tried to forge an alliance with," said Zanal. "Haraak made sure the stories of the wealth here in the west spread. But Otera said these men raped boys. That is not something any warrior I know of would do. Openly, at least. That is why I believe they were outcasts."

"We feared a larger attack," said Riyik. "But if the violence is limited to small raids, there is much we can do to prepare, so that no one again will suffer as Otera and her people have."

That sparked a quiet discussion, with Lanara especially interested, until Otera cut through it in a voice colder than the winter they had just come through. "It is certainly a relief, knowing that monsters are here to protect us. What have we to fear from their kin, now that our land is filled with armed men and horses? Unless of course, they plan to welcome their brothers to join them in ruling our land and our bodies for us. But since no one here is worried, everything must be fine." Otera sent a hate-filled glare to everyone in the room.

"That is quite enough," Janak began.

"Otera," said Kalie, effectively cutting him off, "as the only person in the room who knows just how you feel, I'd like to speak with you privately."

Otera turned her withering gaze on Kalie. "And how would you know anything about how I feel?"

"You said you knew something of my mission

in the east. Perhaps you did not know that nearly eight years ago, I met the beastmen while traveling with a group of traders. I was raped as you were, but not left to rebuild my life with the help of those who cared. The beastmen took me with them, as you mentioned they took some of the other women you knew. I escaped and returned home, but no one believed my account of what happened. I later learned that it helps to talk to someone who has been through the same thing. Of course, at the time, no one else had."

Otera seemed interested in spite of herself, and some of the anger left her face. "And after what they did to you, you returned to their land for more?"

"Well, once people finally believed me, and wanted my help, it seemed the least I could do!" Kalie smiled, aiming for levity, but saw that the attempt fell flat. "My life was nothing but pain and anger by then," she continued in a quieter voice. "Something I think you are familiar with, Otera. I did not plan to survive; only to find a way to destroy the beastmen, so they could never threaten us again. I thought that defeating them would give my death a kind of meaning that my life no longer had."

Riyik reached for her hand, and squeezed it reassuringly.

Otera turned burning eyes to Kalie. "And yet here you are," she said sweetly. "Alive and well and still living with the beastmen. Oh, and you were kind enough to bring them with you, instead of stopping them. And lead enough of them and their horses to blaze a path that any clan looking for wealth and territory can now very easily follow.

Kalie froze under the paralyzing venom of Otera's blame. Her hand trembled in Riyik's, while his did the same. She felt how his whole body shook as his desire to defend her warred with his need to keep the peace and maintain the fragile trust they had all worked so hard to build.

Varena, however, had no such concerns. From her place beside Kalie, the young woman leapt to her feet, fists tightly clenched, and crossed the room to where Otera sat. "You close your mouth, you lying bitch, or I'll close it for you!" she yelled. Varena, although tall for a nomad woman, was not much taller standing than Otera was sitting. In other circumstances, it might have been funny.

"Varena, stop!" Kalie shouted, snapping out of her shock.

Orin and Lanara stood and, flanking her, put gently restraining hands on Varena's shoulders—but no one told her to stop talking, so Varena continued. "You know nothing of what Kalie suffered, or what any of us have suffered! You have no idea what it is to be a slave! Kalie saved more than forty of us from that fate, and left the tribes who would have already conquered this land by now fighting each other, so it might be many seasons before they can try again. And when they do, we will be ready for them because of her, and the warriors she brought here to teach your people how to fight. What have you done to help anyone, Otera? What have you done at all, besides insult everyone you've ever met, and threaten them with a spear you don't even know how to use?"

Otera's face was slack with surprise. She opened her mouth, but suddenly seemed to have nothing to say. Kalie would have hugged Varena if she were not so concerned with decorum. But she knew she would as soon as they got home.

"Otera stopped me when I would have taken my own life," an accented voice said quietly into the silence. Derona, older than the others, with plain features that made it easy to overlook her, held Varena's gaze easily. "And she did much to heal Valeska, although she still will not speak. So do not assume you know all there is to know of her."

"We assume nothing; that is why we have gathered here to learn what we can," Nara said firmly. "But we know bad manners when we see them, and the difference between trying to help and provoking anger." Nara stood, effectively ending the meeting. "For now, there is still much to do to prepare for the Spring Festival, and I suggest everyone return to that." Others stood as people began filing out of the temple. "Ilara, perhaps you and I can help Borik, Durak and Zanal find new living spaces, so Otera can move back into her house."

"That's all right," said Otera. "For now, I will stay in the guest lodgings with my sisters. I do not think we will be remaining here long, and I would not care to sleep where those men have been." She left the temple without meeting anyone's eye, her three companions trailing behind her.

Kalie was silent as she walked home with Riyik and Varena, where Brenia was waiting with the children, and undoubtedly hoping for news.

"Are you all right?" Riyik asked her.

"I'm sure I will be," Kalie replied.

"She had no right to say those horrible things to you," said Varena.

Kalie decided not to wait until they got home. She gathered Varena in a fierce embrace and whispered, "Thank you!" Then she did the same to

Riyik. Then she noticed all four of the other warriors were walking behind them—even Durak, whose behavior at the forge had barred him from the meeting.

"If that woman bothers you again—" Borik began.

"What he means," Garm interrupted, "is that every one of us honors you for bringing us here, Kalie. We promise not to make trouble by dealing with Otera as a warrior of Aahk would. But we want you—and her—to know: you are under our protection."

"We want to help these people," said Durak. At Kalie's raised eyebrows he added, "Yes, even me! I'll admit I was a fool when I first arrived. All that wealth in front of me, and everything so…different from the steppes. But fools like me die where I come from; they don't get second chances! Here, I have one, and I don't want to lose it. And I don't want to see you punished for bringing us here."

Kalie fought to hold back tears. "Thank you," she said, when her voice was hers to control. The warriors escorted Kalie and Varena back home. Riyik, after making sure Kalie was all right, went to speak with his brother warriors. Varena was energetically telling Brenia everything that had happened, so Kalie had a few precious moments to herself.

She knew now that she had done the right thing in bringing the nomads to the land of the Goddess, even if a few might have been better left on the steppes. Otera's cruel words were a small price to pay for that certainty. But Kalie could not help wondering if there was truth in some of the woman's accusations. Had she made it easier for the hordes to sweep into her home? And when they came, as they surely would, would it be, at least a little, Kalie's fault?

Chapter 13

The people continued to prepare for the Spring Festival. Otera remained quiet during this time, sometimes helping to prepare the fields, sometimes walking through the town, listening to and speaking with those who lived here. The new residents from the east all worked especially hard, determined to prove Otera's accusations false.

Lanara helped in the temple of healing, the only one of the four who seemed to remember how to be at ease with others, and to put them at ease as well. Valeska and Derona stayed in the traveler's temple, rarely venturing out.

Since no one from the steppes had ever done any kind of farming, or even seen it, this was a special time, as many found themselves fascinated by the process. Varena, and to Kalie's surprise, Durak, showed signs of finding their true calling. Even Sirak, who had begun to help the men teach weapons and riding to the local children, stopped sulking about the suspension of lessons as he helped with the turning of the earth, the spreading of manure, the clearing of the irrigation channels and the checking of the seeds for signs of rot.

At last came a day of clear weather and the smell of green and growing things which announced the reawakening of the earth. People woke up and felt in their bones that today would be the festival, even before the priests announced it. Despite the fact that most who lived here made their living from trade and crafting, they gathered at the scattered communal fields as reverently as at any farming village.

Everyone scattered wheat seed into the earth, then planted vegetables in their own small gardens. Animals were ritually sprinkled with water, and new lambs and kids counted and blessed.

The sun was still high when the work was finished, so most enjoyed a soak in the hot springs before the bonfire was lit and the feasting begun. There were not yet enough flowers in the forest to provide everyone with a garland, so those went to the children and the pregnant women. But everyone wore at least one flower braided into hair or laced into clothing. All of the pregnant women were seated on cushioned benches, where they had a fine view of the dancing and entertainments, and brought whatever food they wanted.

"This is hard for me," Kalie told the other women as she picked at a piece of perfectly seasoned lamb. "I am not used to idleness—or being waited on."

"I feel the same," said Aldera, a woman nearly as old as Kalie, and about at the same point in her first pregnancy. "They had better let us get up soon! I've never missed a dance at a festival and I don't intend to start now!"

"This year, you have a new role to play," Minda said. "We carry the future of the People in our bodies. Giving up a few dances seems a small price to pay for so important an outcome."

Kalie thought over Minda's words as she felt her baby move within her. It was actually rather agreeable to sit and talk with the other mothers-to-be, and with all the people who came by to bring food, offer advice, or simply visit. Even the ones who insisted on rubbing her stomach for luck were not too annoying, and Kalie couldn't help smiling at this latest reminder that she really was home. Thoughts of what those she'd left behind on the steppes would say about such behavior made her laugh out loud.

Kalie enjoyed watching the dancing—especially when she saw Brenia dancing with Martel, and Varena with Taran. Both pairs made nice couples, she decided. Then Kalie turned to speak with Aldera, and share with her some fried bread dipped in honey. When Kalie looked up, Varena was standing in front of her, Taran nowhere in sight.

"What is it, dear?" Kalie asked.

Varena fidgeted. "I just wanted to let you know…I've decided not to wait until summer. Taran is waiting for me in the woods."

"It's going to be rather wet out there," Kalie said, but in her chest, her heart beat just a little faster. Joy? Worry? Excitement? Perhaps all three.

"But everything smells so good! And feels so alive! I can't wait any longer to be part of it. And Taran's bringing a blanket."

Kalie laughed at Varena's mix of romantic and practical. "Have you been taking that tea I told you about?"

Varena looked away. "I didn't know I would need it until tonight. But I just got some from Sarella. I'll drink it before I meet Taran."

"And you know to keep drinking it every day?"

"Yes, but even if it doesn't work, a baby wouldn't be such a bad thing now, would it?"

"You're too young," Kalie began, then stopped herself. "I prefer that I have my last child well before my first grandchild, but I will be happy with either outcome."

Relieved, Varena grinned. "I wouldn't be the first woman to have a baby the same year as my mother. It's just that here, we might both live to see our great-grandchildren!" Varena gave Kalie a gentle hug, and then ran off meet her lover.

"She does seem young," Aldera told Kalie, squeezing her arm reassuringly. "Yet I know I was about her age when I first came to know the Goddess in that way. And Taran is a nice young man. How did you come by a grown daughter, if this is your first pregnancy?"

So Kalie told her. About Maalke's tent, and the ill-used girl who was his daughter, but a "bastard" because her mother was one of Maalke's slaves, and of Kalie's own hopeless struggle to avoid getting close to the people she had sworn to destroy. By the time Kalie got to the events that had led her to adopt Varena, all the women around her were listening with bated breath, including a very tall woman who stood a little apart from the others.

"Otera?" she said in surprise.

"I would speak with you, Kalie," the woman said in the closest to a friendly voice Kalie had ever heard her use. "But after you finish your story."

Kalie smiled. "A good storyteller always leaves some for later." She stood, and one of her companions automatically reached out to steady her. Adjusting to a new center of balance was a challenge—especially when it changed every day. Another woman handed Kalie her sheepskin cape. "Shall we walk?" she asked Otera.

Otera nodded. They wandered past the bonfire, to where the crowd thinned out, and the sounds of insects could be heard over the sounds of humans.

They walked in silence until Otera began to speak.

"You really lived with them?" she asked Kalie. "Not once, but twice?"

"Yes, I did."

"And did you ever learn…why they are the way they are?"

Kalie sighed. "That question has haunted me for years. I learned some things, though nothing can really explain it all. The land they live in is harsh in a way most of us cannot understand. Searing hot summers, freezing winters. Never enough food or water. I believe it twisted the people who lived there. They made fighting for resources and controlling everything of value into a kind of religion."

"That's no explanation!" snapped Otera. "It makes just as much sense to say they left that place and found a kinder land where they could become better people. Or that the women rose up one day and poisoned all the men. Why would things go one way, and not the other two?"

Kalie thought about it. It was, she had to admit, an interesting question. It also gave her some insight into how Otera's mind worked. But she had no answer, nor did she think Otera expected one.

"I heard tales of your journey to the steppes," Otera continued. "I did not believe them; I didn't really believe in the beastmen, until I met them myself. What you said the other day in the temple, about how no one believed what happened to you that first time? I just wanted to tell you, I'm sorry about that. I guess I was one of those people."

"And then, when it happened to you," Kalie prompted. "You couldn't understand how people could tell you to just get over it; that things would get better, and you could go back to living as you once had."

Otera froze. "Yes," she said. "That is exactly what happened."

"Your world had stopped. How could theirs just go on like nothing happened?"

Kalie was pleased to see that Otera was thinking hard, but Kalie needed to sit down, and the other woman showed no sign of moving. She spied an unoccupied log, one of many which had been dragged to the edges of the gathering place, and began moving toward it. Otera followed. An inebriated couple staggered over to the log, just as Kalie and Otera reached it. They took one look at the two women, and quickly staggered away.

"You're right, Kalie," Otera said as they sat down. "Everything you just said. And what you said that first day, about how talking with someone who's been through the same thing can help."

"But you didn't need me to tell you that," Kalie said, feeling for the first time a stab of envy. "Valeska, Derona, the others—"

Otera nodded. "We've helped each other. Saved each other's lives, if you believe Derona. When I decided to travel here, they would not let me leave alone. Although Valeska follows me everywhere. I don't think she even knew where I was going or why. I don't understand why, but being with me makes her feel safe."

Kalie looked at Otera's threatening bulk and fierce manner, and was fairly certain she understood why Valeska followed her.

"There are four others who survived the attack, waiting for us back in Baratan. And another woman who's joined us from much farther away. We formed a kind of sisterhood. We've been teaching ourselves how to fight. We practice on animals, trying new techniques; new weapons we've developed."

That wasn't what Kalie had been expecting, and she was not entirely comfortable with it. Especially with the way Otera's blue eyes glittered in the moonlight as she spoke. "Your people must appreciate the meat and hides you contribute," she said carefully.

Otera began tearing pieces of bark from the log. "They did. At first. Then they began to worry that our behavior was unnatural. We were causing unnecessary pain to the animals, they said. We were abusing the Goddess's gifts!" Both fists crashed into the log. "Can you believe that?" Otera's voice was shrill. "Abusing the Goddess's gifts! Maybe they need to spend some time with the beastmen to learn what those words really mean!"

"Perhaps the hardest part of all of this," said Kalie, "is learning how to save ourselves from the beastmen without turning into them. That was something that came up, over and over, when I fought to persuade the people of Riverford to allow me to take volunteers to destroy the threat at its source."

"It really was a brilliant idea, Kalie. I'm sorry that you failed."

Kalie bristled. "I did not fail. I simply—"

"Oh, please, Kalie! I'm not blaming you—at least I'm trying hard not to. But the steppes are still thick with murderers and rapists, you've blazed a trail which will lead them straight to us, and you even brought a crowd of them with you!"

"If you want to save your home from the

beastmen, and you are willing to take up weapons and fight, then you should be speaking with the men who followed me here, and not me!" Kalie fought to keep her temper. "They will be happy to teach you to fight—and ride as well, something you will not easily learn on your own—if, indeed, you can ever get horses without their help!"

"They are the enemy! And the fact that you can't see that makes everything you have accomplished suspect!"

"They are not your enemies, Otera, nor mine! But they have trained all their lives to perfect those skills that you and your friends are stumbling around blindly, trying to teach yourselves. Put aside your anger and look at things logically. You need the warriors to learn the arts of war. They need you because there are not enough of them—by far—to challenge the tribes if they come as one big horde. We should be working together, not arguing."

Otera shook her head. "I would rather die free, fighting beside my sisters, than as a tool of the men who came here to conquer. But it may not come to that. I have heard that you discovered a weapon, and used it to escape your tribe. Does it really cripple horses? Even cause them to trample their own riders? If that is true, and you show me how to make it, we will not need the skills of a lifetime to kill the invaders. We'd need to learn only a few new tricks—and a strong stomach."

"Your stomach seems strong enough, Otera. And when enough of the towns and villages have agreed, I will show whoever wishes to learn my new weapon. But regrettably, I do not trust you to use it wisely."

Otera was silent for a time, and then she stood.
Kalie stared up at her impressive stature, and saw how
the moonlight turned her short blond hair into a
gleaming white pelt. "I will return to my sisters with
what I have learned. The journey was well worth it,
whatever you may think of my plans and my
methods." Otera turned to go, and then stopped. "If
you change your views; if those men you brought here
ever betray you, then come find me. There will
be a place for you among my sisterhood."

Then she was gone, leaving Kalie uncertain
how to react. She sat alone in the dark, drinking in the
cool, fresh air of the spring night, until Riyik came
looking for her.

"There you are!" Kalie struggled to her feet at
the sound of Riyik's voice, and he helped her up,
gathering her into a hug at the same time. "Minda said
you'd gone off alone with Otera, and no one had seen
you since. I was worried."

"Otera's no threat to me. Not physically, at
least."

Riyik stared moodily into the beautiful night.
"I wish I could be as certain of that as you are."

"She's more a threat to herself than anyone
else," Kalie said as they began to walk. "Very much
like I was when I returned after my first time as a
captive of the tribes."

"She's nothing like you," Riyik insisted.
"There's something dark inside her."

Kalie wanted to argue; to point out the same
had been said of her, or that everyone around Otera
needed to be patient with her, but she had no idea what
was true at this point. They soon reached their house,
where Kalie was surprised to see Brenia waiting with

the children. Barak and Yarik were both asleep in the room Yarik shared with Varena, while Myla and Liara were giggling and whispering in Varena's bed.

"It seems Brenia's brood will be staying with us tonight," Riyik said, bemused.

"If it's all right with you, of course," Brenia said to Kalie, her normally serene voice strangely high-pitched and rushed.

"Of course," Kalie said, puzzled.

"I'm going," Brenia's eye's slid to the door. Then, in an act of will, she met Kalie's gaze. "I'm going to Martel's home tonight."

Kalie's face broke into a grin. It was the best news she'd heard all night. "Good for you!" she cried, pulling Brenia to her in a great hug. "Stay as long as you like. The children will be fine here."

"I just hope I will be," Brenia muttered. She glanced once more at her brother, as if expecting to be ordered back to her tent.

But Riyik only shrugged. "I always wanted better for you than that fool Hysaak, sister. And Martel is that at the very least. And we all knew we'd have to get used to new ways."

"And I hoped all along those new ways would bring you joy," said Kalie.

"As did I," said Riyik.

Brenia left the house, her nervousness warring with her usual dignified walk.

Kalie kissed Myla and Liara goodnight. "Time to sleep, girls." They quieted at once, and Kalie dropped the door curtain closed behind her.

"Since you're not sharpening your spear to kill Martel," she whispered to Riyik as they entered their own sleeping room, "I guess I don't need to explain why Varena won't be back tonight, either."

"I figured that one out on my own," said Riyik. "It's strange for me; stranger than I let Brenia know. But really, when you think of it, a man can accomplish a lot more when he's not busy chasing other men away from his home, or beating his women to protect their honor."

"This has turned out to be a very good day indeed," Kalie said, sliding out of her dress and into the furs of their bed.

Chapter 14

Once winter had released its grip on the land, the town of Stonebridge resembled nothing so much as an overturned beehive. Travelers arrived, and residents left for journeys to other places. Merchants' packs were heavy with the goods people had spent the winter crafting, including things no one in this land had seen before: felt and unguents made by women from the east, tools of finely carved bone whose evident quality and foreign style, everyone hoped, would bring large profits.

Kalie was too busy to bid a personal farewell to everyone who left, or greet everyone who arrived, but when Casim and his party set out, she walked with them to the edge of town, and then down the well worn path to the sea. Most of those who had arrived with Casim in midwinter had chosen to remain awhile longer in the town, but a new group accompanied him now.

"Is it always like that with you?" she asked the storyteller. "People just leave their homes and follow you?"

"And then reach a point where they've had enough and let me go on without them? Yes. Ever since I began this wandering life."

"How did Darva take your departure?" Kalie asked.

"She was angry, at first. I fear that woman knows only two emotions: anger and fear."

"Don't forget ambition."

"I consider that the offspring of the first two," said Casim. "But I was able to see more in her during our time together. Our way of life is growing on her, slowly. Even if she thinks she has nothing to contribute, I believe she will find something. Especially when she discovers what has happened to her original plan."

The grin on Casim's face sent a spasm of delight through Kalie. "Oh, do tell me!"

Casim glanced at one of his new followers, who took up the tale. "She raged at Casim," the young man said. "Accused him of breaking his oath to her, and swore that her son would avenge her, though he must chase Casim to the ends of the earth."

Kalie laughed. "Is that when she learned that Sirak had made some changes of his own during that long winter when she was too busy to care for him and his sister?"

Casim nodded. "A little praise from the warriors, and some admiration from his students, and Sirak began to see the world differently. And, I suppose meeting a girl who could best him at riding may have helped."

"I hope to be there when she bests him at weapons practice," said Kalie. But the important thing was that Sirak's dreams of conquest and kingship seemed to be fading.

A few days later, it was Riyik she had to see off, along with most of the men who had come with them from the east.

The land was on fire with rumors of nomad attacks, and frightened people doing even more frightening things in response. The council of Stonebridge had deemed it necessary to send delegations made up of the nomads who knew how to fight, and elders of the Goddess lands whose voices were respected, to convince everyone who lived between the Black Sea and the edge of the grasslands to prepare a defense.

"I will be back in time to see my son born," Riyik promised.

"Or daughter," Kalie reminded him. It had become a standing joke between them.

They held each other for a long time.

"Borik will remain here, and Garm."

"Between Garm's weapons and Borik's fighting abilities, we will be safe," Kalie said. "I'm glad you're taking Durak. He may well turn out to be the best spokesman we have. After you, of course."

"We'd best be leaving," Orin said gently. With a last smile, Riyik followed the priest to the path which led north from the town. With them traveled two elderly women who would lend their voices to the warnings of the former nomads, and Orin's eldest acolyte. The horses remained behind, though Riyik was sorely tempted to take them just to speed things up. But the council had overruled him, insisting that the people of Stonebridge needed them to continue training and preparations. And, with only five of them, they could not risk losing even one to mischance, especially the two who were pregnant.

As soon as Riyik's party had disappeared from view, Kalie began her own preparations for departure.

She told no one that she still planned to visit Green Bower, since she knew it would not be a popular decision. But she was determined to learn how her friends had fared before childbirth kept her confined until next spring.

Yet, for the next several hands of days, first one thing and then another prevented her from leaving

Stonebridge.

Yarik became ill, along with many other children in town. It was not serious, but Kalie knew she could not leave until he was well.

Then Kalie became ill, and when she recovered, and was finally ready to travel, Varena— who she planned to leave with the care of Yarik— learned that Taran no longer wished to plan a future with her. Varena had learned to cope with cruelty, hunger and violence in her short life. But no experience had prepared her to cope with heartbreak.

As Kalie sought to comfort her oldest child, the one inside her seemed to be growing with every day lost. She began to wonder if the Goddess Herself was not keeping Kalie in Stonebridge.

Her suspicions were confirmed one beautiful day in late spring, when yet another group of travelers made their way across the bridge to the hilltop town. But these were people were not strangers.

"Larren?" she cried as a tall, self-assured woman with a baby on her back strode across the bridge. Spring flooding had made the bridge the only way into the town from the east.

Behind Larren were Garak and Shula. Kalie ran—or rather, waddled—to the bridge, just as Larren stepped off it, and into Kalie's arms.

"I was just about to begin a journey to Green Bower!" Kalie cried.

"Then I'm glad we reached you first," Larren said, staring down at Kalie's bulging middle. "You're in no condition to travel."

Kalie conceded defeat, but was too happy to care. "Let me see our youngest visitor!" Larren swung her baby around so the pack which held him nestled between her breasts.

"My son, Arlen," she said proudly.

Shyly, Kalie took the warm bundle, and settled him into the crook of her arm as the party walked back into the town. She cooed at his innocent face and wide brown eyes seeing, as she knew Larren did, only a beautiful child, and not a young beastmen. When Arlen began to fuss, Kalie gave him back to his mother, and turned to greet the others.

"You're looking very much alive, Garak," she said, planting a kiss on the big man's cheek.

"Especially for one who would have surely died, had he remained among the tribe," Garak replied with a grin. He inhaled deeply as they passed beneath a blossoming apricot tree. "Everything smells sweeter to me since my brush with death. Or perhaps that's just the smell of life in the west."

"Wait until you've lived in the town a few days, my dear apprentice," said Shula.

"Apprentice?" Kalie asked with a raised eyebrow. "But I thought it was Malor who wanted to study healing!"

"He did, for a while," said Garak. "But he found his hands were simply too well suited for the spear and bow. And he turned out to be a patient teacher of those who wanted to learn the way of a warrior. I, too, wanted to do for others what the healers did for me. And it turned out I had a genuine calling."

"Which was never an option where you came from," Kalie finished.

"There were some raised eyebrows in the temple," said Shula, "when I agreed to take him as an apprentice. But a man who begins training in his

twentieth year has certainly learned things that no one
starting before his tenth year has."

"Let's get you all settled," she told the group.
They continued through the town, slowly enough to
allow everyone a chance to see the sites, and stop to
ask questions if they chose. "Shula, I assume you and
your apprentice—" Kalie shot Garak a quick grin,
"will stay in the Temple of Healing?" Shula nodded.
Kalie turned to Larren. "Will you stay in my home for
the length of your stay?"

"If there's room for two more," said Larren,
cautiously as Arlen began to fuss.

"Of course! Riyik is away, and I want to hear
everything that's happened since I last saw you!"

For the rest of the day, Kalie and Larren
relaxed by the hearth, eating bread and honey, and the
first fresh greens of the season.

"Agafa lived to see the flowers of spring,"
Larren said. "She died only a few days before I left."

"I wish she could have seen more of our
world."

"She had many friends at the end. I think
everyone who met her fell a little in love with her.
And she was lucid until her last moments. Agafa told
me she couldn't afford to grow addled; that if she did,
she might miss out on another miracle of this world.
And that she refused to do."

Kalie smiled, though tears threatened. "That
does sound like Agafa."

"She was not alone or in pain when she died,"
said Larren. "Two things she would have been for
certain in the grasslands."

"And the others?" Kalie asked.

"Most of those we brought have done well in

Green Bower. Sarika is already a respected healer, although she has not taken the vows of a priestess. Saela has become a skilled weaver, and is planning to join with a nice young man at mid-summer."

"Wonderful." It came out a sigh.

"And the big news..." Larren paused for effect. Kalie waited. "At the start of spring, a band of raiders from the steppes attacked the town just north of Green Bower."

Kalie dropped her cup of gillyflower tea. It bounced off her enlarged stomach and landed intact on the soft rug where the two women sat. Spilled tea blended with the pattern in the rug. "And you're just telling me this now? We have to warn the...wait. You don't seem very concerned."

"It probably helped that Malor and Yanal, along with some of their best students were visiting at the time." Larren smiled. "Trying to convince the people there that they would need the skills the men of the east had to offer. The attack came just as the town council was politely telling the warriors that their help would not be needed."

Kalie shook her head. "This is beginning to sound like something out of one of my stories!"

"Except everyone would tell you it was too unbelievable," said Larren.

"True. That is, if it had a happy ending...?"

"Yanal called it 'target practice'. There were only about a dozen warriors—probably bandits, really. They brought no women, no tents and no flocks. Some of the townspeople were hurt, but no one died— except for the invaders. It only took two warriors and five apprentices to kill half, and send the others running back to the steppes."

"Probably because they expected to find easy pickings," said Kalie. "Could anyone tell if they were once Aahk?"

Larren shook her head. "Just outlaws with dreams of greatness. But now our warriors in training have had their first battle—and won! And the people who thought they could just ignore what's coming are rethinking their views."

"And are alive and free to do so," Kalie said, with more venom than she intended.

Larren patted her hand. "It's going better than we could have hoped. A few more attacks like this, and the people of the Goddess will win every time—while getting the experience they will need when the entire horde shows up."

"If these attacks stay small," Kalie fretted. "If the horde waits until we're ready."

"There's no use in worrying about what we can't control," said Larren.

"True," Kalie said, staring into the fire. "But there's something I've kept too tightly controlled. It's time I start showing people how to make horse-killers."

"You won't wait until the delegations return?"

"No. And I want you to take the knowledge with you back to Green Bower."

Chapter 15

As spring turned to the ripeness of summer, Kalie joined her fellow townspeople in sowing and harvesting, and filling the storage sheds with produce. It was normal work for a pregnant woman of this land, and few people urged her to do more than rest often. But to this rewarding work, Kalie added another, more frightening job. She began to teach the people here to make little stars of bone which could cause great injury to any horse who stepped on one.

"Why did you not show us these weapons before?" asked Janak. "They could save us all from the horsemen!"

"These weapons are powerful," said Kalie. "And deadly. They have no purpose beyond inflicting terrible pain to innocent animals, and making it easier to kill men who lie helpless on the ground."

Martel nodded with sudden understanding. "These are not tools, like a knife or a spear, which can be used to slice fruit or put a dying animal out of its misery," he said.

"Exactly," said Kalie. "And in the wrong hands, they can be used against humans as well."

While there were still some in Stonebridge who might doubt anyone was capable of such things, most people simply nodded.

"Let's begin," she told the crowd who had stayed to learn how to make horse-killers. While there was no way to test the weapons on real animals, several human volunteers, wearing heavy leather sandals, stepped, ran over and jumped on the bone stars. Few escaped without at least a cut or puncture wound.

While Kalie was never entirely comfortable with this new weapon in so many hands, the beautiful weather and many joys of the season at least took her mind off her worries.

On a bright warm day with the scent of summer on the way, she bid heartfelt farewells to Larren, Shula and Garak, who were returning to Green Bower with horse-killers and the knowledge of how to make them. Then she took a walk through the town, just to enjoy the changes in the lives of people who had followed her here.

Brenia and her children now lived with Martel. People marveled at the change in the once lethargic widower, as his home rang with laughter and energy, always with the good smells of Brenia's cooking wafting from it. Brenia, now an accomplished weaver, and fascinated by the many dyes available to her, was happier than Kalie had ever seen her.

Darva surprised everyone by moving into the home of another widower: a quiet hunter named Ranal, with no family besides his young son and daughter. Ranal wanted a woman to care for his children while he was away on extended hunting trips, keep his house and greet him with good food and a warm bed when he returned. Few women of the Goddess lands were interested in such an arrangement, but for someone raised as Darva had been, it was perfect. She was now mistress of a fine house, and alone to do as she pleased in it for long stretches. Filled with fur and leather from Ranal's hunts, it reminded Darva of home—or at least the home she had always dreamed of. And, Kalie guessed, the ruggedly handsome Ranal looked and hunted like a warrior of the steppes—but one who did not beat his woman or children.

The only difficulty came when Darva decided she was ready once again to be mother to her own two children. Sirak came willingly enough. He had been living with so many families since last autumn, he was ready to call one place home, and be with the woman who had adored him all his life. But he was dismayed to find Darva so invested in the new man in her life, not to mention his children and the new domain of which she was now a proud mistress.

For her part, Darva barely recognized the adolescent boy who had so little of the steppes about him. Sirak was happy to help around the house, but no longer had any interest in carving out a kingdom in this land, or giving up his work teaching both boys and girls how to ride and fight. Kalie wondered which Darva found more repellent: Sirak's lack of ambition, or his willingness to help his mother by stooping to woman's work.

Myla was a bigger problem. Her memories of maternal love from Darva were few, and she now considered Brenia her mother. Darva wept and screamed that her child had been stolen from her, but gained little sympathy from the priestess who came to assist with the transition—especially when Darva's torrent of emotions upset Myla. It was as if until that moment, Darva really hadn't known where she was. Motherhood carried respect in this land, but not ownership. She was forced to accept that Myla would divide her time between Brenia's home and Darva's until such time as Darva could make amends to her daughter for her earlier neglect. Neither mother nor daughter were happy about the arrangement at first,

but with the help of the community, things slowly
grew better between them.

   Tarella was pregnant, and too happy to make
trouble for anyone. One by one, each of the former
warriors of Aahk found a woman they wished to join
with. All except for Borik, who remained in the house
that had once been Otera's with a series of women
who lived with him for awhile, then moved out.
Whenever Borik found himself without someone to
cook for him or wash his clothes, he appeared at
Kalie's door, looking faintly bewildered, but always
assured of a warm welcome.

   Summer was in full flower, and people were
looking forward to the Summer Festival when Riyik
and his group finally returned home, with several
visitors. Despite the nearness of the Summer Festival,
the people of Stonebridge insisted on throwing a
small, spontaneous feast for the returning delegation.

   Riyik, surprised that he was free to greet his
family, and even bathe and rest before reporting to his
chief as he would have done at once in his old life,
hurried home to Kalie. He grinned at the sight of her
huge belly.

   "I was afraid the baby would already be here!"
Riyik said, embracing Kalie with passion, but careful
about the mound that rested between them.

   "You may wish it was, when the time comes,"
she said, pulling him to the bench by the table where
they took their meals, and bringing out a light snack.
As a traveler herself, Kalie knew Riyik would be
hungry, but she made sure he didn't eat enough to
spoil the feast that awaited them. "First-time births
can be long and difficult. You'll probably spend half a

day pacing a trench in our garden."

"I thought I was supposed to be with you, holding your hand," Riyik said, wrapping a piece of dried meat in small cake of flat bread, and devouring it in two bites.

Kalie snorted, nearly choking on her tea. "I can see why you might think so, but the people of this land are nearly as orthodox about birth being a woman's domain as the people of the steppes. You'll have to wait outside until you're brought news that the baby is born, just like last time." Kalie instantly regretted her words, remembering that Riyik's first wife had died soon after giving him a son with a deformity that should have meant his death, by the warrior's code.

A knock on their door interrupted any response Riyik might have had. "Come in!" Kalie called, rather than waddle across the room to open it. Instead she wiped a spot of grease from Riyik's face, while he hurriedly grabbed a sprig of mint from a bowl on the table and stuffed it in his mouth, trying to chew unobtrusively.

Ilara stood in the doorway. "If you are ready, the council—"

"Yes, of course." Riyik glanced down at his clothing, making sure he was presentable, and strode across the room to follow Ilara outside. He's embarrassed at being summoned, Kalie thought as she followed the priestess and the warrior to the temple. He's used to being where he needs to be without being told.

Before Stonebridge's largest temple, the priests stood conferring. Kalie had been told the meeting would be held inside, but one look at the crowd

wishing to attend explained this last minute
conference. Cushions and stools were quickly brought
outside for the delegation members, elders, and others
whose health warranted it, while a tarp was erected
above them. Everyone else settled down on the
packed earth of the public square, more than willing to
endure the day's heat if it meant hearing the
delegation's news firsthand.

Orin began the meeting by introducing the five
visitors, each of whom represented large communities.
One, a young man from a farming village, had seen an
attack of horsemen first-hand. All were interested in
seeing Kalie's horse killers, and taking the knowledge
of how to make them back to their homes.

Kalie listened, grateful for the shade and cool
drinks people constantly brought her, but not even the
most luxurious cushion could make sitting for long
periods comfortable. She rose and walked frequently,
wishing the constant contractions she felt would give
her some peace. Kalie knew these were harmless
"practice" tugs, and that the baby would not come for
nearly another moonspan. Still, it made the day's
work difficult.

"Many wished for us to stay, and do more
teaching," Riyik was saying. "But they understood
when we explained our promise to return to
Stonebridge. One of the towns in which we left a
large number of horses—and horsemen—last autumn,
will become a central training center, where men and
women from the surrounding areas will come to train."

"I was sent to learn of these 'fortifications'
which were spoken of," said a middle aged woman
from the foothills of one of the distant mountain
regions. "I am pleased to see that much of what you

are doing to limit access to your town may work for us as well."

"I believe our greatest success was in the area of communication," said Orin. "Whether small raid or invading horde, we will use runners—and now riders—to inform neighboring settlements, and bring those who can help repel an attack. And help with the wounded as well."

More reports followed, but by the time the summer sun began to set, and the smells of the feast began to distract even the most focused delegate, one thing was clear: the people of the Goddess lands were ready to fight. More importantly, thought Kalie, ready to organize, and bring aid where it was needed in time to help, rather than just after the fact as before.

"Does anyone else wish to speak?" Orin asked.

Some of those sitting on the hard surface of the common area seemed ready to rise and walk to the feast, but when an old woman stood and walked to the shaded area where the town leaders and delegates sat, everyone settled back down to listen.

"I am Ruleen," she said in a clear voice which could be heard across the crowd. "For fifty-two years I have lived upon the body of the Goddess, most of those years here in Stonebridge. I have seen much in my life, some of it bad, most of it good. But never did I imagine that I would one day hear the people who with whom I have shared bread and life, speaking of killing their fellow humans as if they were organizing a fishing trip, or deciding whether or not to sow a new kind of crop someone has brought from far way."

Kalie sighed and wished she could simply leave. But she stayed where she was, and listened.

"If there is truly no way to make peace with

these 'monsters' you so greatly fear," Ruleen continued, "then we must find a solution that does not involve becoming monsters ourselves!"

"Do you truly not understand?" Durak shouted from his place beside Riyik. "There are men coming to your land who will kill everyone they deem unfit to be their slaves! If I, or any man here they might recognize as a fellow warrior, tried to explain the way of the Goddess to them, they would laugh. And then kill us. You, they would kill before you had time to say anything."

The pressure of Riyik's hand gripping Durak's arm finally stopped his tirade, but Kalie was grateful for his words. Other people of both cultures were echoing Durak's sentiments, many quite loudly.

Nara the Priestess called for silence and got it.

"You spoke of other solutions, Ruleen," Nara spoke loudly into the silence. "What are you proposing?"

"I do not know," the old woman said sadly, but her voice was still strong and her back was straight. Clearly, she was not about to concede defeat or walk away. "I know only what my years have taught me: that things which often seem hopeless when we are young, may turn out, in the course of time, to have solutions which require only great patience and courage."

Beside her, a man nearly as old as Ruleen stood. "If things are truly as bad as you say, is it not better that we should simply leave our homes and start over in a place these men cannot ride to with their horses?"

"How many here agree with Ruleen and Zenek?" Orin called out.

Slowly, about a dozen people stood. Most were middle-aged or older, and most of them had been sitting together throughout the meeting.

When it was clear they would speak only with their numbers, Kalie stood as well. Ruleen's hard expression softened as she gazed at Kalie's bulging midsection.

"I understand your words, honored grandmother," Kalie said. "Perhaps better than most here."

"Yet it is you who have devoted all your hours to persuading the people of the Goddess to become people of the spear," said Ruleen. "You, who have designed a weapon that cripples animals and makes men easier to kill."

"But when I first returned from being the slave of these 'men' my answer was the same as Zenek's. I moved west, and found places to live where horses could not reach me. Marshlands. Mountains. Places of safety can be found. For a few of us. But not even the richest marsh or the most generous mountain dwellers can support the arrival of the entire population of Stonebridge. And there would be fifty times that number if everyone in this part of the Goddess lands were to do as you suggest."

"We do not suggest everyone leave," said a woman who looked to be about thirty years—probably the youngest person in the group. "Only that some of those whose understanding of the Goddess remains pure must leave to preserve that knowledge. We are not complete fools. We know that dark times are indeed coming. If these warriors you speak of come in force, our way of life could be lost forever."

"But if we use their methods," Ruleen

continued. "If we make ourselves the arbitrators of who is worthy of life and who must die for the greater good, then we spit upon the face of the Goddess, and our way of life is lost just as surely."

Kalie sat down abruptly, as another, more fierce contraction ripped through her.

"I'm fine," she said to Riyik and the other anxious people who rushed to her side. "I'm just not up for this kind of debate."

"As always," Nara said with a slight smile, "we have much more to discuss. Now, let us feast, and welcome our guests, and remember our similarities and not our differences."

With that, the feasting began.

Kalie ate a little, and spoke with a few people, but soon decided that what she really needed was rest. While a lavender twilight played beautifully above the hilltop town, she made her farewells, insisted she needed no escort, and began the short walk home.

At least, it should have been a short walk. But the contractions were coming more often as she walked, rather than disappearing as the midwife said they would. Just as her home came in view, Kalie realized she was having trouble walking. It's just up ahead, she told herself, irritated with her sudden weakness.

"Kalie?" asked a concerned voice. It was her neighbor Jula, who was moving toward Kalie at an impressive speed. "Why are you out here alone? Here, let me help you to your home." The older woman quickly had one arm around Kalie's waist and was guiding her to her door.

"I just need some rest; maybe some chamomile tea for my stomach."

"You need a midwife and your family," said Jula. "How could be out walking alone when you're in labor?"

"Labor!" cried Kalie. "No, the baby's not due yet. These false contractions are simply—"

"The real thing," said Jula. There were many people about, heading home from the feast, or returning after bringing children home. Jula hailed several, instructing them to find Riyik and Varena and hurry to get the midwife.

"But it's not time," Kalie said faintly as she fought a wave of panic.

At that moment, a rush of fluid told that her water had broken.

"Well I guess your baby disagrees," said Jula, guiding Kalie into the house.

Chapter 16

Kalie's home was soon filled with women who had given birth, and were ready to offer advice, comforting words, or just a hand to hold. Sarella the midwife arrived soon after, followed by a nervous Riyik. Varena came in next, looking equal parts excited, worried and determined to be helpful.

"Too many people!" Sarella called out. She chose two women. "You and you! Make yourselves useful. Get her birthing blanket, clean cloths and hot water. I will need a lot of hot water. And cool water for her to drink as well!"   Two women Kalie had met early in her stay at Stonebridge moved about her house with great efficiency. They found the leather hide Kalie had prepared on which to deliver the baby, and unfolded it on the floor by her bed. Soon water was boiling and Sarella had all the tools of her trade arranged neatly on a table near the bed.

Varena sat beside Kalie on the bed, sponging her forehead with a cold wet cloth. When the water arrived, she fed it to Kalie in tiny sips.

"Good," said Sarella, sending Varena an approving look. "You're young, but I see you've helped with births before."

"Where I come from," said Varena, sparing a glance at the many herbs, cups, and the strange tool that looked like two spoons joined together, "sometimes this was all we could offer to help. A woman's body was supposed to know what to do on its own."

Sarella shook her head, but had no time to comment on barbarian customs. She instructed Kalie to lie back on the bed with her knees apart so she could examine the baby. Kalie was surprised by how little pain the woman's probing fingers caused her— but that could have been because the contractions were causing so much of it.

"It's too early!" Kalie gasped between pains.

"Your baby thinks otherwise," said Sarella. "You seem close to full term—close enough for the baby to live, at any rate. How near the harvest festival was the conception? Your best guess?"

Kalie was in no condition to explain that on the steppes there was no harvest, or any season called autumn. But she knew why the midwife was asking: the summer solstice was just days away—perfect timing, if the child had been conceived at the autumn equinox.

"After, but I'm not sure exactly how much. Perhaps half a moonspan?"

"Then it's nothing to worry about. Babies can come early by more than that and still thrive."

Quite against her will, Kalie began to thrash and moan. "Give her this." The midwife handed Varena a steaming clay cup. Varena fed it to Kalie as slowly as she had the water, and Kalie detected several herbs she recognized. Bitter, and not even sweetened with honey as she expected, but she knew this brew would help ease the pain.

"Kalie," said Sarella, taking her hand. "You're doing fine. This will be an easy birth—but a slow one. You should have someone with you just to hold your hand and talk you through it. Someone's who's been through it before," she clarified in the face of Varena's indignant look. "And someone who can stay for the whole thing."

"Brenia," Kalie said without even thinking, clenching her teeth against the next contraction.

"Breathe!" ordered Sarella. "Slowly."

By the time the medicine began to take effect, Brenia was there, telling Varena to take a rest, and taking her place on the bed beside Kalie. Martel stood in the doorway, assessing the situation, then blocking Riyik, who tried to push past him.

Kalie sighed with relief when she saw Brenia. Gripping the older woman's hand Kalie's whispered. "Brenia, I think I'm dying. There are things you have to tell Riyik…"

To Kalie's shock, her friend began to laugh. "Why are you laughing?" Kalie was nearly in tears. "I might not survive this birth and—"

"I'm laughing because I said the same thing with my first baby!" Brenia took Kalie's other hand and squeezed both. "Listen to me: I've spoken with Sarella. This is a perfectly normal first birth. You are not going to die. You're just going to reach a point when you'll wish you could."

Unfortunately, Riyik caught some of what Kalie had said. Forgetting for the moment where he was and everything he had learned about the customs of this new people, Riyik pushed his way past Martel, grabbed the midwife by the arm and shouted, "Do something, you fool! I swear by the gods, if you let her die—"

As if it were a cue he'd been waiting for, Martel crossed the room, removed Riyik's hand from Sarella's arm, and with surprising strength, propelled Riyik to the door. "Come with me," he said throwing an arm around the terrified man's shoulders. It seemed a friendly gesture, but he kept Riyik moving at an impressive clip. "We'll get some wine. I'll teach you the toasts we make here for a new baby, and you can teach me the toasts you make on the steppes!"

"We can't toast the baby before he's born," Riyik said helplessly, trying to look back, but finding his view blocked. "It would be bad luck." At that, he shivered.

"Then we'll drink to something else until he's born," said Martel. At that point, they were joined by Borik and Durak.

"I think we'll be drinking to a lot of things before this night is over," said Durak.

Borik nodded grimly.

Back in the birthing room, Kalie tried to explain Riyik's behavior, but couldn't quite get the breath to speak.

"His first wife died giving birth," Brenia said quietly.

Sarella nodded. "I thought as much. Fortunately for everyone, that's not going to happen this time. Relax, Kalie, and don't start pushing until I tell you." She hurried to make another drink for the laboring mother.

After that, things became easier. The pain eased, Kalie learned to breathe with the contractions, and Brenia kept her busy with stories from the steppes and gossip from the town. When Brenia needed a break, another woman seamlessly took her place. Toward dawn, Kalie was able to doze between contractions. While awake, she could swear her companions were repeating the same stories, but soon that didn't matter, as she was no longer sure what was dream and what was real.

And then, just as the sun began to rise, and Kalie finally fell into a reasonable sleep, Sarella was shouting, "Get up, it's time!"

Then it seemed an impossible number of hands were pulling her off the bed, positioning her so she could squat above the birthing blanket, and holding her upright so she could more easily bring the child into the world. Sarella held one hand, Brenia held the other.

"Push!" Kalie answered Sarella's cry by pushing with all she had. There was pain, but more than that, Kalie felt a sense of power. As if, for just a moment, she had become the Goddess Herself, so involved in the act of creation there was no room for anything else. She pushed again with the next contraction, so hard she feared the baby would shoot out of her and strike the ground with the force of it.

"I see the head!" Sarella called from far away.

That's all?

"Again, Kalie!"

Her body responded without any conscious thought, only a tremendous sense of relief.

"Here he comes!" That was probably Brenia.

Then came the most beautiful sound in the world: her baby was crying.

"Just one more push, for the afterbirth," said the midwife, as Varena mopped Kalie's damp forehead and wiped the sweat and tears from her eyes. Sarella cut the cord, and cleaned the still crying baby with simple, efficient motions borne of long practice.

Kalie lay back on the leather mat with a sigh of relief. "My baby?" she whispered.

Mother, greet your daughter," Sarella said formally, setting a linen wrapped bundle into Kalie's arms.

"A girl!" Kalie stared in wonder at the tiny form in her arms, barely aware as the women cleaned her up, eased her into her bed, and tucked her in as if she were the new baby. The baby's cries stopped as she met her mother's gaze. For a moment, they just stared at each other, brown eyes meeting dark blue. Everything about her, from the brown fuzz of hair to the tiny toes—with nails, even—was perfect.

"Can I see my new sister?" Varena asked shyly. Kalie shifted the baby so Varena could see. After a long, serious look, Varena grinned. "Just remember, you're the youngest. I'm firstborn here! Don't get any ideas."

Pushing his way in from behind Varena, Yarik climbed up onto the bed. He stared intently at the baby, but did not look very impressed. "I'm older than you, too," he said. Then, looking around at all the excited adults asked, "When will she be big enough to play with me?"

"Not for awhile yet, I'm afraid," said Brenia, keeping a careful hand on her nephew.

The other women in the room all laughed, then resumed their cooing, and exclamations of how perfect the baby was, and laughing at Varena, who was now running to the door. "I'll go tell Riyik!" She called over her shoulder.

"Good luck being first with that news," laughed Sarella.

Brenia climbed onto the large bed beside Kalie. "May I see her?" she asked. Kalie nodded, but instead of looking at her as Varena had done, Brenia took the baby, setting her on the bed, and unwrapped the blanket.

"What are you doing?" Kalie demanded. "She'll get cold!"

"Yes!" The single word rang from Brenia's throat like warrior's yell of triumph.

"Brenia?" Kalie looked around, making sure the midwife was still there, and wondering if Brenia had lost her mind.

"Kalie, look! It's the same as Riyik's; the same as mine!" Kalie followed Brenia's gaze to the infant's left shoulder, where Brenia was gently tracing a bright red birthmark.

"A strawberry," said the midwife, clearly not sure what the excitement was about, but used to seeing all manner of craziness from relatives. "It's perfectly normal, and the color will fade in time. They often run in families."

Slowly, Kalie began to understand. "Riyik's looked just like this when he was born," Brenia continued. "Haraak never had one. His arms carried scars, nothing more." She bundled the baby back into her blanket, and handed her back to Kalie. "She's Riyik's."

Kalie let out a breath she didn't know she'd been holding. "I hadn't thought of Haraak at all during this whole experience." Kalie held her baby in the crook of one arm, and gripped Brenia's hand tightly with the other. "And now, I'll never have to again. Thank you, my sister!"

Riyik came into the house at a near-run and went straight to the bedroom. Some of the men who'd kept him company during the night waited in the main room, others hovered in the doorway.

"Varena, get food for our guests," Kalie began, before realizing Varena was nowhere in sight.

"It's being taken care of," said Sarella as she bundled up the tools of her trade, kissed Kalie and the new baby on the foreheads and made her farewells. But Kalie could hear the sounds of neighbors moving furniture and setting out food and drink. Then she forgot about all of that because Riyik was kneeling at the side of the bed, his eyes moving from Kalie to the bundle in her arms. He reached out to the baby, and then froze, his hand hovering uncertainly above the tiny, wiggling creature.

"You're all right?" he asked.

"Fine, Riyik. Exhausted, but fine. Now, take a look at your new daughter."

Riyik peeled back the blanket with one finger, as if afraid to touch the infant within. "A little girl," he whispered. "She's beautiful!"

Kalie grinned. "That's not how you do it!" She picked up the baby and set her in Riyik's arms. He looked terrified. "Didn't you hold Yarik when he was born?" she asked, concerned.

Riyik shook his head. "Not until he was much older. And after Yasha died, I left him with Brenia. I was away for much of his first year." The baby began to cry. Riyik looked helplessly at Kalie, who quickly scooped up the tiny creature and put her to her breast. She latched on easily. There was no milk yet, but the cries stopped.

"You'll be able to spend more time with this one. If you want to, that is."

"I want to very much." Riyik was still gazing in wonder at the woman before him who was now mother to a new life that had only just sprung into existence.

"You're not upset that it's not a boy?" Kalie

tried to sound casual and failed.

"No, of course not!" Riyik sounded truly shocked, and Kalie could find no hint of deception. "I already have a son. Now a daughter. And a chance to raise them both."

As if on cue, Yarik freed himself from whichever woman in the next room had been holding him, and came barreling onto the bed. "Careful, little man!' Riyik said, catching him before he could hurt the baby.

"It will be good for you to spend more time with Yarik, as well," said Kalie. "Having a new baby in the house can be hard for someone his age. He'll want to know we still love him too."

Riyik fell on his back—a safe distance from where Kalie sat in the bed nursing the new one—and tossed Yarik up in the air. Yarik squealed as his father caught him, and then tossed him again. "That part, I think I can handle," Riyik said, then began making rude noises with his mouth, which delighted Yarik even more.

"You'll do," Kalie muttered. "So what shall we name her?"

Riyik sat up, surprised. He hung Yarik upside down over the bed to allow himself time to think. "That's not done by the mothers in this land?" he asked.

"Usually, it's both parents who choose the name. Although we can involve as many people as you want to. People love to suggest names."

Riyik shook his head. "We can manage." He settled Yarik on his lap. "What should we name your sister?" he asked, while Kalie nodded in approval.

"Purple!" said Yarik without a moment's

hesitation.

"Purple?" asked both parents together. Yarik nodded, but offered no explanation. It was, apparently, self-explanatory.

"Maybe something more…feminine?" suggested Riyik.

"We can name her Yasha, for his mother," Kalie offered tentatively. A look of sadness clouded Riyik's face for a moment, and then disappeared. "Or my mother," she added quickly. "She died when I was just ten. I don't think anyone has been named for her."

"What was her name?"

"Melora." Kalie's voice was soft with memories.

"That's beautiful," said Riyik. He gazed down at his sleeping daughter. "Just like she is."

Varena entered the room carefully, carrying a steaming mug. "Sarella says to drink this," she whispered, as Kalie set the baby down on the cushion beside her and accepted the mug. "At least two a day. I've already got the herbs brewing for the next batch."

"Why isn't she here with you now?" asked Riyik.

"The birth went well," said Kalie. "It's not like I'm sick, in need of a healer's constant attention."

"Although you'll get it anyway," said Varena. "The constant attention, at least."

That seemed to satisfy Riyik. "We were thinking of Melora for a name," he said to Varena. "What do you think?"

Varena looked again at her little sister. "Perfect," she said.

"Yarik?" asked Kalie.

The boy shrugged and nodded, much more

interested in the string of beads and wooden boat two of the guests had given him.

Riyik and Kalie exchanged very silly grins. "Then it's settled," they said together.

Interlude

Varlas, king of the Wolves of the Gods, sat in the shadowy coolness of his tent, enjoying a break from the searing heat of early summer on the steppes. He also enjoyed the ministrations of his new slave women, taken from various defeated tribes, as Varlas's pack crashed through the west, always victorious, as if they truly were the gods' own wolf pack.

A man's voice outside the tent, requesting entrance, sounded a discordant note to the soft whispering of the women. Normally, Varlas would have been angry at the interruption, but now he only barked an order for the women to leave, and rose to dress.

"Enter," he called to his second in command.

"My king." Garvas bowed briefly, then got straight to the point—one of the things Varlas valued in the man. "The captured warriors have proven most useful. King Kariik plans to move his entire tribe west before the winter."

Varlas gestured for his second to sit, and produced a skull filled with kumis, which they shared. "They have known of the west for years, yet they think to leave now? Fortunate for us, but perhaps not so much for them."

"There is more," said Garvas. "There is much dissent among the tribe. Many do not wish to leave the grasslands, even now." Varlas stiffened, but would not allow his fears to show. Many of his own warriors felt the same way. "Kariik is not the king his father was," Garvas continued.

Varlas laughed. "That much was known to me

before we left our territory in the east. Are you
suggesting he may not hold his crown long enough to
lead his tribe anywhere?"

"It is possible," said Garvas. "Especially if we
remain here until next year, to prepare and consolidate
our newly acquired clans." By allowing the best
warriors of conquered tribes to join the Wolves, Varlas
now commanded nearly two thousand warriors.
"Kariik's men fear his wife more than him. They say
she is a witch, and his plan to move west is her doing.
That land we are to conquer is her home."

The laughter that erupted from the king cut off
at those last words. "Do those men truly believe she
has powers? Beyond what lies between her legs, that
is?"

For the first time, Garvas looked
uncomfortable. "It is something all of them agreed on:
the king is under the power of a witch. And they
believe that many witches dwell in the land of the dirt-
eaters."

Varlas stroked his beard. "That would explain
why the men of that land are so weak. And all the
stories of the women who speak their minds and show
no fear of men." This possible explanation to such
unbelievable tales brought the king no comfort.
Strange lands were challenging enough without adding
dark magic.

"Witches can be killed," Garvas said quietly, as
if reading his king's thoughts. "Or stripped of their
powers." At that, both men grinned.

"Doing so will make a most enjoyable addition
to our campaign," said Varlas. "But first we must
catch them."

"If his own men are too slow," said Garvas,

"we might remove the king of Aahk ourselves. Then add the best of his men to our own pack. At that size, we will be unbeatable no matter what we might face in the west."

Varlas shook his head. "We are large enough already. I have no wish to divide our spoils any further. I only need one man of Kariik's." He met his second's gaze evenly. "One who, for the right price, will betray his king."

"I'm certain such a man can be found," said Garvas.

"Not one who has been captured and tortured. Take a small party under a flag of truce to Kariik and express our interest uniting our two mighty nations. There will be meetings and feasts and much talk until winter. By then the man I seek will have found me."

Garvas smiled in admiration of his king. "I fear the winter will be most uncomfortable for the tribe of Aahk," he said.

Chapter 17

Melora's naming ceremony was made part of the Summer Festival.

Kalie spent most of the festivities curled up in bed with her new daughter, enjoying the company of those who dropped by—usually with food and gifts—and enjoying peace and solitude the rest of the time.

The summer was marked by a bountiful harvest of both crops and trade, and by near silence on the eastern front. Travelers and messengers came through constantly, but only one tale of an attack by a nomad band reached Stonebridge. As was the case in the town near Green Bower, the people of the Goddess fought back, and the few surviving horsemen fled back to the steppes on foot. The extra horses were greatly appreciated, as well as new members for the village, since this group apparently had a few captive women with them. According to reports, the women were recovering nicely, convinced they had found paradise.

"Perhaps things were not as bad as you feared," Ruleen remarked to Kalie one day when they were both picking berries in the forest east of the town.

"Perhaps," said Kalie. It seemed likely, on a day as beautiful and peaceful as this.

And as summer turned to autumn, it became easier still to believe, as a bountiful harvest was brought in, and traders began returning from faraway places, with exciting stories—none of which involved raiders on horseback.

"Motherhood agrees with you, Kalie," Riyik commented one rare night when the whole family was gathered at the table for dinner.

"I've always thought so," teased Varena, who nudged Yarik, who mumbled an agreement around a mouthful of his favorite dish: goat meat, stewed with grain and raisins.

"You know what I mean," said Riyik. "Since Melora came along..." he trailed off, watching his three month old daughter sleeping peacefully in a basket lined with soft rabbit furs.

"I know what you mean," Kalie said. "And I agree." There was a softness about Kalie that was new to all who knew her now—and new to her as well. Even waking often at night to nurse Melora, she slept better than she had in years. The easy rhythms of life and family were all she thought of now.

Most of the time, at least. In her heart, she knew that one day a storm from the east would come and threaten everything and everyone she loved. But if the universe was willing to wait awhile on that, Kalie was happy to wait as well.

And for now, it seemed that it did.

People continued to train with weapons and wait eagerly for their turn at a riding lesson, but it was the birth of two healthy foals that most delighted everyone. The town crafters began to put horse motifs on everything from copper tools and jewelry to woven cloth and clay pots.

Varena found a new love: a boat-maker's son who shared her interest in farming, something he showed a greater aptitude for than boat-building. There was an abandoned farm just outside the town, and the two lovers began to talk of repairing it, and growing flax and vegetables for the rest of their lives. And having assisted with Kalie's birth, Varena was extremely careful to drink her contraceptive tea every day.

Brenia, happier than Kalie had ever seen her, continued to live with Martel, raise her children, weave cloth and brew remedies for the healers. She was reluctant, however, to formally join with him.

"Still feel married to Hysaak?" Kalie asked on the first truly cold day in autumn, as they soaked in the hot springs, luxuriating in the water, and the freedom of having others watching their children for them.

Brenia tipped back her head and slid down until only her face was above the water. "Some days, I can't remember what he looks like. I don't wake up in pain anymore, thinking he's beating me." She pushed herself upright, water streaming from darkened tendrils of hair. "But I still fear a formal joining would somehow bring bad luck to Martel. And that is something I will never do."

"If it's fine with Martel, then it's nobody's business but yours," said Kalie.

"Do you think Varena will join with Noris this winter?" Brenia asked. Unlike farming villages, where weddings were generally held at the summer solstice, or the end of the harvest, midwinter was the usual time in the trading towns, when merchants were finally home, wealth counted and distributed, and people looking for celebrations to break up the monotony. Either that, or early spring, just before the traders left.

"They might. She still seems young to me, but Noris is a fine young man, and I think that farm will be the perfect place for them—and all their energy."

Brenia made a face. "I've seen that place. They should join soon. Only the young and foolish would even attempt a project like that." Kalie laughed.

They were drying each other off when a young boy shouted eagerly from the rocks above that Tarella was in labor, and would her friends come to her house.

"If she's calling us her friends, she must be truly terrified," said Kalie, but she hurried to dress and follow the boy to Tarella's home.

"We are the people she's known the longest," said Brenia. "And she's a much better person than when she first arrived here."

Kalie paused and regarded her sister-by-marriage. "Sometimes, Brenia, you remind me of Alessa."

Brenia looked surprised, but obviously took it as a compliment—as it had been intended.

Tarella's labor was longer than Kalie's had been, and seemed to her to be more painful, despite many potions the midwife plied her with. Or perhaps, Kalie thought, as she sponged Tarella's forehead, this was the one time a nomad woman of any station could vent her pent-up anger by screaming as long and loud as she wanted.

Before midnight, Tarella had a healthy baby boy at her breast, and a completely besotted Varian fussing over her, along with the rest of the family and several neighbors.

Tarella was overjoyed—by her healthy son, and by the gifts Varian showered her with. He had created a set of jewelry made from all the riches which could be found in Stonebridge: shells and amber, copper and gold, even a piece of richly veined blue stone from a land so far south no one knew its name, set into the center of a golden pendant in the shape of the sun. Now, as he hovered over Tarella and their new son, it was clear he would deny her nothing.

And apparently, Tarella had a list. "We will need a new house, just for the three of us," she began. "Your sister should continue caring for your grandmother where they are—she does such a fine job..." Kalie left before she could hear more, but she decided to drop by the temple on her way home, and suggest Nara visit the family, and make sure any changes were agreeable to all concerned.

But that was all she did. In the months since Melora's birth, Kalie had given up worrying about every problem that occurred in Stonebridge, and every word spoken by a former member of the tribe of Aahk. They had been here nearly a year, and everyone—even Kalie—had become a part of this bustling town. She had a beautiful family, good friends and a fine home. Perhaps one day she would take up pottery again, but if not, she was busy enough looking after her family, telling stories and now, serving on the town council.

Winter passed slowly, happily, as even Kalie had to admit that not even the most determined—or foolish—tribe would attempt to travel this far in weather like this. She loved watching Melora thrive, a happy contented baby, who was fascinated by everything. Yarik, now four years old, was proving to be a patient and devoted big brother. He was a good friend to other children as well, as if his early life as an outcast cripple had left him with a greater sensitivity to the pain of others. And if any beliefs in the superiority of boys had been part of his understanding of the world, they were gone now.

The boredom of late winter was broken for Kalie's family and their friends by plans for Varena and Norris's joining, to be held at the Spring Festival. The young couple had spent every spare moment the previous autumn at their future home, shoring up walls, patching the leaking roof, cleaning rot and mildew from the rooms below and planning what would go where. All winter Noris used his boat-building experience to craft furniture, while Varena wove baskets and tanned hides for leather and fur. Kalie even brought up her memories of shaping clay well enough to produce a set of beautiful dishes for the new couple.

When the snow began to melt, and a watery sun offered temperatures above freezing, the people of Stonebridge took to the outdoors, not caring about the cold and mud, simply ready for spring.

It was on such a day that Kalie was with a group of friends in the forest east of the town, gathering the first green shoots, and looking for new things to plant in her garden. She stopped for a moment, her basket half full, at the sound of hoof beats. Horses were approaching.

"Messengers from one of the places the warriors settled?" someone asked

"Too many for that," said Varena.

"Is this the attack, then?" asked a little girl. She did not sound worried. It was just something the adults were always talking about.

"Too slow for that," said Brenia. "And they would be shouting their war calls by now."

Everyone exchanged glances, wondering why no messenger had arrived with news, while Kalie stood frozen, hearing the speculation that swirled around her, as if from a great distance.

Melora began to fuss from her carrier on her mother's back. Automatically, Kalie reached back to pat her baby. "It's nothing, my love," Kalie said.

"Nothing to do with us—"

As the words reached her own ears, Kalie was reminded of a lifetime ago, when she had lived a fragile existence at the edge of town built around a temple of healing constructed beside a mineral spring. Two runners had arrived, and while Kalie had said nearly the same words to her dog, the message they carried had changed her life.

At that moment she knew it would be the same today.

Dropping her basket, Kalie pushed through the bare trees, and hurried up a rocky hillside. The calls from those behind her to come back, to not take her baby into possible danger never reached her ears.

The sound of horses grew louder in the clear, cold air. Kalie stared without blinking until her vision blurred. Finally, she wiped her eyes with her hand, and took a deep breath. When she could see again, a ragged column of riders emerged from the trees below her. Behind them, exhausted warriors walked their even more exhausted looking horses. Women and children stumbled behind.

Leading the rabble, on a horse that looked to be in better shape than anyone else, man or beast, rode a man whose young, but careworn face was one Kalie knew at once: Kariik, king of the tribe of Aahk.

And beside him, patting and whispering to her tired mount as she walked beside him, was Alessa, Priestess of the Goddess Lands.

Chapter 18

"Alessa!" Kalie shouted, even though she knew her friend couldn't hear her. She was about to take off at a run, but by now, others had reached the hillside. They clearly would have prevented Kalie from going anywhere, if she hadn't thought better of it herself. Fleet-footed youngsters had already run back to the settlement with the news.

"Not here!" Kalie said. Striding purposefully back toward the bridge, she saw the others fall in line behind her. "We must greet them on this side of the bridge, and in large numbers. With food and drink, but weapons as well. Varena! Run to the temple and tell Orin to prepare for sick and injured." Varena, the youngest person remaining, took off at an impressive clip. "Minda," she said to the young woman whose infant son was with his grandmother, "can you find some people to help our visitors set up a camp site on this side of the bridge?"

Nodding, the young woman raced across the bridge that the rest had nearly reached. Kalie directed those remaining to fill their water skins from one of the nearby springs, and wait with her, all the while asking herself the same questions everyone else was asking: why had the tribe of Aahk left the steppes in the dead of the winter? And why, after reaching the Goddess Lands, had they continued to travel through snow and rain and mud for another ten to fifteen days while they were clearly exhausted? And why had no messenger arrived ahead of them to share this rather important news?

She would know soon enough, but Kalie felt

much better when people from the town began to arrive, bearing the weight of authority. When Riyik came to stand beside her, she had the sense that somehow, everything would be all right.

As the tide of humanity approached, Orin and Nara strode through the townspeople to take the lead.

"Kalie, Riyik, come stand beside us," called Orin. The couple took their places in the front of the crowd, just as the eerily silent mass of nomads reached them. Kalie was relieved to note that they stopped at a respectful distance from the townspeople.

There was a tense moment of silence while everyone waited for Kariik to speak. Then, Alessa patted her horse gently, and ran to Kalie, flinging her arms around her.

"Alessa!" cried Kalie. Then stepping back, she looked into her friend's eyes and asked, "Is it still you?"

Alessa understood, and clearly took no offence. "I am still a priestess of the Goddess. My loyalties have not been twisted. But there are many here in need of help. My supplies ran out early in our desperate flight."

Riyik stepped forward. "Greetings, Alessa," he said, holding out both his hands. Alessa took them both in hers. "May I present Nara and Orin of Stonebridge?"

The priest and priestess came forward to greet Alessa. "The temples are ready. Those in need will be escorted to them at once," said Orin. "As for the rest, we must ask you to camp here, outside of our town." People moved among the newcomers with water skins and food, as men slid from horses, and everyone crowded eagerly for sustenance.

Finally, Kariik dismounted and walked to the town leaders.

He is afraid, Kalie thought, looking into the king's lean and ravaged face. More than afraid: shell-shocked. His once fine garments were worn and stained, and hung on his gaunt frame. Kariik's only jewelry was a heavy gold pendant with a sun sign worked into it; his badge of office.

Yet he greeted the priest and priestess politely, speaking in his own tongue while Alessa translated. "I bring an urgent message to all the people of Goddess Lands," Kariik said. "A horde from the steppes is massing. They will
be here before summer!"

"It looks to me like one is already here," said Ruleen, holding her basket so tightly her knuckles were white.

"Those I warn you of are many times the size and strength of those few with me," said Kariik. Then, glancing at Alessa, he added belatedly, "We come in peace."

The people of Stonebridge exchanged nervous glances. The nomad warriors numbered over one hundred, with a near equal number of women and children. They were not what anyone would consider "few".

"Let us bring your sick and injured to the temple," said Nara. Alessa began to coax a number of frightened women and children forward from the back of the group, speaking to them as she had to her horse earlier. There were men in need of healing as well, but only a sharp order from Kariik convinced them to cross the bridge and accept help from those they had long viewed as less than human.

Those who remained were already setting up camp, with the help of people from Stonebridge, who brought them food and firewood, and showed them where to get water.   Some of the women from the steppes looked with disgust and barely disguised fear at the strange women who walked confidently and unveiled, working as equals with their men to help strangers.   Others exclaimed over the rarely seen wood they were expected to burn in place of dung, but quickly had several fires going, sighing gratefully at the warmth and the prospect of food. Soon the air was filled with the smells of meat cooking, clothing drying and the snores of those too exhausted to do anything but sleep in the limited shelter of their tents.

"We must speak," said Riyik.

"Kariik, please bring a few of your men and accompany us to the council chambers," said Orin. "And leave someone in charge of your camp whom you trust to…keep order."

Kariik clearly understood, and gave several orders in the guttural language of the steppes. "Alessa will translate—" Kariik looked around for his consort.

"She's in the temple," said Kalie. "Helping with the sick. I will translate." She watched Kariik carefully, searching his face for anger or embarrassment that his woman had left without his permission, but found only a weary acceptance. Perhaps he really has grown into the man Alessa had believed he could be, she thought. Or has at least started the process.

"One thing I don't understand," Riyik said as they headed for the bridge. "Why has no one brought word of your arrival? We set up a system that should have alerted everyone from here to Green Bower—"

Everyone turned to the sound of a lone runner crashing through the bushes. He was covered in mud, from the remnants of his shoes to the short spikes of hair that stood above his red and sweating face. "Can you help me find Stonebridge?" he panted to the first person he saw. "I bring an urgent message from the town of Waterfall, but my partner and I got lost during the rainstorm three days ago!" The man shook his head and took a deep breath. "Horsemen are headed this way and..." he swayed on his feet, overcome by a fit of coughing.

"Well, that answers one question," said Riyik.

"As with any new plan," Kalie said as they crossed the bridge, "there are always a few nits to work out."

Two sturdy men helped the messenger across the bridge to where he could get food and rest, while the rest of the party proceeded to the council chambers of the main temple.

Kariik had brought eight warriors with him. Nara was about to instruct them to leave their weapons outside, but a warning glance from Orin stopped her. She sighed as the sweaty, mud-coated men sat in the newly scrubbed room, then began tearing into the food and watered wine brought to them by wide-eyed acolytes. "The room can be cleaned again," Kalie whispered to Nara. "If a little mud turns out to be our worst problem, it's a blessing!"

Nara nodded in agreement, and then went to stand beside Orin to begin the meeting. Opposite the horsemen, Kalie and Riyik sat flanked by council members. Melora began to fuss, so Kalie shifted her baby to the front, so she could nurse. A few of Kariik's men looked offended, but she ignored them.

Besides, nursing Melora would do more than keep the baby quiet; it would keep Kalie's level of stress down.

"So, king of Aahk, what has made you leave your grasslands at such a difficult time for travel?" Orin asked. "And why have you come to Stonebridge?"

Kalie translated, adding her own question: "Where is the rest of your tribe?" While she probably should have been sitting next to Kariik, she had no wish to. They would all be more easily heard this way as well.

Kariik began with Orin's second question. "We came here because we were told that Riyik and his wife dwell here, and that they are powerful voices in your land. And because we were directed here by many smaller clans who did not wish for us to stay with them." There was uneasy shifting and muttering among Kariik's men. Clearly, many did not agree with their leader's decision to ask for aid—and take no for an answer, rather than simply taking what they wanted. Her opinion of Kariik rose slightly.

Kalie translated and Kariik continued. "Your other questions may be answered together. We fled the steppes when a mighty horde, larger even than the great federation Haraak dreamed of, fell upon us at the start of winter. We fought hard—what you see here is the result of that great battle. Except for the sickest and weakest among us, who were taken in by some of the settlements along the way, we are all that is left of the tribe of Aahk.

There was some whispering among the council, but only shocked silence from Kalie and Riyik. When they had fled over a year ago, the tribe had numbered over two thousand people. More than five hundred were warriors. Barely more than one hundred men had arrived with Kariik.

"This new threat," Kariik continued. "They call themselves the Wolves of the Gods. They come from the east where, it is said, the land is all but dried up. But the western grasslands are not much better. They will come here. Probably before the summer."

"Why do you tell us this?" asked Orin.

Kariik looked startled. "To warn you. And to offer to help you stand against them when they arrive. It is what we heard; that you plan to fight back. We can add over a hundred warriors and horses to your efforts."

"Or, this could all be a ruse," said Janak. Beside him, Garm nodded grimly while Kalie continued to translate.

Kariik looked blank. "Why would you say that?" he asked. Kalie sensed confusion and fear from him, but no sign of deception. Still, that meant very little.

"Your ways are well known to us," Janak replied, the rumble of his deep voice reaching every corner of the large chamber. "But I suspect our ways are known to you as well. Desperate people fleeing through the winter; how could we not take you in?"

"And then when this horde arrives, you would be well-placed to assist in their conquest," Sarella took up the argument. Kalie watched as two or three warriors barely contained their rage at being challenged by a woman.

"That is not why we have come!" cried Kariik. "Those cowards laughed when the rags of our army fled! They let us escape as an insult, knowing all that awaited us was a slow death in the snow."

"And they did not let all of us escape," said another warrior, whom Kalie thought she remembered as Lornak. "My younger wife, my favorite concubine and two of my daughters were taken captive. They took most of our flocks as well."

"My sister, youngest daughter of my father, King Ahnaak, and her two young daughters now belong to the Wolf king, Varlas," said Kariik. "And my son by Mayleen, a daughter of this land, died on the journey."

Kalie's breath caught, and she could not finish translating the last part, so Riyik did it for her. Kalie pulled herself back to the job at hand. She could grieve for the child who might have untied their two peoples later. For now, they had to be certain before trusting any of these people. Even Alessa.

"Yet you insist these monsters know of us." Sarella pressed her point. "Why allow any of you to escape to warn us?"

"They did not 'allow' us anything." Kariik's eyes were hard and his voice cold. "We knew it might come to this when the enemy was first sighted. Since I myself was swayed by fools who swore they would never leave the grasslands for a life bowing to women, I did not lead my tribe west last summer as I planned. My wife swore we would be welcomed—or at least accepted. Yet still I hesitated. I said we would wait another year."

"So when the attack came in the winter, a time when no honorable warrior would do such a thing," said Lornak, "we at least had a plan. Many brave men laid down their lives so that some of us would escape to the west, and someday, avenge them."

"And many women and children laid down

their freedom as well," Kalie said softly in the horsemen's tongue.

Some of Kariik's men looked surprised and angered that the two groups could be compared, but others nodded bitterly. "They, too, bought our lives," said Kariik, facing down his men. "And will be remembered with honor."

"I can attest to the truth of that," came a voice from the open door. "For it was I who decided who would escape and who would be left." Alessa strode purposefully into the room. None of the warriors showed any surprise or offence. Kariik looked relieved.

"Please, Alessa," he said, "sit beside me. Explain to your people that we are not tools of the cursed horde who dare call themselves Gods' Wolves. That we only seek a new life—and revenge against the enemy that nearly wiped the tribe of Aahk from this world!"

Kalie guessed it was the grueling journey, followed by work with the sick and dying that gave Alessa her haggard appearance as she took her place beside Kariik. Yet there was a kind of triumph as well. How many years had it been since the gifted healer had been allowed to practice real medicine, surrounded by people who recognized her skill and revered her for it? What must it have taken to tear her away from the temple of healing just now to come here?

"My partner speaks the truth," Alessa said, meeting the gaze of each person in the room. "The grasslands are dying. I had hoped we would leave the steppes as Kariik said, and arrive here at harvest time." She did not meet Kariik's eye. "But perhaps there is a purpose in our newly diminished numbers; an understanding of just what all of us now face."

"We have much to discuss," said Nara. "But for now, let our guests receive the food and rest they need. How are those in the temple of healing, Alessa?"

"Most, I think, will recover, praise the Goddess, but a few we will lose," she replied. "It cannot be helped," she added, slipping into the tongue of the horsemen.

"Riyik," said Orin, "these men were once your spear brothers. Is there anything you would say to them before they return to their camp?"

Riyik and Kalie both stood, but it was Riyik who spoke. "It is the honored priestess Alessa I would speak with in private, for it was her prophecy that this day would come. For those I once called brothers, my message is simple: your lives now depend on your wisdom and self-control—and your respect for the people of this land. Your first test comes in but a handful of days, for my daughter is to be married then. You are all invited, but if anyone spoils her wedding, I promise you need have no fear of the Wolf pack. You will die long before they arrive!"

Some of the locals looked shocked, but Kariik and most of his men nodded with understanding and respect. Some smiled. Only one scoffed.

"Daughter, Riyik?" called a mocking voice. "When you fled our tribe you had only a crippled son. How then do you have a daughter old enough to wed? Surely you're not speaking of that slave girl your foreign wife brought to your tent!"

Kalie glared at the man who spoke, trying to remember his name. Kelvin, that was it. A close follower of Haraak, back when he held the power. To Kalie's surprise and delight, Kariik turned and struck the man across the face with greater force than Kalie had ever seen him do anything.

Riyik only raised an eyebrow and said in a bored voice, "Of all people, you brought him, Kariik?

"With so many men gone, I had little choice. He has been loyal to me and fought hard by my side." He looked around the room, his gaze moving between Riyik and the priest and priestess. "I humbly apologize."

Kelvin sputtered, and seemed to be trying to lunge at Riyik, but the other men in Kariik's retinue restrained him with ease. They followed two of the oldest acolytes out of the temple. Only Alessa remained behind.

"Well, said Orin as the room cleared. "At least we know the coming seasons will not be boring."

Chapter 19

"It is hard to believe I'm finally home," Alessa said to Kalie and Riyik over a meal at their table. "After so many dreams, I fear this is only another one."

Kalie smiled and did not point out that what Alessa was calling home was a town she had never been to, nor that she had chosen to stay with the horsemen, rather than leaving with Kalie over a year ago. "You told us Kariik would one day lead his tribe to the Goddess Lands in friendship. It seems you were right."

"More like desperation," said Alessa. "But if all goes well, it will lead to the same place." She helped herself to more grilled fish with mint sauce, and closed her eyes, savoring the taste. "I don't think I will ever get tired of the food of my homeland."

"I felt the same way when I first returned," said Kalie. "And I'll give you the same advice I got: take it slow. Your body—"

"—has to readjust to fruit and grain vegetables. Yes, I know." With a sigh, she pushed her chair away from the laden table.

"How many will we have to worry about?" Riyik asked.

"Difficult to say," Alessa replied. "Kariik did a good job of explaining things to the men. It helped that they were so shaken by their defeat—not to mention the loss of their territory and nearly everything they owned. Such a shock makes men more open to the concept of change."

"It may also make some men eager to replace

what they have lost, and salve their injured pride with new conquests," said Riyik.

"I won't deny the possibility," Alessa said, meeting Riyik's gaze. "But Kariik was clear on a few things. Every one of those warriors knows that their survival depends on this alliance. We've told them that every woman here is to be viewed as the wife of a king."

"You've told them; they've heard the words," Kalie said. "But is that really going to change a lifetime's belief that these people are just sheep for the taking?"

A slight tremor in Alessa's hands was all the nervousness she betrayed. "You've already seen Kelvin. There are ten or twelve more like him. The rest, I truly believe are ready to try new ways. Or are simply too used to obeying their king to do anything else."

"We'll need to do something about those men," Kalie said.

Riyik shrugged as if the solution were obvious. "Introduce them to some of our students," he said.

Kalie nearly dropped her berry tart, but caught it just in time. This late in winter, it would have been an offense against the Mother to waste something so delicious. "Riyik," she said calmly, "even the best of the locals have trained for only a year. Men who have trained their entire lives would cut them in half before—"

"There are two or three who fight and ride like they were born to it," Riyik argued. "And one of them is a girl. Well, woman now, I think. Warriors of the steppes are used to training boys without killing them. Although we'd have to make sure they used only practice weapons. And watch them carefully until they learned some respect."

For a moment, all three sat silently imagining what it would be like the first time a warrior like Kelvin was beaten by a woman. Sweeter than this pastry, Kalie thought, washing the last of it down with lavender rose tea.

"I would want Borik to supervise," Riyik added.

"Good idea," said Kalie. "And if that doesn't work, we'll introduce them to Otera."

Riyik shuddered. Alessa raised an eyebrow in question. While Kalie told her old friend the story of the band of female warriors and their leader, Riyik began to clean up, Melora woke up crying and Varena came home with a small crowd of people who had business with all three of the leaders who had just finished their evening meal. Hurrying back to the urgent demands of living, everyone dispersed.

As if her half-serious remark about Otera had conjured it, a messenger arrived the next morning to inform everyone that the great woman herself would be arriving in Stonebridge the next day, or possibly by nightfall. Kalie groaned at the news, but was too busy to give it more attention than that. Despite the chaos and potential danger swirling around the nomad camp, Kalie wanted her main concern to be Varena's upcoming nuptials.

Not surprisingly, this was not easy.

Few of the merchants and other wanderers had as yet left the town, so the additional two hundred or so people had a greater impact than if they had arrived later in the year. Kalie refused to leave the house until the last of the gifts for Varena and Noris were ready and the food she was going to contribute at least planned out in her head.

Then, steeling herself, she marched through the busy town with her head high, strode across the bridge and approached the nomad camp. And while she planned to assist with translations, or anything else that was needed, for a time, all Kalie could do was stare with her mouth open and her legs frozen.

In her dreams, she had never been completely free of the scene before her. The sound of dozens of conversations in a language that had once threatened to wipe her own from the earth, the sight of women wrapped in shapeless black felt moving furtively among the tents, even the smell of meat cooking in oil mingling with odors of people who rarely bathed, threatened to overwhelm her. Kalie searched the crowd for familiar faces, fingering the knife at her waist.

Most of the men were away from the camp, engaged in mock battles. But Kalie recognized some of the women, and that was just as frightening. One limped out of her tent, stooped with the weight of the boy she carried. When one of the healers from Stonebridge came over to examine him, realization hit. The woman was Kara, who had once taunted Kalie about her tales of life in the west, while her son and some other boys taunted Yarik for his crippled foot. Kalie had stood up to that woman back then, but had longed to do more. There were probably others here with whom she had scores to settle.

Yet, for the good of her people, for their future, she could not. And as Kalie looked around, she saw others standing like she was, still as statues, and they too stared at those who had hurt them. Or those they loved.

Darva stood smiling, as if planning her own revenge, but Kalie saw how she trembled and clung to the man beside her. Ranal, her partner, had not left for his first hunting trip of the year and watched who Darva watched, his arm protectively around her waist. "They will make me a slave again, if you let them," she hissed.

"That will never happen," Ranal said firmly. Kalie noticed that he did not offer to kill anyone who tried, but Darva seemed reassured.

Tarella, on the other hand, walked proudly among the hungry, exhausted women, tossing her long blond hair, adorned, not with the veil of a modest tribeswomen, but with jewels, and flaunting her fine clothes and well fed body. Looking for the wife who had once tormented her, Kalie guessed, and so far not finding her. But that didn't seem to diminish Tarella's enjoyment. Kalie should probably tell the bitch to either help out or leave, but somehow couldn't bring herself to stop Tarella from doing what Kalie herself longed to do.

Some of the local women had brought their children to play with the youngest of the visitors, a move of which Kalie approved. It was a slow process however, since the nomad women wanted to keep their children away from the taint of lowborn foreigners. But the mothers of Stonebridge had been wise enough to give their children honeyed fruit and pastries to share. Soon the sounds of laughter and the exchange of names rang through the camp, as children ate treats, chased each other, and used ordinary sticks and balls made from inflated animal bladders to start games.

Brenia arrived with the children. Myla clung to Brenia's skirt. "Please don't send me back to them," she whispered.

"Child, no one is sending you anywhere," said Brenia. "We're here to help them, as the people of this town have helped us."

"I don't want to help them!" Myla whined. "They hurt me! They hurt my mother!"

"Then you don't have to stay—" Brenia began.

Just then, Myla saw her mother watching her. Darva made only a slight beckoning gesture, and a smile that promised safety, and Myla ran to her, burrowing between Darva and the big, strong man beside her. Together, the three of them left the camp and returned to the town.

Kalie searched Brenia's face for signs of regret or loss, but found none. Perhaps some good had finally come of the tribe's arrival. Perhaps good things awaited them in the future. If they could all just survive the present.

Barak barely hesitated before taking the food his mother had given him, and racing to share it with the children of his former tribe. At nearly six years, he probably remembered some of them. Liara waited a bit longer, and then moved slowly toward the older girls, who would be less likely allowed to play. Although far less crass, she moved in a similar manner to Tarella, as if daring those who abused her as a slave girl to even look her in the eye now. But her gifts of food were eagerly accepted, and when Liara found a little girl too weak to get up and play, with a step-mother too busy to care, Liara sat beside her, feeding her slowly, and speaking quietly to her of life in the west.

"Kalie, can you come translate for me?" called Ilara. Kalie hurried over, dropping her anger behind her like unwanted baggage. Ilara was with several women, gathered around the spring in the center of the camp. "Can you please explain that there's plenty of water for everyone, and they mustn't hit each other over who goes first or refuse these so-called 'slave women' access?"

"I can try," Kalie muttered in her own tongue, then put on a stern face and in an authoritative voice translated Ilara's words. It did help, in that things grew quieter, and eventually everyone got their water, but the situation also made Kalie aware of still more challenges.

"I think we'll have to let them work most of these things out the way they're used to doing," she told the priestess. "As long as no one is getting seriously injured, we should probably focus on the bigger issues."

"And what about these women who are slaves? And their children?" Ilara's voice rose at that last part. "How much bigger does it get?"

Kalie looked around. "For now, none of the slaves are asking for sanctuary, or even aware of the possibility. In fact, they're clinging to their way of life as fiercely as the warriors and their wives are in the face of all this terrifying change. We'll have to give it some time before we push for even more change."

Ilara pursed her lips in disgust. "How much time?"

"Days? Moonspans? We'll just have to take it slowly." Then someone else needed Kalie's help and she hurried away.

Later, taking a break to play with Melora,

Kalie spied two women who seemed about to come to blows. Only when one of them spun on her heel and marched away, toward where she was sitting, did Kalie recognize Sarella the midwife. Kalie stood, bouncing Melora up and down, and listened patiently while the midwife raged.

"There's a woman who's going to die giving birth, and these…these vermin won't let me help!"

"Exactly who is preventing you?" Kalie asked calmly.

"That horrid old woman!" Sarella pointed to the one she'd been arguing with. "They call her their midwife!" Sarella nearly choked on the word. "She's got dirty hands, dirt in her hair—which she doesn't even tie back from her face, which is dirty too, and barely knows any useful herbs beyond henbane and tansy!"

"Has labor started?"

"No, not for many more days. It's just—"

"I'll talk to the pregnant woman myself, or I'll ask Brenia to, tonight. Until then, maybe you and I should go see how things are going with the men?"

Sarella started to object, and then laughed. "You're right, Kalie. I can do no good here while I'm this angry. In fact, watching people hit each other with sticks sounds like a fine idea right now, although if anyone a year ago had told me I'd be saying that…" she shrugged, and followed Kalie out of the nomad camp.

In an empty wheat field outside of the town, Kariik and his strongest warriors were busy matching skill with a small group of Stonebridge's trainees.

And everyone lacking more pressing business

was watching.

Once again, Kalie had to admire her partner. Hunger and exhaustion, as well as the shock of such an overwhelming defeat, had weakened the warriors to the point they were well matched with the less experienced townspeople. Kariik wisely chose the same number of his men as there were locals to fight them—about ten for each side. And, Kalie noticed, one of the contenders was Kelvin.

The crowd parted as Riyik made his way to her side. "Most of the warriors too ill or badly injured to fight tried to leave their beds in the temples to come here when they heard about it," he told her. "So Kariik insisted on a small demonstration. Ten against ten. He even promised the men he would choose randomly, since his ten best would not be needed."

"Smart," Kalie agreed. "He won't insult anyone, or start feuds between the men, and can save face if any happen to lose."

"Which is just about to happen." Riyik pointed.

Since the newly arrived horses would need many days of rest and care to be of any use to the warriors, all of the mock battles were fought on foot, with blunted spears and daggers. Swords, still newly arrived among the nomad tribes, were not present, since few remained among the surviving warriors of Aahk, and the new warriors of Stonebridge had yet to learn their use.

Kalie stared in amazement as two heavily padded, helmeted opponents circled each other with spears. The smug arrogance had already faded from the face of Kariik's man as he panted and struggled to disarm the local fighter who had barely broke a sweat.

The experienced warrior leapt in a sudden lunge that would surely have injured his opponent despite the padding—if it had connected. Instead the local fighter, moving fast enough to impress the entire crowd, leapt to the side, and knocked the spear from the foreigner's grip. Then his spear connected with the unarmed man's throat.

No one disputed the outcome. Kariik and many of his men even applauded. When the victorious fighter offered a hand to help his opponent up, it was accepted. The two removed their helmets, and for a moment Kalie hoped to see a woman's face appear on the winner. But it was a man, a farmer she was slightly acquainted with, which was probably just as well.

Several more bouts followed. The warriors from the east, trained since birth in the art of war, won most of them. But not all. And Kalie could see the effect it was having on the men of Aahk. A few more of these, she thought, and respect would begin to grow. And from that, their salvation might follow.

Things only threatened to turn ugly once while she was there. Sirak, now nearly thirteen years old and a fighter of great skill, defeated a young warrior a few years older. The man, humiliated by his defeat, leapt up and, in a move totally against the rules, shoved Sirak in the back while he stood with arms raised to accept the praise of the crowd, knocking the boy face first into the dirt.

Borik growled and moved to intervene, and he was not the only one. But Sirak rose quickly, and shook his head at Borik, choosing instead to glare at his dishonorable opponent. In the silence that followed, the eastern man's rage faltered, as he realized he was being censured by his own side.

"It wasn't a fair fight!" he bellowed. "The mighty of Aahk are half-starved and exhausted from a forced march. While these overfed dirt-eaters…"

"Since when does a warrior of Aahk rely on excuses to explain an honorable defeat?" shouted Sirak. "Or his dishonorable behavior after?"

The other man was about to shout something back, but stopped at the sound of Sirak's accent. "You are of the tribes?" he asked, baffled.

"Once," Sirak said tightly.

"Then I was deceived! Told I was fighting a weak and cowardly dirt-eater, but tricked into fighting a warrior of my own tribe."

"That was not what you called me when last we met, Artev!" Sirak shouted. Artev's eyes widened in surprise. "You called me a slave's bastard and said I'd never be anything more than food for the dogs. And if I hadn't run fast enough, that's what you'd have turned me into! Notice I'm not running anymore. And neither are my people: children of the gods and the Goddess both. You'll find no stronger combination anywhere. And if you want to defeat those enemies you fled on the steppes, you're going to need our help!"

Kariik quickly signaled two of his warriors, and they led Artev from the field, gruffly explaining the new reality as they moved him away. Another pair took the field, but Kalie decided she'd seen enough.

Riyik grinned at her as she made her farewells. "I'd say you took along the right people when you came here, Beloved." He nodded toward Sirak.

"Will wonders never cease?" It was not really a question. "Perhaps some of the men would like to see the town when the contests are over. Or even try a bath?"

"We have been discussing just that," said Orin, leaving his place nearby to join Kalie and Riyik. "I think they should still return to their camp tonight, but a short tour on their way back might be useful. And perhaps some of those who sparred with them might join them for a meal?"

Since we are providing their food lay unspoken. "I will check the supply sheds, and see what more we can spare," said Kalie.

"Just don't give them anything that should be saved for our daughter's wedding feast," Riyik called after her.

"Perhaps some of the women might tour our town as well," said Nara. Sarella looked like she was about to object, then thought better of it and rose to accompany the priestess to the nomad camp.

The short spring day was nearly over by the time the combatants—many of whom shared a new camaraderie with those who had been strangers—and inferiors— the day before—began to travel through the town in small groups. Kalie, intent on the supplies she was counting, along with Martel and Brenia, heard the surprised comments of the newcomers as a pleasant background noise. Yet a part of her still listened for sounds that warned of danger as well: hollow laughter, or comments of easy wealth; whispers of how quickly this alliance might turn into a conquest once the Wolves were no longer a threat.

But mostly she heard awed silence, and questions about who owned the wealth that surrounded them, and confused laughter when the answers were not understood. There were some offended refusals to offers of hot baths; then, surprisingly, a few warriors who said they wished to try one. One man asked a woman walking by if she would help bathe him, to which she laughed and kept walking, while his companion clouted him on the head and reminded him that all the women here were king's wives.

And then Kalie heard the single word "Brenia!" bellowed from very close by, and saw the ground rise up to meet her as a muscular body knocked her over. As someone helped her up, Kalie saw a familiar and hated profile marching past Martel, not even bothering to strike him as Hysaak stood towering over his former wife.

Chapter 20

Brenia moved just fast enough to avoid Hysaak's grasp as he lunged at her. Surprise flashed in eyes already dark with rage and shock. His next move was to swing at Brenia with a fist that might have killed her had it connected. But by then a large group of people stood between them, while several warriors—of both tribes—wrestled Hysaak to the ground and held him there.

Riyik was rushing to join them, but stopped before Kalie. "Are you all right?" he asked, concern for his wife warring with concern for his sister—and desire to kill Hysaak overshadowing all of it.

"Fine," Kalie said, and surveyed the situation, ready to jump in herself if she was needed.

"Hysaak, what have you done?" demanded Kariik, arriving on the scene nearly out of breath.

"More than half their men dead and he has to be among the survivors?" Kalie growled, sounding like Borik.

"What else would you expect?" Durak's face was dark with rage. "Keeping his skin whole is one of Hysaak's few talents."

Hysaak bellowed like a bull, and nearly succeeded in leaping to his feet, dragging several of his captors with him. The confused townspeople, demanding answers, had no idea of the depth of Durak's insult.

Changing direction to what he perceived as an easier target, Hysaak jutted his chin toward Brenia, who stood surrounded by protective friends and warriors and said in a loud, but relatively calm voice:

"That woman belongs to me." He turned his gaze to Kariik. "What say you, my king? I have accepted all of the nonsense you have required—including that we not take the women of the dirt-eaters. Will you now tell us that we may not reclaim our own if they have run away in dishonor? Or that dirt-eaters may take our women as it suits them?" That last question finally brought Hysaak a small amount of the support he clearly expected from his fellow warriors. His captors slowly brought Hysaak to his feet, but kept their hands on him.

Kalie waited for Kariik to point out the obvious, that he himself had witnessed Hysaak dissolving his marriage to Brenia the day they had left the steppes, but Kariik was strangely silent. She saw Alessa hurrying toward the growing crowd in the center of town, but before Alessa arrived, Brenia herself spoke up.

"The last day I spent in the land of my birth, Hysaak, you threw me away. The last words I heard you speak were 'let her die with her brother.' If you require a witness…"

"I need no witness to what I said then!" Hysaak shouted. "And I did not give you permission to speak now! Since it's clear you did not die, you are still mine, to do with as I wish." Hysaak glared at Riyik, and then looked at his brother warriors who stood by their king. "Had you killed the traitors as you should have, Kariik, this would not be an issue now. But you failed, and now my honor is at stake."

"But since you have no honor," Brenia said with a slight smile, "we have nothing to worry about."

Rather than bellowing this time, Hysaak stood completely still. "For that you will die, woman.

Along with anyone who seeks to aid you." Hysaak's eye fell briefly on Martel, but then moved on as if he were beneath notice. But they lingered on Kariik.

If he continues like this, thought Kalie, Hysaak might defeat himself without anyone else's help.

If everything did not fall apart in the next few moments.

Some of Kariik's warriors glanced around uncertainly, others glared at the townspeople with barely concealed rage, but were for the moment, mostly silent. Not so the people of Stonebridge. "You see what they are!" shouted a woman. "These, these…motherless creatures are what some of you thought we could work with as allies!" Others were echoing her sentiments, some going quite a bit farther.

Martel stood close to Brenia, and Kalie could see it was taking all his self-control not to grab her and run away, or at least push her behind him. Finally he whispered, "Is my presence here putting you in greater danger?"

"No,' Brenia replied firmly, and took his hand. Hysaak, still fighting those who held him and railing at his king did not even notice. But there was another in the crowd who did.

A woman detached herself from a group of her nomad sisters, who were watching the proceedings from a respectful distance. Like many of the others, her clothing hung on her gaunt form, and her once lustrous blond hair lay beneath her veil in dirty tangles. A listless baby of about a year old rode on her hip. "It appears your lesser wife has not been lonely without you, dear husband," Elka said.

Slowly, Hysaak's eyes rested on Brenia in a new way, finally taking in the man who stood protectively by her side. "So?" he said, in his calmest voice yet. "You're a little whore as well as the sister of a traitor?"

"Kill her!" Elka hissed. "It is your duty as well your right."

"You've always wanted him to kill me, Elka," Brenia called in clear, strong voice. "Perhaps you should focus instead on helping your husband—for he is mine no longer—before he fatally annoys the wrong person. Or on getting your baby to a healer, before he dies as well."

"You worn out old bitch…" Elka began, but the High Priest of Stonebridge cut her off.

"This has been an educational time for all of us," Orin said. He glanced at Kariik, whose face burned red with humiliation. "So there is no cause for worry or embarrassment. But it seems clear, King Kariik, that not all of your men fully understood the terms that you agreed to. I suggest a group of us, your hosts, join all of you for a meal at your camp tonight." Orin turned to address Hysaak. "For now, let me simply be clear that in Stonebridge, there are no slaves, and no one will be taken against their will, anywhere by anyone. Is that a simple enough place to begin?"

Hysaak, still restrained, called out, "We all knew our king was a fool when he led us here. But now he is condemned by his own mouth. I say that any man who will let these dirt-eaters take our women—or anything else they want—or allow a woman to speak to him as my faithless wife has spoken to him, is no man at all. But Kariik spoke truly when he said this land was fair, and now we are here. Who'll join me in enjoying all the land has to offer, and in showing these sheepmen who their masters are?"

To Kalie's relief, only a few looked ready to follow Hysaak, and none actually made a move to do so. Martel tried to urge Brenia to the back of the crowd, but she refused to move, her eyes riveted on the scene before her.

Hysaak reddened when he saw he had no support. Then he tried a different tack. "If my whore of a wife is here, then so is my son! I call upon my spear brothers to help me reclaim him. Or has your honor grown so weak you will deny me even that?"

This time, there was a muttering of support. Some beliefs could not be overruled by a king, and a man's claim to his children was one of them.

"Release him!" Kariik commanded, approaching Hysaak.

Hysaak's surprise turned to a grin of triumph. "Does the king now see the wisdom of..." Kariik slid his knife across Hysaak's throat in a quick, efficient move. The surprise returned to Hysaak's eyes as he continued speaking, seemed to notice that only blood, not words, came out, and then slowly crumpled to the ground.

To his men Kariik called out: "Is there another man here who will make of me an oath breaker? Who will insult our hosts after eating from their table? Who would endanger all of us—and our children—when we have but one chance left to redeem our tribe?"

There were some respectful denials, and then a scream pierced the air. Elka threw herself on Hysaak's body, wailing and tearing at her clothes. None of the other women approached to offer comfort, although one did pick up the baby Elka had dropped.

Alessa and another healer hurried over and, considering the circumstances, Kalie thought that all three seemed to work together quite well in coming to the child's aid.

People were conferring about what to do next when a new voice joined in. "At least you can all see these animals for what they are. Now perhaps you will finally listen to me."

Kalie did not need to look up to know that Otera had arrived early.

But she looked up anyway.

The tall blond woman had brought a group of at least twenty other women, whom she was instructing in the ways of the beastmen, pointing to the various living specimens as she did. When at last she pointed to Kalie, Otera finished with, "And this is the woman who brought the accursed beasts and all their violence to our homes."

At that moment, Elka leapt from Hysaak's body and rushed at Kalie. "This is all your fault!" she screamed. "None of us would be in this godless place but for you! My husband would still be alive if you had not…"

Kalie grabbed Elka by her hair. Dragging her a short distance, she used her other hand to grab a startled Otera by one of her muscular arms. With a strength borne of a fury she had never known, Kalie marched both women to a nearby storage shed and propelled them through the open door.

"Since you can both agree that everything that's wrong in your lives is my fault," Kalie yelled, "let's find out if there's anything else you can agree on. Maybe by morning, you can arrive at something that's actually useful!" Then, just as both women leapt to their feet and mad a dash for the door, Kalie slammed it shut. From the thud, followed by a yelp, she guessed that someone's face had been hit. She did not care whose.

Kalie leaned against the door to keep it closed, only to have the combined force of both women's might knock her to the ground. The next thing she knew, Borik was lifting her gently to her feet. Then he placed his impressive bulk against the door, feet spread and arms crossed. He looked prepared to remain that way all night.

"Go get some rest, Kalie," Borik said, and Kalie thought she saw him smile.

Chapter 21

The moon had risen and the lavender twilight was fading to black when Kalie awoke. She was in her bed, wrapped around her sleeping daughter. Kalie only vaguely remembered returning home, nursing Melora and falling into an exhausted, dreamless sleep.

Varena and Noris sat on the carved wooden chest near the bed, fingers entwined, and waiting patiently.

Kalie sat up, careful not to wake the baby. "Is everything all right?" she asked.

"We were about to ask you that," said Varena. "But we didn't want to wake you to do it."

"Are Otera and Elka still in the shed?"

"Yes," said Noris. "But probably not for much longer. Everyone agrees with what you did, but Nara says keeping them in there all night is too harsh. She'd like you to let them out, and give them a chance to apologize to you. Then you can all join the feast that's starting…" He glanced out through uncovered window to the first emerging stars. "About now."

Kalie snorted. "Apologize? Those two?"

"You won't be alone," Varena said quickly. "Kariik himself will explain to Elka why it would be a good idea, and half the priesthood will explain it to Otera."

Kalie sighed. A forced apology wouldn't really mean much, but she appreciated the support she was receiving. And it sounded like her presence was required. She quickly changed into a more festive dress and brushed her long brown hair, wondering if she should start looking for strands of grey.

"What about Melora?" she asked Varena. "And Yarik?"

Varena looked proud, almost haughty. "Yarik is at the feast with his father—where no one will dare make fun of him. Noris and I will stay will Melora." She gazed fondly at the sleeping baby. "We'll need the practice."

"Any time soon?" Kalie asked, trying to sound casual.

"Not yet," Noris reassured her. "But soon—or at least, after these troubles are over, I hope."

Kalie thanked them both, and then strolled out into the night, taking slow, deep breaths, and enjoying the quiet. While the town was far from empty, Kalie guessed about half the population of Stonebridge was at the nomad camp.

She reached the storage shed. She could hear nothing from inside, but several people were gathered outside, speaking quietly, and Borik appeared not to have moved from his post at all.

"Kalie!" Orin called. "Are you willing to release the two ill-tempered children you have rightfully closeted together?"

"If that is the will of the council. And I would like Borik to be free to go enjoy the feast."

"I'm fine where I am now," said Borik, but at a gesture from Kalie, he stepped aside.

Kalie opened the door.

Otera and Elka sat against opposite walls, glaring at each other. They looked to the door at the same time. Under different circumstances, it might have been funny.

"Well?" asked Kalie. "Did you find anything else you could agree on? Besides everything being my fault?" She repeated the questions in the nomad tongue.

Otera stood stiffly, and replied, "I do not converse with animals." Then, as she saw the assembled clerics, "And I apologize for my behavior." She ducked out of the doorway and walked toward her lodgings, looking neither right nor left. Kalie wondered if Otera had any idea what she was supposed to be sorry about.

Elka followed, looking from Kalie to Kariik. "I used my time in isolation to mourn my husband, as was fitting," she said. "Since the ugly bitch I was trapped with could not even speak properly, she was not too much of a distraction. If you will excuse me, I shall go prepare to join my husband in the next life."

"Go," said Kariik tersely.

"Will you really allow her to kill herself?" Ilara asked, horrified. Kalie translated, surprised at her own mixed feelings on the subject.

Kariik sighed, looking even older than he had just two days earlier. "It is her right, and our custom, but I suspect your women will find a way to talk her out of it."

"What of her child?" asked Nara.

"That's just it," said Kariik. "We've lost too many people already! There are no women left with enough milk to feed the boy. There are men who need wives—and we're not likely to find them among the Goddess-worshipers!"

"She is a troublemaker," said Kalie. Ilara gasped.

"She is that," said Kariik, his growing command of the local language allowing him to be understood by everyone present. "Were we back on the steppes, at our full strength, I would be delighted to grant her the honor of accompanying her fool of a husband to the afterlife."

"And if things were normal here," said Kalie, "I'd consider it a great step forward to help end that barbaric custom. But there's Brenia to think about as well. Expecting the two of them to live together? Elka did try to kill her, you know?"

"So did I," Kariik said wryly. "Along with your husband and several warriors who are living here now. As Hysaak reminded everyone this morning."

The message was clear enough: everyone involved would simply have to find a way to leave the past behind and live together.

Kariik led the way to his camp beyond the river, where a quiet, but mostly cheerful party was underway. The results of food, rest and medical care were already showing among the tribespeople, especially the women and children. Groups of various sizes gathered around dozens of small campfires, sharing food donated by the people of Stonebridge, supplemented by meat hunted today.

Kalie saw Ranal sitting with another local hunter, and several warriors, all of whom had hunted together that evening. Women were carving and distributing the meat from two elderly stags, while the men seemed to be having an intense discussion of the merits of bow versus spear in a forested area. Several stews containing rabbit and squirrel meat and dried vegetables bubbled at different fires. Children who were not busy eating were playing in the open space between the tents.

Kalie joined a group of women from both cultures. Sarella was ladling stew into bowls and distributing them. They appeared to be in the middle of a discussion about Elka. "Would she truly take her own life because her partner died?" one woman asked.

"It's the only way a woman can be guaranteed an eternity in paradise," explained a woman Kalie remembered as Tilka, a wife from Zavan's clan— when he still lived to lead his clan.

"Paradise?" asked Sarella.

"Like going home to the Goddess," Darva, who was translating, explained. "A place of eternal springtime, where a wife rides beside her husband, without fear of competition or the need to ever work again." Darva smiled bitterly, as if wondering how she had ever believed such things.

"But why not just wait until your gods call you, and join your...what is the word... husbands then?"

The nomad women looked at each other as if such a thought had never occurred to them, and then shrugged. "It's simply the way things are," Tilka said.

As Sarella gave Kalie a bowl of stew, they were joined by Ilara and Alessa.

"What if the wife is a nursing mother?" Sarella asked. "As Elka is. What of her child?"

"Another woman, usually of higher standing, will raise him," said a woman Kalie didn't recognize. "Her husband vows to raise him to know of his father, and thus all are honored."

"Would Brenia take the boy—if such a terrible thing as you describe were allowed to happen?" Ilara asked. "He would at least live with blood kin, as Barak is his half brother--? Did I say something wrong?"

The nomad women were hissing and making signs against evil. One spat on the ground in Ilara's direction.

"Brenia will die a Shadow Woman, cast out of all that is good," Tilka hissed. "She betrayed her husband and her people."

"There is no greater crime," Kara said slowly, as if her hosts were imbeciles. She scanned the other fires, and the people moving in between. "See how she does not dare to show her face even now, while his true wife mourns him." Kara nodded toward the tent from where Elka's wails could be faintly heard.

"Actually," said Kalie, "Brenia is in her home, with her family and friends, mourning Hysaak in her own way." She smiled at the shocked looks several of the nomad women could not hide. "It surprised me too, when I called on her earlier. Hysaak was a man without honor, who nearly beat Brenia to death to please Elka, and then turned his back on her and all he vowed to her when he sensed his own skin was in danger. So why should she mourn him at all? Especially now that she has a better husband and a life without fear and humiliation?"

"What kind of low-born slut could even speak of such things?" Kara began, gazing at Kalie with horror, but not recognition. "Hysaak was her husband! If she could not please him then the fault was hers, and could have been resolved fairly with her death. She does not have the right to simply choose another..."

"Brenia always did have more honor than most in that tribe," Darva added, as if Kara had not spoken. "She kept all her vows to Hysaak; mourning him now is the last of those vows. So of course she will do it." Darva spoke as if to explain, but Kalie could hear the glee in her voice that matched Kalie's own, and for the first time, felt a friendship with Darva begin to blossom. The giddiness that followed made her reckless.

"Brenia will probably ask Martel to leave her bed for a few nights" Kalie said, trying to sound serious, but something close to a giggle escaped. "Something Hysaak would never have done were the situation reversed."

Alessa sighed. "Kalie, we're here to build friendships, not pick a fight." Kalie tried to look contrite, but failed. The other women of the town looked confused as to why any of this would be the cause of a fight.

"But what of the child?" Sarella pressed. "How can there still be women enough left to take him in? And how could any woman leave her child like that?"

"Yes," said Ilara. "There are babies dying now because their mothers' milk has dried from deprivation. And half your warriors have died this past season. If every wife did as you suggest…"

The mood changed abruptly. All thoughts of fighting over whose way was better seemed to disappear. "These are evil times," said Tilka. "Our king says we must adapt to new ways. He is right, of course. And you are right, Lady. She nodded toward Ilara.

Kalie's eyebrows shot so high, her eyes were visible even by the faint light of the fire. "Ilara helped save Tilka's daughter from starvation when Tilka thought it was too late," Alessa said. "And cured her husband of an infected wound."

That would explain Tilka's respectful tone, but not necessarily her openness to new ideas.

"Too many women have lost their men," Tilka

continued. "And too many men have lost wives. So the Great One tells us it is our duty to live instead. To remarry, and give birth to more warriors, and raise the children who are our future."

"He has also said that slaves are to become wives," added another woman. "That there will be no more slaves among the Aahk."

"That shall never happen while I live," said an older woman.

"I did hope you might say that, mistress," hissed the first woman. "Surely our king will not object to you taking your life, if that is your wish."

The old woman gasped, and Kalie realized she was nearly blind, with possible other complications that had prevented her from realizing who sat near her.

"Many of those who are slaves now were once the daughters of warriors," reminded another woman.

"Even so," another said haughtily, "some things simply cannot be allowed." She spoke as one who had departed reality and now lived in her own world.

"Will you tell this to our king?" Kara asked, a touch defensively. "We shall do as he commands, as in all things. But it is hard for many, to endure what has not been asked of us before." She nodded to two women who clung to each other at the edge of the firelight. "They are both honorable widows, yet forbidden to join their husbands in death. As Elka will be."

Kalie moved closer, hoping to offer them comfort in the new beginnings that would be found in this land. One of the women looked up, and Kalie gasped in horror.

It was Kestra, once of the Goddess Lands, who

had followed Kalie to the steppes more than two years before.

"My husband died of his wounds on the way into this strange land," Kestra said in the language of the steppes, but her accent betrayed her. "My daughter too." Her hand strayed to the mound of her belly. "Yet I cannot join them."

"You at least have the hope of bearing a son, that your husband's line will not end," said the woman beside her. "I am denied even that. Yet they tell me I must bear the shame of living; even of marrying another man. So that is what I must do."

"Kestra?" Kalie's voice was barely a whisper. "Do you know me?"

Kestra looked up, and for a moment there seemed to be recognition in her eyes. Then she turned away. "Another shameless whore from this cursed land," Kestra mumbled in a flat voice.

Alessa came to sit by Kalie, putting an arm around her. "This is not your fault, Kalie," she said firmly.

Kalie tried to smile, but only managed a grimace. "You always know what I'm thinking, Alessa. Just as I know that I should never have taken her with us. Kestra was too fragile."

"No one knew that at the time," said Alessa. "Least of all Kestra. You asked for volunteers and she volunteered. It's not as if you had the luxury of turning anyone away." This was true. Haraak had demanded fifty women as tribute. Only thirty two had been willing to join the venture. And most had died on the journey east.

"Will someone please explain this," Ilara cried. "Are you saying this pathetic nomad slave…"

"Was once a woman of the Goddess, who went with me to try to save our world?" Kalie finished. "Yes."

"And she was no slave!" Kara said hotly. The others glanced at Darva, who, though Kalie might have wished otherwise, continued to translate. "She may have been born a mindless barbarian, but a great warrior made her his wife, and a woman of value. Perhaps you should try learning from her example, instead of telling us how we should change to become more like you!"

Sarella stared at Kara, but Ilara, staring at Kestra, ignored her and asked, "How is this possible?"

"The mind can break, just like any other part of the body," Alessa answered sadly.

"Yes, but she's home now! She's safe! She doesn't have to…" Ilara shook her head, looking slightly ill. "Why is she here, and not in our temple of healing?"

"Would you have me drag her there by force?" Alessa demanded. "She has no memory of who she was. She has even forgotten our language! When I chose to stay with the Aahk, rather than returning with Kalie and the others, I worked with her, tried to heal her." Alessa took a deep calming breath and grew still. "You can see how successful I've been," she added bitterly.

Now Kalie put an arm around Alessa. "And that wasn't your fault, either."

"Stop this!" cried Kara. "Hers was a great love story! The kind the poets sing songs about. Why do you try to make it something ugly?"

Suddenly, Sarella began to laugh.

"What is it?" Tilka asked.

"A moment ago, when you spoke of having to learn new ways; all the changes being forced on you, I felt little sympathy. After all, I knew those changes were for your own good; that someday, you would thank us. I now see that there are changes ahead for both of our peoples. And I will admit I myself am more than a little frightened by them."

For a moment, there was silence.

Then, timidly, a nomad woman spoke up. "I would like to learn how you make these garments that you wear, for they seem much finer than felt. If we must abandon the ways of our ancestors, I would like to do so in comfort." There was nervous laughter.

"I would like to learn of your ways of healing," Tilka said to Ilara.

"I would be happy to teach you," replied the priestess.

"And I would like to know what seasonings you put in this stew," Sarella said. "I have eaten many early spring stews, but none like this. Did you bring these herbs with you from the steppes?"

"Yes," said a woman, probably the oldest of the group. "But there's only one herb in there that came not from this place. In my land it is called horsemint. I have not yet had time to search for it here."

Kalie sat back as she finished her stew, and smiled.

Chapter 22

For the next few days, the two groups settled into a guarded truce, as each side learned what would be required of it in the moonspans to come. Kalie heard regular reports, and felt relief each day that blood was not spilled, but was too busy preparing for Varena's joining with Noris to get too involved—for which everyone was grateful.

Kalie sat in her house with Brenia, while their children played outside. They were making final adjustments to the richly decorated linen dress Varena would wear, and discussing items they would each contribute to the feast, when Varena rushed in. She was crying, and so disheveled that Kalie's first thought was that she had been attacked by one of the newly arrived warriors.

"Varena!" Kalie leaped to her feet, spilling the lovely, pale green garment to the floor. Brenia, still as a statue, looked on.

"Oh, Mother!" Varena threw herself into Kalie's arms, and spoke in the tongue of the horsemen. "Noris and I just had a terrible fight! I don't think there's going to be a wedding!"

"What happened?" Kalie asked, holding Varena and patting her back as she sobbed. Brenia, now that she knew the cause of the problem, went to the shelf where dishes and spirits were kept and poured everyone a cup of wine, then gently led the pair to the table. When Varena was ready to disentangle herself, all three of them sat on the benches and took a cup.

"Noris told me yesterday that he wanted to

leave as soon as we were joined."

"Leave?" Kalie was confused. "But your farm…"

"He says there's no point in putting work into something that's just going to be burned to the ground when the horde reaches us. He says there are other farms, farther away, and we should move there. Or just find a safe place to wait out the war, and come back when it's over."

Kalie and Brenia exchanged a look.

"And what did you say to that?" Kalie asked.

"I said we couldn't just leave when our home was in danger. I told him I'd searched for this place all my life, and I wouldn't run away and let my friends die, and that we both needed to stand and fight. Noris said he'd never take a man's life, and he couldn't believe I would either. Then I called him a coward and, well, after that…" Varena began to cry again.

"Varena," said Brenia. "Noris is no coward. He wants to protect you. And I'll wager it's more than just you he wants to take with him."

Varena dried her eyes on the sleeve of her dress. "Well, he has been asking all his family and friends to leave, too. But that's just worse! We need everyone we have to fight when those bastards come here!"

"Varena, Noris wasn't raised to be a warrior, or even understand the idea of war," Kalie said. "If he doesn't want to change all that, it doesn't mean he loves you any less. And Brenia is right. His first thought was to protect you. That sounds to me like a good quality in a man."

"But this is his home! The only place he's ever known. How can he just abandon it and everyone in it? I've only been here a year or so, and I plan to fight!"

Kalie had known that, but hearing it sent a shiver of fear through her. She pushed the feeling away. "Maybe you two just need to talk when you've both had a chance to calm down.

"The joining is tomorrow," Varena reminded her glumly. "And the Spring Festival."

"You wouldn't be the first couple to wonder if the whole thing was a mistake the day before," said Kalie.

"It could just be nerves," said Brenia. "I was so nervous the day before my wedding…" She stopped. "Forget it. Wrong situation."

Riyik, who had come in about halfway through the discussion, spoke up. "Maybe I should speak with Noris."

Kalie was about to tell him that the parents should probably stay out of it, but then saw the closest thing to a smile creep onto Varena's face.

"You'd have to promise not to take any weapons, Father," she said.

Riyik sighed. "Oh, if you insist." At that, Varena's smile grew almost full sized. "And Noris might not be wrong. Many will be going to safety—as much as there will be such a thing when the fight comes. And you, Daughter, will not be fighting at all, unless you practice more. You have a strong will, and you're good with a bow, but you must admit, drilling has not been your main concern since we arrived here."

Varena looked surprised, but had to concede the truth of Riyik's words. She finished her wine and began to pace around the room.

"Varena," said Riyik, "let's you and I take a walk. You'll drive your mother and aunt crazy if you stay here now. Yourself as well."

Kalie smiled as they left. She hoped that the relationship could be repaired; that there would be happiness and hope to remember in the dark days ahead. But once again, even without anyone saying anything, it all seemed to come back to Kalie and her actions.

"If I hadn't brought everyone here, Noris would be looking forward to a normal joining tomorrow," she sighed.

"If you hadn't brought us here, he wouldn't be marrying Varena," said Brenia. "And the horde would still be coming."

Kalie looked at her friend. "How are you doing, Brenia? With Hysaak's death, and all those people from your past?"

"I'm fine. I've avoided the nomad camp, but eventually I'm sure I'll run into someone who will call me names, but that won't matter. Riyik has made sure all the warriors in town are looking after me. The women will only talk, but all of Hysaak's friends and spear brothers will consider it their duty to kill me as an adulteress."

"Doesn't that concern you?"

"It would if Hysaak had any friends, or anyone to call him brother. Kariik has promised me protection. And strange as this may sound, I trust him."

"It does sound strange, but I'm beginning to as well. I just don't like danger hanging over those I love. Especially stupid danger! It's bad enough we have to worry about invading hordes, but this…this goat-dung! Men who think it's any of their business who a woman sleeps with, or that there's some kind of honor in killing her over it!" Kalie sighed. "Yet here you are, calm as ever."

"One of the benefits of my homeland: we don't worry about what we cannot change." Then Brenia grinned, and showed Kalie a copper dagger with a blade as wickedly sharp as Brenia's grin. "Janak gave it to me. One of the benefits of your homeland: I'm not so helpless now as I once was."

"I'm glad to know it. But don't let yourself be alone for a time, all right?"

Brenia's smile softened into something truly beautiful. "I'm never alone here. And I didn't realize until Hysaak died, just how alone I was, all those years I lived with him."

They packed away the wedding finery until a final decision could be made, and then gathered up their children. Kalie insisted on escorting Brenia to her home, despite Brenia's protests that it was only a short distance. Then Kalie had to stay and share a late afternoon meal, since the house was filled with Martel's relatives from outlying farms, who had arrived for the Spring Festival. When Kalie finally insisted on leaving, pleased that Brenia was in good hands, Yarik wanted to stay, and even Melora, who was now crawling, seemed happy to investigate all these interesting new people, and the things they had brought with them to play with.

"Go ahead," called Martel's sister, who had three children of her own, including a baby about Melora's age. "My babes are thrilled to finally have playmates, and I can nurse Melora if she needs it." Brenia and Martel both nodded.

"Thank you," said Kalie. "I don't know when I'll be back, and given recent events, I can't promise their father or sister will come for them." But she knew that was all right with everyone here.

While there was plenty of work to be done, preparing for the Spring Festival, Kalie realized that what she really needed was to be alone for a time. She walked beyond the town, to one of the rocky outcrops with a breathtaking view of the sea. For a long time, Kalie just sat and stared, breathing the fresh sweet air of spring, letting her mind drift, but not arriving at any answers to any of the problems pressing in on her.

Then she stood and walked to Ruleen's house. The place was large, and at one time had been filled with a big extended family. Now there was only Ruleen, her brother—widowed as she was—and her adolescent nephew. The men were out, but Ruleen greeted Kalie politely.

"I came to…" Suddenly Kalie wasn't sure why she had come.

"Come in and sit down," Ruleen said. She led Kalie to a warm and comfortable room, where a fire burned cheerily in the hearth. The room was filled with deceptively simple wooden furniture covered with cushions of brightly dyed cloth. Many fine works of ceramic filled the shelves. The Goddess in all her forms adorned an altar by the hearth.

"Who works the clay?" Kalie asked.

"My mother did, long ago." Kalie noticed that many of the pieces were very old, but well cared for. "Then my brother, although not so much lately. His hands and back grow stiff." Kalie automatically began to think of remedies she would bring over, while Ruleen made tea.

"My mother was a potter as well," Kalie said. "And I was too, for a time."

They sipped honeyed chamomile tea in silence until Kalie was ready to speak again. "When will you and your party leave Stonebridge?" she asked.

"Summer, most likely. We are still waiting to fully understand our mission."

"But the horde will be here by then! Perhaps even sooner."

"We know. We all heard what has been said since the strangers arrived."

"I thought your purpose was to be gone before any of the fighting you disapprove of began," said Kalie.

Ruleen stared at Kalie in surprise, her cup halfway to her lips. She set it down carefully. "We certainly disapprove of fighting, but we would not abandon our own families in a time of crisis. We will be here, to care for the wounded, organize supplies, carry messages—well perhaps those who are younger than I will do that last one. But we will not leave until matters are resolved. And if things go badly for the people of the Goddess, we must try to get as many children away as possible."

Kalie felt her respect for this woman grow. "Do you know yet where you will go?" she asked.

Ruleen shook her head. "Ilara has been seeking visions in the temple. My brother, too, is one the Goddess sometimes touches with such insight. I assume we will travel west at the start. Perhaps there is a hidden sanctuary on some other shore of the Black Waters. The answers will come in time."

They were silent for a time, and then Kalie blurted, "Do you blame me for all of this?"

Ruleen laughed bitterly. "You mean like that ill-mannered child, Otera? The one who thinks the Goddess speaks to her and no one else?"

"Or perhaps she thinks she alone speaks for the Goddess?" Kalie was quite suddenly relieved.

"You and I might disagree," said Ruleen, "but I hope never to become so convinced of my own righteousness that I forget to respect the opinions of others. And blaming you for the arrival of the horsemen would make as much sense as blaming my deceased mother for bad weather. The horsemen would have come regardless. We just disagree on what to do about them."

"Then perhaps we are both right."

"That well may be. I have spent some time with the nomad women, and I am grateful that I had the chance."

Kalie's eyebrows rose in surprise. "What has that experience been like?"

"Very illuminating," said Ruleen. "They are almost like another species, but one where greater communication is possible, than with say, a dog or a bird. Some have been kind, some appreciative, some angry at what has become of them. I find I am not sorry they are here. Their warriors mean hope for our physical survival. Our numbers mean hope for better lives for them and their children. Especially the…what is the word? When a person is owned like property?"

"Slaves."

"Yes." Ruleen stared into her tea, as if seeking answers there. "It helps me understand why this battle you have been preparing us for is necessary."

"Yet, whatever the outcome, you still intend to

leave this land forever?"

Ruleen gazed at Kalie across the shadowy room, now lit only by firelight, as the light outside the window faded. "Someone must remember," she said, sounding for a moment like the Goddess Herself. "Whether we win or lose this war, the people of the Goddess will never be the same. I hope we win, but I cannot ask the Goddess for something that will mean suffering and death for so many. So I and those who share my beliefs will take the wisdom and memories of who we once were, and find a way to keep them alive. Or perhaps hide it for those who come long after we are gone, to someday find again."

"What changes do you foresee, Lady?" Kalie whispered, not sure she wanted to know.

"I believe that in some parts of our world, our ways will be lost completely. In this place, where two cultures have already come together, I foresee a blending; a merging of two very different ways of life."

"That could be a good thing," said Kalie. "Already, Kariik has declared an end to slavery. And when the women of Aahk taste real freedom; discover the feeling that being listened to and respected brings…"

"Yes, those things may well happen. More for their daughters, I think, than those here now. But do you really believe that change shall work only one way? The ways of Goddess will change as well. Perhaps not completely. Women will not easily give up their freedom, any more than men will forget kindness and compassion. But these men from the east bring many gods with them. How will our one Goddess—even in three forms—stand up to so many?

When the faiths begin to merge, what will She become? The wife of their sky god? A distant mother-figure to be remembered only at planting and harvest time? Perhaps just an ancient spirit women call upon in childbirth.

"And what about travel and trade? In a world of dangerous men, will not everyone eventually agree that it makes more sense for only men to be the traders and messengers? When women travel, it will have to be in large groups, with warriors to protect them. They will not wear veils or live their lives in tents, but, eventually, it will simply make more sense for women to stay close to home; concern themselves with the hearth and the children."

Kalie thought of many things she could say: women could still choose to become warriors and travel as they pleased or that staying close to home meant a greater voice in how the village or town was governed. Yet she knew Ruleen had already thought of all that, and it would bring her little comfort. What mattered to Ruleen was the change about to overtake her world. And no matter how many of the old ways survived, the purity and the certainly of over a hundred generations would be lost. Unless...

"So you think to find a place and, what? Bury things that will tell people who live in a future time beyond imagining what we knew and how we lived? What things? And how will they speak?"

Ruleen's gaze swept the contents of her home: goddess statues, colorful cloth, everyday objects of great beauty, made with great care. "The Goddess may speak through many things, to those of our descendants who will listen. And perhaps there will be more than only lifeless artifacts. Perhaps there will be children who can be raised to know the old ways, and teach them in secret to their own children. Whatever the path turns out to be, the ancient wisdom will not be lost."

Chapter 23

Kalie stayed late talking with Ruleen. She arrived home late in a mist-shrouded night, and found everyone already asleep. Melora awoke briefly, and Kalie nursed her and put her back to bed. Then, she too, slept.

Awaking late in the morning of the Spring Festival, Kalie discovered Riyik gone, and Yarik, wearing only a shirt, sitting on the floor, staring intently at Melora, whose hands and face were covered with the gruel Riyik had apparently fed her, as she sucked contentedly on a mutton bone.

"Yarik?" Kalie asked. "Where is your father?"

Yarik looked up at Kalie, then quickly back at the baby. "He had to go out. He told us not to wake you, and that I had to watch Melora until you woke up."

Kalie suppressed a chuckle. "And you've done a fine job. But since I'm awake, please go get dressed." She had just finished cleaning and dressing Melora when Varena came running inside. "Everything's fine!" she cried. "The joining is happening! Will you be ready, Mother? Will my dress be ready?" Varena looked truly panicked for a moment. When Kalie showed her the dress, finished and perfect, she relaxed. "Oh, thank the Goddess! And thank you and Brenia!" Before Kalie could react, Varena ran back outside.

"Well, I'm certainly glad that worked out," Kalie said to her nine month old baby.

As if the lovers' reconciliation were an omen, the day unfolded perfectly. Sun shone in a sky of rain-washed blue, with puffy clouds drifting lazily. The nomads arrived for the festivities clean and dressed in their best.

"Of course, our best isn't what it used to be," said Tilka, trying to smooth the wrinkles out of her stained and much mended felt robe. "Some of the men were able to make new armor, and we were able to make new clothes for those who will be married today, but most of us have had to make do with simply bathing and dressing our hair."

"Alessa was able to get us the ingredients for an acceptable cleansing paste," said Kara, sniffing disdainfully. "Although it seems some of the lower borne women will use water and herbs from now on."

Unbidden came the memory of the paste made of cedar and frankincense which the women of the parched steppes used to clean themselves. The process involved covering their bodies, waiting for the paste to dry, and then peeling it off, along with anything stuck to it, like body hair or scabs, followed by a vigorous rub-down. While Kalie had preferred it to being dirty, she had longed for an actual bath her entire time with the tribe.

"There will be many new things for you to try out," said Alessa. "And you may choose which ones will become part of your life in this new land."

"Let us pray that we will not remain long in this strange land of shadows and ghosts," said Gallia, once the proud wife of a chief. "This time, when our men are victorious, we will return to the steppes and reclaim our home! And our traditions," she added, glaring at several former slave women, who stood together for reassurance. Frightened they may have been, but they held their unveiled heads high, and looked coolly at Gallia.

Others, Kalie noticed, looked at Gallia with the gentle patience people reserved for the senile and the mad. After eight days of food and rest, Kalie had feared that Kariik's people would only be recovered enough to make trouble. Now she saw that most of them were more concerned with making a good impression; with showing off what remained of their wealth, their pride and their honor to those they now considered their hosts. And apparently, they were determined to start by sharing in today's spring festival as fully—and politely—as possible.

"Your people celebrate the coming of spring as well, do you not?" Sarella asked the small group of women she had gotten to know as they walked together to the fields for the turning of the earth and the sowing of the first seeds.

"Yes," Kara said, over the sounds of flutes, rattles and clapping hands as more people joined the procession. "But it is different for us. We celebrate the day on which we leave our winter camp. Those who survived the winter give thanks to the gods. The priests bless the animals on which we depend, and pray for a safe journey to our summer pastures."

"Then we all leave," said Tilka. "The rest of the day is spent walking."

"And if we are fortunate," said Miona, a former slave, "a soft shower of rain comes with us."

Kara glared at the girl but said nothing.

"We gather flowers as you do," said a girl, nearly on the verge of womanhood.

"Will your brides wear flowers today, as ours do?" Sarella asked.

"Yes," said Tilka. "If they were able to find

enough."

They arrived at the first of the fields. Most of the nomads watched with interest as the townspeople performed strange labors in the fields, while the priestess prayed and everyone sang. A few, however, eyed the activities with distaste. Some were clearly offended by the sight of a woman leading sacred rites. Others, Kalie suspected were bothered more by the misguided belief that there was anything sacred about rooting in the dirt like animals—especially when there was urgent business, like fighting a war, at hand.

But no one disrupted anything, and soon Kalie was called away to help prepare Varena and the others for the joining.

Four couples were to be joined that afternoon in the sight of the Goddess, the earth and the community. Then, just before sundown, even more couples would be wed in the nomad camp. Each side was invited to witness the festivities of the other. Afterward, there would be feasting, music and dance, and those on both sides who had planned and labored for it, would learn if their attempt at cultural blending would lead to a new future, or the collapse of a vital alliance.

Sirak suggested that everyone just get drunk together.

Nara suggested they hide the wine.

A compromise was reached by watering the wine, and limiting everyone to two cups. This was easy enough, since only by watering it would there be enough to provide even that much for the larger than usual crowd. The nomads had no kumis to contribute, since they had drunk what little they had on the journey, and the batches they had begun as soon as

they settled into their new camp would not be ready
for some time.

Kalie found Riyik, Brenia and Martel along the
way to where the couples gathered. While Varena had
many friends to help her dress, Kalie's heart soared at
the look on Varena's face when she saw her family—
parents, aunt, uncle-by marriage, even an unruly little
brother and nephew—who would stand with her when
she was joined with her beloved. The fact that Noris
had a rather large extended family, who seemed to be
fussing a great deal over details, made the arrival of
Varena's family even more important.

Varena fought to stay still as Kalie wove a
colorful garland of spring flowers into her long golden
brown hair.

"I remember the last time you wove flowers
into my hair, Mother. When I became a woman and
you invented a Ceremony of Womanhood to celebrate
it."

Kalie smiled. "I didn't invent it; I merely
imported it. Had you been raised here, it would have
been as normal to you as the changing of the seasons."

"And here I am at my wedding, ah, joining,
and it is a far sight better than what would await me on
that side of the river." Varena nodded toward the
nomad camp.

"Hold still!" cried Kalie. She glanced at
Brenia who was making last minute adjustments to
Varena's dress. It was made of fine linen, dyed in the
vivid green of new grass, and brilliantly embroidered
with the darker green needles of pine trees and beads
made of tiny shells and lustrous freshwater pearls.

"And I remember your wedding, Kalie,"
Brenia said. "Though only from the back of a crowd

of well-wishers. I clapped and trilled until I was hoarse."

Kalie nodded. "Hysaak would not allow you to participate in your own brother's wedding. Not to contribute to the feast, or even to use your tent to prepare me. I remember little of the whole thing, but I know I'd have been far more comfortable in your tent, than wherever it was they put me."

There was an awkward silence, as melancholy seized Brenia's normally serene expression. "But you are here now, at my daughter's wedding, and it will be far more beautiful than either of ours were," Kalie said, hugging Brenia tightly.

"And I could not have a better family to stand with me while I pledge my future to Noris," said Varena, squeezing in to embrace them both.

"Careful, you'll muss your hair!" said Brenia.

"Can I finally see what I look like?" One of the other brides surrendered the mirror of polished copper, and Varena gazed in wonder at the beautiful woman looking back at her. While the women to be joined that day began giggling and whispering together, the families enjoyed a brief moment to relax.

Martel had been explaining the order of events to Riyik, who Kalie was sure already knew, but listened politely anyway. Flashing Kalie a mischievous smile, Riyik walked over as if deeply concerned. "Now, sweetness, I think I know what to do, but in case I forget where I am and try to offer Varena to Noris in exchange for thirty horses…"

"Don't worry," said Kalie. "I'll kill you."

Two senior acolytes began to circulate among the couples, leading them to the field where the ceremony would take place. The families sorted themselves into orderly groups and followed.

They reached a broad, rolling hillside clothed in fresh spring grass and dotted with orange and yellow wildflowers. At the top of the hill Nara waited, while musicians played behind her. The view was breathtaking: the field stretched to a steep drop to a forest below. The effect was of a flowery green field that met a brilliant blue sky in one endless line.

Varena and Noris were the youngest to be joined that day, though not by much. The second bride was only a season older than Varena, her partner the same age as Noris. Next came a woman of about twenty seasons, though still a first time bride, joining with a man of nearly thirty. Last, and sparking the most discussion, was a couple in their fifties. Each had been happily married for nearly thirty seasons, but widowed for the past ten. As they had been living together for several years, no one was quite sure why they chose today to make it official, but they were welcomed the same as the younger people.

Spectators, both local and foreign, began to gather until the field was full. At a sign from Nara, the music stopped, echoing briefly across the open space.

"On this day of new beginnings," she began, "we call upon the Goddess in all Her forms to bless the joining of those who are here to create new beginnings of their own. May each couple find joy and laughter in their union, to keep them young at heart as the first of spring. May they know a bountiful harvest of children and all that they build together. May they know contentment as they reach the winter of their lives, and share their wisdom with those who come after." Then she called the first couple forward.

Varena strove for dignity as she was quickly

surrounded, then pulled forward by Kalie, Riyik, Brenia, Martel, Barak, Yarik, and most of the easterners they had arrived with. There was giggling and good-natured pushing, but the newcomers had been warned that this ceremony was not to be the rowdy affair of a nomad wedding. Noris arrived, somewhat more nosily, surrounded by his family. Riyik stood perfectly straight-faced as the mother of each new partner led their son and daughter to the priestess, who solemnly bound their right hands together with a green dyed cord.

The ritual was repeated three more times, and then each couple was led to whatever dwelling would be their home for the foreseeable future.

For Varena and Noris, this was a rather longer walk than the others. Kalie, Riyik and the rest of the entourage, walked with the couple to the old, but well built house which was now theirs. Sanded and repaired on the outside, and freshly whitewashed on the inside, the house was indeed ready for habitation. After fumbling with the door with their right hands—still tied together—Varena finally managed to open it with her left hand. Crossing the threshold together, the new couple ushered their guests inside.

"How long do they have to keep that rope on?" Durak asked.

"Until they figure out how to untie the knot without breaking it," Kalie replied. "Usually that's when they sit down to their first meal."

"Good thing that priestess didn't tie their legs together, too," said Borik. "We'd still be helping them get here at sunset."

The house consisted of a large main room, with a ladder leading to sleeping quarters on the second floor. A kitchen, with a newly dug storage pit beneath, sat nearby. Wedding gifts filled the house in the form of furniture, cooking utensils, beautiful pottery plates, cups and bowls, and baskets of food. Kalie knew that a new bed of carved wood and a feather mattress waited in the room above, for Riyik and Martel had worked on it all winter. Blankets woven by Kalie, Brenia and their many friends adorned the bed.

Varena blinked in surprised. "None of this was here the last time I was! I thought it would take days of work just to make the place livable, but it's all been done for us!" She stared at her new home, the white walls mellow in the afternoon light that came through the uncovered windows, as if she had been brought to the tent of a king.

"What did you think our families and friends have been doing since we announced our intention to join?" asked Noris.

Varena, who had been raised in a place too different for her partner to understand, merely shook her head. "But what are we now to do with our days?"

At that, raucous laughter erupted from everyone, settled and nomad alike. A few people began to make some earthy suggestions, but Norris's mother loudly announced it was time for the guests to leave. Amid much hugging and well wishing, the families filed out.

"I thought we were going to share a meal," Borik grumbled, although less loudly than his stomach.

"The feasting will begin after the next set of weddings," Kalie explained. "Which should be starting soon."

"Leaders from both sides agreed that we should

arrange the timing of the weddings so all who wanted to could attend both," said Brenia. "The evening will be for feasting, so each side could enjoy what the other had to offer: food, drink, music, dancing—"

"A good way to bring our two peoples together," agreed Garm. "And young Sirak may have had the right idea when he suggested we all get drunk together. It's worked before when warriors have needed to form alliances."

"It's also led to a lot of blood being spilled," said Brenia.

"I'm not sure I'd take advice from a boy of thirteen on something this important," said Martel. "Even if he's proved himself redeemed in many ways."

"He and those like him are the future," said Riyik. "We'd be wise to listen to them, although I agree that watering the wine was a good idea."

As the sun slanted toward the west, the next set of joining began.

The tribesmen had moved several of their tents to allow a long, smooth path from the forest to the river. Tents and trees were festooned with ribbons and pennants, and everyone was dressed in their best. Here, as before, music filled the air, but it was the heavier sound of drums, shrill whistles and ululations coming from women's throats.

As the curious townsfolk watched, a cluster of horsemen emerged from the trees. These, Kalie knew, were the grooms, the men to be married. There were at least twice the number of couples here as in the earlier ceremony. Then, from the largest tent—Kariik's she realized with surprise—came an equal number of women, robed and veiled from head to toe.

Then, from all around, trilling women rushed to surround them as if for protection.

Kariik stepped forward, dressed in all new clothes—made from local cloth, but sewn in the eastern style. As he opened his mouth to speak, all music and talking ceased.

"Friends both old and new," the king began, "We have suffered many hardships to reach this time of rebirth. That those days might be forever behind us, we call upon our gods to witness our commitment to them and the future of our tribe. In the year just past, many have lost mates; many have lost children. Tonight we celebrate new marriages, which will create new families, and strong new ties to our new allies."

Kalie winced. Kariik had never been a very good speaker, but he had improved greatly since she had first met him. Still, she hoped he would soon stop talking.

He did. "Warriors!" he called to the men on horseback. "Claim your brides!"

What followed was a noisy chaos that Kalie suspected frightened even those of her people who had been prepared for it. The men on horseback charged the group of women, all of whom began screaming and rushing around. The horsemen shoved aside the women attendants as each plucked one of the brides from her feet and flung her over his horse. While no one was hurt, it looked dangerous enough. Then each man wheeled his horse and went crashing through the forest, or over rocky hillsides, while the crowd gave a mock chase, laughing and shouting, before returning to the camp.

"What are they doing?"

Kalie turned to find a terrified Sarella clutching

Kalie's hand and staring wide-eyed at the scene before her.

"Looking for an open field to consummate their marriages," Kalie explained.

"Why an open field?" asked Sarella.

"Yes," said Ilara. "That sounds more like something we would do."

"Something about the sky god having to bear witness that the marriage is sealed," Kalie said. "Afterwards, they will return and the men will feast while the women wait in their tents for their new husbands to come to them, wanting more sex."

Sarella and Ilara both made noises of disgust. "Perhaps we can tempt some of the women to join the celebrations," said Ilara.

"Perhaps," Kalie said doubtfully. "Kariik would not dare forbid it, but the women themselves might refuse to go against their traditions." She looked up and saw Otera, her many followers hovering nearby, watching the proceedings with a kind of fascinated delight.

"I love how these animals make no attempt to hide what they are," said Otera, approaching the group. "If you hadn't decided to stake our entire future on an alliance with these creatures, it would even be amusing."

Kalie was about to turn and walk away, when she felt Sarella grip her hand again, but in a different manner. "I find it interesting how you daily become more like the horsemen, Otera," Ilara said. "But not amusing at all."

Otera's pale skin flushed. "It is you who have become more like them!"

Kalie looked around at the feast taking shape in

the nomad camp. Across the river, in the center of
Stonebridge, another feast was being prepared. Kalie
experienced a strange sense of double vision. The
feasts she had attended for the first eighteen years of
her life, merged with those she worked to prepare as a
slave on the steppes. Both were happening now.
Kalie could choose to help roast whole animals at the
fires near her, or cross the bridge and help make salads
of spring greens and set out the honey cakes which had
been baked earlier in the day. She could feast as the
wife of a warrior of Aahk, or as an honored mother of
Stonebridge.

Perhaps tonight she would do both.

"I shall help lay out the feast," Kalie said to the
group of women. Then, to Otera, "Perhaps you'd care
to help. Unless you've forgotten how to do that as
well." She left before Otera could respond.

Much to everyone's surprise, the evening went
extremely well. People from both cultures crossed the
bridge throughout the evening, joining into the
festivities of each. The folk of Stonebridge celebrated
as they had the year before, with music, food and
dancing, much to the delight of the warriors—and
many of the women—of Aahk.

And the nomads, too, celebrated in the same
three ways. But the dancing was unlike anything the
people of the Goddess had seen before: men danced in
groups, with swinging spears that met and struck with
sounds like thunder and simulated battle, yet also held
a kind of alien beauty to those watching. The hunters
had killed a huge boar, which had begun making
trouble for the local farms. The meat was delicious,
and, like the dancing, different to the palates of the

western folk. Then someone—Kalie never knew
who—got the idea of inviting musicians from both
sides to meet at the bridge, and play together.

The music they created that night was haunting
and magical. The story of the endless grass and
forbidding sky of the steppes, told with drums and
sticks and bone flutes, blended with the wooden flutes
and harps that told of trade routes and the earthy
smells of forest and field. Men and women of
Stonebridge played together, while the few female
musicians of the tribe kept well away from the men.
But the music was too intoxicating for the players to
keep apart for long. Musicians, as they always will,
want to know how a new tune is played; how another
instrument works. After meeting in the middle until
the bridge was impassible, they played with great
enthusiasm to a large audience on each side.

Then leaders from both sides came with food
and drink and much applause, and asked them all to
clear the bridge, but please continue the concert in an
open space on the side of the nomad camp. This, of
course, brought more people, and the dancing soon
moved to where the musicians played. The dancers,
too, combined the various styles. Kalie and Riyik had
more practice at this than most, and were soon in the
center of the crowd. Kariik and Alessa had also
practiced, but lacked the stamina to stay for long. Or
perhaps it was just that their concentration was divided
between showing their peoples what was possible, and
watching them, to make certain there was no trouble.

Kalie was soon called away, at Kariik's request
to tell stories to the warriors.

"I truly am slipping back and forth in time,"
Kalie said, and then finished her wine and followed

the young warrior who brought her the king's request. Request, she thought. Not command.

Riyik escorted her to where the audience waited—once again made up of people from both sides of the river—and said, "Plain water is better than wine for this kind of work." Then he handed her a drinking bag made from a leather covered sheep's bladder, filled with cool water.

"Your first gift to me!" cried Kalie. "I thought I'd lost it!"

"I found it when we were helping Varena pack her things. Tonight seemed the right time to give it to you again."

Kalie grinned, suddenly feeling all was right with the world. "You should probably wander and keep an eye on the crowd," she said, somewhat reluctantly.

"I think I should be here, listening to you tell stories," said Riyik, the love he felt plain in his rain gray eyes.

So Kalie walked proudly to the space reserved for her between the tents, and surveyed her audience. For a moment she wondered if she still knew how to tell the tales the warriors liked. Then from across the years came the memory of the first story Kalie had created for her captors. "It was on a day like this, in early spring, when the two mightiest of the clans of Aahk were on their way to the great summer gathering," she began, and launched into the still popular, "Battle of Spring Trail."

It was dark when Kalie finished, but the festivities were still in full swing. She walked with Riyik for awhile, always on the lookout for trouble. But once again, there was none. To Kalie's surprise, many nomad women, including a few of the new brides, were also out and about, many without veils, enjoying food and conversation, or dancing for their men.

Then one of the brides looked up from the small group of women she was speaking with, and Kalie gasped. "Kestra!"

Fear sparked in the woman's eyes, and for a moment it looked like she might run. Then she collected herself, calmly pulling her veil over her hair and around her shoulders, but leaving her face uncovered.

The other women backed away. Kalie gestured for Riyik to continue without her. Without a word, he did.

Kestra met her eye, and then looked away. "You are Kalie," she said, although it seemed more a question.

"Yes, Kestra. We left a town very much like this to travel together—"

"My name is Jalisa!" Kestra snapped. "My first husband, the great warrior Saryk, honored me by giving me the name of his beloved first wife, who died shortly before he married me."

Kalie rocked back in surprise. Alessa had not told her about this. Unsure how to proceed, she asked, "Do you remember when your name was Kestra?"

Kestra's face grew hard. "I know I was once a dirt-eater. I remember very little. I did not want to return here, but our king said we must. I did not want to marry again, but I knew I must."

"Kariik said you had to marry another beastman?" Kalie was outraged. How could he? And why didn't Alessa tell someone so it could have been prevented?

"The king said nothing of my marriage, other than to bless it. But I knew if I did not, I would have nowhere to go but back...there." Kestra glanced with distaste across the bridge. She put her hands protectively on her bulging middle. "And the great Saryk's son would be raised to be..." She shuddered and did not finish the thought.

Kalie took a deep breath and let it out. Then another. "Your child, Kestra, uh, Jalisa, boy or girl, could grow up to be any number of things in Stonebridge. Including a warrior, if that's what he wanted."

"Well, now I don't have to worry about it. Alrik is one of Kariik's most trusted advisors, and his greatest warrior. He has promised to name my child Saryk if it is a boy, and raise him as his own son. And my status shall be higher than any woman's in the tribe, except for Alessa. What more could I wish for?"

Kalie stared at the woman who had followed her into the beating heart of their enemy so long ago. "When you find out, Jalisa, come to me, and I will help you find it."

She turned and walked away. Kestra did not call her back, but Kalie doubted she would have heard. She wandered the two camps for the rest of the night, stopping only briefly at her home, to nurse Melora and settle her and Yarik for the night. Then she resumed her wandering. Kalie didn't know what she was looking for, yet somehow, little by little she found it.

Shortly before dawn, a mist arose, and Kalie felt as if she were an invisible spirit. She watched bleary-eyed warriors stumble back to their tents, sleeping children carried home, and the few who managed to get drunk enough to pass out, helped inside homes, or in the case of the warriors, left snoring on the ground.

First light found Kalie sitting on the highest ground in the area. She could see all of Stonebridge laid out before her like a magnificent carved toy emerging from the rising mist. The nomad camp was barely visible in the distance. When she turned around, Kalie could glimpse the sea, still covered in its pearly shroud.

The previous day and night had been a time of balance, when day and night were of equal length—something that happened only twice each year. When the sun rose today, it would stay just a little longer, and tonight would be just a little shorter.

A tipping point had been reached.

And as Kalie breathed in the cool morning air, and watched the sun come up in a glory of pink and gold, she knew that another tipping point had been reached. A time of great change was at hand. She didn't know where it would all lead, but for once, Kalie felt no fear, nor any guilt that she was the cause of what would come to pass.

She knew only that she wanted to be part of it, and to live to see the new world that would be born.

Chapter 24

The season that followed the Spring Festival was as different from past springs as the festival itself.

True, many hunters and merchants left the town as they had in years past. But many more did not. And even those who did travel carried messages and weapons, or escorted those who would train fighters or swell their ranks.

Many of Kariik's warriors returned east to find family they had left behind to be cared for in the smaller villages, further reducing the strain on resources in Stonebridge. To the relief of many, Elka and her new husband were among those who left. Kestra (Kalie refused to call her Jalisa) remained. Her husband, Alrik, was indeed one of Kariik's closest advisors, and soon proved to be one of the best teachers of riding and fighting for those who arrived almost daily to learn the arts of war. Alrik also worked tirelessly with the more advanced students who had learned everything Riyik and Borik could teach them.

The town of Stonebridge began to look like a military camp. Of the eighty warriors who remained with Kariik, many continued to live in their tents across the river. Others, however, came into the town to give settled life a try.

"It's the way of the future," a young warrior explained to his wife, mother-in-law and former slave who was now his second wife. "You will learn the skills of cloth-making and bread-baking, and I will grow closer to those who run things here. And we will all enjoy the wealth of this new land!"

Several houses in town opened up as a few families decided to move west, away from what would likely be the site of a major battle. Borik also left the large house where he had been living alone, to return to life in a tent with Kariik's warriors.

"He's never really been comfortable living in a house," Riyik told Kalie.

"After all the time he's lived here?" Kalie was baffled. "But he seemed so…content. I don't recall him saying a word about not liking…well, anything, really."

"He's never been much of a complainer, either."

"That's certainly true," sighed Kalie. She watched Borik pack his few belongings, while a large nomad family waited to move in. "How will he fend for himself without a woman in his tent?"

"He won't have to," said Riyik. "Ah, here she is."

Kalie looked to where Riyik was looking, expecting to see one of the women from Kariik's group, perhaps encouraged by Alessa. To her utter shock, it was Ilara the priestess who walked with a pack on her back to stand with Borik. The head on her petit frame barely reached his chest.

"She wants to learn more about the tribe," said Alessa, stopping to explain, and smiling at Kalie's expression.

"This is…well…this is certainly one way to do it," Kalie said.

"And as Borik's woman, she can go anywhere safely, and speak to anyone. No one wants to be seen as offering insult to someone belonging to a warrior of his size and strength," Riyik said.

Kalie insisted on making a meal for the couple's first night in their new tent. The brief time she spent with them, between the lavish compliments of her cooking, Kalie became convinced that this was yet another insane step toward a happy outcome to the war they faced.

Spring was barely past full flower when the messages began to arrive. The horde was on the move. They would reach the eastern border of the Goddess lands before summer. And they were bringing the entire tribe.

"Everyone?" Kalie asked at the meeting where the messenger had just brought his news. "Families? Herds? Everything they own?"

"We knew it was a possibility," said Orin. "Kariik described the conditions on the steppes as desperate."

"But we expected warriors!" said Garm, away from his smithy only because of the importance of the meeting. "Families and flocks will slow them down—"

"Giving us more time to prepare," Nara said.

Those who once called themselves warriors of Aahk looked at each other nervously.

"What is it?" asked Nara.

"This means they are coming to stay," Kariik explained. "They plan to take this land. Not wealth and food and slaves, but the land itself. They mean to rule here." He glanced at the priest. "As Orin said, they are desperate. Even as the most powerful tribe on the steppes, these so-called Wolves, will have no place to return to if they fail."

"Which will make them even more dangerous," said Martel, stating the obvious.

Amid whispers of how this might change things, a girl on the verge of womanhood spoke up. She sat beside Sirak, and was known as the only girl to ever beat him in a fight. "You're forgetting the most important thing in all this," she said.

"And what would that be, Analie?" asked Orin.

"How we are to make room for all of those women and children after we kill all of their men," Analie said simply.

Sirak grinned. "She's right, you know. No one here will allow them to die, or be sold as slaves next trading season."

"Assuming we can keep them from killing their children and then themselves after their men are defeated," Alessa added.

Sirak nodded, deep in thought. "But now we'll have to kill their men, not just drive them back. The women will have nowhere to go, nor any way to support themselves here. I suppose we can show the folk of the Goddess the pleasures to be had in taking many wives…"

Analie batted his head playfully—at least Kalie hoped it was playful. She liked the confidence with which the two young people, soon to be a couple she suspected, spoke. Everyone would need that confidence soon. But she also knew that for many at this meeting, the war they faced had just become real for the first time.

"The spring rains were light this year," Janak said.

"Even if they'd been normal," said Alessa, "this river would have still been too low by summer to create any real barrier to the horses."

A large group of people stood on the bridge, looking down at those who waded in the shallows. For now, the bridge was the only way into the town on the hill. But that would change by summer.

"Horses will cross it easily by then," said Riyik.

"There's always the chance that the horde will be defeated before they get this far west," Sarella began, but stopped at the looks cast her way.

"This is actually the ideal place to defeat them once and for all," said Riyik. He began to tick off reasons on his fingers. "There is the forest the warriors must ride through—a perfect place for traps and ambushes. There's a large, well-armed population atop high ground. And there's this river, which, if it would just cooperate, could trap the horde as if between a pair of pincers." He glanced at the Janak to see if he had the right word.

The smith nodded, and smiled grimly. "So what you're saying is all we need to do is devise traps which no one on either side has ever thought of, make a lot of arrows, and find a way to raise and lower a river at will?"

A few people chuckled, and Riyik seemed to be searching for an appropriate reply when Varena spoke up.

"If one person can create horse-killers, then enough of us working together should be able to come up with a few clever traps. And we've already got a huge supply of bows, arrows, and the people to use them."

"And more being made every day," said Orin. "The problem is the river."

"Maybe not," said Varena, staring upstream

from her place on the bridge.

After waiting a few heartbeats, while Varena stared, deep in thought, Orin prompted gently, "What are your thoughts, my dear?"

Varena came out of her daze, blushing crimson as she realized how she had just spoken to an important leader—and a man.

"Don't worry if it will sound foolish, or even impossible," said Nara. "Those are likely to be just the ideas we need."

"It's just…" Varena now looked toward her new home, the farm that was not quite visible from the bridge. "I know I'm new at this, but the first thing I learned about farming was the need to bring water to the seedlings; that sometimes rain is not enough. So people learned to dig ditches to carry water from a watercourse to the fields."

"Irrigation," Otera said impatiently. "What do you think you can do? Bring water to the river instead of from?" While her tone was mocking, it was clear Otera's own words caused her to stop and think— along with most of the people who heard.

"Not quite," said Varena. "It would be…what do you call it when you put stones across flowing water to create a pond, or to dry up some land for building?"

"A dam," said several voices at once.

"I don't know where the source of the river is, or if there would be enough water," said Varena. "But if we could…capture enough of it, and lower the river right here to something the warriors would find easy to cross—"

"We could release the water when we chose to!" cried Janak. "Varena, you're a genius!"

"I agree," said Kalie, smiling proudly at her daughter. "But there will be much to learn before we discover if this plan will even work."

"And if it does not, then another one will," said Nara.

Janak conferred with Garm and a few of the other crafters, as well as some farmers. Kalie went to the rocky beach to sit and nurse Melora while dipping her bare feet into the cool water, as the day was unusually warm.

"Where's Noris?" she asked Varena, who came to sit beside her.

"Getting the boat hidden in the scrub at the shore," Varena said neutrally. "He's agreed to stay, and he works very hard on the farm, but says he'll sleep better knowing we have an escape route that the horses can't follow."

"He's very wise to do that," said Kalie. After a moment's silence she asked, "How are the two of you doing?"

Varena's smile told her mother what she thought of the physical side of the partnership. "Actually all of it's good," she said. "As long as we don't talk about the coming war."

"Which I'm sure is rather difficult."

Varena sighed, but then smiled again. "We manage. I keep telling myself that this time next year, I will be trading the flax we're growing for all sorts of good things, and eating the last of our stored vegetables, while watching the new ones come up in the fields. And perhaps anticipating the birth of our first child." At Kalie's look of concern she added, "Next year! Not now. I drink the special tea every day."

Janak approached with an old man who had recently arrived from one of the small villages to the north. "Omel here has an idea of where we might place the dam. It's over half a day's walk, so we'll leave tomorrow at first light to see it. Would you care to join us, Kalie?"

She patted Melora's back until she burped. "I wouldn't miss it."

Water pounded down from a rocky hillside in a cascade that made hearing anyone difficult. Then it flowed down a gentler slope, breaking off into channels through a land too rocky for farming. The main channel flowed uninterrupted to Stonebridge, and then beyond to the Black Sea.

"There are certainly enough rocks to build this thing!" Alessa shouted.

"Lumber, too!" Janak called, pointing to a small stand of trees, digging into the soil between rocks.

"Why do we need lumber?" Kalie asked, keeping Melora occupied by swinging her through the spray that rose like a fine mist over the lower channel.

Janak nodded downstream, and the group followed him to where conversation was possible. "We'll want to be able to breech this dam quickly when the time comes. The simplest way to do that would be to use logs to bolster some of the larger rocks. We set the logs across flat rocks. When we're ready, two or three people will put their weight on the section of log that sticks out past the rock it rests on." With his hand, Janak demonstrated the other half of the log lifting as the first half lowered.

It took a while, but most of those gathered

understood that using the logs as levers would pry enough rocks away to create a slide.

"And then the pressure from the captive water will do the rest," Kalie said, impressed.

"Sahrene would have loved this," Alessa said wistfully.

It took Kalie a moment to remember the skilled crafter who understood the earth so well, and had once devised ingenious ways to bring water to dry lands, using ditches and even gates to control the flow. Sahrene had been one of the first to die after they reached the grasslands three years ago.

They spent the night in the nearest village, still over an hour's walk from the falls. It was a good opportunity to scout the land, as they always did now, seeking routes the horsemen might use, and ways they could be blocked. At the village, they saw defenses being prepared: a ditch dug in a circle enclosing the houses, with sharpened sticks at the bottom, pointing up.

"We plan to cover it with sections of grass cut from the meadow," said the headman, pointing to the currently waterlogged stretch of green. "That way, the horses will fall through as they ride and land—" He shook his head unable to continue. "I never thought I'd live to see the day when we worked at ways to kill our fellow humans."

Kalie left that one to Alessa, and went to settle Melora for the night.

They left the next morning, after a short survey and a long discussion brought agreement that the village's water supply would not be harmed, and thus the dam could now be built.

"I hope there will be news when we get back,"

Alessa said. "Even if it's what we've been dreading, it will mean we can finally do something besides prepare."

Kalie wanted to warn her friend to be careful what she wished for, but in her heart, she agreed with Alessa. Riyik and some of the others had left the same time as Kalie's group, to ride through the lands to the east, helping with preparation, gathering intelligence, and, most dangerous of all, trying to determine exactly where the horde was now, when they would reach the first settlements, and what could be done to lead them to a place of the defenders' choosing for what they hoped would be the final battle.

"We should have settled somewhere farther east," Kalie said. "Riyik and I. Stonebridge is so far west, the war could be over before they reach us!"

"Only if we're lucky," said Alessa.

"And if we're not, thousands will die and the land left in ruins before they get here. If they get here at all!"

"You chose the right place, Kalie," said Kariik, striding up to walk beside the two women. "We already know that Stonebridge is the right place for the real battle. All the rest will be skirmishes and ambush."

"During which many will die," Alessa said.

"Unfortunately true," said Alrik, who always seemed to be wherever Kariik was. "But if enough goes according to plan, our enemy's forces will be greatly reduced. They will be exhausted and afraid. The strangeness of the forests alone may do much to sap their will to fight."

"So why come this far at all?" asked Janak. "That's what I don't understand. The villages to the east will be easier targets. Once they've burned them to the ground and taken what slaves they can, won't they just pitch their tents and settle?"

Alrik was about to answer, but Kalie spoke first. "Not enough grass there for the horses and flocks. What they need is north, along the Black Sea, and in the fields around Stonebridge and the large farming villages close by. Not to mention more water than they've ever seen in their lives." She looked at the river, beside them, low in its banks as they drew closer to home.

"But more important than any of that," Alrik said, "is what's here in Stonebridge." They had gone up a low hill, and in the distance, could just see the town, crowning a much higher hill. "It's the promise of wealth that makes men like this leave everything behind and travel through land that feels cursed by evil spirits. Their king will want more than a place to pitch his tent."

Kariik nodded. "Gold, finery, metal tools and weapons. Food stores meant to last years will provide feasts for many nights. And of course, slaves." He looked ashamed for a moment, then straightened and met the gaze of each of his companions. Including the women.

"But there are many places with all of that in this part of the world!" said Janak.

Again, Kariik nodded. "So our real job will be to convince this king that the place he wants to lead his horde is Stonebridge. And he must believe that it was his idea." He grinned at Alessa, who blushed slightly at the memory of how much of that she had done to Kariik. "Honored wife, do you have any sisters we might send to Varlas?"

Chapter 25

Kalie kept busy over the next few days, practicing with her bow and helping to come up with ideas for bringing the horde to Stonebridge—and defeating them once they got here. Everyone was aware that it would take more than horse-killers and a well-timed flood to accomplish that.

Yet they continued to make the deadly bone stars, dig ditches to be filled with sharpened sticks, build their dam and store food for a possible siege. Most important of all, Kalie thought as she approached the busy forge, were the new arrows.

Janak had more than just Garm to help him now, as skilled refugees arrived in Stonebridge from villages that would have no chance against the horde. Places which lacked forest cover for ambushes, or the manpower—or willingness— to mount an effective resistance. At least a dozen men and women, plus a few young apprentices, labored to create knives, spearheads and arrow tips of copper.

"But not pure copper," Janak was explaining as he demonstrated. "Copper is too soft. Strangely, it's the impurities that make the metal strong enough to hold a point that will punch through leather armor, or an edge that will break a flint blade."

"What kind of impurities?" asked a woman who had left her own forge and brought her family here just days ago.

Janak nodded to Garm to answer. "More than one type will work," said the young former nomad. "The best is a kind of weak, gray metal that can sometimes be found by the copper."

"Soft plus weak equals strong?" asked a man. Everyone laughed.

"We discovered it by accident," said Janak.

"Like most important discoveries," said an old woman.

"There's also something in the copper veins some distance from here," the smith continued. "Almost a kind of powder. It's dangerous, though. It can make the miners sick, but the metal strong." People grew serious. This seemed the perfect metaphor for what was happening to the people of the Goddess, as they made ever more compromises and sacrifices for their goal of defeating the invaders.

"What we need to do," said Garm, "is try different combinations, and test the results."

"An opportunity I would relish," said an old smith from a village near Green Bower, "if time were not so short."

With that, everyone got to work.

"Are the arrowheads ready?" Kalie asked Garm.

"Soon." Garm nodded to where steam issued from a huge vat of water.

Sirak arrived a moment later, carrying a spear. He went straight to the master smith, even though it meant waiting until he was finished answering an apprentice's question. "This is what we need!" the boy said eagerly without preamble. "This spearhead. It doesn't grow dull, even after five mock battles! You told us to tell you which ones—"

"Yes," said Janak, taking the weapon and studying it intently. He was soon lost in his own calculations. Two of the apprentices brought the arrows Kalie was waiting for. "You'll need someone to help carry these," one of them told her.

Kalie saw that the girl was right—but that was a good thing. They were going to need a lot of these.

"I'll help," said Sirak. "I'm headed back to the practice field anyway."

Kalie admired the way the boy, although now at thirteen years, nearly a man, hefted the heavier of the two wooden crates while she lifted the second. He had certainly changed, she thought as they walked to the practice field, where the newest recruits would learn the art of fitting the points to the wooden shafts and attaching the feathers that would make the arrow fly true. A small amount would be used in practice, the rest kept back for actual battle.

Suddenly Kalie asked Sirak, "What's happened to you? What caused such a change?"

Sirak's open, confident expression disappeared, becoming guarded. "What do mean?"

Kalie had not wanted that to happen, so she lightened her tone, and tossed back her long brown hair. "Only that when you first came here, you and your mother meant to rule this place with you as king. Something seems to have changed. Or should I be worried?"

"You knew about that?" Kalie saw that Sirak was actually ashamed.

"I figured it out," Kalie said, deciding not to go into detail that would embarrass Sirak further. "But now I have to worry about at least a dozen new warriors, lately arrived with Kariik who might have the same ambition. So I'd like to know what changed for you. And could we make it work for them?"

Sirak nodded gravely. "There are a few in that group we'll have to worry about. They remind me of myself." His mouth twisted in bitter amusement. "Ambition is probably the hardest thing any Aahken warrior has to give up to make a life here."

"But you gave up yours?"

Sirak stopped and looked at Kalie. His expression was not the least disrespectful or condescending. "I traded it for new ambitions. Who needs to be a king, and spend his whole life worrying about a knife in the back from rivals who will always be there, when there are so many other things to be?"

"Like what?" Kalie asked as they resumed walking.

"A great warrior. A teacher of great warriors. A hero. That's what I want to be the most. I want to be the man who defeats those arrogant fools who dare to call themselves Wolves of the Gods. I want to save this new world so I'll always have a place in it." Kalie started to interrupt, but Sirak continued quickly. "I know: I'll have a place here no matter what. But I want more. I want to earn it."

"You could have earned an important place in the tribe if you'd stayed—"

"Ha! That's what they say! But that's not how it is; not for the son of a slave. Once I figured that out, everything changed. That, and seeing that all the wealth and comfort my mother wanted so much already belonged to her, so it stopped being my responsibility. If she spoils it for herself again…well, I can't help that. I like having different paths to choose from, and knowing it's me who gets to decide. And Analie. I never thought I'd like a girl who fights like a warrior, but I like her."

They had reached the practice field. Kalie was moved almost to tears by Sirak's words, so she just smiled at him, and handed off her crate to a large blond man whose family had been arrow makers for as long as Stonebridge stood. Sirak hurried off to his students. Kalie took a rare moment to look around. No one had the luxury to just be a spectator, unless they'd been ordered to watch a particular bout by an instructor. Everyone was busy learning, teaching or practicing with weapons or horses, and the sense of time running out was everywhere.

And then Kalie spied an amazing sight. Otera, and most of her followers, were practicing with men from the east. Not the new arrivals; none of Kariik's band. But Durak and Zanal were there, along with several of the men and women of Stonebridge who had trained the longest. Kalie went to join them.

As they practiced with spears and daggers, it became clear that these women worked as well together as any formation of warriors Kalie had seen. Some showed real skill, and all responded well to criticism—although better from women, Kalie noticed, than from men. Next, the coaches led the students to where the horses grazed. Kalie felt a pang as she saw Blossom. How long had it been since she'd been astride her old horse?

"Have any of you been on horseback?" she asked one of the women.

"This is our third day training," she replied. "But only about half of us show any promise."

"Maybe I can help," Kalie said. "At least I can offer an additional horse. And she's a good one for getting acquainted with the idea."

Kalie worked with the women for the rest of the day. Afterwards, they went to the hot springs to bathe and relax, and Kalie finally found time to speak with Otera.

"What changed your mind about working with us?" she asked bluntly.

Otera seemed ready to challenge Kalie's use of the word "us". Then she leaned back in the water until only her face showed and stayed there for a long time. Emerging slowly, water-darkened hair plastered to her face, Otera shrugged. "I want my new tribe to be the best warriors in the land. And, much as I may wish otherwise, that means learning from creatures who know nothing else. At least they have their uses."

"The warriors from the east or the warriors of Stonebridge?" Kalie asked innocently.

Otera shot her a dirty look at which point one of her followers jumped in. "None of these people have harmed any of us," said a red-haired woman. "While it is hard for some of us who have had dealings with men from other tribes, we have to stay focused on what matters: keeping our world alive."

"And that means learning from the best," said another.

"Only until we're better than they are," said Otera.

Kalie looked at the women soaking in the lovely water, stretching out on the rocks around the pools with soft towels providing comfort, combing each other's hair or massaging pain from overworked muscles. In the shadowy world of the underground cave, they could almost be any harem in any tent on the steppes. Except that the camaraderie was much friendlier.

"Would you like a massage?" a very young woman asked Kalie as she climbed out of the pool and began to dry off. "I'm pretty good."

There was laughter and good natured gibing. "She's great!" said Otera.

"Yes, thank you," Kalie said. She stretched out and the girl went to work on her back and shoulders, clearly knowing just where stiffness from practicing with a bow all day would be.

"Malana doesn't much like the water," said one of the others. "But given her experience with it, it's no surprise."

"Ah, but a river is what brought me to all of you," said Malana, and Kalie noticed her accent. One which matched her blond hair and eastern features.

"You're from the steppes!" Kalie cried, turning to get a better look at her.

"Don't jump like that! You'll undo all my work." Kalie obeyed, but knew she wasn't as relaxed as a moment before.

Malana redoubled her efforts. "I was once a chief's daughter," Malana said.

"Which tribe?" Kalie couldn't help asking.

"A very small one. They no longer speak my name, so I shall return the favor." The bitterness in Malana's voice was not lost on Kalie.

"What was it? Defying your father? A rival's lies?"

"I was raped by the man I was supposed to marry after my father broke the betrothal in favor of a better alliance. Him and all his clan."

"Yes, of course," Kalie said, trying to unclench. Malana really was very good; it would be wrong to waste her efforts. "Their way of declaring war with your father. And forcing him to kill you. Very...artistic."

"You seem to know a lot about my old life."

"I was a slave in the tribe of Aahk for a time," Kalie said casually, as if speaking of a summer season. Malana's hands fell gracefully away, and Kalie sat up. "That was wonderful. Thank you. So how do you still live?" she asked, getting dressed.

"I jumped into a river to spare my father the grief of killing me." Malana moved on to another woman who had badly strained nearly all her leg muscles learning to ride. "The river brought me to the Goddess Lands. Strange how easy it was to shed all I knew of life, and replace it with something so—"

"Scandalous?" asked Kalie.

"Different," Malana said firmly.

Kalie had many more questions, but sensed it was time to leave. She bid the women farewell, feeling a lowering of barriers and a lessening of mistrust. It had been time well spent. Plus, she had gotten a great massage.

It was only after she reached the trail which led to her home did Kalie remember the question she had most wanted to ask. What did Otera mean by her new tribe?

Later that night, Kalie lay alone in her bed, missing Riyik, but comforted by the warmth of Yarik and Melora's small bodies as they slept peacefully beside her (just for tonight, she told them).

It wasn't Riyik's absence that kept her awake. At least not just that.

The latest messengers put the horde of the Wolf at the border of the land of the Goddess. The fighting would begin any day, and Kalie could do nothing about it; not even witness the first, monumental clash.

She knew well enough what the plans were. When she closed her eyes, she could see the map that covered the floor of main temple, complete with every plan, every trap, every contingency that had been devised.

In her mind, Kalie listed each one, as if that would bring sleep:

Nearly half the villages on the eastern border had been evacuated. Some had taken everything useful with them, refusing to participate in the killing which would come.

Others left gifts for their uninvited guests: horse killers, poisoned food and water, and pit traps filled with sharpened sticks that had been smeared with dung.

Villages surrounded or backed by forests would only appear abandoned. Warriors hiding inside would engage the enemy, then retreat into the woods, where more warriors would harry the men of the Wolf while—hopefully—allowing everyone to escape into the trees.

Other traps and ambushes stood ready farther west.

The king of the invading horde had a following of two thousand warriors. If everything went perfectly, the people of the Goddess could hope to kill or disable a third of them. That left over twelve hundred angry barbarians to reach the rich heart of the west. And Kalie doubted everything would go perfectly.

Somehow, all those warriors would have to be brought to Stonebridge, where traps, a flood and sheer numbers of people fighting for their homes would stem the tide.

And that was the final piece of the puzzle. Two groups of volunteers were gathering, but neither had yet to engage the enemy.

The first consisted of women who would allow themselves to be captured, and would beg their masters not to approach the Goddess's sacred city of Stonebridge, with its stores of gold and virgin priestesses. The second would be a small group of warriors of the steppes who would ride to the king and ask for the honor of changing to the winning side, in exchange for information about the dirt-eaters and the traitors who now ruled them.

Kalie, who had already tried something close enough to the first plan, had voted for the second. But there would be a high risk of failure either way. And an even higher risk that both were suicide missions.

She was tired of suicide missions.

She was tired…

Interlude

King Varlas faced the setting sun and scowled at the shadows of the demon trees that tried to reach out and grab him. A lesser man would have backed away from this unnatural place, so different from the clean lines of endless grass meeting endless sky, where an enemy could be spotted far in advance. Lesser men had backed away from the foreignness and danger that lay before him. But King Varlas was not a lesser man.

He turned, pleased to have the sun behind him and his warriors arrayed before him. The women were setting up the tents along the river they had just crossed, where horses and men had finally been able to drink their fill. Beyond the river stretched the grass of home, but dry and parched in the searing summer heat. There was nothing there that would feed the horses; only goats and sheep could live off of that.

"Warriors!" he called. At once the men formed up into neat groups of forty—fifty in all, each led by a chief Varlas trusted. It was not so much their loyalty to him he trusted, but rather their greed and ambition. Varlas knew he was perhaps the first king in history who need not worry about whispers in the dark or reckless plots. For Varlas, slayer of kings, who now lived in a tent filled with the wealth of those who had thought themselves the rulers of the steppes, their wives and daughters even now awaiting him and ready to serve him in the most intimate ways, had brought his men to a land that would satisfy all of them beyond the dreams of avarice.

"We have endured much hardship to reach this land, and our trials are not yet over. But if we have the courage to face down the superstitions and fears that have kept weaker men out, we will soon ride unopposed across this land of witches and dirt-eaters. Who fears the ugly women who think they own this land?"

"None here!" shouted two thousand voices.

"Who fears the half-men who bow to these women?"

This time the answer was laughter.

"Then let us ride through these trees and pull down their wooden hovels, burn their 'villages' so grass can grow for the purpose the gods intended—to feed our herds. Until then, our horses can eat the grain they have grown for us, while we feast upon the meat those fools thought was theirs, and enjoy the pleasures to be found in showing their women who in truth their masters are! Let us roast these so-called men beside their sheep and drink kumis from their skulls!"

Cheers filled the campsite, chasing away the strangeness and the fear. For in truth, there was nothing to fear. A few traitors could not turn dirt-eaters into warriors, no matter how desperately they might have tried. Thousands would die in the season to come. But thousands more would become the slaves of the king's conquering army. That was Varlas's secret plan: for the first time, men as well as women would serve the warriors of the gods. Whatever luxury a man might require, whether it be gold, fruit, wine, a saddle that matched his armor or twenty women in one night would have what he desired. And it would be the honor of these witless savages to provide it for them.

Lost in his dreams, Varlas felt his manhood swell. He dismissed his men and made for his tent.

The food would not be ready for a while. Before he sampled the pleasures of the wild women who thought they could resist him, he would enjoy the princess he had taken from that fool Kariik, and perhaps her two young daughters as well. Maybe all three together. Varlas grinned.

Chapter 26

"—The monster laughed, but Owl only flew higher than his fiery claws could reach and looked down. She coughed up a mouse she had eaten earlier, and dropped it upon his head. For a moment, nothing happened. Then—"

Kalie stopped her story midsentence at the urgent tapping upon her door. Melora was already asleep, but Yarik was waiting for the end of the story.

"You already know the rest," she said, for it was one of his favorites, and kissed her step-son on the top of his head. "So finish it with your inner voice, and I will be back soon."

She tucked both children in again, and hurried to meet the impatient whispers of those outside her house.

It was still light outside, the sky deepening to twilight, with the summer solstice just two hands of days away. Kalie had been avoiding meetings lately, but one look at the messenger at her threshold, and she knew that she had to go. She knew also that Riyik had not returned, or the young man would have told her.

Most of the town seemed to be making their way to the temple, despite the late hour. Minda stood in her doorway, her baby fussing in her arms, and watched her parents trudge down the lane.

"Minda, will you--?"

"Of course. I'll hear if they need anything, or Yarik will know to come get me."

Kalie nodded her thanks, and joined the stream of people, all silent, all pretending they didn't already know what the news was.

Once again, the people gathered outside the temple, where there was enough room.

Taran, once a fisherman, and Varena's first lover, had ridden out with Riyik and Borik nearly a moonspan ago. But a year of training gave him the look of a warrior of the steppes. "It's begun," he said simply. "The horde crashed into our lands about two hands of days ago. The first two villages they reached were abandoned."

"Did that give the invaders the confidence we hoped for?" asked Nara.

Taran nodded. "They gorged on the food, and set their animals to feed on the crops in the fields."

"The grain could not have been ripe yet," said Alessa.

The messenger shook his head with a tight smile. "Some of the horses were already getting sick when I left. It will likely continue, until they find enough grass." No one wanted to say anything hopeful yet and Taran continued. "The next village was one filled with traps and poison. Many invaders died. Others are likely too sick to recover without a skilled healer—which they do not seem to possess."

The brief, ragged cheer which arose from about half the gathering was cut short by Ruleen's voice. "And do we now rejoice over the suffering and death of others?" she asked.

Some might have wished to answer, but Orin quickly interjected a question. "Had the real fighting begun before you left?"

"Only one battle that I can bear witness to," said Taran. "And that was enough."

Everyone in the courtyard held their breath.

"The town of Dancing Waters had left oil

smeared all over their houses, as well as pit traps outside. While this time, the beastmen knew to avoid the traps, and were careful searching the houses, the hidden archers were able to set the place on fire from a distance. Just not a safe distance. Some beastmen were killed, but many townsfolk as well. Those who fled beyond the falls were captured more easily than we expected. I believe most of them are dead." Taran's eyes said that he hoped they were.

"And how many invaders dead?" The words sounded pulled from Nara's insides.

"I can't say for certain, but at least forty, and many more injured or sick. They were still moving as one body when I began my journey back here."

"It may well be in our favor if they continue moving as one body," said Kariik. "Their king would have planned to divide his forces after the first easy victories, after his men were drunk on pride and loot." At that nearly everyone smiled. "But having lost so many men in those first skirmishes, he may now be unwilling to do so."

"I agree," said Taran. "We shall know soon. There will be many more scouts, bringing many more messages as the battles are joined."

"Thank you, Taran," said Orin. Food and drink had already been set before him, but he seemed only now to notice. Before he could take his first sip, however, Kalie heard words leaping unbidden from her own mouth.

"And the men you rode out with, Taran?"

Many had left with him, but Taran knew what Kalie was asking, so he got straight to the answer. "When we saw how things stood, Riyik insisted on remaining to lead the fight. And Borik insisted on staying to guard Riyik. In a more personal message to you..." Taran hesitated, but at Kalie's expression continued. "Riyik said: 'Tell Kalie I love her. I beg her forgiveness for this decision, but as I once came to this land as a conqueror, I must seize this chance to make amends. Tell my children I love them and will see them soon.'" Borik said, "I will see that Riyik returns to you safely, or there will be no safe place in this land for me." Then Taran began to eat.

"That sounds like both of them," Kalie heard herself say. Someone seemed to be helping her remain upright, although she didn't remember standing up. Then she turned and walked back to her house.

"I'm not leaving until you eat something," Alessa said the next morning. Brenia sat beside her. "You don't have to talk about it, but you need to keep up your strength."

"I'm fine," Kalie said, shoving a piece of bread in her mouth, and chewing almost well enough. She managed to choke down some tea without choking on the bread. "I'll sulk a while longer, and then I'll get back to work. There's too much to be done for anything else." The suggestion that her two friends leave was clear in Kalie's expression.

They only sat silently until Kalie burst out, "He could have at least told me that's what he was going to do! Did he think I would fall apart like some fragile blossom? Or try to stop him somehow?"

"He may not have planned this!" said Brenia. "You heard: when they saw how things stood, he decided to stay. If Riyik's leadership could make the difference between victory and defeat—"

"Does he think he's the only one competent to

lead?" Kalie snapped. "That not one of the seventy who traveled with us--?"

"He may well be," said Alessa. "We weren't there; we didn't see. Which brings us to the real problem: you want to be there, too."

Kalie ate some strawberries, and tried not to look at Melora playing quietly off to one side. "If it did not come down to a choice between leaving a baby who needs my milk, and fighting by Riyik's side, I would already be there, not sitting here helplessly, wanting to kill him, yet afraid someone else really will!"

"There are others who can nurse Melora if you choose to go," said Alessa.

Brenia had not displayed shock in a long time, but she did now. "Alessa! How could you suggest a mother leave her child and risk her life doing what—"

"Men do?" Alessa finished. "Better she should go with our support, knowing her children are cared for, than twisting in the wind until she runs off without thinking or planning. Haven't you seen her caught between two conflicting duties all this time? And what it's doing to her?"

The knot inside Kalie began to slowly come undone, and for the first time since last night, she almost smiled. As usual, Alessa had seen the problem, and laid it out with simple grace. "I'm being pulled two ways and I don't know what to do," she said quietly. Alessa and Brenia each set a hand over one of Kalie's, and for a time, the three just sat there.

The people of Stonebridge prepared for the refugees that the latest messengers had told them to expect, while Kariik helped make room by selecting thirty of his warriors to accompany thirty local warriors to aid the fighters who were steadily falling back toward the west. They were to leave the next morning.

"I wish he'd send all of them!" said Darva. "Things are so tense now, and you know how men get when there's no enemy to focus their energy on."

Kalie knew. They sat with a group of women, filling baskets with healing herbs, while Brenia demonstrated a new way she had discovered for stitching wounds. The local healers were impressed; for all they knew of healing, few here had any experience treating injuries inflicted by tools of war.

"They're already fighting each other," Kalie said. "I'm glad Kariik is sending so many warriors to the front lines, but he should have done it sooner."

The nomad women in the group looked at her angrily, and some made the sign against evil, but no one said anything. Kalie took a moment of satisfaction from that.

It was short lived, for momehts later, a scream pierced the air. Even though it came from the west, near the path to the sea, everyone was on their feet and armed in moments.

A weeping man came toward the temple, carrying an unconscious young woman. The screams were from the victim's mother, joined by others who saw them. Kalie made way for the more experienced healers, but quickly assessed the situation from where she stood. The woman lived, though badly beaten. And it was clear from her torn clothing and the blood on her thighs that she had been raped.

Alessa bit her lips until they, too, bled. "I really thought we'd get through the whole war without this," she said as she joined the healers.

Kariik arrived while the healers were still working, and curtly ordered all his men—including those who were to leave in the morning—to form up before him.

"Ladoka fought her attacker," Nara said, showing no emotion. It was clear from Kariik's face that he wished she would. "One of them will have injuries that will tell the story."

However, with the recent fighting among them men, and even the mock battles, many men bore cuts and scratches on their arms and faces.

"The man who did this could save us all time by confessing!" Kariik shouted.

"Don't you mean bragging?" Kalie muttered. Then to her surprise, a smirk on the face of a young man in the second row, who sported a black eye and a split lip, showed just that.

A crowd had gathered, eerie in their silence. Some had been busy with preparations for the Summer Festival just moments before. Now Kalie wondered if the festival would happen at all. The people here had been pushed to their limits by an invasion many had no way of comprehending. But this, from someone they had been convinced to accept as an ally, might finally push them too far.

Alessa came out of the temple of healing. "Ladoka has named her assailant," she said, her voice carrying. "She is not ready to face him, but she will be soon."

"Tell us," said Kariik. "Everyone here knows she will have spoken the truth."

"Charnak," Alessa said, as if pronouncing a curse.

Kalie was already looking at him, for it was the man who was smirking. Then she remembered: he had fought Ladoka in a practice bout, and she had won. Charnak had been angry and humiliated, but he had not been the first to lose to a woman. Most had dismissed his promise to regain his honor as hot temper and empty threats. A mistake, Kalie realized.

He stopped smirking, but showed no sign of fear or regret that she could see. "Charnak!" Kariik shouted. "Step forward."

Kalie was relieved to see that most of his brother warriors pulled away from Charnak or looked at him with disgust or anger.

"I did nothing wrong," he said defiantly.

Kariik moved closer to Charnak, who bowed to his king. "How do you reason that?" Kariik asked softly, but everyone heard him. "Were you perhaps missing the day all my warriors took an oath to treat all women of this land as the wives of chiefs?"

Charnak looked considerably less confident, but persisted. "This one doesn't count," he said simply. "None of the ones who play with weapons and pretend to be men could ever be chief's wives! And that girl I had," a grin appeared on Charnak's face, quickly smothered. "She's had half the warriors you brought here, my king. And plenty of her own dirt-eaters who won't even try to fight. Hardly the behavior of a chief's wife. Clearly she gave up the protection we promised of her own free will."

"So that's reason enough to break your oath, make your king forsworn, and possibly destroy our alliance?" asked Garm, his smithing hammer shaking in his hand.

Charnak glared. "I did everyone a favor! That

girl beat me in a rigged game of combat, with rules
and blunted weapons, and even our own warriors
acting like teachers breaking up fights among boys!
Well, now I've shown her what real combat is! No
one's going to yell 'stop!' and discuss the merits of
technique in a battle. So the women can all just stay
home like they're supposed to, and leave the fighting
to the men. Besides," he grinned again. "After we
sparred the first time, I said I wanted a rematch. She
said I could have one whenever I wanted. So I did.
Just now."

Kariik stared at Charnak for at least thirty
heartbeats. Then, he struck him hard in the face.
Charnak fell back, and with no one nearby to catch
him, landed hard in the dirt. "Alrik!" called the king.
"I believe this man is your nephew. Do you wish to
speak for him?"

Charnak got angrily to his feet. Alrik stood
before him. "How did my brother ever spawn such
filth?" he asked. To Kariik he said, "He broke his oath
and betrayed his king. What else is there to say?"

"What?" cried Charnak. "Uncle! You can't
mean that!" This time, Alrik hit him.

"Enough!" called Orin. "Kariik, it is time for
you to take your men and leave. When Ladoka is
ready, she may decide Charnak's punishment."

"What?" Charnak repeated. "For doing what
any man does with a whore? This is insane! If
someone wants payment for her use, then fine,
although it's hardly fair—no one else had to pay—"

"His punishment is death," said Kariik.

"That is not our way," said Orin.

"But it is ours. I cannot undo what has
happened, but I can at least make certain nothing like

this happens again. I will offer my apologies to Ladoka if she will see me. If she wishes me to spare her attacker's life, I will. But my instincts tell me it will be better for everyone here, even Charnak, if he dies cleanly, and that others may learn from his mistake."

"Uncle!" Charnak shouted, clearly expecting Alrik to put a stop to this madness. "Even if you're angry with me, I know you won't let them—"

"I believe Kariik may be right," said Nara. "Since the only alternative by our laws would be castration."

Charnak fainted.

When he came around, only Kariik and a small group of warriors, including Alrik were with him. Charnak was led to a secluded spot across the river, near the nomad camp. Ten witnesses from the town, including Ladoka, watched as Kariik stood before the young man, and cleanly put a spear through him.

Kalie was not present, but she was told that Kariik had knelt before Ladoka and begged her forgiveness. Ladoka had graciously told the king that only Charnak had wronged her, and that his debt was paid.

The next morning, Kariik marched out of Stonebridge with sixty of his warriors. The last twenty remained in town under Alrik's command, with orders to continue training with the more than two hundred fighters from the local population, and to guard the dam.

Chapter 27

With Melora strapped to her back, and Yarik comfortably settled in Brenia's house, Kalie made her way to the group who struggled to build the dam. The town, although less crowded than it had been just days earlier, had become oppressive. She needed to be part of her land's salvation, and if it couldn't be on the front lines, it would be here, designing something new, as she had once designed tiny stars of bone which could shift the tide of battle.

The work and camaraderie she found at the construction site did much to ease Kalie's fears and anger and the empty place left by Riyik's absence. An old farmer who had built dams in his youth was in charge, and several other skilled technicians assisted him. Everyone else, including Kalie, carried rocks, cut and shaped logs, and dug ditches that would drain off water until the dam was completed.

They worked through the Summer Festival, which suited Kalie fine. She was in no mood to celebrate. But when the long day drew to a close, everyone put down their tools and gathered wood for a bonfire. The food brought from home became a feast, and tired workers found they still had the energy to sing, although the songs were fraught with melancholy, and not the usual tunes chosen for the shortest night of the year.

When a column of people, heavily laden with food arrived just at sunset, even Kalie had to smile. And when she saw that Varena and Noris were among them, she cried.

"I couldn't miss my sister's first birthday!"

Varena said, tossing Melora in the air and cooing at her.

"I wish her father were here as well," Kalie said.

"Soon, Mother, he will be." Varena's simple faith finally opened Kalie's heart to the magic of the night. She joined in the singing, now the joyful songs of the season, and the prayers that this sacred night would be celebrated next year, and not forbidden by new owners of the land and its people. No one stayed awake through the short night, but retired early to be ready for another day of work.

And as if in answer to their prayers, the dam was finished the next day. Not by magic like in one of Kalie's stories, but by hard work through a long day, and by the extra work provided by the people who came to celebrate the solstice. That night, the temporary canals were blocked, and the artificial lake created by humans was finally seen in all its glory.

"It's beautiful," Varena said simply, and it was. The water was a cloudy blue, with tiny rivulets adding to it in a sparkling silver spider web.

"This will only hold a short time," the project leader said, pointing to the incoming water, too small to make a difference as they watched, or even in the course a day. But slowly, the level would rise until eventually it would spill over their carefully built wall. "Within a moonspan, we must release it, or lose all of our work."

"Somehow, I don't think we will have to wait that long," said Aldera, while her daughter played with Melora.

"We need one more thing," said Kalie. "Horsemen. Warriors who can look at this thing we've built, and tell us what Vargas and his men will see if they happen upon this place."

"Yes," said a smith who had come to lend his expertise. "If they know what it is, they'll destroy it, and flood the river before their main force arrives at Stonebridge."

"Or simply prevent us from breaching it," said the leader. "Then their army can just ride across the little stream that was once a river, and take the town without a fight."

"Oh, there'll be a fight," said a woman who followed Otera. "Just not one we're likely to win."

Messengers were sent to bring the few remaining warriors of Kariik's band, since they were the newest to the west, and would still see things with a nomad's eye.

While they waited, the work crew rested for most of the day—something nearly everyone had forgotten how to do. Then Melora took her first step, followed at once by Aldera's child, and for awhile, Kalie forgot everything else.

Late that afternoon, a group arrived on horseback, led by Alrik. Kalie was surprised to see Kestra with him, despite having given birth less than a moonspan ago. Still, she looked well enough, if you could call her vacant stare healthy. She seemed barely aware of anything—not even her healthy new son. Two other warriors had brought their wives, so they made a cheery enough group.

The party dismounted and for awhile just stared at the huge wall of stone and logs, and the newly made lake behind it.

"So what do you think?" Kalie asked Alrik. "More importantly, what will Varlas and his men think?" She stood next to him, trying to see the structure she had helped build as the men of the steppes saw it.

"Hard to say," Alrik said, rubbing his bearded chin. "Not a weapon, I think. They will have seen enough strange dwellings, built of wood and stone, so this will probably look more like some kind of temple."

"Or bathing place," said another warrior. "But no, I don't think they'll bother with it, except to drink from the lake and water their horses."

"What do you think of posting a team of warriors here, to make sure the water breaks free at the right time?" asked one of the workers.

"Definitely," said Alrik. "It's crucial to the defense of Stonebridge."

The others agreed, most of them more interested in removing the stones from their horse's hooves, and getting away from this rocky, hilly terrain.

Then, too soon for Kalie's comfort, they were heading back to the once beautiful town that was now an armed camp.

She stretched out every rest break for the joy of watching Melora's first baby steps. Once, close to the town, when they splashed in water that barely reached their knees, Kalie held out her arms, and Melora ran to her getting close enough before stumbling so that Kalie could catch her up and swirl her around in the misty, rocky stream. Cuddling Melora close, inhaling her clean baby scent, Kalie knew she could never leave her to fight a war.

Once back in Stonebridge, the dam builders, nicknamed "Beavers," found a much smaller town than they had left. Other than Otera's band, who were preparing to leave in a few days, only twenty of Kariik's warriors remained, with sixty of the town's new warriors to fill the ranks.

"Warriors can be recalled quickly to shore up our defenses," Orin explained. "And over half the town can use a bow or throw rocks when the time comes. But for now, fighters need to be where the fighting is."

"And there is news!" cried Garm. "Some of it even good!"

There was always news, thought Kalie, who at that moment wanted nothing more than a long soak in the hot springs, and someone to rub her sore feet. But she stayed to hear what Garm had to say.

"The scouts who brought it have already left," said Garm. "The fighting is still many days to the east, and many people are fleeing west. Your horse killers are making a huge difference, Kalie. The horde has lost many men, but if they continue to lose horses at this rate..." He trailed off, never having contemplated such a thing.

Sirak, arriving with a group of friends, took up the story. "The traps have done all they can. The warriors know how to spot them now. But our metal weapons are much better than theirs, and that's making a big difference!" He looked proudly at Garm, who merely shrugged. "The scout said one of every four men who came to our land are dead or injured. Can you even imagine numbers like that?"

Kalie could but did not want to. She focused instead on the pleasure of hearing Sirak referring to the land of the Goddess as "our land."

"The bastards are getting more brutal, though,"

Sirak continued.

"Sirak, we don't need to go over that again," Garm began.

"But it's important!" cried Josan, a boy who had once fallen under Sirak's spell to bring the ways of the steppes to this land, but who now trained by his side—and was better than Sirak at wrestling and hand to hand fighting. "The bad men are killing everyone they can! People who don't fight back. People who fight, and then try to call for a time to help the wounded. The scout said they're raping women to death." Josan paused as if trying to remember what that meant. Sirak looked away as if wishing he hadn't brought any of it up.

"That's enough!" Garm said, effectively dismissing the young people. He looked at Kalie with sympathy. "It's to be expected, although now it appalls me. But this whole tribe came here expecting easy victories and lives of untold luxury. To suffer so many defeats at the hands of men—and women—they consider inferior...it's too much for their pride. They have to strike back somehow. But you didn't need to hear the gory details."

"Yes, I did," said Kalie.

She moved slowly through the town on her way to reclaim Yarik from Brenia, watching the walls and fences being built to connect the outer houses, creating, in effect, a walled town—and platforms for firing arrows down at an enemy who would have to shoot *up*.

The next day brought news of another kind.

"The beastmen have found a defense against the caltrops," said a grim-faced priestess who brought, along with news, a request for healers to accompany her to the fighting in the east.

"Leather boots for the horses?" asked a leatherworker who had been working on such a solution to protect their own horses.

The messenger shook her head. "One would need to possess a soul to think that way. These beasts have been using their own people—slaves, sick people, young warriors who don't prove themselves in battle—to walk out ahead of the horses, and 'find' the stars. With their feet."

There were a few exclamations of horror, but far fewer than there would have been a year ago, Kalie thought.

"Then we must not use them," said Ilara.

"That's what the people east of here are saying," said the foreign priestess.

"Hence the need for more healers," Kalie said. "With less chance of them returning home safely.

The priestess glared at her. "What else can we do?"

"What happens to the nomads who are used in this fashion? After they 'find' a caltrop that is?"

"I'm told that if the wound is severe, they are left behind to become food for predators. Or to starve."

"Then they can be rescued!" Kalie's words were echoed by several others, all excited by the possibility of a good turn of events.

"Yes, that is the one good thing, I suppose. But only those most gravely hurt are left. The rest are kept to be used again. And those we can help may be crippled for life."

"Let those to the east stop using them," said Kalie. "And let us think of a way to rescue those *testers* by the time they reach us. For I do not intend to fight that battle without my stars." She walked away, deep in thought, unaware of the admiration in the eyes of those who watched. Or how most of them stood just a little straighter as she passed.

A few days later came the news they had all been dreading.

"The horde has taken a town," said the hollow-eyed young man who sat in the temple, drinking cup after cup of wine, as if to drown out what he saw. And he hadn't actually seen anything.

"It's large; Starfall is nearly as large as Stonebridge, but not so rich, nor as easily defended. The people there tried, though. Arrows from rooftops. Ditches filled with spears. Even fire, but...this time the horde just kept coming. From two directions. When they breached the town, people tried to run. They had a plan, and knew that many have escaped from other towns and villages, especially if there was forest nearby. But this time, it was as if a special group of beastmen had orders to capture those running while the rest secured the town."

"But some must have escaped," Orin prodded gently. "Or you would not know the story."

"Yes," said the messenger. "A child who hid in the forest for three days without food. Then two women escaped from the town and found him. A pair of scouts found all three, and brought them to a village, deep in a marsh, safe from the horses—for now at least. The things those women described—" The young man shuddered, then reached for more wine.

Orin took the pitcher away, and brought the

man tea and broth instead. "I know it is hard, but you must finish your message. Then you can rest in a temple, where healers and those who have seen other such horrors can help you."

The man nodded, and sat up taller. "It's just that what happened in Starfall does not match what I was told to expect. When all of those of the town who still lived were brought to the main square, this king, Varlas, ordered his men to choose from among the women. They selected mostly young and pretty women but others too, most of the women of the town, in fact. The people of the town had heard…had expected they might be raped and made slaves. But the beastmen…they gathered in groups around each woman…only about two hundred women and about seven invaders for each woman. They raped them until they died! All of them! The beast Varlas said they were not fit to be mothers of warriors. Only the women of the horde would be allowed to live in the town from now on!"

"And the men?" Otera asked, her voice clear despite the crowded room.

"They killed nearly all of them. But they made it last many days." The messenger hung his head. "I was told they kept only old men and women, a few of the younger women and some children. And most of those they…marked somehow. With fire, or hammers, so that they would be crippled, and unable to leave. One of the women who escaped is older, with a twist in her back. She thinks the beastmen thought her already crippled, and unable to run, so they didn't watch her so well. But she overcame her challenge early in life, and runs well."

"Does the horde mean to stay in town?" asked

Alrik.

"It seems so," said the messenger dully. "They lost many men and many horses. The younger woman said she thinks they may hope to rest in the town and regain their strength. But at such numbers, the food and grass will be gone within a moonspan, and there is much forest nearby. The beastmen fear the forest, and so do their horses. But the boy said they were cutting down trees when the three escaped."

Orin thanked the messenger, who was led away by two acolytes. The discussion began at once, of what could be done, and what should be done, but Kalie heard little of it. She did hear Otera's terse, but polite farewell. "We have our marching orders," the tall woman said.

And I have mine, Kalie thought, and slipped out of the temple like a ghost.

Chapter 28

She would have simply walked out of the town
with a few hastily gathered supplies if Alessa had not
stopped her.

Kalie tried to explain that yes, she could just
leave without saying goodbye to her children, because
saying goodbye would hurt too much. And what if she
cried or said something foolish? That might be the last
memory they had of her, and besides, Yarik had
already lost one mother, and a serious goodbye might
frighten him.

But Alessa was relentless. More importantly,
she wasn't trying to prevent Kalie from leaving. So
Kalie nursed Melora one last time, and told Yarik he
would be staying with Aunt Brenia again, and she
would see them all as soon as she could.

Then Alessa checked Kalie's provisions, and
repacked everything, adding a few things, but knowing
Kalie had to travel light. "Drink a cup of this tea every
morning," Alessa said, adding a pouch containing a
blend of herbs. "It will help you keep your milk, if
you're not gone too long. Express some every day;
nurse another woman's baby if you can, while Minda
and Aldera nurse yours."

Wordlessly, Kalie hugged Alessa.

"You're not riding Blossom?" Alessa asked.

"She's gone with the all the others. I don't
even know which group took her. Probably just as
well."

They walked to the bridge, Kalie memorizing
the town that had become home to her in such a short
time. From the bridge, Kalie looked down at the

water, now a tiny stream that had once been a river. The day was hot, and many people sat on both banks, dipping their feet in the cool water. Despite her serious mood, Kalie felt a fission of pleasure at the sight of nomad women who were barely distinguishable from the locals.

While a few stubbornly continued wearing their felt robes, most had taken to wearing the lighter local fabrics, although they still covered more of their bodies than the settled folk did this time of year. Most still wore some kind of veil, but now only to cover their hair, and these too were lighter and more colorful than before.

Sitting apart from the others, close to where the bridge ended, was Kestra. Kalie paused a moment, then walked the few steps needed to see what the other woman was doing. Kestra was piling pebbles from the riverbank into a tower, talking to herself in a sing-song voice as she did. A pile of twigs sat beside her, and now and then, Kestra would slip one between some rocks. As Kalie watched, Kestra pulled on one of the twigs, and the tower collapsed. Then she began again, talking all the while.

"How long has she been like this?" Kalie asked.

"Just the last few days," replied Alessa. "But she's been getting stranger and more distant for at least the last moonspan."

"Where's her baby?" Kalie asked with concern.

"In her tent. Kestra's happy to nurse him when he's brought to her, and plays with him for awhile. Then, she just seems to forget about him. Ilara has been staying with her since Borik left, looking after Saryk and doing most of the cooking."

"And sharing Alrik's bed?" Kalie asked.

"Probably. I can't see Alrik allowing her to stay under any other circumstances. And you know Ilara. She's determined to get inside the minds of these people."

"Like someone else I know," Kalie said, but then her attention returned to Kestra. She could make out most of the words, because they seemed to be part of a story.

"The rabbit was caught in a trap. The hunter slept, for he was not yet hungry and the sun was warm. When at last the hunter went to collect his meal, he found the rabbit had chewed his way out of the trap. And then the rabbit ate the hunter."

Kalie and Alessa looked at each other in shared confusion.

"Look after her, Alessa," Kalie said. "If her mind can't heal, at least keep her safe."

"I will," Alessa promised. The unspoken "as safe as anyone can be" was understood.

The two women embraced, and then Kalie skirted what was left of the nomad camp, and headed into the sparse forest and down the rocky hillsides, walking nearly half the day without seeing anyone. Grateful for the solitude, she worked on various plans to free the captives of Starfall, to draw the horde into a battle at the foot of Stonebridge, to singlehandedly defeat the Wolves who preyed on her people.

The sound of horses caused Kalie to slip behind the nearest tree and freeze before she even knew what she was doing.

It wasn't much of a tree, and Otera spotted her easily. She slowed her horse, and seemed about to speak, but Kalie just started walking again, not looking at Otera, or the line of women behind her. About half were mounted, the other half walking.

Otera rode her horse beside Kalie, keeping the pace so those on foot could keep up easily. Kalie continued to ignore her. They walked this way until close to sunset.

"Taking the battle to the enemy alone?" Otera finally asked.

Kalie said nothing.

"Excuse me for asking, but didn't you already do this once before? Marching off on your own to defeat the beastmen? As I recall, it didn't work out too well last time."

Kalie kept walking, but looked back along the silent column behind Otera and finally spoke. "Actually, the last time I tried this, it was with about thirty naïve women behind me, all thinking I would lead them to victory. And things didn't work out too well for them. Have you told your followers that story?"

"Yes, but you're the storyteller, and besides, you were there. Why don't we find a place to camp, and you can tell it tonight."

"Because I'm trying to forget it!" snapped Kalie. Why was this woman being nice to her? "At least this way, I can only get myself killed."

"That would be a waste. Ride with us, and maybe we can help each other."

"I don't have a horse!" Kalie was tired and her feet hurt, but she wasn't about to share a fire with this group.

Otera laughed. "I know. But I know who has yours!" She held up her hand and the other riders stopped, rather messily, although only two horses

actually bumped into each other. Kalie nearly laughed
at what Riyik, or any steppes warrior, would make of
such ill-prepared recruits.

"Danarie!" Otera called. "Walk awhile. Kalie
will ride your mount. Or, should I say, hers?"

"Blossom!" The word was out before Kalie
could stop it. For her part, Danarie, an older woman,
walking stiffly and rubbing her backside, seemed
relieved.

"I should have known that riding all day would
be different from riding a few times in a large circle,"
said Danarie. "You're welcome to her."

Kalie leapt easily onto her old friend. And
Blossom did seem happy to have her there.

"Do you people really think you're ready for
this?" Kalie asked.

"As ready as anyone ever is," said a woman of
about twenty years. "Another year of training would
have been most welcome, but this is what we have."

They continued along a narrow trail until they
came to a likely place to camp: flat ground, grass, a
freshwater spring and plenty of branches on the
ground for a fire.

The women, twenty three of them, Kalie
counted, went efficiently about the business of making
camp. Kalie saw to her horse, and then strode across
the clearing to where Otera sat on a log, supervising.
"All right, Otera, why are you being nice to the
woman who you blame for singlehandedly causing the
downfall of our civilization?"

"I never thought it was your fault alone," said
Otera. "Although, I'll admit, I probably sounded like I
did."

"To put it mildly," Kalie muttered.

"I have mellowed some," said Otera. "Or, at least I've learned to be less of a bitch."

Kalie laughed. "You sound like a horsewoman! What other words in their language have you learned?"

"Just the swear words and insults. But they have so many of those, I could probably have an entire conversation with their king, given the chance."

Kalie felt her spirits lift at the change in Otera—not to mention the image of Otera speaking with a captured enemy king, which made her want to giggle. But she was still wary of this angry woman, so Kalie waited.

"I'm sorry for the things I said to you," Otera finally said, nearly through shut teeth. "And, yes, you were right about the need to learn this cursed new art called war. Those warriors you brought were good teachers. But we're out of time, and you know more about our enemy than any of my warriors, save Malana. And you have more experience actually fighting—and riding—" Otera rubbed her back, "than any of us."

Lanara, who Kalie remembered was a healer, began bringing a pain-killing tea of willow bark and chamomile to the women who had ridden, and offered massages to the sorest. "Stay with us, Kalie," she said. "No one wants to see you killed, or worse, captured again. We've all got a better chance of surviving if we work together. And I think you'll find Otera is a different person when she's in the company of only women."

Otera glared at Lanara, but said nothing.

Kalie thought about it. "What's your plan?" she asked Otera.

Otera shrugged, suddenly seeming at a loss for words. "I'd like it to sound better, but it comes down to posing as a group of helpless women, and letting them chase us into an ambush."

"Didn't the first few villages already do that?" Kalie asked.

"Very successfully!" said Danarie.

"At first," said Kalie. "But the beastmen have gotten wary of such traps."

"It was my thought…" Otera looked morose, as if speaking of the plan out loud showed its flaws. "It was my thought that a group of only women, especially women carrying weapons and dressed in armor might…distract them."

"Amuse them, more likely," said Kalie. "But that could be exactly what will give us the advantage. It would only work with a small scouting party."

"Of which there are many," said Lanara, sitting beside Kalie, while others began to pass around the food: cakes of dried meat, fruit, and fat, with flat bread. Water from the spring balanced the dryness, but also made small portions ideal.

"Yes," added a woman Kalie remembered as Derona. "In fact, starting tomorrow, we'll have to be on watch for them."

"That close?" Kalie nearly dropped her bread. This was news to her. But welcomed news, for it meant that the time of waiting and worrying was finally over. Let the battle finally begin, she thought.

"So what were you going to do, all alone, Kalie?" asked a pretty girl, barely a woman. "I'm Erobia, by the way."

Kalie thought about it. She wished she had a wonderful story about a secret weapons and plan which would allow a single woman to accomplish what a hundred warriors could not. She had certainly created enough of those tales when she lived as a slave among the Aahk. But tonight, the truth was less exciting.

"Just gather information, and find a group I could join. One that stood a chance of making a difference."

"And have you found that group?" Otera asked.

"I think I may have," said Kalie.

There were smiles then, and quiet words of welcome. Soon after, they prepared for sleep. Kalie was relieved to see Otera posting as guards the women Kalie would have chosen herself. They were silent and alert, and had obviously done this before. Otera and two others would take the next shift. It was well planned, at least.

As they lay in their bedrolls, Kalie whispered to Otera. "You do realize that if we are caught, these men will rape us before taking us to their king as prizes?"

From the darkness she heard Otera's voice, as cold and brittle as ice. "Realize? Kalie, I'm counting on it."

Chapter 29

They traveled through land that was nearly untouched by war. Except for the walls—fences, really—thrown up around villages, and farmers practicing with weapons in the fallow fields, Kalie could almost imagine the world was still the same as the one she had been born in.

They stopped at each village for news, and were always offered food and a place to sleep. That at least hadn't changed. Messengers remained busy, but the only thing anyone was talking about was Starfall: how long would the horde remain there, and whether this would be the battle that would decide the future.

As they traveled, Kalie became better acquainted with the strange assortment of women Otera had collected and trained. She already knew that Lanara was a skilled healer, whose calming presence was a deeply appreciated counter to Otera's stormy moods and intensity. The two often spent evenings at the campfire discussing remedies and techniques, especially in the new area of battle wounds.

Kalie learned that Danarie was the best with a spear, and that Derona, much to her own surprise, took to horseback riding like she was born to it. Valeska still had not spoken since being assaulted more than a year ago, but was deadly with rocks, whether launched from her sling or simply flung from her strong right arm, which, with her newly developed muscles, no longer matched her left arm. Kalie sometimes practiced with her, when she needed a break from her bow or throwing sticks. Young Erobia was highly skilled with the bolo which could tangle a horse's legs, as well as being the best scout in the group. Griva, once an apprentice healer, divided her time and effort between helping Lanara, practicing spear-throwing, and learning the beastmen's language.

All of them had experienced the same sexual violence that Kalie had, or lost friends, along with any sense of safety or ability to fit in with the world they had been born into. Although Kalie had not expected to, she found herself growing comfortable with these women, in a way she had not felt with anyone since her ill-fated journey east nearly a decade ago.

After five days they came to a wide marshland with a village in the middle of a man-made island. Kalie had seen such places before on her travels, and the sense of safety she felt once they had been ferried to the village was profound. No horse could make it through the sucking mud of the place. In fact, without local guides, death by quicksand was a frightening possibility.

"This is the place where the survivors of Starfall went," Kalie explained. "We'll need to talk to them if we're going to be part of any attack on the horde."

"This is the place I'd like to lure the beastmen," said Erobia, her youthful features clouded with hate. "Let them drown here, or be helpless in the mud while we fill them full of arrows!"

They received a friendly, but somewhat strained welcome. The village was filled to capacity with refugees, and food was being carefully rationed. But there were warriors here whom Kalie knew and messengers as well.

"We'll eat only the food we brought," Kalie

promised the leaders. "And we'll be gone tomorrow.
But we must speak with many people here." She
looked around at the tilting wooden houses, smelling
musty in the perpetual damp, the hordes of insects kept
away by the greasy paste the people here smeared over
their bodies and the peat fires which gave more smoke
than light or heat, and knew that one day would be
enough. Otera and the others seemed to feel the same
way.

But the people here ate well, and despite the
number of extra mouths, insisted the newest visitors
have at least a little of the food they had prepared. The
duck migration had been bountiful this year, and Kalie
couldn't resist a portion of crispy roast duck, and a few
bites of tasty fish. She graciously turned down the
skewers of frog and lizard meat, although Lanara was
quite fond of the way the cooked snake here, and
allowed herself a small, second portion, when pressed.

After that it was all talk, which was no bad
thing, for the first thing she learned was that Riyik was
alive and well, and heading for Starfall.

Then there was the delightful surprises of
familiar faces, and news of old friends. When she
went to speak with a group of warrior discussing what
they had learned from the marsh people about
defenses, she found Malor, last seen back in Green
Bower.

"What are you doing all the way out here?" she
cried, slipping into the language of the east.

Malor answered perfectly in Kalie's milk
tongue. "The duty I swore to uphold when I left the
steppes with you, Kalie. The protection of the people
of this land. We're trying to make certain the Wolves
of Fools don't get this far west."

"And Starfall?" she asked.

One of Malor's comrades answered. "Several bands are there now, testing their strength, and preventing them from leaving, but we have too few men, er, sorry, warriors, for a full frontal assault. What we need is to break them into small groups, and lure them to where we have the advantage.

A woman who had glared at the former nomad's use of the word "men" shook her head. "King Varlas is a brute and possibly a madman, but he's not that stupid. Numbers are his biggest advantage."

"But only until they run out of food and grazing," Kalie heard another say. Whatever he said after that was lost as she recognized the woman who had just spoken.

"Saela?" she cried. "Is that you?"

And the little slave girl, barely older than Varena grinned up at her. No longer a girl, and most definitely not a slave, she stood proud and tall, and comfortable in her leather armor, and with the long dagger she sharpened as the conversation continued.

"What happened to you?" Kalie nearly squealed, pulling her outside where the heavy night vapors acted to dampen sound. "When I last saw you, you were so…"

"Weak? Frightened? Clueless?" Saela laughed. "Yes, I was all those things. But not anymore."

"I thought you wanted to learn to weave and sew."

"I did. And then I realized that all the wonder my new life held would be snuffed out if someone didn't stop Varlas and his horde. And then my new family told me I could study that instead of weaving, if I wanted." Saela's eyes were hard, but there was a reckless joy in their depths as well. "And I wanted."

Kalie would have loved to talk all night with her old friends, but there was too much work to be done.

A short visit with the three survivors from Starfall produced little new information, but they had created a good map of the town and the surrounding villages, forests, and other features. Otera got busy copying it onto large piece of leather which could be rolled up and easily carried. Lanara worked with the other healers, who were still trying to help the three recover from their ordeal.

Kalie was up most of the night, walking around the island, and speaking with the men and women who had created the island in the lake, and those who drained the nearby swamps to create farmland.

In the morning, she presented her idea to those interested in hearing—which included most of the town.

"I believe we can finally create the path which will lead our unwelcome guests to the field below Stonebridge where we will defeat them, once and for all." She pointed to the struggling farms and half-drowned meadows between the marsh and the forest beyond. Past them, the way they had traveled, were more marsh and lakes. Those who lived there traveled the land using rafts and narrow plank walkways.

"See this land as a horseman would," Kalie continued. "Forests are dangerous. Water cannot be crossed. If you were to remove those planks you walk on, and drain enough marshland to create a pathway, and drain enough water from the meadows so horses could walk without getting bogged down—"

"You'd have a long, thin ribbon of green!" Malor said.

"Leading straight to Stonebridge," said Lanara.

"Not quite," said Kalie. "There would still be about a day's ride through forest and hill we couldn't do much about. But the point is there would be grazing for the horde's animals, and land that will be open enough to make them feel secure."

"What you are describing will take time!" said a middle aged man, who had done this work all his life. "If these monsters are to be here in half a moonspan as you say, there is no way we can have these changes finished—"

"Perhaps they do not need to be finished," said one of the warriors born in the east. "The beastmen need only see this as their only way through the land. The water-meadows need be just dry enough to keep the horses from shying away. Wet green grass will be a feast for them, and seem like gold to the warriors, for it means healthy mounts."

"It will not stay green for long without water," said a priestess. "You will change the land in a way that may do it much harm."

"The farmers who live there would lose their farms, at the very least," said one of the marsh people.

Kalie nodded. "Yes, the crops nearly ready for harvest would have to go to the beastmen, and the owners would have to flee."

"But they would think we'd given up," said an old woman who had helped to create the farmland. "They would have food—and a strip of grazing land so thin they would have to keep moving west to keep the animals well-fed and strong."

"And, if necessary, we could distract them with small bands of warriors who would attack from the forest and then quickly disappear."

"Enough to convince them that there's something we don't want them to find in the west?" said a grizzled old warrior. "That could work."

"But only if the people here agree," Kalie said, meeting the eye of the man she recognized as the strongest voice in the council. "The changes we make to the land could alter things for years to come. Even your marsh could be affected."

"All the people of Goddess Lands are making sacrifices," he said in a voice that carried easily. "We can hardly sit safe in our marsh and do nothing while monsters ride across our lands. I say we at least try it." He shot Kalie an amused glance. "You realize you are suggesting something that has never been done?"

"Oh, she does that a lot!" called Saela. Laughter rippled through the fog, and the inevitable meetings began.

"I forgot how persuasive you can be," Otera said, and they prepared to retrieve their horses and continue east. "You know, if this works, we might keep the enemy out of Stonebridge altogether. Get them lost in the forests, gather all our warriors together and form two groups...we could trap them between two forces who know the land. One waiting for them in the forest, and the larger force, pouring out of Stonebridge. They'd be cut off from food and grazing land."

Kalie nodded. "Brilliant." Then, for the first time, she grinned at Otera. "Did you just say 'our warriors'? Men and women? East and west, together?"

Otera grinned back. "Yes, Kalie, I did. I might prefer to win this war with just twenty-four women, but I'm not a fool or a madwoman. No matter how it looks. Now let's find those messengers and send them to carry these ideas to all of our people."

That afternoon, they were on their way to Starfall.

Interlude

King Varlas sat in a wooden chair covered in luxurious furs, finer than anything he had ever owned in the grasslands. His new "tent," a structure built entirely of valuable wood, contained even more luxuries, some quite unknown on the steppes. The woven cloth was softer than a girl's skin, the strange foods delicious, and the wine—amazing. Varlas had come to enjoy this drink quite a lot.

But everything had come at a greater price than he could have imagined when he led his people west.

Nearly half his men, killed by dirt-eaters. Not all the defenders were dirt-eaters; he knew from fighting them that some were warriors of the steppes, as good as any of Varlas's own men. But for every warrior raised as he had been, at least three had been born to the dirt. How, then had this happened? And with so few horses…but now the enemy had many more horses. His horses.

But at last there had been a victory. Varlas now lived in what had surely been the home of the king, in greater luxury than any king on the steppes. Many of his men had joined him in these strange living spaces, for the comforts they offered were significant. Besides, if he was to rule his people, a king must be seen taking for himself the best his new subjects had to offer.

Yet once again, even in victory, almost nothing had gone according to plan. There should have been beautiful women to fill the tent of every man in Varlas's horde, for these dirt-eaters bred like rabbits and this "town", as it was called, had been filled with hundreds of them. But after a moonspan of ugly deaths at the hands of enemies without honor, who hid like cowards and left traps and poison to do their fighting for them, his men craved revenge more than they craved the usual celebrating after a victory. Especially one delayed by so many defeats.

So Varlas had done what was necessary. Torture and death for those who had dared to defy the Wolves of the Gods. Humiliation for those who were spared, especially the women, who dared to take up arms, and make a mockery of true warriors. Only after that were spoils divided, and the men at last able to rest in safety, and enjoy all that they had fought and sacrificed so much for.

Yet he could not escape the fact that not everyone Varlas had defeated had died at the king's order, or in pain. When his men had found the rooms beneath some of the largest buildings, called temples, they had expected to find even greater treasures. Instead they found the bodies of whole families, children nestled peacefully between their parents, empty cups beside them. His men muttered of trickery or madness. The priests spoke of curses. But Varlas knew these people had taken their own lives—and their children's—rather than live as slaves. That knowledge sat uneasily on him. It was not the way things were done. People, even dirt-eaters, were supposed to know their place. Defeated tribes accepted their fate. Their women should be fighting for a place in the bed of a king. Or any mighty warrior who possessed them—and the power to raise them high. Instead...

Varlas flung his goblet across the room, where it struck a wall. It was gold and set with jewels, and made a satisfying thud. His new slaves froze, as they had learned to do when the king was angry. Varlas snapped his fingers. His second wife looked up from anointing her body with the scented oil the new slaves made for her, gave a curt order, and a woman quickly picked up the goblet and brought it to her master. The cup was dented. "Fix it!" he ordered the slave. She in turn gave it to another woman, who scurried from the room.

It made no sense, and infuriated Varlas like few other things had, but these women did not know how to be slaves. They barely knew how to be women. His wives and the new concubines Varlas had acquired from the death of so many of his men had to spend much of every day teaching them.

Yet they could fix anything—men or women, it made no difference. Sickness, injury, that goblet. There was always someone here who could do things his mightiest warriors or most powerful priests could not.   They did these things willingly enough; Varlas's lesson to those he spared had seen to that. Yet sometimes he had the strange sense that it was not fear or cowardice or awe of his greatness that motivated them.

When his queen lay sick and surely dying, these women, shorn and scared as Varlas had ordered, had brought her back from the abyss. The same with some of his men, even now recovering from wounds that should have been fatal. If they were witches, their powers should have vanished once they'd been raped. But if they still had their powers…No! Varlas shook the thought away. They obeyed because there was no choice, as all conquered people did.

Varlas stood, and left the house without

needing to duck through the doorway as he would have in a tent. He walked proudly through his new domain where his men enjoyed their much needed rest, and slaves scurried to do their bidding. Some of his men chose to live traditionally, in tents set up beside the town. Each of his chiefs owned a woman whose beauty had been spared. A few were already pregnant, but even those favored ones behaved strangely, showing little gratitude for their good fortune.

The tribe would rest until the all the food these dirt-eaters grew was brought in and readied for transport. Then they would move west. To the prize that waited beside water so large the far bank could not be seen. Varlas's man in Kariik's pitiful rags of a horde had everything in place. All the Wolves had to do was ride across this strange land that was their new home, and claim what the gods held for them.

Chapter 30

This time as they traveled, Kalie and the others found evidence of the changes wrought in their world. Burned out villages, and farmland turned into battlefields. There were unburied corpses they had to avoid at Lanara's orders, and pitiful bands of refugees who they helped when they could, and prayed for when they could not.

If they had been careful before, they were careful to the extreme now. And when they passed an abandoned village in an area otherwise untouched by the beastmen, every one of them felt their presence. "They're here," whispered Otera.

Kalie looked around, feeling exposed. There was a copse of trees with a stream running through it within easy running distance. The start of a forest lay not far beyond it. Somewhere east lay Starfall. Other than that, there was scrub and thorn bush and grass; easy to see why the horsemen might be headed here.

All the women were on foot now. After a seeing the difficulties some of them had managing the horses, Kalie began to see them as a liability, rather than an asset. Only three of their members could ride as if she were part of her animal, as a steppes warrior could. This was not the time to learn how to work with a horse, Kalie had insisted. When they met a group of their own warriors who had lost a skirmish with Varlas's men, it was an easy decision for the women to give their few horses to the survivors. Lanara had done what she could for them, but the speed of the horses might mean the difference between life and death for the worst injured men and women.

Now, Kalie knew, some of her companions were wishing they still had the horses. But everyone froze as they had trained to do. Everyone sniffed the air and looked for movement. Then the wind brought it: the faint, but unmistakable scent of horses, and men who did not bathe. Then, the smell of stale kumis and grease.

A few moments later, Kalie could see them, a dark smear on the horizon. They appeared to be a raiding party, but it was impossible to know their exact number. And they needed to know their exact number. The smear disappeared into a ravine. Water, Kalie guessed; they would water their horses, and then replenish their own supplies.

Otera looked at Erobia, who had the keenest eyes. Hopefully, thought Kalie, she could also move quietly enough to keep them in her head. Erobia moved silently through the bushes, always keeping downwind. As long as the wind didn't change, they might have a chance. Erobia disappeared, although Kalie could swear she had not taken her eyes from the girl. A few moments later, she slid back into the copse.

"Sixteen of them," she whispered.

Kalie would have counseled retreat. They had all been warned that a two to one advantage was needed in a fight with steppes warriors. But she knew Otera would not listen. And if she were honest with herself, Kalie was ready to stop running and hiding.

Otera divided the women in half. Twelve would take their weapons and hide in the forest. The other half would wait for the enemy—or if necessary, catch their attention. "The half who remain," she said with a grin, "will run screaming to the forest as soon

as the beasts give chase. Five of us will be caught."
She waited for volunteers. Kalie, who would be in the
safety of the forest, was shocked when four women
stepped forward.

"Otera," Kalie began, very aware of the limited
time. "They will rape you; possibly kill you."

"And in doing so they will divide their forces,"
said Otera. "And expose their... vulnerability."

Kalie sensed that some of this had been
planned before she joined the team. But she knew her
job, and it was time to go. It was essential that her
group be hidden in the woods before the enemy
arrived.

Choosing one of the first large firs she came to,
Kalie shimmied up the trunk to a sturdy branch,
stopped to catch her breath, and then climbed higher.
Climbing a tree with all of her gear was harder than
when she had last practiced it. The others fanned out
around her, some, like Kalie, in the trees, others on the
ground, hiding behind the largest trunks.

Kalie had a good view of her twelve
companions, splashing in the stream, laughing and
making all the noise they could. The raiders came into
view, spotted the girls, picked up speed—and still
Otera did not give the order to run. Kalie was
beginning worry that if they kept up their playacting
much longer, the men would smell a trap.

Just then, Otera screamed, echoed by the
others, and they all began running toward the forest.
Several women, she noticed, wore very little, all of it
wet and clinging to their bodies. Yet she knew that
every one of them carried weapons. Otera and two
others grabbed spears from gear scattered beside the
stream, and flung them at the horsemen, while the

others got closer to the forest. By now, Kalie could hear the men laughing—although one seemed to have just lost part of an ear. Faking being a poor shot after months of training was a difficult thing, Kalie knew.

The spear throwers turned and ran for the woods, far behind the others, except for two who lagged behind. As the horsemen rode close enough to catch them, Kalie knocked an arrow, and tried to slow her breathing. Her knuckles were white on both the bow and the string.

Two of the men each managed to grab a fleeing woman, but the others, well practiced, avoided their grasp. Danarie even managed to cut the hand of the man reaching for her. At that, the leader called an order, and the men moved their horses to block the escape of the three women, slid from their horses, and caught the women nearly in a single motion. Another order brought all the warriors to attention.

"You men!" He called names and pointed, dividing his group in half, just as Otera had done. "Go get the rest and bring them to me!"

Some of the men eyed the forest with anger and fear. Others eyed the struggling women with lust and resentment.

"Don't worry!" The leader shouted with a grin. He laid a struggling Erobia across his knees and playfully swatted her bottom. "There will be plenty left for you when you get here. More if you hurry and get your own!" With that, the eight warriors rode for the trees. The remaining men, all on foot now, settled down to enjoy their spoils. The three who had to wait their turn with a woman moved about in a perimeter around their comrades, weapons drawn, and watched the area more sharply than Kalie liked.

The coarse laughter and vile comments coming from the men, along with the sound of clothing ripping and women screaming made Kalie fear she would be sick. But even now the sounds of the women were different from what she remembered of her own experience. And they were about to change in a way no one had heard before.

"Can you believe it?" laughed the man on top of Derona. "They have weapons!" He laughed again as he twisted the knife from her hand, and then ripped the axe from her belt—along with the belt and most of the clothing beneath it.

"We'll teach you how to be real women," laughed the one on top of Otera as he pried her legs apart. "Who knows, you might even like it!" He shoved into her, and his laughter became a scream. The scream grew as Otera rolled on top of him, reached between her legs and removed the knife from the folds in her body where it had been hidden.

"Yes, I think I will!" she cried, stabbing her captor in the stomach, and then in the chest. All four of the other women were now using similar small knives on their attackers.

Kalie drew back and fired, catching square in the back the man who already had his lance poised to strike Derona. Her next arrow missed the second guard, but avoiding it caused him to move directly into the path of Griva's spear. The third guard had Erobia in his grasp as her rapist, barely scratched, lunged at her with his dagger. A rock on the back of his leather-armored head caused the guard to drop Erobia and turn—and then drop like a stone himself as Valeska's second rock caught him square in the forehead. Erobia scrambled to avoid her captor's blade and failed, but the cut along her back and shoulder was not fatal. As her opponent moved for a second try, Erobia lunged at his exposed crotch with both hands, twisting, pulling and with a leap worthy of a cat, burying her face between his legs and biting. Quite hard if his scream was any indication.

Forcing her attention away from the amazing view in the distance, Kalie focused on the eight riders below her. Arrows, spears, and rocks rained down on them. Bolos tangled the legs of two of the horses, and their screams as they went down, crushing their riders, were the only ones Kalie regretted.

Four mounted men made it out of the forest alive, though all were wounded, and one slumped in his saddle and lagged behind. Kalie slid from her tree and followed him almost leisurely. Then she saw Trisa, pinned down by a rapist, who despite the knife in his back, twisted Trisa's hand and planted the girl's own knife into her throat.

Otera, only an instant too late to save Trisa, uttered a scream unlike anything Kalie had ever heard as she smashed in the back of the man's skull with an axe before he had a chance to look up.

With a bolo, Lanara toppled the horse of the wounded man who was trying to flee. Kalie stared a moment, then returned to the fight. She had not thought the healer would pick up a weapon of any kind. But from the corner of her eye, she saw Lanara made no move to harm the warrior, only wept as she cut the throat of the screaming horse whose leg she had broken.

Three men escaped on horseback, one pausing to pick up a wounded companion. Of the rest, nine lay dead or dying, while the three remaining were tied up to await interrogation.

Standing in shock for a moment, the reality of their victory began to seep in. A ragged cheer arose from deep inside them, filling the land. But it died as the bodies of four young women were laid out before Lanara.

Trisa and Area were dead. It was clear from the look on Lanara's face that Derona would be soon. Lanara gave Kalie a cup of wine mixed with syrup of the poppy, nodded toward Derona, and hurried to tend Griva, who despite the blood that covered her from a dozen different wounds, might yet live.

While Malana and Valeska assisted Lanara, Kalie gently lifted Derona's head and fed her the pain-killing drink in tiny sips. On her other side, Otera held her hand. It was only then that Kalie noticed Otera's other arm was broken. When Derona slipped into a deep sleep—one from which she would not awake, but would at least be free of pain—Kalie took hold of Otera's good arm. "Let's get that arm splinted, shall we?"

Otera did not seem to hear her. "She was with me from the first day the world changed. And she never left my side." Otera's voice was raw with emotion and unshed tears.

"And she never regretted even one of those days." Kalie felt stupid; she didn't even know if that were true. But it was all she could think of to say. "She lived to see her dream of revenge. To make it happen."

"It's all any of us dreamed about," said Otera. "Just now, when we killed those men, when the others went running back to their chief, beaten by women, I felt...I don't know how I felt. Whole, perhaps. I dreamed of it ever since…. But I never thought that living that dream would mean losing three of my sisters."

Kalie was about to point out that no one fought a war without losing friends, but thought better of it. Then Lanara, finished with Griva, who now slept fitfully, came and sat beside Otera. "I need to fix your arm," she said.

"Leave it!" snapped Otera, but eventually allowed Lanara to splint it, accepting nothing for the pain but a stick to bite on. Kalie suspected that Otera might require pain for sustenance as much as she needed food, but again kept her thoughts to herself.

By then, the three prisoners were fully awake and becoming noisy. One, Kalie knew, couldn't help himself, although, as any warrior of the steppes, he was trying to keep silent. He was the one Lanara had felled from his horse, and he was bleeding badly, with at least a few broken bones. The second had been hit on the head, and was just now regaining consciousness, and looking around in confusion. The third, and youngest, was badly bruised and probably had a broken bone or two, but even so, his words surprised Kalie.

"Get that bitch who heals over here!" he shouted. "And bring some wine!"

At that, Otera nearly smiled. She started to move in the prisoner's direction, but Malana held her back while Lanara finished her work. It was Kalie who reached him first. She squatted on her heels, staring intently into his eyes. They were hazel, and filled with hate.

"What's wrong?" he asked, gritting his teeth against his pain. "Can't you half-demon cunts understand me?"

"Unfortunately for you, some of us can," Kalie
said. She put the point of her knife against his chin,
and slowly moved his head up, until the position was
painful, and fear began to replace the hate in the young
warrior's eyes.

"I want to ask you something," she continued.
"If you answer truthfully, you might live through the
night. Or at least be granted a warrior's death." She
leaned closer, pricking the man's skin enough to draw
a few drops of blood. He held his breath.

"You came to our land, murdering and raping,
stealing from real men and women like the lowest
scavengers that you are. Now you attacked what you
thought were helpless women, and finally got a small
part of the justice you deserved. So why do you think
anyone here is going to help you?"

Those hazel eyes were wide with shock. Kalie
pulled her knife away and waited. When he could
speak the young man's voice was respectful and tinged
with fear. "We were told that dirt-eaters were weak
fools who try to make friends with everyone. And that
your witch-women are under some kind of spell that
forces them to help everyone, even enemies. I...I
thought I need only command you."

"In part, you are right," said Lanara coming to
stand beside Kalie and her prisoner. Malana stood
beside her, translating everything the two had said.
Kalie translated the healer's words for the prisoner.
"But we help everyone, even cowards like you,
because it is our sacred calling. Because it is the right
thing to do. Do you even know what that means?
Kalie, do those words even translate?"

"They translate," she said. It was clear from

the man's face he understood a woman had just called him a coward.

"Tell that ugly crow she will die for those words!" he shouted.

"Before or after she heals your wounds?" Kalie asked as Lanara went to help the man with the most serious injuries. "Really, coju," she uttered the insult mildly, which made it worse. "Why do you speak to us this way? Are you wishing for an even more painful, humiliating death than what you dole out to your victims?" She nodded to Otera. "That one wants to castrate you before she even starts asking you questions. Do you think after what you did to these women, anyone will stop her?"

Again the fear was back, and this time Hazel Eyes couldn't push it away. "You can't do that!" he whimpered. "We...we are your masters. We were only doing what warriors do. And you're just women. You shouldn't even be allowed to hold a weapon! Where are your men? I demand to speak with the person in charge!"

Kalie grinned as Otera's shadow, longer than usual in the westering sun, fell over them. "As you command, Master. She's right here."

Chapter 31

In the end, Otera castrated Hazel Eyes and the man who had been knocked out briefly. Then she stabbed Hazel Eyes in the gut, cutting his throat when his screams no longer pleased her. Lanara would not let Otera near the man she was tending, but it proved to be unnecessary. He provided enough useful information about the details of Starfall and the forces occupying it that at last Otera was persuaded by her own followers—many of whom had been sick during the interrogation—to leave the two men behind in the morning.

Kalie, who once might have enjoyed watching Otera work—or even participated in it herself—now wished only to walk far away from the sights, sounds and smells in front of her. But Malana had already done that, so Kalie was forced to stay and translate.

"How many warriors are in Starfall?" Otera asked the injured man whose name, Lanara had learned, was Talik.

"About twenty four satraps," Talik said, seeming puzzled as to why a woman would want to know.

"A satrap contains forty warriors," Kalie explained.

"And how many captives?"

Talik drank the wine Lanara gave him and shrugged. "Not even one in each tent. The wives have been complaining. They expected many slaves."

Kalie caught Otera's good arm to stop her from striking Talik. "You've caused enough pain for one day," she said roughly. "Ask your questions so we can be gone from this place!"

"How long do you mean to remain in Starfall?" Otera asked.

"The last of the food will be used in a great feast in about two hands of days. Some will remain to rule in our king's name. The rest will ride west, to complete our conquest."

"Where?" Otera looked like she was about to leap out of her skin.

"A rich town, near a great water, with enough grass for our horses, and room for our tents." He drank more wine and began to drift off to sleep.

"Wait!" Otera shook him. "Will you travel as one horde, or in many groups?"

"I don't know," said Talik, and this time, Otera let him sleep.

"We have learned much," Otera said, looking ready to drop from exhaustion.

"I'm surprised he spoke so easily. Even after what you did to his spear-brothers." Kalie looked up and saw that Malana had returned, and was looking away from the mutilated corpse of the arrogant man whose name they did not know. "Warriors like him will usually die under torture before giving up information to the enemy."

"Perhaps he thought we were too weak or stupid to do anything with it," said Otera. "Or perhaps keeping his balls was more important than his so-called honor." She stood up and began to speak to her warriors about their great victory today, and the loss of friends who would never be forgotten. Kalie walked away, into the gathering shadows of dusk until the only sounds were the soothing murmur of crickets. She sat, watching the sky grow dark, and the campfire light up in the distance, until Lanara came to join her.

"How's Otera?" Kalie asked.

Lanara shook her head. "I don't want to talk about Otera."

"How about the others, then?"

"Fine. At least as fine as anyone who's experienced such violence, and committed it themselves can be." Lanara's tone suggested no one was fine now, or should be. After a long silence she asked, "Why did he speak to us that way, do you think? The rude one, giving orders and shouting insults while he was tied up?"

"Yet another question I don't have an answer for, although I really wanted to know. I meant it, when I asked him. Perhaps Malana would know."

"I've already asked her. If she knows, she's not saying."

"I suppose…did anyone get his name?" Lanara shook her head. "I suppose he answered as truthfully as he could. Nothing in his experience prepared him to see women as anything but subservient and easily frightened. And everything he was told about us must have convinced him that no matter what happened—even a defeat he couldn't believe in—he could bully his way out of it."

Lanara cocked her head, considering. "Like his rudeness was a kind of weapon after he'd lost all his others? That even tied up on the ground we'd bow to his natural superiority if he just pushed hard enough?"

"Something like that." Both sighed, still mystified. Kalie asked, "How are you, Lanara? You used a weapon, lost friends and then used your skill to save a man who did things that surely made your skin crawl. It can't have been an easy day for you, either."

She could sense Lanara smiling in the darkness. "It wasn't easy for any of us. But if someday I can tell my grandchildren about it, and it's nothing to them but a scary story on a winter's night, it will have been worth it."

The next morning, the women packed up, riding the horses of the men who had attacked them. The two surviving men were left untied by the stream with food, medicine and water bags, but no weapons.

"Can't you leave Morik a knife?" asked Talik. He stared at them, especially Otera, through haunted eyes, as if they were demons from a nightmare who stubbornly refused to let him wake up. "After what you did to him…" Talik paled and turned his eyes away from his spear-brother with the bloody bandage between his legs, who starred with empty eyes into the sky. "He cannot live this way. Could you not…?"

"And the women you've raped?" Danarie asked. "Did you ever ask them how they would live with it? Did you ever ask the parents whose children you murdered if they wanted to live? Or cared about the answer?"

"But that's different!" Talik began. "Those things are just a part of war. This—"

"This will be a part of war from now on, for as long as your people choose to wage it," said Otera, calmly mounting the horse which had once belonged to the party's leader. "Please tell your people that, if you ever see them again. And tell them that, from now on, a man who does not know how to use his penis properly will have it removed. I'm sure if you give it some thought, you will see the logic of it." With that, she signaled her people and headed east.

They were soon back to hiding in whatever cover could find, which was limited. As they approached the town of Starfall, it became clear that everything that would burn was now a smoldering pile of ashes, and small trees and bushes that survived the fire had been pulled out by the roots. From a rocky hillside, Kalie and two other scouts saw the forest that had once nestled the villages surrounding the town. Most had apparently resisted burning, perhaps because the unseasonably damp weather of late. Several large trees had been brutally hacked to death, stumps standing like jagged teeth; a testament to the rage of men who could not abide anything they could not control, but most of the forest still stood.

Kalie looked away, and got her first look at the enemy, firmly settled in their new home—and her old one.

Varlas's men rode a perimeter around the outer villages that had once clustered around the town like baby ducks around their mother. Most were deserted, some burned to the ground. In the distance, a large group of rag-clad, skeletal men and women worked to bring in the last of the grain from a wheat field, under the watchful eyes of mounted warriors. Similar work seemed to be going on at the edge of Kalie's vision. In empty fields and in open land outside of the town, warriors drilled, exercised their horses or enjoyed food and women under the few remaining stands of trees. None, Kalie saw at once, would provide cover for an attack, which was probably why they still stood.

Where two villages once stood, over a hundred felt tents squatted bleakly. Because it was mid-day, most of the horsewomen were busy preparing food for

their men. Kalie finally got her first look at the
women and children of Starfall to be spared the
beastmen's slaughter. She could see only a few, and
from a distance, but it was clear that they were hungry,
sick, ill-used, and something more; something she
could not identify. She watched as a nomad woman
knocked a little girl down for some invisible
infraction, and then began beating her with a switch.

Kalie had seen enough. She ghosted silently
down the hill, disturbing not a single pebble. Danarie
and Malana did the same. Back in camp they gave
their report.

"The forest is nearly intact," Danarie told them.
"Room enough to shelter us all for several days. And
hopefully, feed us." Their supplies were nearly gone.

"There are probably at least one thousand
warriors spread out there. And others out scouting or
raiding," said Malana

"There are not enough tents for all of the
people gathered here," said Kalie. "At least half of
them, men, women and children, must be living in the
town."

"Strange," murmured Malana. "Those men
hate being enclosed. And the women distrust anything
new."

"Perhaps not so strange," said Lanara. "The
houses were designed for comfort, and are filled with
luxuries. Soft beds, rich furs, even fragrant wood for
burning, given the types of trees that grew here. And
still grow," she added hastily.

"Could they be trying out a new way of
living?" Danarie asked with a worried frown.

Otera shook her head. "It doesn't matter. For
now, we must reach the forest, find food, and plan our

next move. We will wait until dark."

Kalie wanted to go home. She had not nursed a baby since leaving the marsh-dwellers, and Alessa's tea was nearly gone. Each day she seemed to express less milk. She missed her children, and did not support the belief that twenty women, some injured, could take on a horde of over a thousand brutal, well-trained fighters with nothing but anger, determination and metal weapons.

But turning around now and making her way home alone seemed like a worse idea. When night fell, Kalie was ready with the others.

Since the invaders had little experience with the forests of the west, they lacked the tools and experience to successfully remove large trees. But they had done enough to create a clear area over three hundred paces wide between the space they occupied and the nearest cover. The quarter moon and cloudless sky helped the women find their way quickly, and without stumbling over exposed roots, but made it harder to blend in with the night.

They were nearly to the woods when a shout made their blood run cold. "More target practice!" called a voice in the language of the east.

"These dirt-eaters never learn," laughed another.

As one, the women ran for the safety of the trees, not daring to wonder if the beastmen might have overcome their fear and be waiting for them inside the forest as well. But it wasn't likely any of those on foot could outrun horses and find out.

Kalie, one of the few on horseback, knew it was her job to cover the escape of those on foot. When the pursuers were close enough, she turned in her saddle and fired an arrow—a trick the horsemen had yet to perfect. Me as well, she thought as the shot went wide.

But she tried again, along with Otera and the three others who rode, while the rest went screaming toward the forest.

"Hey!" called the leader raising a fist, and causing his men to slow down and bunch together. "Those are the witches who attacked Brenak and his men!"

More like fought back against their unprovoked attack, thought Kalie, taking advantage of the brief pause to turn her horse and ride with the others toward the trees.

"Varlas wants them alive!" cried the horseman. "Get them! Now! Don't let a single one of those witches escape!" They spurred their horses to unbelievable speeds.

No hope now, thought Kalie. But the thought of being taken alive, after the insult they had offered that arrogant king turned her blood to ice. I will make them kill me, she thought. They will not take me alive again. At that moment, Kalie's horse foundered, pitching her head over heels to the ground. She rolled as she had been taught, broken bow dangling from her shoulder, dagger ready.

A greasy hand grabbed her arm, twisting viciously as the warrior tried to pull her onto his horse. But Kalie knew what to do. Using her good hand to rescue her dagger from her captive one, Kalie dug the blade into the horse's flank. His scream made her forget her own problems for a moment, but now it was Kalie's attacker who pitched forward, struggling to control his foundering animal, and allowing Kalie's escape.

She ran, but now the battle was mostly occurring on foot, the warriors just as relentless that way as mounted. She had nearly reached Otera, who, still mounted, turned and held out a hand pull Kalie up behind her. Then Otera's body went rigid, her hand falling from Kalie's. Two men worked to pull the large woman from her horse, while a third grabbed Kalie from behind. Kalie stared in horror, expecting to see a spear protruding from Otera's back. Instead, blood matted her blond hair. Otera had been hit a glancing blow, and was only stunned. Regaining consciousness while the men were still grappling with her, she began to fight.

The startled warriors nearly dropped her. Had Otera her full strength she might have escaped. As it was, they held on and began stripping off her armor— and then the clothing beneath it. "It's her, their leader," said one of the men. "The one who controls all the others; makes them act like they're warriors instead of women."

"They're women, all right," the one in charge said as he untied his belt. "I intend to show them just how true that is. Hold her down and I'll let you go next."

"Varlas has special plans for this one," argued the underling.

"Varlas said to make sure there powers are gone, first," said the man who held Kalie. "And everyone knows the way to do that." Kalie felt his erection hard against her back. "Watch the show, pretty thing," he said into her ear, licking her face with a tongue that stank of kumis and meat. "If you learn something that pleases me, I might—"

He gasped and let go of Kalie, clawing at the arrow that had appeared in his neck. The man about to rape Otera leapt up and raised his spear, only to have his head split in half, brains and blood spraying around the axe still embedded in it. Even in the dark Kalie recognized the only man big enough to wield and axe that size. He freed the axe and gave chase to the third warrior, who didn't get far.

"Borik?" she cried.

And then the smaller man beside him was beside Kalie, the bow he had used to kill her captor still in his hand as his other reached out to Kalie.

"Are you all right?" Riyik asked, his face white in the moonlight.

"I am now," said Kalie.

Chapter 32

Warriors were pouring out of the forest, but they were allies; men and women wearing the leather armor in the style of the west. The fighting was intense; everyone, even Otera who should not have been able to, joined the battle, until Varlas's men finally retreated.

"Hurry!" yelled a familiar voice, and Kalie realized it was Kariik. "Everyone, to the forest. "Ladies, stay behind one of us. The ground is covered in horse spikes."

"I thought you had to stop using them," Kalie said. "Isn't Varlas using his captives to test for them?"

"He was," said Riyik. "But too many of them just scampered up the trees and escaped."

"Escaped the warrior's arrows?" asked Lanara.

"They were usually too distracted to do that," replied Riyik. "You see, we always keep at least a few of our own in the forest to cover any escape." He gazed hungrily at Kalie. "Like yours."

Kalie felt the same hunger for her lover, but had too many questions. "Isn't the forest where you live?"

"We'll show you where we live," said Kariik. "Just be very careful to disturb nothing."

Through twisting paths in the dark forest, Kalie and her companions followed their allies—about thirty of them—to a rocky clearing. Surrounding the rocks were a perfect circle of very large, very old trees.

"This looks like a temple," said Danarie.

"It was," said a warrior who had probably been a priestess before the horde came to her land. "Those trees were planted long before memory. And as you probably know, in ancient times, temples were often connected to a network of underground caves."

Kariik led the way through an opening Kalie would not have seen had Kariik not just disappeared into it. Carefully, one at a time, everyone slipped though. Borik was last, squeezing himself in with great difficulty.

Rough steps were carved into the rock as they descended a tunnel, which in turn, opened into a large, dimly lit chamber. It was roughly circular, lit with oil lamps and containing perhaps one hundred people, who were engaged in activities ranging from sharpening weapons to repairing gear, cooking food and even playing games with dice and chips of colored stone. Bedrolls and other gear line one wall.

"Our healers are set up over here." Kariik indicated a short tunnel which led to a side chamber. While not injured, Kalie was curious, and wanted to make certain her friends who did need care got the best. Inside the small, but better lit chamber were all the familiar sights and smells of bundles of herbs hanging from drying racks, pots of ointments, and low cots arranged in a neat row. An elderly man, middle aged woman, and a boy and a girl on the verge of adulthood fell to work as if they'd been working together for years.

"My sisters first," Otera said, as the women tried to lead her to a padded leather pallet. She turned to Borik, who had also followed the injured. "I didn't need your help!" she snapped. "I was doing fine by myself. It will take a lot more than a mere two of them to kill me. I just wanted you to be clear on that."

"Of course," Borik said with a nod. Someone

finally got Otera to sit down to be examined, and Kalie sidled up to Borik.

"I think that was her way of saying thank you," she said.

"I know," said Borik.

"I'd still like to wring her neck. You saved her life and she—"

"She's a proud woman," said Borik, as if Otera's behavior was not the complete opposite of how a steppes warrior acted when his spear brother saved his life. "I understand."

Kalie watched Borik watching Otera, wondered at the strange image that stirred in her mind. Borik? And Otera? Definitely not. And she would not wish Otera on a gentle soul like Borik.

The next thing she knew, Riyik was leading her down a twisting maze of tunnels to a small chamber, obviously for sleeping small groups. "Where are our children?" he asked as soon as they were alone.

"With your sister. There are plenty of women to nurse Melora until I get back."

"Do you still have your milk?"

Touched that a man of his background would even know of such things, Kalie nodded. "For now."

"I should be angry at you for leaving them, and running off into danger like a fool," said Riyik. "But I'm too happy to see you."

"Good," said Kalie, pulling him closer. "Because I've just now gotten over my anger at you for running off into danger without even telling me."

"I didn't plan it this way," he said wrapping his around her and squeezing her until she nearly forgot everything else. "But we both knew when we brought danger to this land, we would have to be in the front of it."

"How many live here? Do you have a plan to move against the horde?

"About three hundred warriors are here, although not all at the same time. We scout and coordinate with similar groups hiding in caves, and canyons. As for plans? Too many! At least one for every group here."

"How many groups?"

"Kariik leads the remains of Aahk. I speak for the far west. About four others from other corners of this land. Of course, because we represent this land, everyone has an equal voice."

"No wonder nothing gets done," Kalie sighed.

They looked at each other, each thinking there was something they could do, although it had nothing to do with defeating King Varlas and his men.

Then a shout for everyone to meet in the main chamber put a stop to that. With a shared sigh and one last kiss, Kalie and Riyik joined a line of people streaming down the tunnel in an orderly fashion, and then filling the main chamber to capacity. The various leaders Riyik had mentioned stood against a mostly smooth wall of rock, with faded images of animals painted on it. Riyik went to join them.

To Kalie's surprise, Otera, covered with bandages and a new cast on her arm, followed him.

Kariik spoke first. "Our new Lady of Battle has brought important news," he said nodding to Otera. "It appears our spies—those who went to gain Varlas's trust and were never heard from again—may have succeeded."

"Varlas intends to move the bulk of his warriors to the very spot we have chosen for battle," said Otera. "Probably very soon."

"That would make sense," said a man who spoke for the lands around Green Bower. "Those locusts have stripped the land of everything edible. They'll have to go somewhere, or send out many more parties to bring food in."

"Which hasn't gone well," said another man, "thanks to our attack bands, harrying their every step."

"If the marsh-dwellers have succeeded in the plan we left them with," said Kalie, "the horde will likely travel in the direction of Stonebridge, whether they plan to or not."

"But the amazing thing," said a young woman, who had been training in a distant village when her home of Starfall was attacked, "is that they seem to want to go there. All we have to do is let them, and wait for them at the river with all of our forces."

To Kalie it sounded a little too amazing; that there was something here she should be seeing, but could not.

"But Varlas plans to leave men here to hold Starfall—and our few surviving relatives," said a local man. "If we allow them to stay dug in as they are, we'll have to fight two battles. And we're looking at hunger and homelessness this winter, even in the best outcome."

"That is a terrible thing," said one of Kariik's warriors. "But if Varlas wants to divide his forces, I say, let him! Fighting two small groups has a better chance of success than one large one."

"Especially after the way you people botched the first battle," said the warrior beside him. Probably brothers, Kalie guessed, noting the family resemblance. "If you'd made a better stand, Varlas wouldn't be living in your chief's lodge, and your people wouldn't be waiting for rescue."

"We're not as experienced as your people are in the ways of murder and death," a local man said hotly.

"You say that like it's a bad thing," said the warrior, looking confused.

"Let's stay with the matter at hand," Riyik said quickly. "Two battles or one?"

There was much arguing back and forth. Kalie could see the wisdom of both, although she preferred a single battle at Stonebridge—as long as her side could determine the conditions under which they fought.

A hush fell over the room. Kalie looked up to see an elderly priestess leading a small group into the chamber. They were emaciated. Some limped on badly injured feet. And the women among them were bald, but for a few tufts on their scalps like badly shorn sheep.

Kalie knew at once that these people had recently escaped Starfall, and more, she realized what she had seen, but not understood, while spying on the occupation.

"What happened to your hair?" Malana asked.

Several people were helping to settle the group on blankets and cushions brought by healers, and a few threw Malana reproachful looks for her tactlessness. But Kalie knew that everyone who arrived with her wanted to know the answer. Especially when, on closer look, scars left from burning and cutting became apparent on many faces and arms.

One of the women spoke up quietly. People strained to hear her. "I am Riana. After the fighting

was over; after Varlas had…won. After the monsters
had killed so many of us," Riana caught her breath.
Someone brought her water. "Varlas announced that
any woman who had taken up arms and pretended to
be a warrior would be denied the…" Riana choked,
drank more water and continued. "The protection
women were normally accorded after a battle."

"We later learned that meant the chance to
entice our masters with our beauty and willing ways,"
said another. "To bear their children and become
concubines rather than slaves."

"Not that anyone would have done such a
thing," said a third woman. "But Vargas made quite a
show of stripping us of our beauty." She fingered her
shorn scalp, and gingerly touched the ragged scar on
her face that had been treated with soothing ointment.

"He said if we thought we were warriors, he
would allow us the privilege of looking like warriors."
With a gasp, Kalie realized that the marks cut or
burned into many of the women, and some of the men,
were a kind of parody of the scars and tattoos that the
warriors wore. As she met Malana's gaze across the
room, Kalie saw Malana had seen the same thing.

"Then they gave us to their women, to learn to
be slaves, and thus keep our lives a while longer."
Riana's voice was devoid of emotion. "Some of those
women seemed happy at first. They would have
slaves to do the work who would not be of any interest
to their husbands."

"But our ugliness was not much of a deterrent,"
said a girl of about thirteen years.

"Some of the men seemed to find it exciting,"
said another. "'I've never fitted my shaft into a
warrior's cunt before!' That's what the beast I was

given to used to say when he…" She stopped, then got up and left the chamber.

"They did not mutilate the little girls, or cut their hair," said Riana. "They said it will be the job of the beastwomen to teach them proper behavior; how to be modest women. So someday they will know the joy of pleasing a man and perhaps even becoming a wife."

"How many…" Otera seemed to be having trouble finding her voice. "How many…? How many captives are still there?"

A man spoke up. "About three hundred when I was last there. Fewer now for certain. I am Cresson, and I spent much time with this monster Varlas, for I studied the nomad tongue when I was an acolyte for many moonspans before they arrived. I foolishly believed I could broker a peace between our peoples." Cresson snorted, but that seemed to cause pain to the cuts and burns on his face.

"How did so many of you escape?" Danarie asked.

"Some did when we were sent to show the warriors where the horse spikes were, using our bare feet," said another man. "If we were injured we were left behind. To die, I suppose our captors thought. But we were picked up by our friends here."

"Always watching," said Borik.

"Others escaped up trees, although many died that way," said Riana. "And the rest slipped away at night, or on foraging expeditions." She looked puzzled. "It was as if those beasts thought that once we had been tortured and named slaves, we would never think to grab the first opportunity to leave, despite knowing the land, and having friends close by."

"Capture while trying to escape meant death by torture," said Cresson. "Perhaps they thought that was enough frighten us away from trying."

Kalie knew now why they had been allowed to meet the survivors of Starfall and its villages. There was no question of abandoning those who were still captives, not even for the advantage that splitting the enemy forces might prove later in the war.

They had to get those people out now. And they had to reduce the number of able-bodied warriors as much as they could in the process. Kalie suspected most people here were looking forward to that part.

"I have an idea," she said.

Chapter 33

"I should really learn to keep my mouth shut," Kalie said early the next morning as two women from Starfall fitted her in the rags they had been wearing, careful to make sure both knives strapped to her thighs were concealed. Dyes made from berries would resemble scars in various stages of healing. Or so they hoped.

"Like that's ever going to happen," said Riyik, already dressed like a captive. He ran his hand over Kalie's newly shorn scalp. "Your beautiful hair!" he sighed.

"If I live, it will grow back. You're the one I'm worried about, Riyik! Your muscles are bulging through those rags, and you're far too well-fed! At least I lost enough weight recently to almost pass for one of them."

"I'll be in the fields, where the overseers will be too drunk or too busy with the women to notice. And we won't need much time. Kalie? Promise me: no extra heroics. We get in and out as planned, and save as many as we can. We won't be able to rescue everyone."

"I promise. I want to be gone from here as much as you do." Kalie kissed her lover, and met his gaze. "You promise me the same." Riyik did.

They joined the other six members of their party. Malana, whose lovely blond hair was gone, looked nervous. As Otera was even now reminding her, she had never been on this kind of mission. But Malana, like Kalie and Cresson, who was also going, spoke the horsemen's tongue. Gathering intelligence was as important as all the other things they would be doing. Otera would have shaved her head in a heartbeat, but her broken arm and other injuries were keeping her back this time.

Darvo, a young farmer who had escaped during the original attack was going to try to rescue his family, and perhaps atone for running from the fight in the first place. Riana had insisted on coming, and was joined by Selima, recently escaped. They had no trouble looking the part. It seemed to Kalie that only their burning hatred of the tribe and desire to rescue those still captive kept them from collapsing under the weight of their fear.

The nomad camp was still waking when the women, carrying firewood approached. It was a slave's job, and no one would question a few industrious slaves getting the wood early in the hopes of pleasing the women whose moods meant life and death to them. The men would have a harder time slipping in among the field workers. Kalie offered up one last prayer, and hurried to her work. She built up the first cooking fire she came to as high as she dared on this hot summer morning. At least this time she would be posing as a slave for less than a day, and not more than a year.

She passed the morning working among women too exhausted and dead inside to notice a new face. But when she whispered to them that help had arrived, and to be ready to run to the forest as soon as the signal was given, they noticed, and they began to spread the word. As she cooked a porridge made from the grain and fruit the true owners of this land had grown, keeping her head low, Kalie felt, more than heard the message spreading among the people of the

Goddess.

"We will have to put the plan into effect soon," said Malana. "The wives can already see the change in their slaves." It was true; the mood in the camp was shifting like the warm wind blowing through. But the wind was blowing toward the dry wooden buildings of Starfall, just as it had the last few days. As long as it continued like that, their plan had a chance to succeed.

"The horsewomen and their children are nearly finished eating," said Kalie. "Selima and I can clean up. Go arrange the distraction like we planned, and tell Riana to get the strongest ready to help the weakest. Then get into position." Everyone nodded and went to their posts.

By now, Riyik and the others would be helping to store the harvest. Hopefully in sheds that were upwind, but there was no help for that. A scream made Kalie drop the pot she was scrubbing. A beastwoman was beating a slave—but it wasn't the slave who was screaming. The skinny bald woman had risen up, grabbed the switch from her startled mistress, and struck back. And kept striking. While horrified wives began screaming and rushing to help their friend, other slaves, armed with sticks and rocks turned on their tormenters.

It was a sight anyone who had ever been a slave dreamed of seeing, and Kalie wished she could stand there and watch it. It was the distraction she had ordered; the easiest one for these desperate women, fueled by rage, to create. But Kalie's part was crucial. With a burning stick in each hand, she ran to the tent farthest from the town. The wind was strong at her back as she plunged the first brand into the felt tent. Heavily impregnated with the natural oil of sheep's wool, the tent caught fire at once. With the second brand, she set the next tent on fire.

Malana, meanwhile had run with her two brands to the edge of the wood-built town of Starfall. The wind carried the fire as they had hoped, and soon the proud conquerors were reduced to a screaming mass of confusion. "This way!" Kalie shouted, determined to lead as many people as she could to the temporary safety of the forest, and the warriors waiting to cover their escape. But the distance seemed so much greater than it had this morning when she'd arrived.

No matter, these people knew their land, and there were enough level headed women here to help lead. "Come with us if you want to live!" she shouted to the screaming horsewomen. They were past the last of the tents, coughing on oily black smoke, when the first warriors opened fire. An arrow knocked Riana off her feet. Another pinned a fleeing captive to a burning tent.

Fools, thought Kalie, dodging more arrows as she tried to free the woman trapped against the tent. They should be saving their families and their horses, not killing warriors who were finally fighting back. Weren't they supposed to respect their enemies?

The newly freed slave was dead, her body already burning. Kalie started to go to Riana, but was stopped by a sound from within the tent. A baby was screaming.

"No!" she moaned. She had to get out of here. She had promised Riyik; promised everyone, and the plan was actually working. But as the flames licked the tent, the cries growing more desperate, Kalie took a deep breath, covered her face with a rag torn from her clothes, and ran inside the tent. Flames were everywhere and the tent would collapse into a bonfire at any moment. But there was the baby, miraculously untouched, and nearly within reach.

Kalie pushed a leather cauldron into the fire that was trying to reach the baby, slowing it only a moment, as the hungry flames worked to devour the tough leather. Scooping up the baby, she ran back out, full tilt into a screaming warrior with a lance raised and poised to strike the woman at his feet. With her free hand, Kalie slid one of her knives from its sheath at her thigh, dropped to her knees and replaced it— point first—into the matching thigh of the warrior. He screamed again and drove his lance at Kalie, who barely scrambled out of the way in time. He made a grab for her, and would have caught her by her hair— if she'd had any. Pulling the sobbing woman to her feet, Kalie dragged her from the inferno, knowing that if another attack came, she would have no free hands with which to fight.

But now the captives had their own warriors to cover their escape, and the enemy was too busy fleeing the fire to do much damage. But the desperate screams from within the town made clear that many would not escape. Kalie could only hope that most of them were enemy warriors, and kept running.

In the midst of the heat and stench, Kalie felt something warm dripping down her front. Tearing away her rags, she searched for the wound, only to find her milk was flowing. The baby's cries had awakened it.

She pushed its tiny rosebud mouth onto the breast that felt heaviest. The cries stopped and a wonderful feeling flowed through Kalie. She dropped the hand of the woman beside her, who by now was able to keep up on her own, and kept the baby balanced and nursing through the whole run back to safety and freedom.

They regrouped in the forest, but only briefly. The wind was keeping the fire at bay, but that could change any moment. Under Kariik's direction, over six hundred warriors fought to protect the injured and the newly freed captives, and to force Varlas and his superior numbers toward the green path to the west.

It worked better than any of them had hoped. While the fighting was hard, and both sides took casualties, Varlas seemed eager to go exactly where his enemy wanted him to.

"That seems strange," Kalie said, finally able to sit down, clean the soot from herself and the baby, and begin to search for the child's mother.

"Not really," said Ealak, a warrior who had come with them in their flight from the steppes nearly two years ago, and settled in a village just a few days away. "Varlas is a greedy man who wants to rule his people from a place where he can impress them."

"A rich town, high on a hill, surrounded by pasture is too good to pass up," said Riyik.

Something still sounded wrong to Kalie's storyteller's ear, but she was too busy being grateful that she and Riyik were alive, and mourning those who didn't make it to have time to think on it. Besides there was this baby… "A girl!" Kalie cried, when she finally had time to look." Cleaned and fed, the child, about six moonspans, seemed healthy enough. "Could she belong to one of the captive women?" she asked Selima.

The younger woman shook her bald head.

"None of our babies were allowed to live. Only children over three years, and few enough of those. And our women have long since lost our milk."

"A horsewoman's then," said Kalie. "No matter. A life saved is a sign from the Goddess."

"You will keep her?" Malana, conscious, but injured lay on a blanket nearby, being treated by a healer. Of the eight who had infiltrated the enemy stronghold this morning, Riana was dead, and Cresson likely to follow. At least sixty of those they had gone to rescue were dead or unaccounted for. But over two hundred had made it alive to freedom.

"If we can't find her mother." Kalie looked at Riyik. "What do you think of another daughter?" she asked.

"She's already done us the favor of keeping your milk flowing," he said, smiling through weary eyes. "Something Melora will appreciate when we get home. What shall we call her?"

"Riana," said Kalie. Many of the freed captives, still mourning those they had lost, seemed pleased by Kalie's decision.

"Would you have kept the baby if it had been a boy?" Otera asked.

"Of course," Kalie said, wondering if Otera was serious, or trying to provoke another argument. But she seemed genuinely curious.

"Raising the child of my enemy," Otera mused. "I'm not sure I could."

"I already have," Kalie said. "Have you forgotten Varena?"

"Ah, yes. I had forgotten. Not the girl herself—she's quite memorable. But that you found her among the beastmen. I actually like the idea of raising their girls. It's a way of saving them. But a boy?"

"We'll save them, too. Many, I hope. Raise them to respect women, honor the earth, value peace…they're not born violent you know."

"Sometimes I wonder," said Otera, deep in thought.

"It's time to split up," called one of the battle leaders. Riyik and the others working in the field had managed to "liberate" most of the food stores before fleeing both fire and angry warriors. They had enough supplies to allow the exhausted refugees a chance to rest and recover for several days, with enough left to get them to a place of safety, in this once rich land, where the resources had been almost completely stripped, or begin rebuilding Starfall if they chose.

Kariik would lead the bulk of the warriors back toward Stonebridge along a route which would parallel that of Varlas, collecting more warriors as they went. If all went according to plan, this army would reach the enemy's flank just as the first warriors crossed the shallow stream into Stonebridge. Then, at the signal of three flaming arrows, those guarding the dam would breech it, causing a flood which would both sweep away many men and horses, and trap half the horde on the far side of the river, where the second army would be waiting.

Even if everything went according to plan, the outcome was uncertain. And how often, Kalie thought, did anything go according to plan?

But she bundled baby Riana under her breast and joined Riyik and the other twenty or so riders who would head west along a different route from Kariik's, raising the call for warriors and taking out any scouting parties they might meet along the way. The baby might be a complication, but no one said anything.

It was good to be going home, Kalie thought, as they traveled west that evening. They stopped to eat their share of the rations taken from Starfall, and get a much needed night of sleep. Kalie nursed Riana again, and then settled into her blankets with Riyik, feeling that life was almost normal.

They broke camp early the next morning, hoping to travel a great distance this first day; perhaps even reach Stonebridge in less than ten days.

As they prepared to leave, a hunter from one of the lost villages of Starfall, came back from checking his traps, sucking his bleeding hand. "We would have had rabbit stew at mid-day," he called. "But that little beast turned out to be a fighter! He chewed through the snare, and attacked me when I tried to pluck him up."

A few people laughed. One called out, "Never underestimate your opponent!" which drew more laughter.

But Kalie froze. From across the land, Kestra's words from the day Kalie left returned to her, and at last Kalie recognized the story the broken woman had been babbling. It was one of Kalie's own from when she led her group of volunteers across the wilderness to pose as slaves among the Aahk. She had wanted to keep up the other women's spirits during the grueling journey that had killed so many of them. So she told stories in their own language about how they would trick their enemies and destroy them from within.

But concerned that one of the warriors might

have learned their tongue, Kalie had hidden them in the metaphor of children's stories. Like the arrogant hunter, killed by a tiny rabbit. "All those stories were all about defeat coming from where you least expect it!" she said aloud.

"Kalie?" asked Riyik. "What is it?"

"A trap, I think." She explained to Riyik what Kestra had been saying, and as she did so, suddenly recalled what Kestra had been doing. "She was playing with piles of stones, like a child or a madwoman. At least that's what I thought at the time. But she was slipping sticks in among the stones, and then pulling them out so the rock pile would collapse."

"The dam!" cried Riyik. "She was trying to warn you. But of what?"

"That our confidence that the dam will save us is misplaced? That someone we trust or underestimate…"

Borik approached, looking concerned. "What is it?" he asked. "Everyone is ready to leave, and they can see something is wrong."

Kalie turned and look at the rest of the party. Suddenly, everyone seemed suspicious to her. There were only three women besides herself. Most of the men, as well, were local people, trained by the warriors who had come here with Kalie. Besides Borik and Riyik, only Ealak and Malor were from that group. "Did any of these men arrive here with Kariik this winter?" she asked.

Borik shook his head. "All of those are with Kariik now, or back in Stonebridge. What is it?"

"Someone has warned Varlas about the dam," Riyik said, putting it together.

"Not just the dam," said Kalie. "The entire

plan. That's why he took all his men west so easily. All he needs to do is prevent the dam from breaking, and his men—his entire remaining horde—will ride into Stonebridge like children jumping over a puddle."

"And with over a thousand warriors," said Riyik. "He will never be dislodged. All the advantages that made Stonebridge so easy to defend will belong to Varlas."

"If that's what's happening!" Kalie shook her head in frustration. Riana sensed her distress and began to whimper. "It could just be wild imagining!"

"I've never known your instincts to be wrong, Kalie," said Riyik.

"Nor I," said Borik.

Their faith in her helped calm her, and allowed her to trust herself. "But how? And who? If we could find the traitor—"

"We won't," said Riyik. "And it might not have been a traitor. One of the spies we sent to ingratiate himself with Varlas might have been tortured into revealing what he knew."

"Or, one who rode with Kariik," said Borik, "changed sides for real. It doesn't matter. What matters is getting to the dam in time to break it when Varlas reaches the river."

"How many are guarding the dam?" asked Riyik.

"Only about thirty when I left," said Kalie. "They only thought they were waiting for a signal to open it. They're strong, many are warriors, but they're not any kind of fighting force."

"Let's go," said Borik.

Chapter 34

They rode as never before. Even those raised to the saddle as nomads had never ridden this desperately. For those who had learned to ride only in the last year it was a nightmare. Yet no one gave up.

On the second day, Kalie was forced to leave Riana behind in a small village, mercifully untouched by the war. The pace they were keeping was not safe for a baby. Kalie nursed the child she was already beginning to think of as hers one last time, grabbed a few hours sleep, and left Riana with a kind mother of three who had plenty of milk.

"I will return for you," Kalie promised the little girl as she rode off.

Wherever they stopped for food and rest, their numbers swelled. Newly made warriors who had stayed to protect their homes joined Kalie's band once they learned what was at stake. Messengers and scouts who found them joined as well.

On the day they knew they would reach the dam, their numbers had tripled. So it was a band of sixty, mostly exhausted, mostly inexperienced warriors who reached their destination, just after midday. The sickening sounds of battle reached the band before they could see anything. But soon enough, all were swept into it.

"Varlas must have sent a hundred warriors!" Kalie cried in horror as she leapt into the fray. Most of the men and women stationed at the dam were already dead, but the last few fought on with courage that would be remembered forever. At the sight of their deliverance, they fought even harder, while Kalie,

Riyik and all the others surged forward.

Arrows flew, fighters and horses fell, but most of the fighting was hand to hand. Kalie found a somewhat protected spot to fire arrows from. She chose her targets carefully, as forces from both sides slipped on the rock piles that made the dam, or grappled with each other along the top. The rocks were slippery, and each time someone lost his footing or a body was pushed over the edge, rocks fell in showers, and the dam was weakened.

Kalie fired her last arrow and saw it fatally strike an enemy warrior through the neck. As she drew her dagger and waded into where the fighting was thickest, she nearly laughed at the irony of it. Neither side could afford for the dam to break. Varlas's men had orders to keep it intact at all costs, while Kalie's side needed to hold it until the order came to breech it. Yet they were fighting in the middle of it; right on top of it, even. An untried piece of construction that would kill them all if they knocked out the wrong support in the course of the battle.

Laughter bubbled up in Kalie's throat, and for a moment she thought she was going to run as mad as Kestra. They would all die together, and for nothing!

The next thing she knew, a grinning warrior wearing the blackened leather armor of the Wolves lunged at her with a lance, as if he were still on horseback. Thoughts of madness fled as Kalie dodged the lethal tip and tried to move in close to score him with her knife. Long though it was, the weapon left her at a decided disadvantage against a lance.

The warrior laughed. "Put down that toy and I'll let you live!" he shouted. "I have no wish to sully my honor by fighting a woman!" He swung at her sideways, knocking Kalie off her feet and drawing blood. "Had enough?" He reached for her, giving Kalie the opening she needed. Springing up, she sliced her blade across his unprotected forearm. The warrior bellowed, and Kalie doubted he would ever hold a weapon in that hand again. Unfortunately, he was as deadly with his left hand, though evenly matched now that they both held only daggers.

The enemy warrior was relentless, pushing Kalie back to the edge of the dam. Then, his head exploded, and Borik was pulling her to safety.

"Thank you," she panted, but Borik was already back in the thick of things.

And then it seemed the tide was turning in their favor. Alrik was leading the reserve forces Kariik had left behind in Stonebridge. He backed slowly to where Riyik was holding his warriors together, fighting as a perfect unit. If Riyik could just keep the center from collapsing, thought Kalie, they might carry the day.

Alrik drew closer, shouting something to Riyik that he could not hear in the chaos. Alrik pointed, and as Riyik turned to see what he was pointing at, Kalie saw Alrik raise his knife, close the distance between them, and bring the blade down toward Riyik's back.

"Riyik!" screamed Kalie. At the same instant she uttered the useless warning, Kalie flung her knife at Alrik. While designed for throwing, the distance seemed hopeless. Yet the weapon caught Alrik on his face, just below his right eye, spoiling his aim. His blade landed in Riyik's shoulder with a sickening thud Kalie could swear she heard. Riyik went down and Alrik leapt upon him, pinning Riyik and rendering him helpless to prevent the second blow.

As Kalie struggled helplessly against the

human tide to get to Riyik, Borik slammed into Alrik. The two men grappled, but Alrik could not match Borik's strength—or his rage. With a scream of "Traitor," Borik pushed the other man from the dam where he slid down the steep side, collecting a landslide of small rocks along the way, to land unconscious at the bottom.

The dam was collapsing, as leaks of all sizes sprang from between the rocks. The battlefield had become a moving, scratching thing of mud and rock, like something out the nomad's own hell. With Alrik gone and the place they had been ordered to hold turning on them, Varlas's men began to retreat.

Kalie reached Riyik at last, one of the few moving toward the dam, while others—everyone, it seemed—were running away from it. "Get a healer!" she screamed, trying to staunch the flow of blood from his shoulder, and wondering if she should remove the knife.

"Get him away!" cried another warrior, and Garm was there, helping Borik to carry Riyik to safety.

"Wait!" called a woman. "We have to hold back the water until we get the signal!"

"No help for that now!" called another voice that seemed close to Kalie, although she would not take her eyes from Riyik to be sure. "Get away, everyone, or you'll be crushed or drowned."

On a nearby hillside—the same one Melora had taken her first step, Kalie realized—Riyik was laid with the other wounded. "This man needs a healer now!" Kalie screamed, but the healers were doing their jobs exactly as they had been trained, and Kalie knew there were more serious cases.

Then Alessa was by their side and Kalie nearly

wept with relief. "What are you doing here?" she cried.

"I had a dream that I would be needed."
Alessa was focused on Riyik, but she spared a quick glance at Kalie. "The same night Alrik announced he was taking a group of his best men to guard the dam."

Kalie collapsed against the hillside, her vision blurring. No one knew what to do. The blood-red sunset felt like a message of doom.

Then a shout caused Kalie to look up. Three flaming arrows flew in a perfect arc.

The signal to break the dam.

"Thank the Goddess," someone was saying. "It would not have held much longer." People were taking their places with levers and long poles, muttering about how the damage had changed things.

But they did it. While Alessa and the other healers continued to work as if nothing was happening, a great rumbling shook the earth. The water burst free and filled, then overfilled, the riverbank that had for so many days been nothing but a trickle.

The war was on, and Kalie could do nothing but hold Riyik's hand and pray. Then his eyes fluttered open, as Alessa stitched his wound. "Go," he said weakly. "Get our children. Finish this."

Kalie gripped his hand tighter. "But for our children, I would never leave you."

"It should have been me," Riyik said, the words fading, as exhaustion and whatever Alessa had given him finally claimed him.

"Go," said Alessa.

Chapter 35

On horseback, Kalie reached Stonebridge before dark. There she found a scene of such chaos and terror she wanted to turn around and leap into the sea behind her.

The river had swept more than one hundred men and horses to their deaths, and trapped hundreds more on the eastern bank. There, Kariik and his men had already gained the upper hand by the time Kalie arrived.

But hundreds more, including King Varlas himself, had gained the town, and fighting was everywhere. Even if they won, Kalie wondered how much of a town they would have left. The screaming and clang of weapons was different from the battle of the steppes, she thought as she frantically tried to reach her home. There were no women shrieking in fear, running down the streets, making themselves perfect targets for men seeking prizes. Any woman who was outside in this battle was fighting. And the arrogant invaders were fighting in desperation, not glee. This might mean something, but for the moment, Kalie could not think of what.

Her house, when she finally reached it, was dark and empty along with all the others in the area. And then she realized: anyone not fighting would be inside the temples. Dodging a cursing horseman whose hair was on fire, Kalie made her way to the temples. The fighting was heavy in the clear areas outside, but only because the beastmen had correctly guessed that everyone they viewed at prizes would be inside.

What they had not expected was the well organized human shield surrounding each sanctuary; the men and women who were fighting for loved ones inside, and the strategies those of lesser fighting skill had developed this long and frightening year.

In frustration, many warriors contented themselves with plundering empty homes, only to find many weren't quite empty. Varlas's men were dying at an alarming rate.

But so were the defenders.

Kalie was easily recognized by a woman she had trained with, and admitted to the clean, empty open space where the temples clustered. Like an ocean of calm in a sea of chaos, most were filled with children, adults who would not fight, and people treating the injured. She saw Ruleen and her followers, working as they had promised, caring for wounded of both sides.

In the next temple, Kalie found Brenia and Martel, calming singing to their children and hers. Here, it was almost quiet enough to hear the singing. Picking her way through other groups and trying not to step on anyone, Kalie finally reached them. Yarik ran to her at once, and Melora, fussing her way toward an all-out tantrum, cut off her crying when her mother wrapped her in her arms.

"She nursed recently," said Brenia. "But she might want to—"

Melora latched on to Kalie's breast at once, nursing briefly and mainly for comfort. "Varena and Noris?" asked Kalie.

"We don't know," said Martel. "They may have gotten to their boat with some of the others, and taken to the sea. Or they may be safely hidden in their food cellar."

Or they may have gotten caught in the middle of all of this, Kalie worried. "I have to go out there," she said.

"Do you have any weapons?" Martel asked, eyeing her critically, and seeming concerned by what he saw. She couldn't blame him: she had been about to join a fight unarmed.

"Come with me," he said. "I'll take you to the weapon cache." Kalie noticed that many who were not praying or tending the wounded were repairing weapons.

Melora clung to her mother, and screamed when Kalie gave her back to Brenia. I will be back, she silently promised both herself and her children.

The next temple they went to had been converted into a forge. Janak, red faced and bellowing orders to his many apprentices, was determined that if his side lost, it would not be for lack of the right tools. Kalie suspected that if they won, his efforts could be the reason. She added pieces to her armor, two more knives, some throwing sticks and a spear. She did not think a bow would be useful in the close quarter fighting of the town.

From the moment Kalie left the protection of the temples, she was caught up in the whirling, noisy world of blood and body parts, war cries and cold determination.

Later, she would be told that she fought like a demon; that no one had seen the like. She would remember little of it. Her vision narrowed to a red-tinged tunnel, through which she could see one snarling, black-clad man after another. With spear and knife she fought, killing, wounding, running, until it all became a blur. Once she nearly killed a man on her own side, so lost she was in the frenzy that had taken her.

The cry of the hunt awoke Kalie to fact that she had been spotted as danger who must be eliminated. At least six men were chasing her down a dark lane with empty houses on either side. She dodged between two buildings, knowing better than to enter one and become trapped inside. Another group came from the opposite direction, trapping her. Two men she did not recognize died trying to protect her.

In a move these beastmen should have been familiar with by now, Kalie scrambled up the wooden side of a house, using the low thatching to vault herself onto the roof.

Then the night was lit up with flame. When Kalie could see again, the house she stood on was in flames. It would only be moments before the dry thatch which kept her out of reach of her enemies became more deadly than they. Warriors gathered to cheer for her demise. "Come on down, so we can have some fun before we kill you!" called one.

"You owe us that much for the trouble you've caused!" said another.

"Let's just watch her burn!" said a third. "Who wants to fuck a bald cunt anyway? I'll bet her daughters and sisters will be more to our taste!"

The jeering became undistinguishable, and now other houses were burning. Kalie flung her throwing sticks into the crowd, finding the occasional grunt of pain satisfying. It was, Kalie realized, the moment where she had to choose how she would die.

And she didn't like it.

And then, her salvation arrived. Not with a

troupe of her own warriors, or even a single fighter like Borik who was worth ten, but with the arrival of Varlas, King of the Wolves, riding in all his gaudy splendor to see the unnatural woman everyone was speaking of brought down.

The roof she stood on was burning now, but Kalie stood for a full ten heartbeats, taking in every detail of Varlas's armor, hair, and even how he sat his horse. Then, as the section of roof next to her gave way, he moved forward for a better look.

Knife in hand, Kalie jumped, landing full force on the arrogant king who had come to claim her land as his own. Struggling, they fell from the horse, landing with Varlas on top of Kalie. For the first time in her life, that was exactly how she wanted it.

Weapons bristled around her, but Kalie was in little danger as long as she had these fools' king as her shield. With her knife at his throat, she pried herself into a sitting position, the thrashing horse guarding her back, the king covering her front.

"Drop your weapons or your king dies!" she screamed.

The men froze, but no one backed away or lowered a weapon. Most simply readjusted their position to get in a killing shot before Kalie could cut Varlas's throat. She had to act fast. "Tell them to drop their weapons!" she hissed in the king's ear, sliding the knife up his face until the tip rested against his left eye.

"Step back! Lower your weapons!" he shouted to his men. "I'll handle this demon-bitch myself!" With that he twisted with such force that Kalie was nearly thrown off. The horse that had protected her got himself upright and bolted. Only Varlas's arrogant order saved Kalie's life.

Leaping like a cat, Kalie mounted the king like a horse, pulling him off balance once again. He sat heavily, Kalie still on his back, and the rage he felt at looking like a fool pulsed through every part of him. This time, Kalie removed his left eye with her knife. While Varlas howled, she again whispered in his ear, but this time it was to make a deal. The only deal that could prevent her home from becoming a funeral pyre.

"Tomorrow, Vargas, you can be a one-eyed king, or you can be hanging from our temple roof with your balls stuffed in your mouth. You choose!"

As Kalie's knife moved to his remaining eye, Varlas yelped, "What are you talking about?"

"This war will kill both our sides if we don't stop it now," said Kalie, loud enough for everyone in the growing crowd around them to hear. "Do you even have enough men to rule us now if you win? Do you think my people will forget their Goddess and their honor and join your side to replace the men you've lost?"

"I wouldn't take such filthy cowards as my warriors!" shrieked Varlas. But the men around him knew their enemies were no cowards.

"Good, we don't want to join you either. So let's try this. There will be much empty land with no one to work it. Some of that land will suit your needs quite well—whether you continue your nomadic life, or decide to try your hand at farming. You and your surviving men, and any women who choose to go with you will be granted your own territory. We will make a treaty, which you will swear by your gods to uphold. If any of your men break the treaty all of you will die. And you will end up back on the temple with your balls stuffed in your mouth."

"Who are you to make such an offer?" Varlas demanded. "Queen of this land?"

"If that's who I need to be," retorted Kalie. "Or you may call me Keeper. A keeper of the ancient wisdom." But only one of many, she thought.

Chapter 36

The night had grown too dark for anyone to
know who they were fighting, so a truce was declared.
The sun was cresting the eastern hills before all the
dead were laid out and the wounded gathered for care.
And by the end of the day, an agreement had been
reached between the two warring sides, although as
Ruleen reminded everyone, only one side had wanted
the war.

There were meetings and discussions, but the
most immediate concern was disposing of the dead.
Neither side was allowed the rites they would have
liked, for the piles of bodies were far too deep and the
weather was far too hot. To avoid pestilence, bodies
had to be burned, or piled into ravines and covered
with earth and stone. The only dead who were able to
insist on strict adherence to ritual were the wives of
Varlas's warriors, who filed to the burial sites wearing
their best clothes and jewelry, only to lay down beside
their husbands and stab themselves, or be strangled by
surviving male relatives.

"Amazing," said Otera as she watched.

"One word for it, I suppose," said Kalie,
turning to leave. She'd seen enough of it while living
with the tribe. All she wanted now was to go home
and care for Riyik and see her children. And perhaps
have a long hot bath.

"It will at least leave us with fewer mouths to
feed," Otera persisted. "Since our brilliant leaders
have decided that feeding those who will soon return
to kill us is a fine plan."

"While many of us go hungry this winter,"

Danarie said bitterly.

Before the hostilities could officially end, however, there was the matter of Alrik, whose misfortune it was to be taken alive. In a trial which Kalie would have preferred to miss, and Riyik did, Alrik was brought before Kariik and the leaders of Stonebridge, and made to answer for his treachery.

"What did Varlas offer you to betray your king?" Kariik asked, looking and sounding like more of a king than ever.

Varlas stood watching the proceedings, but spoke up from his place. "I offered him nothing! He came to me before our tribes even left the steppes. He promised me he could deliver the best this land had to offer. In exchange, he would rule the territory of his choice, as a brother king."

Kariik paled. To learn that greed or the sight of the odds might have changed a man's allegiance was bad enough. But this…? "So you were a traitor from the start," the shaken king said.

"No man who holds with his gods or his honor is a traitor!" Alrik retorted. "You would have had us bow to women, and give up all that made us men—and warriors! You murdered my nephew—a good man who took nothing that was not his by right—and all for what? A life of digging in the dirt like worms? Of trading instead of taking? Of handing your balls to your wife, and then asking her permission to let you use them? It is you who are the traitor, Kariik!"

"But it is you who will die a traitor's death, while I go on to lead our people to a bright new future. And I notice your 'brother king' did not offer to share your fate."

At that, some of Alrik's smugness slipped, but

he only said, "And what of my dear wife, who helped me every step of the way? Who showed me how the dam could be used to defeat you, rather than save you? Will she not share my fate? Or will you spare a traitor for no better reason than it has a cunt instead of a prick?"

Kalie hated this bastard. There was no way Alrik could prove his accusations, but the fact was, given Kestra's mental state, he could easily be telling the truth.

"Let her die with her beastman husband!" shouted Griva. "She could have returned safely to her old way of life. She chose his instead."

The smile on Alrik's face made Kalie want to scream.

"Kestra will be secluded in a distant temple of healing until she regains her sanity, or until she dies," Alessa said. "Let that be the end of the matter."

"The real Kestra was strong enough to find away to warn us," Kalie added. "Despite her fear of her husband. That should count for something."

She wasn't sure it would, but it would have to be enough. Already Alrik was being stripped naked, his hands tied to the back of a horse, with enough lead rope to allow him to run behind the racing stallion for as long as he could. After that, he would be dragged to death.

Kalie went home to sleep beside her husband, warm and alive, and nearly free of fever, although still far from recovered. He would not sleep until Kalie had told him everything that had happened.

"I can't believe I never saw what Alrik was," said Riyik.

"None of us did," said Kalie. "Least of all

Kariik."

"I thought he was one who would lead the others to a better future. When I looked at him, I saw…"

"Yourself?" Kalie gathered Riyik into her arms. "You've been away from treachery for far too long, my love. You've learned to see the good in others, but not always the bad."

"On the steppes, that would be a fatal weakness," said Riyik.

"Not here," said Kalie.

"Only because we won. This time." Riyik ran a hand over the short tufts on Kalie's head, where her hair was starting to grow back. "But perhaps with you at my back, I don't need to worry about next time. I won't forget it was you who saved me from Alrik."

Kalie settled contentedly into his arms as Riyik drifted off to sleep. "We've saved each other," she whispered. "Too many times to count."

The bridge had held, though the water was still barely an arm's length below the bottom of it. Nothing remained of the nomad camp on its eastern side. And here it was that Varlas, with six of his warriors, met with Kariik, and six of his advisors. Orin was not bothered by playing the role of a subordinate, nor was Riyik, who should still be in bed as far as Kalie was concerned. Between them, Janak and Borik lent a certain gravity to the proceedings, and Kalie and Alessa stood to remind all of Vargas's people exactly who their neighbors would be from now on.

It was agreed that more than oaths would be required for the former enemies to live in peace, especially after the fighting nearly flared up again when Varlas learned he would have to give up his captives, including Kariik's sister and nieces—along with any women who wished to leave. While few of women took the opportunity, such a blow could have cost Varlas his kingship.

So both sides agreed to exchange hostages. Two of Varlas's sons would live among the people of the Goddess for year, and two boys (both acolytes, but now elevated to the status of princes) would live with the nomads. But Varlas, who had been reduced to nothing but five hundred men and a few horses, would now have flocks and gold, and his remaining women would learn how to make the fine fabrics he had come to crave—all courtesy of the settled folk. He would choose to see it as tribute from inferiors, but in fact it carried the subtle warning that all of it could be taken away as easily as it was given.

Kalie, who had been roused from a two day sleep to attend the ceremony, planned to spend little time at the feast that followed, but she knew there were people she must speak to—perhaps for the last time.

"Have you decided where you will go?" she asked Ruleen as they sat with the other Keepers, sharing thin stew and watered wine.

"At last, yes," said the older woman. "It was given to my brother in a vision. There are many islands in the Great Southern Sea. Some, we believe, house the oldest temples to the Goddess still standing. We will travel there, and teach the ancient wisdom to any who wish to learn, and hide the treasures which tell the stories, so whatever may happen, the Goddess will never be lost."

"I wish you the blessings and the protection of

the Goddess," Kalie said formally, but she also meant it.

"And you?" she asked Otera who was already directing her women in packing their things.

"North of the Black Sea there is a barren wild land, with decent grazing, and almost no people," replied the tall woman, whose face and body were now covered in scars and her blond hair shorter than ever. "We will create a new tribe of horse warriors." She smiled wickedly. "But only women. We will be an entire tribe of women."

"Won't that make having a next generation rather difficult?" asked Kalie.

"Oh, we'll visit men in places like this at least once a year. But I think our numbers will grow mostly from recruits. And since our nearest neighbors will be Varlas and his rabble, the rest of you may someday be grateful for our presence." Otera gazed of in the distance. "We shall take an oath to protect each other—but also anyone in need of help. And, like Ruleen and her Keepers, we will never let the Goddess be forgotten, though we shall worship Her in a new way."

"May the Goddess smile upon your new life," Kalie said, taking her leave.

Crossing the bridge back into the town, she found Kariik alone, staring into the water. "My king—" she began formally.

Kariik glanced up at her and smiled. "Not anymore," he said. "And never yours."

"What's happened?" Kalie asked, growing concerned.

"You probably know that I never wanted to be a king in the first place."

She began to relax. "That I did. But I did not think a king could step down other than into his grave."

"On the steppes, perhaps. But here?" Kariik sighed and threw his arms wide. "For the first time, I have choices."

And Kalie laughed with the sheer joy of how often she had heard those words this past year. "And where will your choices lead you?"

"Hunting, riding, teaching those of your people who want to be warriors. Who knows what else? I am finally responsible only for myself. Those of my tribe who wish to keep with the old ways will leave with Varlas in the morning. The rest will find lives for themselves among your people. I'll stay here because this is where Alessa will be, but..." He trailed off. Kalie waited. "I do not think we shall remain together. Ours was never a love match. And she will have many duties. And...most likely take other men. Now that I'm without a wife and a crown, I may have to learn how to court women—for the first time."

"Speak with the priestesses in the temples," said Kalie. "I'm sure they will be happy to provide instruction."

Kariik chuckled. "And what of you, Kalie?"

He was, she realized, the first person to ask her. "I don't know yet. There will be no shortage of work for me here. I suppose my calling now will be to create a new world out of two very different cultures."

Kariik raised an eyebrow. "You will not seek to convert us all?"

"To what?" Kalie retort was sharper than she intended. "I have killed my fellow humans, and I do not regret it. The Goddess I worship now has many new aspects. I barely understand them myself, so how can I teach others?" Then suddenly, Kalie found her question answered, although she had meant it rhetorically. "I think, after all this time, I may return to pottery. I will create images of the Goddess in her form as Mother—a mother bear, fiercely protecting her children."

"I look forward to seeing them," said Kariik. "In fact, I may want one to guard my tent—or house, or wherever I land." To her surprise, Kariik reached out and offered a tentative embrace. To her greater surprise, Kalie accepted it.

"Good luck," they both said at once.

She found Riyik, engaged in debate with two of Varlas's men, despite his promise to return home to rest as soon as the ceremony was over. "Time to go home, dearest," she said firmly, placing a hand on his good arm and tugging, none too gently.

Riyik smiled and nodded to the warriors. "I look forward to continuing our conversation."

"Is this what our king's 'peace' will bring us?" asked one. "Am I now to be ordered about by my wife?"

"No more so than before," laughed the other.

Home at last, Kalie and Riyik lay upon their fur covered bed. Yarik was asleep in his own bed, while Melora and Riana shared a crib. Kalie had not only kept her milk, she had enough for both of them.

"There are so many orphans," she mused. "What do you think of taking in one or two more?"

"I think we'll need a bigger house," said Riyik.

"That can be arranged," said Kalie. "Once the land has recovered and the crops are in, and trade has resumed."

Riyik chuckled, even as he drifted off to sleep. "An amazing people you are, my love. Men came to enslave you and destroy all you had, yet you speak only of rebuilding, and teaching them to be your friends."

"It's the way it has always been in this land," said Kalie. "So perhaps it will continue for a while longer." Then she drifted off to sleep in Riyik's arms.

Epilogue

"Are you sure you have everything?" Kalie asked Melora, as they left the house she had been born in thirteen years earlier. It was a large house now, with a second story, and many rooms, but soon it would feel empty.

"I'm supposed to travel light Mother, remember?" Melora, who had only recently completed her Ceremony of Womanhood, had been determined to join Otera's Amazons since she was five years old. The day had finally arrived.

They walked to the temple, where seventeen-year old-Yarik would soon complete his apprenticeship and be initiated as a healer. Alessa had seen the gift in him early, but even she was surprised by his skill. He would be one of the great ones.

"Time to leave, sister?" Yarik asked, his limp still noticeable, but never an impediment. He tugged one of Melora's honey brown braids.

"Once father arrives," she said impatiently.

Kalie and Yarik exchanged a knowing glance. "He has a special gift for you," said Yarik. "One I think you'll find worth waiting for."

Varena and Noris, followed by their noisy brood of children approached, although they had already said goodbye at a rowdy feast at their farm the night before. That farm wasn't so isolated any more, as the town had grown out toward it, and other farms crowded in, to meet the food needs of a growing population.

"I wish Barak and Riana could be here," said Melora.

Barak had traveled the long trade route to the Great Southern Sea, to find out if the life of a sailor would appeal to him, and to see how Ruleen and her Keepers fared. Riana, now an acolyte, had traveled nearly as far as Melora would today, to study some of the oldest mysteries with an elite group of priestesses.

Riyik arrived leading the most beautiful silver gray mare his daughter had ever seen. And Melora had cared for little beside horses since early childhood.

"Oh, Father, she's beautiful!" With practiced ease, Melora swung up and settled herself astride the animal.

Kalie's mount, beautiful and beloved, though never quite able to replace Blossom, stood waiting patiently beside the excited filly.

"I'm afraid after all these years, I will need help," she said, pushing a strand of gray hair behind her ear and turning to smile at Riyik. He boosted her into the saddle. Kalie was grateful the journey would be short, but she was not looking forward to returning alone.

Then, as she turned to say goodbye to Riyik, Kalie found him mounted on his own horse, bedroll and saddlebags behind him, clearly ready to leave.

"Riyik, you can't come with us!" Kalie was both scandalized and regretful. "You know the rules the Amazons have about their new recruits. No men may accompany them."

"Perhaps it is time for those Amazons to learn that a father might wish to see his daughter safely to her new home as much as a mother does. And if they do not, then I shall wait for you at the edge of their territory until the initiation is complete."

Kalie glanced at Melora, but she showed no

sign of concern or embarrassment at the strange nature of parents—only a barely contained impatience to get started on this journey. "It's better if father comes with us," she said finally, turning her horse as if she meant to leave by herself if the two old folks didn't hurry. "You'll be glad for his company on the way home."

Kalie sighed as a great warmth filled her. Yes, indeed she would.

"The town has changed," she said to Riyik as Stonebridge fell away behind them.

"This whole land is changing," Riyik replied. "I think for the better. Don't you?"

"In some ways. But not all. Ruleen was right when she predicted that most of the traders and scouts and messengers who traveled the land would be men now."

"Sadly, it is safer that way," said Riyik. "But many of the tribes who follow the old ways have turned to trading instead of raiding, and the Goddess has been accepted by nearly all of them."

"Only as the consort of the great thunder god," Kalie sighed, thinking again of Ruleen and her predictions.

"But there are women in every trade and craft and council in the land," Riyik argued. "And many of them began their lives as the property of warriors. And don't forget the stories of great cities rising across the islands Barak has gone to visit, where Ruleen's people are now leaders. I look forward to learning more about that when he returns."

Kalie nodded, her good humor restored. "And our daughter will soon become a warrior in a sisterhood which has no equal."

Riyik grinned. "I have heard that Varlas's youngest daughter plans to join them when she comes of age."

At that news, Kalie laughed out loud. But as the fertile land fell away behind them, and barren lands, suited only for the hardiest of animals and humans rose in the distance, she wondered if the day might come when the sky god would replace the great earth goddess entirely. But that time would be long in the future. And if it truly did come to pass, it would not mean the end of the way of life Kalie knew, for there would still be women warriors. And there would still be their opposites in distant places who kept alive the memory of a goddess of peace and cooperation.

The world would never be the same as the one Kalie was born into. But as she rode with her man and their daughter in companionable silence, she decided that the one they had now was a fair trade.

Note to my Readers:

My journey to bring these books to life has been no less amazing than Kalie's own journey. I have loved hearing from those of you who have posted comments and reviews, every bit as much as I have loved writing these books. I look forward to hearing from all of you as time goes on.

But as one journey ends, another begins. Kalie's story is finished, but lately, others have been tugging on my imagination, demanding that I write their stories as well. Most notably Otera. (Can you imagine saying no to someone like her?) If anyone would like to read a book (or series) about Otera and the founding of the Amazons, please let me know, through my website, my Amazon Author page, Goodreads, Facebook (my page or the Prehistoric Readers and Writers Campfire) or e-mail.

I won't start writing Otera's story unless I know there's an audience, but until then, please consider taking an entirely new journey with me through my next novel, *From the Ashes*, which will be released in the summer of 2015. *From the Ashes* is different from any novel I have written. It's alternative history, in a world where Nazi Germany has won WWII. But it's also very different from the host of others in that genre.

For everyone who has gone on Kalie's Journey with me, please accept my deepest thanks for reading my books and coming this far. And for those who come on other journeys with me in the future, I look forward to our time together.

Sandra Saidak graduated San Francisco State
University in 1985 with a B.A. in English. She is a
high school English teacher by day, author by night.
Her hobbies include reading, dancing, attending
science fiction conventions, researching prehistory,
and maintaining an active fantasy life (but she warns
that this last one could lead to dangerous habits such
as writing). Sandra lives in San Jose with her husband
Tom, daughters Heather and Melissa, and two cats.
Her first novel, "Daughter of the Goddess Lands", an
epic set in the late Neolithic Age, was published in
November, 2011 by Uffington Horse Press. Learn
more at **http://sandrasaidak.com/**